It Takes Time

Rylee Smith

Published by Rylee Smith, 2024.

This is a work of fiction. Similarities to real people, places, or events are entirely coincidental.

IT TAKES TIME

First edition. October 4, 2024.

Copyright © 2024 Rylee Smith.

ISBN: 979-8227275394

Written by Rylee Smith.

For Paige,

Here it is!

Chapter 1

"Surgit," a deep voice hissed in the dark. Claws of icy fear grabbed my heart as I froze in response. I didn't have a clue what the voice said, but let's be honest. That was hardly my first question when confronted with a male voice in my bedroom. Not that that happens to me often.

The dim glow of streetlights glared in uniform slits through the blinds, giving me just enough light to make monsters out of the shadows. Maybe I'd just imagined a voice in a language I didn't speak, and was only going crazy. What a comfort. Not for the first time, I found myself wishing that my twin sister Tamryn hadn't moved out and left me here alone in our childhood bedroom.

At that moment I really wished I'd had some kind of weapon. Tamryn had a small revolver she bought at her new husband's encouragement, but she had taken it with her. The best I had was a stuffed dog and a box of tissue for when my nose ran at night. Unless my assailant had spring allergies, that wasn't going to do it. My best plan was no plan at all. The helplessness made me sick to my stomach as I waited for another sound.

He- or it- didn't speak again. With a rush of adrenaline I leaned off the bed and seized my phone, yanking the charger out of the wall as I moved to turn on the phone's flashlight. Before I could, though, I noticed my screen was lit up with a video of a man.

He was standing behind a podium in front of a dry erase board, in what appeared to be a college lecture hall. It was impossible to tell without knowing the dimensions of the room, but he looked enormous. Even beneath his white dress shirt, it was obvious that he had a strong body with rippling muscles, and he could have been well over 6 feet tall. I was already starting to forgive him for waking me up.

I slapped my hand to my face and sighed heavily, unplugging my phone from the dangling charger and leaning back into bed with it. Did I really think there was someone hiding in my room? Ridiculous.

The relaxed smile left my face as the apparent professor's eyebrows contracted in confusion. He waved at the camera slowly, as if trying to get the attention of someone behind it. An orange logo rested to the right of his head, advertising for the app that was already open: *IEducator.*

"Salve," he said uncertainly in his smooth voice, then waited for a response. Before anyone in the video could respond, a notification popped up on my phone, inviting me to "Translate to English." I tapped on the message, and suddenly he laughed softly and shook his head.

"Ah, I'm terribly sorry," he smiled. A smile suited his tan, masculine features. "I guess you don't speak Latin." I waited to see who he was talking to, and whether they would respond. They didn't. If a man who looked like that had something to say to me, I'd jump at the chance...

"Excuse me," he finally said. "Girl in the dark. Do you speak English." My heart jumped. Looks like I had my chance. How did I get connected to a video chat in the middle of the night? Sure I wanted to talk to him. But not like this. I searched for a button to cancel the call and escape, because I was not ready for this. There wasn't one. I jerked the neck of my t-shirt away from my throat as I tried to still my rising panic. There was nothing else to do. I shut off my phone.

Despite the successful evasion, my heart still slammed in my chest. I counted the lengths of my breaths: four seconds in... six seconds out. Eventually I settled down and pulled on my sheet, ready to shrug it all off and try to go back to sleep. This would all seem less embarrassing in the light of day, when I was refreshed. In the morning I'd wake up and say "Hey, that guy doesn't even know who I am. What do I care if he thinks I'm rude for hanging up on him?" In the morning, that would seem even remotely convincing. Right?

I would have no such luck.

Of its own volition, my phone turned back on and I found myself face to face with the same man from before, who was now standing right against the camera. How did that even happen? I ran my finger over the rubber that covered my phone's power button. It was still there, and from all appearances should have been working. But here I was, looking at a phone screen that was definitely on. My phone had betrayed me.

"Listen, do you want to learn or not?" Though his words were harsh, he couldn't keep a twinkle from creeping into his eyes. "You can't just turn me off."

That was probably true. I'd tried the whole turning him off thing, and it hadn't gone so well the first time. He might have thought it was kind of funny the first time, but I doubted he'd have the same reaction again. Anyway, there was only so much rudeness I could tolerate putting out. I wasn't used to hanging up on people. I sighed weakly, accepting my lack of options. He was still there, looking at me, and I was just going to have to talk to him. The pounding of my heart urged me to get up and get on with it.

I leaped out of bed and stumbled to the light switch, halting suddenly as dizziness told me my blood pressure struggled to respond to the action. When I recovered somewhat, I dropped to a sitting position on the carpet and held the phone up to create a more flattering angle of my face. If I was determined to answer him, and at this point I was, I might as well look halfway decent while I did it. There wasn't much else I could do to improve my appearance beyond running my fingers through the mussed up layers in my hair.

Did I want to learn or not? That had been his question. It was one he'd probably intended to be rhetorical, but that didn't mean

I had to take it that way. Now that I was here, in the middle of the night, with a handsome stranger on the phone, I could hardly remember signing up for this in the first place. Whatever I'd decided before, I was starting from scratch now. Tamryn had suggested this app because she thought it might give me some sense of meaning, or at least something to do with my time. She'd heard me complain about my lack of job enough times that suggesting it was probably the only way to maintain her sanity. I couldn't blame her, except that she only had to hear me worry about my joblessness once a day (ok, sometimes more). I had to hear it on a running loop in my brain 90% of the time. If learning history from the IEducator app made me feel like I was enhancing my resume and improving myself, then it was worth it. That was still the goal, right? Of course it was. Just because the professor gave me more of a Hercules vibe than the teachers I'd had in the past didn't change anything. Hercules, whatever his real name was, stood waiting for my answer.

"Uh, yeah. Yes. Please. I'm down. I mean I'm interested. Yes." It wasn't quite the Gettysburg Address, but I got my message across somehow. My breath caught when he grinned approvingly.

"Wonderful. Tomorrow then." With that, the professor and his classroom disappeared, replaced by an empty white screen. I had no choice but to shelve my confusion and try to get some sleep.

#

To my enormous shock, I woke up to a bright morning. I hadn't expected to be able to sleep after the night's events. My hand shot out and grabbed my phone before I could even think of it.

My heart sank. There were no notifications on my screen- no messages from the app to tell me that my mystery professor planned to speak to me today. Maybe it had been a dream. It didn't seem like a dream, but maybe the quarantine was starting to give me cabin fever.

It wasn't normal to be forced inside for weeks by a pandemic. Maybe I was losing it.

Or maybe it was eight o'clock in the morning. I remembered exactly what he'd said (and how smooth and strong his voice was when he said it): "Tomorrow then." Not "The second your eyes open in the morning I'll be calling you." Maybe this was why I was still single.

Still, I was awake now, and there was no chance I'd go back to sleep and risk missing a call. Or worse (much worse), answering the call later in the morning, still in my pajamas. I was done sleeping, and there was no sense in trying to reverse that. Might as well take advantage of the extra time.

I dug a blue one piece bathing suit out of my top drawer and pulled it on. I was halfway down the stairs when I ran into my mother, who was drinking what was probably a protein smoothie but looked more like a glass of mud. I'd never managed to get into that whole protein smoothie thing. Didn't she know you could make a milkshake instead? There was protein in milk.

"Swimming," she said, pushing her glasses back up her nose from where they'd been displaced when she'd taken a drink. "That's good exercise. Don't forget sunscreen."

Like anyone could forget the dangers of the sun in Tucson, when it was beating down constantly. I nodded my assent to the superfluous advice anyway. Giving advice was one of my mom's specialties. Being a teacher ran in her bloodstream. I'd always envied people like my mother who knew exactly what to do with their lives. The rest of us just had to wing it. Winging it, it turned out, was not as easy as the term suggested. Sometimes winging it meant laying in bed at night, staring at the ceiling (or, ok, at the top bunk above you if you lived like a 10 year old like I did) and wondering if you'd ever do something in your life that justified your existence to the world.

A light breeze bravely pushed through the morning heat, brushing over my exposed skin when I stepped into the backyard. I flinched against the cold mist of the sunscreen as I sprayed it haphazardly on myself. I'd probably missed more spots than I'd actually reached, but I liked to think it was the thought that counted.

After a few minutes of allowing my sunscreen to set, I made my way to the pool and descended to the first step. I tried to focus on the cool water, already warmed enough by the sun to be welcoming instead of jarring. This was my favorite time of year for swimming, before the water started to feel like bath water, but close enough to summer that the cold didn't shock you into your bones. I swished my feet in the water, squinting against the sun's bright reflection on the surface, and tried to enjoy the moment. Instead, my mind went back to the man on the phone last night.

He was unreasonably good-looking. It wasn't fair to be that attractive, actually. I'd always been a sucker for a man with long hair. Just because he was cute, though, didn't mean I wanted to date him. Okay, it certainly didn't hurt. But he was also a professor, which probably meant that he had a good brain under all that beautiful hair. I was willing to find out, at least. I took another step into the pool, letting the water envelop my legs. An internal voice I usually preferred not to listen to argued that whether I'd want to go out with him wasn't the only question.

Did he want to go out with me? Should he? I was a college graduate with no real job, no plans, and I was living with my parents indefinitely. That wasn't the sort of information someone would want to put on their dating application. Actually, I didn't like this line of thinking. As if it could dissolve the thoughts, I let myself fall into the water and sink until my head was submerged. My hair floated around my face, and I blew fine bubbles from my nose.

I had plenty to offer this guy. Just because I didn't know exactly what to do with my life didn't mean I wouldn't do anything worthwhile. Intention counted for something, didn't it?

I kicked off the bottom of the pool and set to swimming easy laps, picking up speed as I got warmed up. I counted my laps carefully, whispering the number out loud at the end of every few laps to avoid losing my place. Somewhere along the way I'd decided to swim 100 laps, and despite the arbitrariness of the goal, I was dedicated to it.

"Twenty," I whispered, taking as deep a breath as I could manage without losing my momentum. My feet slid as I kicked off the wall. How did this guy end up teaching history for an app, anyway? Did they put up advertisements on job sites for that kind of thing? Maybe I could do something like that.

Teaching. I kicked harder against the water, swimming faster. Good for sexy app professor man, but not the job for me. I'd learned the hard way through a stint of substitute teaching that being an educator required patience for the antics of kids, and a thick skin. I was pretty sure I didn't have either one. It would be better to find a job that focused on my strengths.

By the time I made it to 100 laps, I'd all but forgotten about the man from the app. As I climbed out of the pool and made my way back inside the house and up to my room, I was back to my usual reverie about where I'd be in five years. The best answer I'd managed to come up with was "somewhere." It wasn't much. It didn't belong on a resume, and it wouldn't sound very impressive in a job interview. Still, it was a start.

Anyway, it was better than "nowhere," I decided, drying my hair with my towel.

My father's voice shook me from my reflections. From somewhere near the stairs I heard him shout, "I'll be right back!" The stairs creaked as he made his way up. Two light knocks announced his presence before he pushed open the door.

"Good morning, Lane," he smiled, as professional as ever. I noticed for the millionth time in my life how much my parents really belonged together. They were both teachers and both treated family life a little bit too formally. They even both wore glasses, as if as a sign that if they weren't born perfect, they did everything they could to rectify that, including their vision. "There's someone downstairs to see you. You didn't tell us you were seeing a man."

I'm not sure I would anyway, I thought quickly, before the significance of his statement set in. I wasn't seeing a man. Not from an online dating profile, not from my former college classes, not from anywhere. The only young man I spoke to on a regular basis was my brother-in-law Levi. I quashed rising nerves, but I couldn't help some small part of me imagining scenarios of what Prince Charming might have finally come to my door.

"I'll be right down. Tell him I'll be right down," I told my dad with forced neutrality. Somehow, my voice came out even, if a little fast. I barely waited for the door to close behind him before I tore off my bathing suit and threw open my closet door. Something nice. Something cute. Something flattering. It had been so long since I'd needed the perfect outfit.

I settled on a short red t-shirt dress and yanked my hair into a hair tie that I found lying on my dresser. I'd have liked to put on makeup, but I settled for scrambling to the bathroom and swiping on deodorant. I was pretty sure my priorities were solidly set on that one. With a deep breath, I strolled confidently down the stairs.

There was no one standing by the door. My confidence deflated, but I fought against the discouragement. It was okay, he was probably with my dad in the kitchen, waiting for me. Whoever he was.

"Hello, I'm Lane. How can I help-" I began as I turned the corner into the kitchen. My question died in my throat.

Chapter 2

Standing in the kitchen, staring into the open pantry like he lived here, was the professor from the video call last night. I swallowed. This wasn't what I'd meant when I'd agreed to talk to him today. I was mentally prepared for a video call. Distant. Safe. The type of interaction where you could pretend your screen was frozen if you were really in a pinch. Something about pretending to be frozen in person didn't work as well. I tried to breathe evenly, even as my lungs suggested I take as many breaths as I could fit into a minute. I resisted. Just because I was nervous didn't mean I had to act like it. It was hard to seem calm, though, when the man was even more intimidating in person.

I was right to say he was huge. He must have been 6'3" or 6'4", with arms that could crush anyone or anything that got in his way. If it weren't for his outfit, he'd look like a warrior. In place of his professional teaching attire, he wore a plain black t-shirt and jeans.

"Tamryn?" he asked, closing the pantry and coming to look at me more closely. He raised an eyebrow. *Well, I* just *said my name was Lane*, I thought, but I was used to the twin confusion.

"No, my name is Lane. Wait- you know Tamryn?" It had taken me a second to realize how weird his mistake really was, but now I was stuck on it. How on *earth* did this strange, beautiful man know Tamryn? I didn't know any strange, beautiful men. Not even one. Why wouldn't she have introduced me? I thought we were friends! What good was having a married sister if she didn't funnel all of the hot guys your way? We were definitely going to have a talk about this.

"Oh, no, not really. I just thought... you looked... like a Tamryn," he stammered, running his fingers through his long, dark blonde hair. I got a strange feeling, beyond the slight thrill that went through me when I made eye contact with him. No, I was actually more focused on what he'd said, and the bizarre tone he'd used to say it. He was obviously hiding something. I was hardly a human polygraph machine, but even I knew that was the worst lie I'd ever heard. Why would he lie about knowing Tamryn? If they'd had some kind of fling before Levi, I definitely would have known about it. Plus, he would've been able to tell us apart, I liked to think. We were identical twins, but the people that knew us managed to tell the difference. I didn't have much time to think into it too closely, because he continued. "My name is Gannicus. I'm here to teach you about the slave revolts, like you requested."

Gannicus, like the gladiator who helped lead the Spartacus slave revolts two thousand years ago. I'd initially balked when I told Tamryn I needed direction in life and she suggested I download a history app, but maybe she was onto something. This was certainly a change from my daily habit of late, which included watching Netflix and eating all day. Wait, though. Had she told this guy where I lived? Because I sure didn't. Except, that didn't sound like something Tamryn would do.

"Oh, like the gladiator. That's cute, I like that. I get it. Very immersive. Anyway, *Gannicus*. How did you know where I lived?" My dad looked up quizzically from his morning grapefruit, pushing his glasses up his nose to take a closer look. Gannicus grabbed my arm and led me out of the kitchen and into the living room. I wasn't too focused on the confusion of the moment to notice how big and warm his hand was.

"No, not 'like' the gladiator, the gladiator. You gave the app access to your information. Didn't you read the syllabus?" He stared at me expectantly, as if anyone is supposed to read those things. As if reading my mind, he added, "It said 'Please read.'"

I just shrugged and glanced away. Who was this guy that thought people actually read into an app before they accepted all the terms? Maybe if I had, though, I'd know why he was so intent on staying in this character. Arguing that he was the same gladiator from the slave revolts was a bit of a hard sell. While his dedication to the bit was kind of cute, it was also a little weird. It would've been like if I went to Chuck E Cheese and the guy in the costume acted offended that I didn't believe he was a real giant rat.

"Ok wait a minute here. Sorry, did you say *the* gladiator? As in the guy that lived over two thousand years ago? I get the theme you're working with here, interacting with history and all, and I appreciate it. But last I checked my brain does work and I am capable of rational thought, so we can skip past the pretension part. But really, I appreciate it. It's a cool idea."

My rambling was interrupted by a roaring bark of laughter. I jumped, startled by the volume.

"Well I believe you now," he laughed. "You're certainly not Tamryn. She accepted it all a lot more quickly."

Tamryn had accepted it more quickly? So he *did* know Tamryn. That much was obvious, but he'd sure given it up quickly. I supposed Tamryn must have experienced the unusual methods of the app because she was the one who recommended it to me. I knew she didn't read the terms and conditions of the app either, because no one did, but maybe someone had told her how it all worked ahead of time, so she'd know to just go along with the schtick. If she knew this behemoth was going to come to my house, meet our dad, and claim to be a slave from before the birth of Christ, though, why wouldn't she have given me some kind of *warning*? Still, knowing that Tamryn had gone through this made me feel a lot safer with it.

Might as well go along with it. I started to head towards the couch, where we could be comfortable for our conversation. Gannicus was looking somewhat absently towards the kitchen, like he was forming a question. Maybe I could grab his hand and lead him over to the couch with me, as a way to get his attention. Was that flirtatious, or was that weird? Weird. It was weird. Instead, I waited for his eyes to fall back on me and motioned for him to follow, sitting on the couch expectantly.

"Do you happen to have any wine?" Gannicus asked, standing despite my invitation. I glanced at the electronic clock under the tv.

"It's... not quite 9 a.m."

"I'm from a different time zone," he grinned, the corners of his eyes crinkling with genuine humor.

Though I was growing skeptical that Tamryn would knowingly send me this apparent alcoholic, I compliantly stood up and went to the kitchen to seek out wine. I waved awkwardly to my dad and prayed he wouldn't comment as I pulled a bottle from the pantry. Fortunately, he was too engrossed in the book he was reading about the life of Elvis Presley to even see my wave, much less notice what I was taking from the pantry. I let my hand fall to my side.

When I came back, Gannicus was sprawled out on the couch, intently reading a pamphlet my mom had left on the couch about teaching college online. The pamphlet looked small in his hand. I let myself look for half a second more than was necessary, at the way his long hair pooled on the arm rest behind his head and one tree trunk-like leg was sort of crossed over the other. He really belonged on the cover of GQ. I tossed him the bottle when he glanced up at me. Though I had my hesitations about giving wine to my morning guests, I had to acknowledge the sudden glow of warmth in my chest when he smiled.

"Let's get down to business then," he said, taking a long drink from the bottle. "You want to know about the war from someone who lived it. Thank you for choosing IEducator. Your participation keeps the tradition of history going, and will provide a strong foundation for the future. Please remember to rate the app in your app store, and recommend it to your friends." He ran through the speech like he was counting his years suffering in purgatory. His expression set off a twinge of sympathy in me, but I didn't even really know why.

"The first step is to prove to you that this is real, that I am who I say I am. You can look at my battle scars." Even as he took off his shirt to reveal a muscled landscape of the evidence of deep cuts across his chest and abdomen, his voice continued in that uninterested tone. The makeup to create the scars must have been exceptional. They were as beautiful as they were macabre, and definitely believable. For an app I'd never heard of before Tamryn recommended it, iEducator had quite a production budget.

Before I could stop myself, I was reaching out to touch the memory of a long gash across his pectoral muscle. I could feel the raised scar. It didn't smudge, and my finger came away completely clean. More than that, though, I could just feel the difference between special effects and real scars. That was not makeup. I looked at his face, where his eyes were waiting to look into mine. They were deep and serious. His full lips were set in a firm line.

My face burned. What was I doing? He was a stranger, and here I was touching his bare chest? That was unacceptable. It was creepy. Clearly I'd crossed the line.

"I'm sorry," I said, shifting back to sit further away from him. It wasn't much, but there wasn't much to say.

"Worry not," he said, an easy smile returning to his face after a beat. "It's all part of the experience."

Despite the confidence of his reassurance, my stomach churned. For that one moment, there had been a difference in the air. Through a slight, involuntary tension of his muscles, through a barely perceptible narrowing of his eyes, he'd communicated a discomposure he'd meant to keep hidden.

Before I could remind myself that he was a stranger, and that I'd already acted too comfortable once, I tilted my head to the side and stared at him.

"Are you sure?" I almost whispered.

He knit his eyebrows together and shook his head, keeping his lips turned up.

"Certainly. This is what I do. My focus is you getting the whole experience."

Right. This was an acting thing. He was here to play a character, and teach me about the 70's B.C., when his character had lived. I'd already decided to go along with the act, so there was nothing to do but keep doing that. So the guy had battle scars from some war where they used knives or swords or whatever instead of bombs and guns. That could be a real thing. Maybe he had a pet tiger. The point was, the battle scars didn't prove he was actually here from the distant past. His hesitation didn't mean he was asking me to understand him. If I didn't want to make an actor's job harder, I'd better get us back on track.

"Cool," I muttered, glancing away from where my eyes had settled on his tan, athletic chest to a safer place on the carpet. "Let's hear about the war."

Chapter 3

We sat on the couch for the next hour as Gannicus told me his story. It all started when he was a slave in a gladiator training school in Capua. There he met Spartacus, a strong-willed man who inspired faith and courage in anyone who met him. It was this man who united the gladiators in an escape effort. Once they were free, it wasn't as easy as I might have thought. Roman praetor Gaius Claudius Glaber and his army tried to head them off at Mount Vesuvius, but they managed to surprise the Roman army and get them to flee. They continued to stay ahead of the Romans, gathering more slaves and even free men to join them.

"You should've seen us," Gannicus said, pride shining in his eyes. "We crushed the Romans under our feet. They were terrified of us. What started as an attempt to free ourselves turned into a mission to fight against the injustice of Rome. Spartacus, Crixus, Oenomaus - they were strong leaders for a while." His grin wilted, and a hardness crept into his eyes.

It was an abrupt change, and it threw me off guard. He was really invested in this explanation of his. I was too, but I was just interested in a compelling story. Gannicus, on the other hand, was clearly affected. I'd been to my share of plays, but he made those actors seem like amateurs. Even the little mannerisms that I would think were subconscious seemed to go with his character's story. He would rub his hands together for a moment, pushing his thumb against the other palm in some gesture that seemed to be between frustration and anguish. When he ran a hand through his hair, it was with an intensity that made it seem like his hair was getting in the way of the heroes of the story.

"Then Spartacus got us into a mess. We went down through Italy, with the idea that we'd get to Sicily and recruit more for our army. Problem is, he made a deal with Cicilian pirates to help us get there—no good bastards. They left us with no option but to cross the Strait of Messina on our own. Didn't work. We tried to react and keep moving through mainland Italy, but Crassus - sorry, Marcus Licinius Crassus - trapped us on Melia Ridge.

"Well, what could we do? Sit around and wait to starve? Not likely. We waited for the perfect moment to face Crassus. In the middle of a night cold enough to freeze your testicles off, with a storm raging, we struck when they least expected us. It wasn't easy, but our army got through the gap in their defenses and we were on our way."

The bottle of wine laid on the couch, forgotten in the drama of his story. I was right there with him.

"I couldn't forgive Spartacus for that. What kind of general gets his men into a storm like that? And now that we knew how strong we were, why not go right back into the heart of Rome? Take them down, make them pay for the slavery we suffered. Castus, a brave man and a friend, decided to join me when I took matters into my own hands and separated from Spartacus. We took quite an army with us, some 30,000 soldiers."

That was apparently the end of his story. It didn't sound like much of an ending to me, but this wasn't my show. With a relaxing of his posture and a sigh, Gannicus stood up from the couch, reaching down to claim the bottle of wine that I certainly did not invite him to take home. I didn't argue with him.

"Well, Lane, that's the end of your first lesson. There might be a test. There might also be... opportunities for extra credit," he leaned into me with this last line, winking playfully. Something swooped in my stomach, like the feeling of a drop on a rollercoaster. He laughed out loud when my jaw dropped of its own volition. He was definitely having too much fun with this teaching position.

When I said as much, though, his smile lost its radiance as he nodded unconvincingly. I hoped I hadn't hurt his feelings, somehow belittled his efforts. Should I say something? I stood up and followed him as he left the couch. Maybe I could tell him that he did a really good job or that he could be a famous actor if he tried to go to Hollywood or something. Or was that worse? Maybe if I implied he was an actor he'd go on about how I didn't read the syllabus again. I didn't know how to make up for it if I'd said the wrong thing, but I thought saying a second wrong thing would definitely be worse, so I just let him put his t-shirt back on and stroll towards the door.

"If you want another lesson," he said as he reached for the door knob, "you know where to find me." I breathed out a "thank you" as he closed the door behind him.

I would certainly be requesting another lesson.

I tried to have breakfast after he left, but the excitement of the morning was getting to me. I pushed the Cheerios around the bowl, only managing to take a few cold bites before I shoved the bowl away. Listening to Gannicus' story had been interesting, but only now that he was gone did I realize how overwhelmed I really was. There was a lot to unpack. He'd known my address and just showed up; that was something. What else did the app know about me that I'd apparently agreed to? But I hadn't stumbled across the app. It had been recommended to me by the person I trusted and loved the most.

If the app Tamryn suggested had included a few free PowerPoint lectures, I wouldn't have been too shocked that she'd been pretty vague about it. In fact, when she'd initially suggested it, I didn't even notice that she'd shrugged off my few casual questions. Now that I knew the experience was so... immersive, it seemed too strange that she hadn't given me any information. If it was anyone else, I'd be suspicious. But this was Tamryn. If there was something I didn't know about her, all I had to do was ask. So that's what I'd have to do now.

I picked up my phone and video called her.

"Hey!" she greeted from her position at her desk. I could see her school notebooks at the edge of the screen. I ignored a small pang as I wondered again if maybe I should follow her lead and just go to law school. She'd be starting next year. What elusive dream career was I even waiting for anymore? It would take me a few months to study for the LSAT, but maybe it was time to just do that. She broke my thoughtful silence. "Did you try the app?"

"Yes. I have a question. What the hell?" I thought that summed it all up pretty well.

She laughed, making eye contact with someone off camera. Levi must have come into the room. She whispered something to him that I thought sounded like, "She tried it." The pounding of feet on the hardwood floor announced his arrival as Levi stormed up behind her to see me on her screen.

Levi was a handsome man, with short black hair and hazel eyes. He had strong principles, and loved Tamryn. Still, I couldn't understand how she could choose to marry anyone after meeting Gannicus. Something about him set him apart from other men. Wait, what was I *thinking*? I had literally *just* met the man today! For all I knew, he was exactly like everyone else. Just because he was exactly the physical specimen of my type, didn't mean he was anything more than a pretty face. Even though the thought was technically a possibility, I couldn't bring myself to feel convinced by it.

"What class did you take?" Levi asked in his deep voice. His eyebrows were raised expectantly, and he leaned in closer, as if he was afraid to miss my answer.

"I took the one with Gannicus," I said slowly, watching them carefully for concealed reactions. If Levi's dash into the room hadn't told me he'd also tried the app, common sense would've stepped in. Tamryn said it had changed her life when she was pursuing her history major, and it was in those history classes that she'd met Levi. Maybe they'd bonded over their love of the app, or downloaded it together for a group project or something. Whatever it was, it was safe to say that Levi knew something about the app, and I was eager to know how much that was. I didn't need to bother with the subtlety. Their eyes widened. She gasped and he smiled a slight knowing smile. Tamryn actually clapped.

"Isn't he something? Did he take off his shirt?" she asked. Oh. He did that with everyone. That was just part of his act. I was surprised to find that I was disappointed. I wasn't surprised because I didn't know I was attracted to him, but just because it was so unrealistic of me to think that he had done it especially for my benefit. Did I think he showed up at my house because he wanted to date me? Disappointment wasn't an appropriate reaction at all. Fortunately, I had too many questions to dwell on it for long.

"Yes, he took off his shirt. Ok now tell me what the hell is going on!" Tamryn glanced at Levi, a question in her eyes. I didn't have to hear the question to know she was asking his advice on what to tell me. Levi didn't either. He almost imperceptibly shook his head. I knew I wasn't supposed to catch it, so I kept my mouth shut and let a slight narrowing of my eyes speak for me. Tamryn pursed her lips, unsure of whatever decision she'd made. Who told Tamryn she was allowed to keep secrets from me? Secrets were for people without twins! I was about to drive over there and kick Levi's ass for suggesting she not tell me. But then he started to give more information, so I decided to forgive him.

"It's just what you think. The app lets you meet historical figures. They come to your house and tell you about their experiences. Just be careful, because some of them are less friendly than Gannicus," Levi said. He looked at me intently, gauging my attention to his words. "When you have someone, don't let them out of your sight."

This conversation wasn't answering questions so much as it was raising new ones. There was one fact I did have to acknowledge though. Levi just implied the historical figures were really from the past. That I shouldn't let them out of my sight said there was something odd going on here, beyond a clever way to have actors teach history. He was suggesting that some of these people were dangerous, and not with the intention to warn me away from an app that hired sketchy employees. No, he said it as if it was an unavoidable fact of dealing with people from the past. Who were real. I wouldn't have believed it from anyone else, but I trusted Tamryn and Levi. I wasn't sure I believed them, exactly, because that was impossible. I knew if it was a joke, though, I could get them to give it up.

"Do you swear it's not a joke?" I asked Tamryn, staring into the phone's camera so it would look more like I was staring right into her eyes. Tamryn and I would never lie to each other. Ever.

"Yes. I swear it's not a joke," she said carefully.

Huh. My stomach dropped at the simple words. It wasn't a joke. Despite all reason, I believed Tamryn when she said it. I couldn't help it. If Tamryn said that these people were really from the past, then she believed they were really from the past. Was she crazy? Had she fallen for some really bizarre scam? Or was she right?

I tried to ask about her experiences, but she kept brushing off my questions with the insistence that I "have my own unique experience with it." I did get Levi to nod when I asked if these people were really from the past. I didn't quite know what to make of that. Mostly because it didn't make a modicum of sense. How could Gannicus have gone from fighting in a slave revolt to sitting on my couch? It defied logic.

"How did they get here then? If this is real," I asked, at the same time that Tamryn announced that she had to go, she had another online class. "Wait! Seriously -" She hung up anyway.

Chapter 4

The more I thought about how sincere Tamryn and Levi had been, some part of me wondered if he really could've been Gannicus, Celtic leader of a branch of Spartacus's rebellion. If he was, he didn't hop on a plane to get to Arizona. He'd have to have gotten here with time travel. My first thought was *Back to the Future*, but I tried to be open-minded. Technology was expanding every day. Certainly the smartest of scientists would've considered the issue. There were way too many movies about it for them to not even look into it. Time travel was theoretically possible, right? Multiple dimensions or something. Time dilation? If only I'd been confronted with this problem when I was trying to settle on a major. I'd have majored in theoretical physics if I had known I'd be in this mess. Okay, maybe I'd have befriended a theoretical physics major, at least.

As it was, I decided to do my best to use the tools I had. Apparently knowledge wasn't one of them. But I did have an app.

My heart began to beat faster as I found the app on my phone and tapped on its icon. I swiped a few fingerprints from my phone's screen with the bottom of my shirt in a pathetic attempt to stall or something, but it didn't last long. So I dug through the features until I uncovered the syllabus for "Interacting With The Past." It was high time I read one of these things.

Syllabus (Please Read)

Thank you for being a part of IEducator. We are proud to offer a variety of courses to expand your mind, all free of charge. Education is a gift that we must all work to bestow upon each other. This is no ordinary class.

This course offers you the chance to speak with people who really experienced historical events. It may be difficult to come to terms with this possibility, but we invite you to do further research into the realities of time travel.

You won't find a textbook recommended, or coursework suggestions. Instead, we offer you guidelines on how to stay safe and have fun as you interact with the past:

1. Feel free to start as many courses as you like, as often as you like. There are no commitments.
2. If you wish to visit with an instructor more than once, simply choose that course option as you did the first time.
3. Instructors are available 24/7. Please allow for some error as the app attempts to predict your sleeping habits based on your time zone.
4. You cannot delete your information from the app. However, our privacy policy will protect your information.
5. **Do not** encourage instructors to leave the address that is listed in your user profile. You do not have to provide this information; it is already on the app.
6. Please keep in contact with the instructor for the duration of the hour, until the lesson is completed. At that point, they will be transported from your address.

This course aims to create an experience that you will remember for the rest of your life, and to spread knowledge wherever we can. Please help us in our mission by rating the app in the app store and sharing it with your friends.

I kept scrolling. Surely I'd missed something. Maybe a paragraph about what to do when there was a gladiator in your living room. I'd have settled for a single sentence, in fact. Instead, it was all frustratingly vague. All I had was the suggestion that I do my own research. What was I supposed to do with that? Put it in Google?

A quick Google search revealed that sure, time travel wasn't theoretically impossible according to Stephen Hawking. I took to a scholarly article database accessed with my old University of Arizona Student ID, and found articles insisting on the existence of time travel. I wouldn't normally take them at face value, but Gannicus had been very convincing. And peer-reviewed articles had to be true, right? Anyway, the articles reported that it was a new technology, just beginning to be tested in the real world. Just because it was new to me didn't mean it didn't exist. I liked to think I was reasonably intelligent, but that didn't mean I was an expert on a subject like this.

So maybe time travel was a possibility. Maybe the professors on the app were really from the past. Maybe Gannicus was really a gladiator?

If only I lived with a historian who could help me, I thought sardonically. I abandoned my internet searching, clearing out the tabs in my phone as if to erase the evidence of my investigation. It was time to turn to a live source. If anyone would be willing to teach me about history, it was my mom. She'd been doing it my entire life - invited or not. I certainly wouldn't be able to tell her about the app; she couldn't even figure out Facebook half the time. She definitely wouldn't be open minded about the possibility of time travel. At the very least, though, she knew something about the Spartacus slave revolts and of Gannicus. I could ask her what history remembered of him, and see if his story added up.

"Hey, Mom," I said when I found her working on her computer. Her black hair was tied loosely back, and her glasses were slipping down her nose again. "You remember that guy Gannicus, from the Third Servile War?" She turned in her faux leather computer chair, enthusiastic to discuss history with someone who didn't need her class to graduate for a change. She was used to teaching college freshmen who paid more attention to the stickers on their hydroflasks than they did to her. I pressed on, encouraged. "What ever happened to him?"

"He died in battle, at the Battle of Cantenna. I think it was... 71 B.C." She nodded, as if to confirm her own statement. I was surprised I'd gotten an answer so quickly. There wasn't any interrogation as to why I wanted to know this information suddenly. Maybe she was just happy I'd asked. That made me feel a little guilty for never really asking her about history before, actually.

Wow, died in battle. I wonder what that must have been like. Did he know it was coming? Or did someone stab him in the back, sending him to his death before he'd even had time to fear it? Then again, it didn't really happen, did it? If my understanding of time travel was correct (and it wasn't much of an understanding), wouldn't someone have to get to him before he died? I wondered how lucky he felt to be spared from such a ghastly death.

By using the app, maybe I was helping the people involved by participating in the program that saved their lives and gave them a second chance today. The app might be able to save even more people if it had a lot of customers. I could tell my friends about it, and maybe it would grow in popularity. That was doing something meaningful, wasn't it? I clung to the idea that months after graduating college without a clue what to do with my life, I might have achieved some semblance of productivity.

"Was he a good guy?" I asked, before I could ask myself why on earth I would utter a question like that. It sounded more like a question you'd ask about a man you were interested in dating, not a dude who died a couple millenia ago. What was I going to ask next? *Does he have a girlfriend?* That would be only a little more ridiculous. My mom frowned, adjusting her glasses so she could more effectively scrutinize me.

"I suppose so," she said, drawing out the words as if to give herself time to stop them if she changed her mind. "He fought against slavery, so he stood for something important. I'd say he was considered an admirable figure. There's not much about his personality."

It wasn't much - or anything, really - but I digested it anyway. He did fight to free himself and other slaves. That meant he was brave, and that he was willing to die for his beliefs. That certainly was a positive. *He's against slavery* wasn't really a high bar for a potential boyfriend, or even friend, though. I was pretty sure everyone I knew had the same opinion on slavery. No, the only way to find out what kind of guy he was was to talk to him myself. Besides, I couldn't even be sure that he was really from the past. Just because time travel was real didn't mean *he* was. Wouldn't it be cheaper to claim to pull people from the past than to actually do it? It might be worth getting to know him either way.

Whatever questions I had for my mom faded away as I made a plan for tomorrow. I'd want to choose his name on the app and request another lesson. This time I'd be ready. I'd get up earlier to do my makeup and curl my hair.

That night when I went to bed, I locked my door as quietly as I could. It wasn't like my parents to barge in without knocking, but I didn't normally plan to video chat with gladiators, and I wasn't taking any chances. My dad saw Gannicus this morning. If he knew I was talking to him again tonight, my parents would start talking. Once my mom got wind of it, the whole extended family would be set on fire with the news that Lane was finally talking to a man again.

I settled onto my embarrassing old bunk bed and took two slow breaths. My stomach flipped, begging me to get on with it and talk to him already. I forced myself to look at the issue in context. This was nothing but a casual meeting, and asking him for another class wasn't any kind of risk. If he declined, he was just busy with another student. So there was no reason to be nervous, no reason to focus too much on my heart thudding against my chest. How did I ever go on actual dates in the past? I was struggling to ask this guy to do his *job* and teach a class. I supposed this time was a little different. It was a lot easier to interact with guys I only sort of liked. I liked this one a lot, and thought he was really attractive and had really nice hair and...

Ok, trying to relax wasn't working. It would be better to just get on with it and make the call. I opened the app, scrolling through the options until I found his class. As soon as I did, I tapped his name in an instant. No point dragging it out any longer than I already had.

This time he appeared promptly, standing in the same classroom as before. His eyes lit up in recognition when he saw me. My breath caught. Well, there he was. I wondered how much time he spent there in that room just waiting to be summoned. It was pretty late here; I was just about going to bed. Just how long were his shifts? I hoped my call would break up the monotony of the night shift. Of course, that was assuming he didn't get calls from girls - I meant students - all the time, at all hours of the day. It would be a good thing if he did, because that would mean his career would be going well. It *would* be a good thing. I *meant* that. Even if they were girls.

"Hello there, girl in the dark," he said, his white teeth flashing an amused smile. I admit I did leave the light off again, but I was all ready for bed. I couldn't risk him catching a glimpse of my retainer. Now that I thought about it, I probably could've spent less time thinking about the call and more time getting ready for the call. I really did plan to go to bed after this, though. Besides, I was going for casual.

"Are you free tomorrow? Say, 9 a.m.?" I asked. The question came out clear and strong, like there was nothing about the man that made me nervous at all. Good for me. I was just a student interested in learning a bit more about history. For all he knew, that could absolutely be true. With just as much dedication to my act of serenity, I tried to breathe slowly and evenly as I waited for his anwer.

Instead of answering, he turned towards the white board behind him. For a horrifying second, I thought maybe he would totally ignore my question. That would totally obliterate the usual platitude of "the worst they can say is 'no.'" Fortunately, I didn't have to sit in terror for long. Taking a red marker off the ledge at the bottom of the board, he scrawled "Lane" on the board followed by the number "9." He turned back and grinned casually, apparently satisfied with the adjustment to his schedule. It looked good up there, my name, in his rushed handwriting. 9 a.m. was early enough that I wouldn't have to spend the whole day getting anxious about our meeting, so it was perfect. I waited, just smiling in response to his makeshift schedule on the board, but he didn't say anything else.

Well, I guessed that was it. I'd wanted to make a plan for tomorrow with him and I had. The interaction should have probably been over now. I took a breath to say something, but I didn't quite know what to say. So I mumbled a weak, "Ok, thanks" and hung up. Not my best work, but talking around a retainer is a higher plane of difficulty.

Tomorrow. Tomorrow I'd be ready.

Chapter 5

My alarm didn't go off.

As soon as the memory of the night before hit me, I sat up to check the time on my phone. 8:50! No. *No!* I didn't have time for this! That was 10 minutes to get ready! I couldn't become irresistible in 10 minutes. Why were alarms even invented if they didn't work? Maybe I'd go back in time and yell at the guy who created them for not making them more reliable. I gave myself one second to gasp, wonder what happened to my alarm, and flail around uselessly before I hurled myself out of bed and tore through my dresser drawers like someone had hidden jewels in them. I seized a casual enough outfit.

This would just have to be my second day putting off breakfast, which was very unlike me. Talk about interrupting my priorities. Instead, I smothered on foundation with as much accuracy as my time crunch would allow. I smeared the tan liquid over my cheeks and under my eyes. I didn't have time for this. I swiped on mascara. It wasn't enough. I swiped it on again. And one more time because it wasn't right. Shit, I was going to be late. I took a quick glance in the mirror. It was passable. I didn't have time for perfect. I had to go get the door before my parents did.

I got halfway down the stairs before I remembered I'd better brush my teeth. There wasn't time, really, but this was important. Somehow I managed not to choke on my toothbrush in my hurry and made it downstairs before the doorbell rang. I tried to open the door slowly, when it did, casually, and not tear the door off the hinges like my adrenaline was suggesting I do.

There he was, just standing at my threshold and waiting to be invited in, like he didn't even know I'd woken up 10 minutes ago. Maybe this would turn out ok.

"Hello, Lane," Gannicus smiled. A black SUV pulled away from the house, as if the driver had been waiting to make sure I opened the door.

I invited him in, staring at his broad shoulders as he walked through the door. I wasn't sure if he was really a gladiator, but he sure did look like one.

"Can I get you anything to eat or drink?" I asked politely, glad that I had something to say right away. I smoothed out a wrinkle in my shirt and tried to even out my breathing. Only now that I wasn't running up and down the stairs did I realize how out of breath all the drama of the morning had made me.

"No need," he said, and I started towards the couch. But he strode past me into the kitchen. "I can help myself."

I couldn't help but laugh at his boldness. I followed him into the kitchen and grabbed myself a banana nut muffin off the marble counter. I gestured to the others, wrapped in cellophane, but he smiled and shook his head. Instead, he opened the white wooden pantry door to investigate what we kept inside. I waited while he considered his options, apparently putting some thought into the choice. After studying the pantry, he settled on a bag of Doritos, and a box of Lucky Charms, a bag of beef jerky, and a jar of honey-roasted peanuts. He carried them in a stack to the couch. This class may have been free, but I would certainly pay for it in food.

"Should I continue telling what happened in the rebellion?" he asked, after swallowing a mouthful of Doritos.

He barely looked over as he asked the question, choosing to focus on the bag of chips instead. The question had probably been more of an opener than an actual request for information; he'd assumed I'd want to hear more about the rebellion. And I did. But there were more pressing issues. If Tamryn wouldn't give me more information about her experience with the app, then I'd just have to get the answers myself. There was something here that no one was telling me, and I didn't like to be out of the loop.

"Actually," I said carefully, "what I really want to know is how you know my sister." I took a bite of the muffin, but I had trouble swallowing it as his face took on a beautiful thoughtful expression.

"Well, I had the pleasure of meeting Tamryn in the same way that I met you. She was interested in my services through the app. We had a very insightful conversation about battle strategy, and whether I thought there were any parallels between our revolt and the American Revolution. I have to admit I'm not all that well-versed on that, but we do go through a basic historical class before we're set up as instructors on the app..."

Why would Tamryn call him just to talk about the American Revolution? I remembered enough about her history finals to realize an essay question comparing the American Revolution to the slave revolts wasn't totally out of the question. She must have gone right to the source to study for her test. Tamryn, apparently, had seen the app as an opportunity to learn history, not just to meet cute gladiators. Well, her loss.

"She was very polite and intelligent, but that was one of the last times we spoke. When I saw you, I figured she was getting back to her historical lessons. You really do look alike, though I can see the differences now." As he said it, he looked at me intently, as if preparing to explain what those differences were. I didn't ask. My least favorite experience as a twin was being compared to my sister. Someone had told me years ago that they could tell us apart because I had "a bigger forehead." It was an experience I didn't need to repeat. I imagined myself through his eyes, but I had no way of knowing what he saw. I was almost tempted to ask what the differences were between my sister and me, just to hear him describe me, when I was distracted.

The light shining through the open living room window was catching on a bright spark of gold on his hand. It was a ring, unlike any I'd seen before. I wondered if it was from his time—and if so, how I could get my hands on it. If I were going to find out whether he was really from the past or not, knowing whether his ring was authentic would go a long way.

"Where did you get that ring?" I asked suddenly, interrupting his examination of my face. I so hated to do that. If he had any interest in looking at my face, I wanted to encourage that behavior as much as possible. This was important, though, so I didn't really mind when he looked down at the ring, as if just noticing that it was there.

"It was a gift from a generous benefactor. He was impressed by my performance in the arena. He tried to purchase me from Vatia, the owner of the training school, but he had no such luck." Before I could respond, Gannicus held out the hand with the ring and let me look at it.

"It's beautiful," I said, trying to come up with a plan to keep it so I could show it to my mother. "Hey actually, it looks like it's been awhile since it's been cleaned. My mom has a cleaning kit. Want me to go ahead and do it for you?" My heart slammed in my chest, like I was attempting to rob a bank. It really did feel like I was. I also wasn't very enthused about telling him that I thought his ring looked dirty, because that was actually pretty rude. But I needed to know if he was legitimate or not, and getting a historian to check out that ring was the best plan I had.

"Be my guest," he said smoothly, taking off the ring and dropping it into my hand. It had a width of about 6mm with raised intricate designs of the same gold as the rest of the ring. There was a dark stone in the center, but I didn't recognize what kind. It was lovely.

I hoped it was evidence that he meant what he said. His face was sincere, and I wanted to believe whatever he told me. I slipped the ring into my pocket as casually as I could. The plan had been far easier to execute than I'd imagined. Maybe I had a career in theft.

"Ok, so how 'bout you tell me how the rebellion ended?"

He took a deep breath and laid down on the couch, laying his arm over his eyes. I leaned back into the leather of the couch and settled in for a long story.

"Well, it didn't end so well. Spartacus and the rest of the army were defeated by Crassus in the mountains in Petelia. He died in battle. Those that managed to survive the battle were crucified along the Appian Way. They wanted to make it clear that that was what happened to those that stood against Rome." He raised his arm to rub his forehead as he closed his eyes, drawing his eyebrows together.

"I would not have made it that far. Crastus and I made our final stand in the battle of Cantenna. I suppose he died on the battlefield, but I never saw for myself. One moment I was fighting the Roman army, the next I was staring at an unarmed man wearing strange garments." He looked down at his blue Henley shirt and added, "Something more like the clothing I wear now.

"I had no time to inquire about the stranger, so I turned my back on him and returned to my opponents. In the next instant, I was stung sharply by an unseen insect, and felt myself losing consciousness. When I awoke, I was in a new time." As he finished his story, he began to fill his hand with an unholy combination of Lucky Charms and beef jerky. He tossed it all unceremoniously into his mouth.

For such a strange story, he told it so casually. If I had a story like that to tell, I'd have made a big show of it, and gone into excessive detail about my feelings in every moment. I guessed he wasn't like that.

"Well, that's good, isn't it? You avoided dying in battle," I said after a moment of quiet, in which I had sat there, aghast, watching him eat.

He sat up and looked at me seriously, opening his mouth for a second only to softly close it. My heart skipped when he leaned forward and spoke again.

"No, Lane. It is not. Celtic men find glory in death on the battlefield. I, a slave, was going to bring honor to my people and to myself. Maybe I'd have earned a favored place in the afterlife. Instead, I lost consciousness in battle and was spared death, yes, but it was my rightful death." I watched as he ran his fingers through his long blondish hair, staring absently at the ground.

I wasn't quite sure how to respond. I heard what he was saying, but it wasn't like I really *understood*. It seemed to me that avoiding death was a better deal than dying with honor, if I really had to pick. Still, I put my hand on his knee and met his eyes when he lifted his head again to look at me. It felt like this was the right thing to do for him.

We sat there for a minute, just looking at each other. I wondered if he wanted to know me as much as I wanted to know him. Something in his eyes told me that maybe he did.

"You've put in a lot today. Why don't I tell you about my history?" I offered, nervous that he'd turn me down. After all, what stake did he have in my story? Instead of turning me down, he picked up the bag of Doritos and settled back on the couch, grinning as he waved to indicate that I had the floor.

"H-hello," I stammered, realizing I had no clue what I was going to talk about. I grinned anyway, recognizing the silliness of my presentation. "My name is Lane Elizabeth Reid. I was born here in Tucson, grew up here in Tucson, went to college here in Tucson..." My words slowly petered out as I heard my story through the ears of an outside listener. I hadn't really gone anywhere, hadn't done anything. This was supposed to be cute, but it was taking a turn towards embarrassing instead. Especially when I considered his life, and all the stories he had to tell.

When he noticed I was starting to lose steam, Gannicus reached out and briefly squeezed my hand, smiling confidently.

"I graduated college recently, and I'm gonna be somebody special. I don't know how, but I know I'm gonna do something important." It wasn't really information; I wasn't really saying anything. But I still needed him to know. I needed myself to know, too.

He smiled a small, soft smile, with a seriousness in his eyes that made me uncomfortable. It was sweet of him to be so supportive, but I didn't want him to feel sorry for me because my life was lame. I stopped for a moment, digging through my recent memories for a story that would take the focus off of my hesitation.

"I used to be a substitute teacher," I finally said enthusiastically, excited about the stories that job gave me to tell. "I once had a kid eat a dead fish in my class."

I jumped a little at his loud bark of a laugh. Since it was obvious I had his attention, I continued.

"Yeah! He was about 16 years old and they had a goldfish from a class project that died. Some other kids told him that they'd pay him $40 to eat it. I told him what he did outside of class was his business, but he wasn't about to eat a dead fish in my classroom. That was, unfortunately, the wrong thing to say. As soon as class was over he took the dead fish with him and ate it outside."

Gannicus laughed heartily at the story, and his mirth was contagious. Before I knew it, we were both laughing so hard my stomach hurt.

"I knew a man at Capua," he breathed, barely containing his laughter, "who ate a living rat."

"A live rat!" I gasped. It was terrible, really, but my sides hurt from laughing as I waited for more.

"He wanted to pose as strong to the rest of us," he said, breathing steadily again. "He did not succeed."

We traded a few more stories, laughing and cringing in turn. An hour passed way too quickly. We might not have noticed the time, but I heard a car door slam shut from the street outside. When I looked out the blinds, I saw a man in slacks and a polo shirt walking away from a black SUV and up to the house.

"You'd better go," I said, watching the man make his way up to the door. Gannicus nodded and stood up, collecting the snacks in his arms and taking them back to the pantry. At least this time he didn't take them with him. When he was safely in the kitchen I felt the ring in my pocket, wondering if he'd remember he gave it to me. I quickly pulled my hand away when he came back into the room.

"Think about what you'd like to discuss for tomorrow," he said, opening the front door and turning to face me. *Tomorrow?* I reminded myself desperately I'd just met this man, but that did nothing to quell the adrenaline that shot through me at the idea of even another hour with him. Another hour that he'd suggested.

As if reading my mind, he smiled slyly and said, "Yes, tomorrow. Hopefully that gives you enough time to see if that ring is real."

Maybe I hadn't been as smooth as I'd thought. My cheeks flushed when I imagined him seeing right through my plan the whole time. Did he think I was a liar? Or did he think the story I'd told about cleaning the ring was ridiculous? Somehow I didn't think so. We'd been genuine with each other today, and my gut told me that he forgave me for being less than truthful about the ring. The feeling was based on absolutely nothing I was conscious of, but it felt right anyway. As far as keeping the ring tonight, it didn't really matter that now he knew why I'd wanted it. I still had to go through with it, if I wanted to find some modicum of proof of his story.

I just stared at him as he laughed and walked out the door, closing it behind him. Tomorrow. I'd better work fast then.

Chapter 6

As soon as the SUV had driven away, I burst into my mother's home office. She was sitting at her oak computer desk, surrounded by stacks of papers and books too long to be appealing to anyone. Her computer screen seemed bright, even with the sun shining through the large window behind her.

I considered my approach here. Discussing a guy I liked wasn't usually something I'd do with my mom, and I'd already decided not to tell her about the time travel thing. Was that still the right decision? Maybe if she knew the whole story she could help me assess the ring carefully, considering all the aspects of the story that were and weren't realistic. Or maybe she'd say I was naive for believing him at all, and that it was completely ridiculous. Maybe she'd say that I should know better than to take the word of a man I didn't know, just because he was attractive and seemed nice. Was that the reason I believed him? I really didn't know. I just knew that in my gut, what he was saying felt like the truth. That wasn't nearly enough evidence to convince someone as pragmatic as my mother that time travel was real. The technology was too new for her to have heard about yet, and Gannicus handing me a ring wasn't going to change that. No, I'd been right before. She didn't need to know the details.

"Mom, I need your help," I blurted, reaching into my pocket and bringing out the ring. She closed a tab on her computer and turned around, holding out her hand when she saw what I had. I waited with bated breath while she took off her glasses and held it up to her eyes for a closer look. It would probably be a good time to explain what I needed help with, or what she needed to be looking for, but I was spellbound as I watched her consider the piece of jewelry. I wanted to know her whole thought process on whether it was authentic, and I hadn't even asked her yet. I just wanted her to tell me that it was.

"Wow," she said finally, after a short examination. She looked at me for a moment, her eyes slightly narrowed. I shifted my weight to my other foot and tried to look casual. I was fairly certain that I failed. "Where did you get this?"

"A friend of mine. Kailee. Her boyfriend gave it to her," I lied quickly. Lying was hardly my go-to, and it showed. The best I could manage in this moment was to try not to cringe, to avoid completely showing on my face that I knew my story was doubtful.

"Kailee? I thought you said she'd left to stay with family in Pittsburgh when the quarantine started. When did you manage to get it? Did she mail it?"

"Uh, Mom, I really don't know. Whatever. Can you just help me find out if it's really a historical artifact? From the late 70's B.C., maybe 80's, I'd guess." She raised her eyebrows at my dismissal of her perfectly valid questions, but she took out a magnifying glass from her desk drawer and looked at the ring. That was a huge surprise, knowing her. My mom didn't like inconsistencies and things that didn't make sense. She leapt at the chance to catch people out in mistakes like a cat waiting for a mouse to leave its hole. She must have been pretty curious about the ring to let it slide. I tried not to seem too eager, but I couldn't help but shift my weight from foot to foot as we examined it. This felt like a moment of truth.

"Garnet intaglio..." she muttered, making an appraisal that I didn't understand. I didn't catch any other words, though she said a few more quietly to herself. Finally she put down the ring and the magnifying glass. She shrugged slightly, and for a second I deflated. She didn't know if it was real or not. I was back to the beginning in my search for knowledge of Gannicus, and I'd embarrassed myself by taking his ring for nothing.

"I'm really not an expert on ancient jewelry. But I have a friend at the U of A who might be able to help. Will *Kailee* be needing her ring back today?"

I shook my head, but I did want this to move along quickly. The quicker we got to see my mom's professor friend, the less time my mom would have to ask me questions. Anyway, I needed to give Gannicus the ring back. I ran out of the room, grabbing her purse from the kitchen and dropping it in her lap. Just knowing I was one step closer to learning about Gannicus made patience impossible. What if he was making the whole thing up, and I was making a giant clown out of myself? Was I like a kid hiding out to catch Santa?

To my relief, she consented when I suggested we leave for the college right now, and called her friend on the way to confirm. The school might be closed for quarantine, but apparently Roger wasn't going to let that get in the way of his office hours.

I turned up the radio as we drove, listening absently to a song by the Eagles. Now that we were on our way, maybe I'd be lucky enough to avoid my mom asking any more questions.

"Your dad told me a man came by the other day. I thought I heard a male voice in the house this morning," she said. *Shit.* She allowed her gaze to leave the road just long enough to flash me a grin. There was a slight hesitation in her grin that gave away her awareness that this was unusual territory for us. I looked away. A twinge of guilt kept my eyes firmly fixed on the road ahead. We might not be the type of mother-daughter duo that shared everything, but she was trying right now. That didn't mean I was about to spill everything about Gannicus, though.

"Yeah, I'm... taking a class. Kind of an immersive thing they're doing," I replied, even though I knew there was no way she'd accept it as an answer. It *was* the truth, but it sounded impossible even to me. *Imagine how ridiculous it would sound if you told her the whole truth,* I added to myself.

"Alright. But just so you know, Lane, if you were seeing a man, you could tell your father and me. We just want you to be successful and happy," she said. I inwardly cringed at the unnecessary addition of the word "successful" in this context. We weren't even talking about my lack of career right now, but it had to make an appearance in the conversation anyway. Alright. Maybe I felt less bad about keeping her out of the loop. I just nodded my head and focused on the road.

Roger's office was on the third story of the building. It was a small enough room that his desk took up half the space; his bookshelf and two plush guest chairs took up the rest. At his invitation, we settled into his chairs. While Roger and my mother caught up, I tried to learn something about the professor from his office decor. He had an assortment of books on ancient Greece and Rome. I wondered if any of them mentioned Gannicus, even in passing. I hated to admit it, but I'd have settled for a footnote.

"Let's see what you've got," Roger said to me, interrupting my thoughts. Here it was, the moment of truth. He hadn't started by asking where I'd gotten the ring, so that was a good sign, at least. Apparently he wasn't particularly nosy. I appreciated that, since I didn't want to remind my mom of my feeble backstory. I dropped the ring into his pale, outstretched hand and looked back at him. Roger was younger than my mother; he looked to be in his mid-30's, maybe early 40's. He had a pale, skinny face and brown hair so dark it might have been black.

Roger took his time examining the ring, going so far as to take a book off the shelf and flip through the pages, comparing the ring to the book's pictures. There were too many pages. Thousands of pages (ok, tens of pages, but that's a lot) would pass between each picture of a piece of jewelry. Once he actually stopped on a ring, and I started to say, "That's it!" He just kept shaking his head and moving on. I was getting discouraged. All of these rings looked the same.

Dragging it out, he took out a magnifying glass for a closer look. I wanted to tear the ring and the book out of his hand and check it myself already. Finally, with little fanfare, he smiled and declared the ring "authentic," as far as he could tell. My stomach dropped.

Authentic? Gannicus was telling the truth. Holy shit. A mix of excitement and relief flooded through me, but the feeling faded quickly. What did this actually mean? That he'd lived in 71 B.C.? Or that he had a ring that was an authentic historical artifact? If I was being honest with myself (which I sometimes liked to do), I knew the second option was a whole lot more likely. If I went to a thrift store and bought an ugly old dress from the 1800's, that wouldn't mean that I'd grown up in those days. It was just a historical object. Still, I was one step closer to his story being the truth. The ring was real, as far as Roger could tell. That was something. The ring wasn't just a prop. Maybe Gannicus really had gotten it as a gift from an admirer from his arena days.

Roger and my mom made smalltalk while I had my internal debate, discussing the way the quarantine lockdown had affected them and their coworkers. I smiled absently, pretending to listen to their stories and even managing to nod and laugh in the right places. The whole time, though, I was wondering if Roger had any more information for me. Maybe I just wasn't asking the right questions. I'd asked if the ring was real, and he'd said yes. If I wanted another answer, I'd probably better ask another question. A degree in journalism was serving me well, after all. I couldn't very well ask if Gannicus was who he said he was. Maybe I could ask if the book mentioned gladiators receiving jewelry from fans. Yeah, that was a reasonable question I could ask.

I missed my chance. My mom stood up and announced she was ready to leave the office. Well that was fine, I'd come to find out if the ring was real and I'd found out. That was good work for one day. We could leave. Part of me was relieved that I didn't have to come up with more questions, or worse - explanations of where those questions came from. Unfortunately, my mother excused herself to go find a bathroom, leaving me alone with Roger. Here was my chance again, and I was starting to think I might back out of taking it. Somehow I'd reveal too much information and he'd think I was losing my mind. It was too hot in his office, I noticed. No, I wouldn't ask for more information. I'd wait for my mom to get back and we'd just leave.

"See to it that he gets his ring back, will you?" Roger finally said, making me jump. He indicated the ring in my hand with a jerk of his chin.

"What? Who?" I gasped. I racked my brain for everything I'd said during the meeting, wondering when I'd told him anything about the owner of the ring. I hadn't. I'd remember.

"Gannicus. IEducator, right?" Oblivious to my pulse quickening, he took out his phone and held it up, giving me time to find that little orange icon on the screen. "I, too, was interested in taking a course on ancient Rome. I thought it looked like his, and the time period here confirms it."

I should have been excited to hear that. I should have been smiling right then, leaning in closer to hear more from him. Instead, my face was just getting hot. I wasn't sure why, but his response made me want to storm out of the room and never see him again. Sure, I'd wanted Roger to tell me exactly what he'd just told me, but now it seemed too easy. I hadn't even asked. For all I knew, Roger was just messing with me by saying the ring was legitimate, trying to go along with the story of the app. Maybe I really was the kid waiting on Santa, and he was just another adult humoring me. That was irritating.

"It's ok," I said dismissively. "You can tell me he's just an actor."

Roger's forehead wrinkled. Rather than argue, he motioned for me to take a look at the book he had been examining earlier. On the open page was a ring eerily similar to the one I held in my hand.

The caption read, "Golden ring of ancient Roman aristocrat. Circa 83 B.C."

Right, the ring was real. We'd covered that. I frowned at Roger, and he continued.

"I doubted it at first, too, when the Chair of the History Department introduced the other professors and me to the app. We actually met the creator at a conference, though, and his presentation on time travel was exceedingly convincing. None of us, nor our friends at other universities, have been able to find fault with any of the instructors on the app. In fact-" Roger stopped and smiled casually when he saw my mother coming into the room. Apparently the community college professors hadn't been treated to the same course on iEducator, because Roger didn't seem to want my mother to hear the rest of what he was going to say.

I shoved the ring in my pocket instinctually. My mother raised her eyebrows, but seemed to quickly brush it off as we thanked Roger for his time and left the office.

"In fact," what? What had Roger been about to say about the other instructors on the app? More importantly, what else might he have said about Gannicus? I guessed it didn't really matter. Roger had told me his opinion - he thought Gannicus was legitimate. His explanation was too specific and reasonable to just be someone playing along.

As we made our way across the campus lawn, I tried to maintain a neutral expression. My mom glanced at me a few times, enough for me to know she was wondering what was up with me, but she didn't say anything about it.

We talked about her classes as I drove home, but I thought about the ring and its owner the whole time. Though I wanted to hold back, I found myself thinking of him as the real Gannicus more and more.

Chapter 7

He's supposed to be a teacher, I thought repeatedly that night as I tried to focus on my yoga workout. He's only doing a job. I raised into a pathetic attempt at Downward Dog, too inflexible to keep my heels on the ground. Just because I knew he was really a gladiator didn't mean anything about our relationship had changed. In fact, didn't it make it less likely to work out now? For all I knew, he'd had a wife before he'd been rescued from the middle of the battle and brought to this century. Then again, he'd never mentioned a wife. Something told me participating in a slave revolt didn't lend itself well to having a family.

The yoga instructor on my laptop screen leaned down into a Child's Pose. I followed her example, closing my eyes and breathing out through my nose. I tried to focus on being calm and mindful and sensing how my body was feeling in that moment or whatever she was trying to suggest. It wasn't really working. Yoga probably encouraged clearing your mind, but that wasn't going to work for me right now.

I didn't know that a gladiator would like a girl like me, even if he was single. What did I know about what gladiators wanted in a wife? They probably had entirely different societal standards and expectations. How was I supposed to know how I stacked up against those? Actually, I didn't know what guys from my own time wanted either. So what was the difference?

The instructor came back up into a Downward Dog, and I groaned under my breath. What was her obsession with Downward Dog, anyway? It was the worst yoga position. It did nothing but remind me that despite my efforts, I was as flexible as a new pencil. I made an attempt anyway, letting my mind wander to more relevant issues.

When had I even decided I needed to have a relationship with Gannicus? The whole point of joining this app had been to better myself, to spend my time learning. Meeting a guy had never been the goal. There was a whole list of classes on the app, a world of historical figures that I could meet. I should go and meet one of them. Maybe there was a guy from the wild west that I'd like to talk to. Or, imagine it, a woman. I could take the class and actually attempt to learn about history instead of just trying to get a boyfriend. That was a thought.

I finished my workout, collapsing on the floor. I stared up from where I was lying on my back, imagining pictures in the random pattern of the popcorn ceiling. Did those little white dots kind of look like a sword? I considered what Gannicus would look like with a sword in his hand, charging onto a battlefield. It wasn't an altogether unpleasant image. Off to the right from the sword, I thought I could make out a heart shape, and my mind wandered to romance movies, and whether I'd have something like that someday. Actually, now that I thought about it, maybe I was being too quick to move on to other instructors in the app. I had all the time in the world to try out the other classes. I should really focus on this one with Gannicus for the time being. It was good to specialize, right? Definitely. And if I was focusing on his class, I should really try to do my best at it.

I headed into the kitchen and dug through my mom's cookbooks, searching for a cookie recipe.

I spent the next couple hours baking cookies for him, like normal students do for their teachers all the time. Or something.

When Gannicus showed up at my door the next day, I was dressed in a flattering v-neck tank top and short skirt. My hair was curled, which was cute the last time I looked in the mirror. I'd smiled, fluffed it, and turned my head around to admire it. Now I doubted it. It was too much. Was this my wedding? Did he invite me on a date? What exactly did I think was the point of this meeting?

I pulled my hair back into a ponytail before I opened the door. Now there was still effort, but not so much that he'd read into it. Right?

"Hello," he said, stopping to give me a quick once-over. I pulled at my skirt awkwardly, but he smiled easily like he didn't notice. "You look lovely."

Was that a genuine compliment or a pity compliment? Could he tell I'd tried to dress up? The ponytail was definitely the right call. I was worried about being overdressed as it was. If I had gone with the curled hair left down, I definitely would've felt out of place. Still, he didn't seem like he felt sorry for me. He was standing closer to me than was probably necessary, watching me without trying to hide it. I thought I should say something, break the silence. Instead, I ran away.

I strode quickly into the kitchen and brought back the cookies, holding them out like a trophy.

His eyes lit up, and I hoped using his obvious love of food had been a good way to surprise him.

"Thank you, Lane," he said. He didn't say anything else about it, but he took a cookie off the plate and ate it in two bites. For a quiet moment he closed his eyes and smiled. Even after we'd settled on the couch for our lesson, I noticed him looking at me thoughtfully, like he was trying to figure something out. Inappropriate for a teacher or not, baking cookies had definitely been the right call.

We spent the hour as we had before, discussing his experiences in the slave revolt, but we managed to pepper in details of ourselves along the way.

"Your favorite color is yellow?" I asked, my hand brushing his as I reached into the bag of Cheetos. It was silly, the way my heart beat faster because I touched his hand in the pursuit of powdered cheese.

He shrugged, staring thoughtfully at the wall as he chewed a handful of the chips.

"The sun always came up. Wherever I went, wherever I was forced to go, I could count on that. It is one thing that never changed from my time to this. I like the sun, I like yellow." I stared into his eyes when he glanced back at me, nodding carefully. It felt like a deeper glimpse into his personality than I'd expected from such a juvenile question, and I was afraid to make him regret being so open. It also happened to be a striking contrast from my own answer. Before I knew it, I was laughing. He blinked at me.

"Is that funny?" he asked, a smile spreading on his face despite his raised eyebrows. He wasn't self conscious about his words, even though as far as he could tell I must have been laughing at him. There was a turn to his lips that suggested he was waiting to laugh with me.

"No!" I said, putting my hand on his knee. I looked at it there, resting on his jeans, for just a second before I took my hand back. "My answer is just dumb. My favorite color is ballet shoe pink, the color of Regina George's dress in the movie *Mean Girls*."

"Certainly," he said with mock seriousness. "I am not familiar with the George girl but I could see that."

I laughed at his response, letting the mood in the room lighten. Still, as I watched the crinkles at the corners of his eyes when he smiled, I thought about the solemnity of his answer to a simple question like "What's your favorite color?" My answer was true, but ridiculous. I didn't have the devastating life events to change my answers to every question that was posed to me. If I'd had his experiences, I didn't know that I'd be able to laugh them off like he did. I kept a nonchalant expression, but I wondered just how different we really were. It seemed like he'd lived at least one lifetime longer than I had. I wondered how he'd changed in those years of fighting, who he was before. The more I learned about him, the more I wanted to learn.

When the hour was up, I wanted to get my clocks fixed. There was no way time had really gone by so quickly.

Before he left, he locked his eyes on mine with mock intensity.

"Can I have my ring back, or have you sold it?" he joked. I laughed and grabbed it from the coffee table where I'd left it for him.

"Do you believe me now?" he asked, leaning down to look into my eyes as he put it back on his finger.

"Yes," I said. I was surprised by how intensely I meant it.

"Well, that is fortunate. I do not often have to ply women with jewelry for them to believe my words. They usually accept whatever I say." He actually winked when he said it. My face fell.

If it weren't for the wink, I might have thought his words just came out douchier than he meant them. Unfortunately, I saw the wink. It was there. He was used to attention from women, used to them drawn into his every word. Maybe I was just another girl giving him attention. This was his job, after all, to get people to be engaged in his lessons so they'd keep using the app. His being charming and convincing women to hang on his every word was just another part of that skill. What a stupid thing for me to be surprised by.

I thought about our conversation, about the way we'd shared little details about ourselves, and the connection had seemed so real. I'd found myself waiting in anticipation of what he would say next, and collecting each smile of his like I could cash them in for a prize at the end of the hour. Or maybe they themselves were already the prize. Did I really think I was the first girl to have that experience with him? That he'd reserved all his charms and kindness for me, a random girl who'd signed up to use his app? Of course not. He was just being nice to me because it was good customer service. The extra flirtatious vibe I was getting was just him using his natural charm to improve my experience as a customer.

And that was his right. He was teaching me history; he wasn't my boyfriend. Any extra feelings that I'd assigned to our interactions were nothing but my own interpretation, and my own fault. I'd been over here making him cookies dreaming about some kind of a future together, and the poor guy was just trying to do this job. There was no reason for me to feel any kind of way about what he'd said, or how many girls were all over him. So I told myself I'd just had too many cookies as I said goodbye and closed the door behind him. That had to be the reason my stomach suddenly hurt.

The chill of the night air tickled my bare arms as I examined my surroundings. Though I had never set foot on this ground before, a voice in my head whispered that I was in northern Lucania, a place now called Basilicata. An enormous mountain stood proudly at my side.

I froze in fear when I heard the sound of ground crunching and turned to see a small army of men creeping forward from the foothills, many of them on horseback. Their large red shields and metal helmets brought back memories of movies I'd seen: they were Roman soldiers.

"I seem to be lost," I said as boldly as I could when their lines approached me. My words fell on deaf ears as they dissolved right through me like ghosts, horses and men alike, coming through whole again on the other side of me. Maybe it was me who was the ghost. I followed them, though I wasn't sure I wanted to see where they ended up.

Around a bend in the hills, we came upon a camp. It was quiet; everyone must have been asleep. I looked up at the sky, gasping softly when I saw a million shining stars. There was no modern light to pollute their brightness. However I got here, I was no longer in the 21st century.

The Roman army I'd joined was yelling, causing a commotion as the men in the camp began to wake up and emerge from their makeshift tents. My body went cold as I recognized one of the men who appeared from a tent.

He had the same long, brownish-blonde hair, but instead of jeans he was outfitted in some form of animal skin, maybe leather. His chest was bare, but his arms were wrapped in the same material. Gannicus was beautiful here, in his own world. I didn't know how, but I knew he wouldn't last long. I may not have known how I got here, but I knew this was his final stand.

Gannicus and his rebel army took up their swords and approached the enemy; clashes of metal announced the meeting of swords. Only a few men had fallen, blood mingling with the dirt as their bodies landed. When the battle was just beginning, the Roman soldiers turned and ran. Why were they running? They were the ones who initiated this fight.

I ran to follow them. I wasn't the only one. I heard Gannicus's army yell before I turned to see them giving chase to the Romans. Giving up my head start, I slowed down to run next to Gannicus, watching beads of sweat fall down his forehead. I skidded to a halt when we turned around a hill and came face to face with the Romans. The Roman cavalry ran to the back of their standing army.

It was an ambush. Gannicus and his men were no match for a direct battle against the Romans, who were waiting in formation.

"Run!" I screamed, reaching to shake him by the shoulders. My hands went right through him, flailing desperately. He charged forward anyway.

"Please! You'll never win!" Tears ran down my face like a Tucson monsoon rain.

No one heard me as I fell to my knees in agony and waited to see Gannicus die like the others, his blood staining the pages of history forever.

I woke up crying. I sat up, pressing my fingers to the wet spot my tears had made in my pillow. Even as I saw the first rays of dawn through my blinds, the heaviness weighed on my heart. *It wasn't real. It was just a dream. Man, I must have it bad for the guy.* Except, it was real. I knew in my heart that that was what really happened to him, what should've been the end of him. I laid my head back down and sobbed, letting the tears wash the misery out of my soul.

When I began to feel better, I took my phone and Googled Gannicus's last stand. I found the historical account in acceptable detail, but as I read through it I realized I didn't need some historian's guess. I already knew what happened to Gannicus; I had just been there.

I needed to see him. But I needed to leave him alone. This was the first time I'd had feelings strong enough for a man that playing hard to get wasn't a given. This time, even the idea was a slow burning torture.

Chapter 8

The smart thing to do would be to just let him go. He obviously had plenty of other women who were interested in him, and he knew it. My feelings for him were clearly getting out of hand, if my dream was any indication. There was no way I should be having nightmares about him, crying over him. Letting go of the idea that we could be something was the best way to protect my heart.

Alternatively, I could just see what happened with him. It's not like I was signing myself up to marry him. There was no commitment in just going on a few more dates, or lessons, or whatever, and seeing where it went. I wasn't really taking that big of a risk. Sure, I'd be disappointed if I found out he was a jerk. But wasn't I already disappointed by the prospect of never seeing him again? Yes, I was. Why resign myself to that right now, when I could still have a little bit of hope? Yeah, that was the better choice. Continue, but continue with caution. I could wait a bit to reach out to him again, and give him some time to consider these questions the way I was.

One day. That was how long I managed to keep away from Gannicus.

With each passing hour I wondered if I might allow myself to open the app, just to talk to him on the phone. Surely talking on the phone was a small enough act that it wouldn't even register in his brain as an indication of whether I was too into him or not. Of course, if it was that small of an action, why did I want to do it so badly? I had myself there. No, it was better to give him time to miss me.

I considered it a miracle when I made it to noon on Saturday. Then I broke. Waiting that long was enough, wasn't it? It wasn't like I needed to make him forget all about me.

"Hi there," I said when his face appeared on the screen. He was sitting on his bed, leaning his back against a pillow. "You're probably off the clock because it's Saturday, huh?" I gave him an out, just in case he wanted to be left alone, but I hoped he'd say that he wanted to talk to me any day of the week.

"Off the clock? Where is the clock?" he said instead, bewilderment coloring his features. I couldn't help but laugh.

"I'm sorry, I meant you probably don't have to work because today is Saturday."

"Actually, I'm available for calls every day of the week," he said, shrugging. I couldn't see how that worked. Wasn't it illegal for a job to force you to be available all the time? Maybe being on call was allowed because he technically wasn't working. Doctors had to be on call, right? It must have been something like that.

Oh, right. I had to say something out loud in response.

"I'm sorry," I said finally, after an awkward pause in which we just stared at each other. "I didn't mean to bother you. I want you to have free time." I really meant it. He deserved time for himself.

"Do you want to come over to my house to hang out tomorrow?" I blurted, before he had a chance to confirm my worst fears and say that he did want time off. He could still say that, but at least if he did he'd know what he was missing. I hoped. Did he know what the term "hang out" even meant? The broad smile that spread over his face suggested that he did.

"I'll be there in," he checked a gold watch on his wrist that certainly didn't come from his time. "24 hours." I beamed, but I told myself that it was a casual, measured beam.

My parents were still out of town when I woke up on Sunday, judging from a picture my mom sent that morning of the ocean. I hoped they wouldn't come back until after Gannicus left. If they didn't see him, I didn't need a story to explain who he was or what he was doing in our house. It was easier that way.

At 11:55, I dashed downstairs in an off-the-shoulder t-shirt that I'd specifically chosen to seem attractive but casual. My stomach protested against the nerves that I was becoming better accustomed to after all of this time with Gannicus when I watched the clock pass by each minute. Finally my eyes were blessed with the numbers "12:00."

I paced in front of the door while I waited. Nothing happened.

A light knock on a window across the room shocked me all through my body. It came from the backyard. I was supposed to be home alone. My heart thumped in my chest as I crept across the carpet towards the window, hoping and praying that whatever made that sound didn't enjoy killing people. I took a deep breath and tried to remind myself that Gannicus would be here any minute, and he was a gladiator. If there was someone hiding in my backyard, I'd put my money on Gannicus. Was that offensive, to say that I would bet on him? Because people used to watch him fight in the arena and probably bet on it? I made a mental note to find a better phrase. The point was, this wasn't even scary because I was barely even alone. My heart was determined not to remove itself from where it had lodged in my throat, though.

When I made it to the window, I was just ready to see what was out there. I yanked open the blinds, my hands clasping the hems of my shirt in terror.

Oh, wow. It turned out I was right when I'd told myself not to be scared. Excited, maybe. But not scared.

There was Gannicus's enormous frame standing in the backyard, a pink rose in his hand. It looked like the ones that were growing in the bush just to his right. He casually tossed it behind him when he saw me, as if he'd only picked it absentmindedly. There was something intimate about seeing him throw it away at the sight of me, like I'd caught him in a personal moment. It was endearing. This was definitely better than being confronted by a serial killer. As a matter of fact, it was better than most things I could think of. I probably wouldn't have minded taking the rose that he threw on the ground, though.

"I'm gonna meet you out there, then," I said loudly, pointing. He nodded, following my gesture with his eyes. When I walked away from the window and couldn't see him anymore, I remembered to be nervous again. Gannicus was here, at my house. I smiled despite myself. If all we did was sit around and talk, I had a feeling that would be just fine. There was something comforting about being around him. Even though I didn't know him well, and the very sound of his voice made me shiver, I felt safe with him. I stepped towards the backyard more quickly, like I couldn't wait to be reunited with him, but something stopped me as I walked through the kitchen. Before I went outside, I decided to grab a box of Twinkies and a bottle of wine to take with me.

"This is a new bottle of wine, since some boar came in here and stole my last bottle," I grinned. I tossed him the box of Twinkies but I was nervous about throwing the bottle, so I carried it over to him. Something about throwing it badly and watching a wine bottle shatter all over the ground didn't strike me as particularly romantic. He set it on the table and dropped the Twinkies in his lap, forgetting both of my offerings in an instant as he pulled me towards him and kissed me, long and slow. Forget butterflies- there were pterodactyls in my stomach. It was only once he released me that he began to investigate the Twinkies.

I sat in a deck chair across from him, watching him open the box. *That* guy just kissed me. In real life. I wondered if the smile on my face was more of a goofy grin than I was going for. I tried to look more casual. Anyway, who knew how much time we had before my parents got back from their trip? I didn't want to waste it just thinking.

"So," I said, just to get him talking. "What's our lesson about today?"

"Most people want to know what it's like to be a gladiator." He unceremoniously shoved an entire Twinkie in his mouth, not noticing my baffled expression. Was it even enjoyable to eat it like that? I settled for grabbing one and taking a reasonable bite. I did want to hear what it was like to be a gladiator, if he didn't prefer to avoid the subject. I remembered my dream and suppressed the urge to shudder. From what I could tell, his life made for great stories, but I didn't think I'd want to be the one to live it. What was it like to be him? I guessed this was the point of the app. You could spend your whole life studying the way gladiators- or any other person from the past- lived, but it wouldn't help you know who they really were.

"If that's what you want to talk about, I'd love to hear it. I know the gist of how it worked by now," I said, referring to our past conversations, "but I want to hear about how it *felt*."

"In many ways, it was glorious." I didn't expect that answer, or the expression on his face, like he was relishing a favorite memory. I'd expected more frowning, more hesitation, like it was painful to pull the memories to the front of his mind. Instead, he leaned forward subconsciously, like he was excited for me to take in every word. So I did. I listened intently as he told me about the importance of battle to his people. He didn't say anything about how he was thrust into the role of a gladiator as a slave, and I didn't ask. I was afraid to embarrass him. Besides, I loved the radiance in his eyes. Instead, I let him keep up his bravado as he told tales of his exploits.

"When I entered the arena, armed with a shield and a sword, the crowd was wild with passion. Sometimes they allowed my opponent to live once I had defeated him, sometimes they didn't. No matter to me, I never lost."

"How do I really know that, though? You could be making yourself out to be better than you are," I kept an innocent expression, so he wouldn't catch on to the fact that I was just teasing him. It worked; his face broke into an incredulous expression. My heart skipped at the playful spark that lit up his eyes as soon as I said it. That had been my intention, but it still managed to catch me off guard.

"You don't think I could defeat any man who tried?" he asked, standing up from his chair. I swallowed. Now that he was standing up, towering over my chair, I realized how big he was. No wonder he always won in the arena. Well, no reason to give in too easily. He didn't need to know I believed him just yet.

"How should I know? You're the only gladiator I've met," I laughed, but stopped suddenly when he reached forward and scooped me up, like I weighed nothing. I instinctively grabbed at his t-shirt to steady myself; it was surprisingly soft. He just grinned as he carried me out the pool gate and unceremoniously tossed me into the pool. Hey! I blew out my breath under the water indignantly, the slight shock of cold sending a jolt through me. That wasn't what I'd expected him to do.

In the few seconds that my body sailed through the water to the bottom, I created my plan for revenge. He'd gotten the upper hand by throwing me in the pool, but I wasn't about to let that stand. I wasn't the type to let someone else have the last word. Besides, I had an evil plan. Everyone loved an evil plan.

I held my breath as long as I could and kept to the bottom. My buoyancy tried to bring me to the surface, but I fought it as well as I could, pushing up against the water. When I couldn't manage it any longer, I allowed myself to float up to the top, weightless. I broke through the surface of the water, splashing with feigned panic and sinking again.

"I- can't," I gasped as I desperately threw my mouth out of the water, "swim. Help-" It was actually pretty good exercise, this pretending to drown. Actually, though, I'd been on the swim team in high school, so it was safe to say I had the swimming thing down pretty well by this point in my life. I wasn't even sure what it looked like when someone drowned. But I doubted he'd have too much time to analyze whether my drowning looked authentic enough or not. I wouldn't have won any Oscars for the performance, but it did its job. The next thing I heard was a splash as Gannicus leapt into the water to my rescue.

He wrapped an arm around my waist and dragged me to the surface. I let him carry me, wrapping my hand on his arm and looking at him innocently. It was really sweet of him to save my life like this. Not that he really had much choice, or that I'd really needed it, but it was sweet anyway.

"I'm sorry," he said, pushing the wet hair out of my face. He was holding me tight against him, searching my eyes. His eyebrows were furrowed with concern, waiting to see if I would forgive him for endangering my life. I said nothing, because my mouth was full of pool water. He continued, explaining what probably seemed to him now like a terrible joke. "I didn't know you couldn't swim." Instead of responding, I spit the water into his face and laughed. He jerked back instinctively, his jaw dropping in mock outrage that was marred by a smile that fought against his attempt at seriousness.

I took advantage of his moment of shock to dive out of his arms and sprint away, exhibiting the swimming ability he didn't know I had.

Unfortunately, I didn't get too far. He was on me in a second, diving out to grab my ankle and pull me back. Laughter bubbled out of me in a shriek as I was yanked back through the water.

"Admit it, I got you," I said, coming face to face with him.

"I suppose you did," he said, smiling easily as he brushed my cheek with his thumb. His thumb left a trail of warmth on my face that seemed to linger after he'd drawn his hand away. I was already in his arms, yet somehow the extra contact still managed to make an impact. I didn't say anything. We just looked at each other. I took as much time as I could to stare at the drops of water on his eyelashes, and those full lips. He was like art, but a kind of art that wasn't subjective; everyone had to admit that he was beautiful. When I decided I could manage taking a break from staring at him, I leaned in and kissed him. His lips tasted like chlorine, but his mouth still had a hint of sweetness from the Twinkie.

It started out as a sweet kiss, simple and romantic. There was more, though. More kissing, more tongues intermingling. Before I knew it we were both breathing heavier, me taking a break from his lips to lightly suck on his neck below his ear. His wet t-shirt stuck closely to his chest, letting me feel his hard muscles through it. I felt small compared to him with my legs wrapped around his waist, my hips grinding against his jeans.

I saw animal hunger in his eyes when he pulled away for a moment and looked at me. My body was thrilled to see it, but unfortunately for everyone involved, my mind stepped in. He went back into the kiss, but after a moment I pulled away. It wasn't fair to him to let things keep escalating when I knew I couldn't let them go on too long. I understood that intellectually, but that didn't mean it was easy to follow through on. Especially when he looked like *that,* the sun shining on his skin and his wet hair clinging to his cheeks. He closed his eyes and sighed, as if he was facing an insurmountable task by allowing the kissing to end.

"Gannicus," I whispered. "We'd better stop before this goes too far." I ducked under the water to escape his response. I needed to tell him I would probably never let it get too far. That was the next step in the process here. A conversation. I popped my head back above the water, wondering if he'd have anything to say in protest. He was looking towards the back door, as if wondering if someone might come out at any moment and see us.

He kissed me lightly when he turned back, smiled, and swam towards the pool steps. I followed, only slightly relieved. I was glad he wasn't making an issue about it, but that didn't mean it wouldn't ever be one. But that was the future. This was now, and it was a beautiful day, and we were having fun together. Right now I needed to focus on the moment, and not listen to the voice in my head that told me as soon as he knew everything about me he'd lose interest. Even if that were true, we weren't at that point. We were here, and here was magical.

Water dripped from his clothes as he took a towel off of the pool gate and held it out to me. I wrapped it around myself, worried that if I tried to say anything he'd hear my erratic breaths. The towel was warm from sitting in the sun, and I pulled it tighter against myself, closing my eyes against the dry cloth. Finally I regained the ability to speak. I returned to our former conversation, to questions that had been floating around in my head since before we'd jumped - or before I was thrown- into the pool.

"If you loved fighting in the arena so much, why did you join Spartacus in his rebellion?"

Joining a rebellion was dangerous. In his case, it would have been deadly had he not been rescued by time travel. That wasn't something you just joined for fun, to kill some time on the weekends. Clearly the rebellion was a cause he'd put his whole being into. Why? He'd made being a gladiator sound like an adventure, like something he actually looked back on fondly.

He sat down on the edge of the pool, dipping his feet in the water. Rings of water spread out from the spots where he put his feet in, until he pushed them away by moving his feet slowly under the water.

"It was exhilarating in the arena. But life wasn't solely in the arena. We trained everyday, getting to know the other men. I wasn't always so lucky as to fight a man I had never seen. Some of them were good men—my friends." He took off his soaking wet shirt and used it to dry off his hair. I tried to think of something insightful to say. What did you say to someone who'd been forced to kill? It was a serious disclosure, and I wanted to do it justice. I came up empty, so I just sat beside him. The cement around the pool was hard and scratchy on my bare legs, but I tried to sit still.

"I'm sorry. I can't even imagine," I finally said. It wasn't much of a contribution.

"Slavery is no way to live. A man can only survive in service to his own will." He didn't look up, but instead watched our feet make ripples in the pool. I silently agreed.

We spent the rest of the hour sitting in the sun, taking turns drinking from the bottle of wine. We talked casually, sometimes leaving comfortable silence that we didn't feel like we had to fill. That was something I didn't know I was capable of, but with Gannicus it wasn't awkward. When we made our way back into the house, I made a concentrated effort not to ask when I'd see him again, and succeeded. The nature of the relationship made it more difficult for him to initiate our next meeting, but I had to take a chance and expect that of him anyway.

My personal rule for men would just have to extend to the specific gladiator breed: if a man wanted me, he'd make it known. I deserved to be with someone who wanted me just as much as I wanted him, and I wouldn't settle for anything else. If Gannicus was that guy, and I really, really hoped he was, then he'd make sure he got to see me again.

Gannicus wrapped the wine bottle in his still damp t-shirt and grabbed the box of Twinkies in his other hand. I followed him through the house and to the front door, where he stopped and turned to me.

"I am going to take the wine," he said, "and these cakes." We both laughed lightly, short but genuine. His face turned more serious, pragmatic. "Have you adjusted the settings on the app? You can set it to allow me to contact you and propose meetings." I tried to keep my smile friendly and almost neutral, but I knew my eyes danced. This was exactly the sort of move I was hoping for from him.

Though it was unnecessary to get his help on this simple technical task, I leaned my back against him and held up my phone, letting him point out the next steps and show me how to change the settings. I was happy to accept help if it meant an extra excuse to be close to him.

"I should go before they come to collect me," he said when it was done. "I'll see you soon." He kissed me tenderly, running his hand down my damp hair.

Chapter 9

It was only a few hours after he left that I heard the groan of the old garage door opening, announcing my parents' return. Though I knew there was no way they could possibly guess that Gannicus had been here, or that we'd gone out on Thursday, part of me waited nervously to see if my secret would be revealed. They'd have to find out about Gannicus eventually, but I was thinking later was better than sooner. Was our wedding too late?

Fortunately, nothing my parents said gave me any indication that they wanted to hear more about my love life. *Unfortunately,* I was ambushed soon after their arrival with another unwelcome discussion of my career prospects. I was beginning to think my parents thought of *my* career and its development as a group project that we would all be graded for very soon. If that was the way they saw it, they definitely thought I was slacking on my part.

"So, Lane," my father began, dragging in the last item from the car, a large black suitcase. "We were wondering if you've given any more thought to a job search." He made his way over and sat at the base of the stairs, as if he were expecting an in-depth answer that warranted interrupting his unpacking to sit and listen.

For a few agonizing seconds, I was mentally transported to a rendering of my parents sitting in their beach chairs in San Diego, having a deep discussion about how their daughter had now been a college graduate for months, and was still procrastinating the process of becoming an adult. I imagined their mutual looks of concern as they contemplated how to overcome this dilemma. I really could've done without that mental experience.

The answer to his question, of course, was no. The entire time they were gone I'd been extremely focused on a goal that was of the utmost importance to me, and I thought I'd used my time very wisely. Unless getting Gannicus to like me was a job that paid rent, though, I had a feeling that wasn't going to count. It wasn't that I didn't care about getting a job. I had been thinking about it for months. I'd just taken a little break from worrying about it in the past week or so, and I had to admit that it felt good. Feeling good, though, also didn't pay the bills.

"Well," I said, trying to think of something quickly. "Maybe I'll become a doctor." My father's lips quirked into a reluctant smile.

"You're not going to be a doctor, Lane," he said. His thoughts probably drifted to the same point that mine did: the last time I'd had a vaccine I'd fainted, and I couldn't hear people discuss illness without feeling queasy.

"We did have an idea," my mother cut in from where she was standing by the front door, leaning on her suitcase. She had apparently decided not to allow my dad to be sidetracked. "What if you went to law school? You've always had the perfect skills for law." I briefly considered rolling my eyes, but thought it might not be the most mature response.

"I know, Mom. You told me that one before. I don't want to do it." While I actually didn't mind the idea of going back to school for three more years, I was fairly certain I didn't want to be a lawyer at the end of it. I wanted to have a career that was important and made a difference in the world, but I didn't want to work my whole life away either. I didn't know much about it, but I knew law school was too hard to go into just out of obligation. It was also a great way to go into enormous debt, which was only worth it if you planned to stick with law after graduation. This was my career I was talking about. If I could avoid it, I didn't want to settle.

"I'll check online and see if there are any jobs I want to do," I said before she could push the lawyer issue. I was doubtful that an open job search would bestow on me my calling, but it was a somewhat productive activity that would appease my parents. Besides, it would give me something to do besides think about Gannicus.

I brought my laptop to the backyard where I could get fresh air and avoid prying eyes. How did one go about finding a job? My eyes drifted past the pool gate to the striking aqua of the water. I thought about how it had tasted on Gannicus's lips... No. I was trying to be productive here. I was going to focus.

The reason for my hesitation in just choosing a job was that I wanted to make a difference in the world. Did that even mean anything? I tried to consider what a better world would look like, in a realistic way. I wasn't going to run for president or invent a cure for cancer, but I could make a positive impact if I thought it through. What were my values? I opened a new document and typed the things that were important to me.

1. Family
2. Justice
3. Life
4. Religion
5. Love

I was fairly certain I could scratch "love" off the list as far as a useful job description, unless I wanted to try my hand at the oldest profession. I did not. Family was important, but what kind of job could that give me? A job involving families was a job involving children, and I'd already experienced that unique hell as a substitute teacher.

What about justice? That translated to jobs. I pulled up a job search website and typed the word "justice." By attaching the resume Mckenna's sister had helped me create, I was able to apply for a list of jobs with very little effort, and honestly with very little attention to what the jobs actually entailed. I'd narrow down which jobs I actually wanted if I heard back from any of them, which my past experience in job hunting suggested I would not.

Applying for jobs with no idea of your passion was like writing an essay with no idea what point you were trying to prove. It was time consuming enough to give yourself a pat on the back, but it was unlikely to yield any useful results. I finished it anyway, hitting "send" on the last application, one to a nonprofit organization.

It wasn't clear whether I was much closer to finding a lifelong career, but at least I'd taken a step in a direction. I thought I'd remembered someone giving the advice to just keep moving in any direction if you didn't know what to do. On its face it seemed like a good recipe for getting lost, but in this context it did seem better than nothing.

Though I thought I deserved to reward myself for the hard work, I instead decided to torture myself further by agreeing to watch a horror movie with my mom that night. She was always trying to convince me to watch them with her, but I usually shut it down. This time, though, she'd caught me when I was daydreaming about Gannicus, and the residual joy caused me to betray myself.

We sat on the couch with all of the lights off when night came, the usual contented quiet of the house taking on a sinister heaviness as I waited for the movie to start. I felt a little lighter when I saw my mom next to me, her enthusiasm clear on her face. At least I was sacrificing my psychological wellbeing to make her happy.

I held a blanket in front of myself protectively for most of the movie, trying not to turn away. The movie she chose was called *A Rush of Blood,* about vampires decimating a small town. I was a *Twilight* aficionado, so when I heard the idea of the movie I was relieved. It turned out that this false sense of security just made me all the more susceptible to the fear.

As we commiserated over the creepiness, though, I had to admit that it *was* kind of fun. There was something exhilarating about fearing creatures that couldn't actually hurt us. Maybe I'd been too harsh on scary movies. I had always been one to avoid the feeling of fear, but by the end of the movie I wondered if I should give in to that morbid curiosity more often.

As long as I could be sure that I wasn't in any true danger.

Chapter 10

I didn't hear from Gannicus the next day. Instead, I filled my time by video chatting with my friends and online shopping. I was proud of myself for my meager efforts at distraction.

My cacophonous default ringtone woke me up at 9 on Tuesday, earlier than I was planning to wake up. I looked at my phone, surprised I'd accidentally turned the sound on in the first place. The screen showed the orange icon that I recognized as the iEducator app, ringing to get my attention. Well, it definitely had my attention. I couldn't think of any reason I'd have a call coming from the app, except for a call from Gannicus. Oh no, I wasn't ready for a call. I hadn't done my hair. I probably looked like I'd just crawled out of my grave to terrorize a rural town. Oh well, there wasn't much I could do. I certainly wasn't about to cancel the call so I could put on some makeup. I swiped to accept the call, already smiling in greeting before Gannicus even appeared on the screen.

"Good morning, beautiful," he said, his seductive charm pulling me in as usual. *Beautiful.* He wouldn't have said that if he didn't mean it, right? Right. He thought I was beautiful! Generally I didn't disagree with him, but it was certainly nice to hear. I wasn't the one most fitting of that description this morning, though. Gannicus's hair was pulled back into a lazy low bun. I knew no artist had ever created a masterpiece like it before. He interrupted my insights to ask a question. "Are you free tomorrow?" I'd cancel my own funeral to see him.

"Maybe," I said, smirking. "Yeah, I guess I can squeeze you in. Why not today? You have a date with someone else?" I started to laugh, but stopped when he only gave me a half smile. Maybe that wasn't a cute joke. I thought it was pretty cute, though.

"Actually I do," he started to say, and then realized he'd made a dire mistake. My stomach twisted slightly when he said it, as if I had any right to feel that way. We weren't anything near exclusive. I had no claim on him, and I knew that he was popular with women. I didn't have to like everything about him, but right now it was early enough that I did have to accept it. Apparently he wasn't thinking the same thing, because his eyes widened and he waved the hand that wasn't holding his phone in a panicked sign for me to let him explain. "Wait. That answer was not right." I saw my own features harden into a stony expression in the corner of the screen. "No, I do not have a date. I do have another class today."

Oh. That was perfectly harmless. A small rush of embarrassment tried to creep in and tell me that I shouldn't have reacted negatively in the first place, since I'd *just* told myself that he wasn't mine. It was summarily squashed by a much larger feeling of relief, which stomped it out like a cigarette butt. Gannicus having a class was cool and interesting, and an enormous difference from him choosing to spend time with another girl romantically while I was over here pining over him.

"That's exciting," I said, not feigning my supportive attitude. "Do you know who they are?"

"A girl. Well, woman. I would say she was just a few years older than you, judging from the glimpse I got. It looks like word of the app is spreading, which looks promising for Davidson." I nodded thoughtfully, like I was analyzing the success of the app. It certainly was interesting that people were trying it out. Anyway, was this woman pretty? What was her name? What did she do for a living?

"What if it spreads to a lot of people? Would they have you travel a lot?" I asked instead.

"Well I know they launched it to the University of Arizona first. From what I've heard, the eventual plan is to offer lectures to accommodate high numbers of people. Apparently it takes time for these things to take off."

"Yeah, that makes sense," I said, even though I honestly didn't have the foggiest idea how an app became popular. There wasn't much else to say, so I let him go before I could ask any questions about the girl he was meeting. "Let me know how your class goes."

As we said goodbye and hung up, I wondered about his class today. Was the woman beautiful? Would he take off his shirt to show her his scars? Would they laugh a lot? There was no point in wondering. He'd probably make the lesson as engaging as possible, because he had an amazing personality and that was his job. He'd probably go through the whole shirtless routine to prove his authenticity, and it was none of my business either way. I would probably never find out, and assuming the worst wasn't doing me any favors. I'd have to fill my time thinking about something else.

Hey—if Gannicus was spending his time using the app today, why shouldn't I? I downloaded it just to learn, right? Just because I ended up falling in - *growing attached to-* the first man I met on there didn't mean I couldn't use the app for actual educational purposes. I actually liked learning about history from the actual person who experienced it, and that would probably be true even if the teacher wasn't Gannicus.

I opened the app and perused my choices, deciding what type of lesson I'd want to do. These were all real historical figures, so they'd all be interesting. The wild west, the Renaissance... what was that? That one looked interesting. I felt the ghost of last night's horror movie thrill when I came across a class called "The Real Dracula." Now *that* sounded like an exciting way to spend an hour. When I chose the class, I was confronted by a warning popup that told me, "This course is not intended for children or sensitive users."

I was something of a sensitive user. I considered myself pretty easily creeped out, at least. Watching a vampire movie had been out of my comfort zone, so meeting a man considered the "real" thing might be too far. But this was about having a new experience, branching out. If I wanted to learn something useful and interesting, it might be scary too. I was ready for that kind of challenge. Anyway, it was just information. It wasn't an immersive experience in bloodletting. With a light thrill running through me, I hit "Accept." I hoped it was the right choice. My stomach churned as I waited to see the instructor for the day on the screen.

"Greetings." I heard a nasally voice before I saw its owner. He had an accent that I couldn't quite place. I must have had the movie on my mind, because I just thought it sounded like a vampire. Shortly after he spoke, I saw his face on the screen. He had a skinny, pale face with a pointed chin and a well-kept black mustache. "My name is Vlad III Dracula, though I am known to many as 'Vlad the Impaler.'"

Ok, Vlad the Impaler. My teacher. There was no reason at all to be nervous.

"It's nice to meet you," I said in a friendly voice despite my nerves. I held my phone up carefully, letting him see my face, lit up by my phone's screen and containing no traces of fear. "You free right about now?"

Vlad blinked for a moment at my casual tone, as if he wasn't used to people being so flippant. Interesting. I thought most people used humor as a coping mechanism.

"Yes. I will be at your residence shortly."

I reminded myself to stay relaxed and easy, because he was just a teacher. There was an internal struggle, though, because having a stranger over to my house was nerve-wracking on its own. Entertaining houseguests was as scary as vampires. Especially because this one creeped me out. Maybe that was mean, though. Just because this was the guy that the story of Dracula was partially based on didn't necessarily mean he was a bad guy. Here he was, teaching history to the public. I felt a little bad for assuming that he was creepy, based on what? The fact that he had an accent that I associated with old monster movies? Or the fact that he had sharp, severe features and intense eyes? Those weren't things that he could help, or things that indicated what kind of person he was. The fact that he was referred to as the real Dracula was another thing altogether, but I was trying to talk myself out of being afraid, so I pushed that thought away.

When I heard a knock at my door almost an hour later, I took a deep breath and went to open it. I struggled a bit with the door handle in my hurry to greet my visitor. The most uncomfortable part of meeting someone was right at the beginning, and I wanted to get it over with. There he was, wearing a long red coat with large golden buttons and a red cloth hat. His expression was serious, but didn't necessarily suggest a negative emotion. Though he lacked Gannicus's impressive height, his appearance on the whole evoked in me a feeling of awed intimidation. I wasn't about to let my discomfort keep me from following through and being polite, though.

"Hi," I said awkwardly, letting him into the house. "Can I get you anything to eat or drink?"

"Do you have the blood of my enemies? Many say I have enjoyed dipping my bread into it," he replied, grinning sardonically. I laughed, making it sound as sincere as I could to hide the chill that went up my spine. He was getting right into the role, and that was a sign that he was good at his job. The role was telling stories that really happened, to him, about his own life and history, but I tried not to get ahead of myself. He said people *claimed* he drank human blood, not that he did.

"Well, did you?" I asked, following his lead when he settled into a seat at the dining room table. The wooden chairs were straight-backed with thin cushions on the seats, painted in a light blue. The simple modern design looked strange against his historical red coat.

"Perhaps," he said simply. Oh, great. I didn't have any blood of the enemy in the pantry. I wasn't even sure I had bread, actually. I'd probably better make a trip to the grocery store. Or make a trip out the front door and run for my life. Either oblivious or apathetic to my reaction, Vlad continued like this was an everyday occurrence. I supposed it was, for him. "I inspired the story of *Dracula,* you know. Would you like to discuss my treatment of enemies?"

At this point, I wasn't sure if I *would* like that very much. If Gannicus was really from Ancient Rome, and by now I truly believed that he was, that meant Count Chocula here meant what he said too. So the stories he told me were probably true, not just scary stories told around a campfire. For the first time, I realized that the app didn't just rescue the good guys. There was at least one person with a class who was known for brutality, and he was sitting in my dining room with me, alone. Just waiting to tell me how he was the person whose existence inspired the creation of a classic monster. Somehow, he was offered a job with the app anyway. The last part was some comfort, though. There was no way the people that ran the app could afford to send maniacs out into the world unaccompanied. So whatever Vlad had to say, it was probably more tame than he was letting on. He was probably just coached on the theatrics to make it more interesting for listeners. And it certainly was interesting.

"Uh, yeah. Please go ahead," I muttered, staring down at the white wood of the table and reminding myself that it was just a conversation.

"Let me start my tale at the beginning. My father was ruler of Wallachia, in a place I believe you now call 'Romania.' My father, my brother, and I were captured by the Ottomans when we deigned to grant them a diplomatic visit. They told my father they'd free him if he agreed to leave my brother and me behind. He thought it best for the family, so he returned home alone. He was eventually ousted from power in spite of his efforts and killed by the local aristocracy."

Yikes. I imagined Father's Day was probably pretty far down this guy's list of favorite holidays. No wonder he was so creepy. It was probably some kind of defense mechanism to hide the pain he felt from being abandoned by his dad. I leaned in almost imperceptibly, a nearly unconscious gesture to make him feel more welcome. I was starting to feel guilty for judging him so quickly. Here he was, just trying to use his time to share history. His schtick was a little off-putting, but the app probably had a wide range of presentation styles to appeal to all of the viewers they hoped they had once it took off. It was an interesting strategy. I listened quietly while Vlad continued.

"Soon after my father died and my brother Mircea was buried alive, I was freed from captivity with one singular aspiration: to rule Wallachia. I was successful, but it was not easy to rule Wallachia. The Ottoman Turks pressed in at all times. I allowed them an audience with me in 1459, and they refused to remove their hats. I could not allow that disrespect, for their religion or for any reason. But if they really wanted to keep them on, I would ensure that they never took them off."

Well, that was fairly tolerant of him, considering his attitude seemed so much against them. It sounded like he was really dedicated to helping them follow their religious rules. Maybe Vlad was even sort of supportive.

"I had their hats nailed to their skulls."

Oh. My stomach turned. Somehow worse than what he'd said was the way he said it. Almost casually, except for the hint of smugness that he couldn't keep from revealing in the slight upturn of his lips. He wasn't just telling the story to expose a bitter past, and he was probably not going to explain how he spent the rest of his life trying to redeem the horrors he'd committed. No, he was actually proud of torturing people. He thought it was *clever*. Before I could stop myself, I started to imagine the blinding pain of a nail piercing skin, the blood-curdling screams. Sweat prickled the back of my neck. I glanced past Vlad to the front door, wondering if I could escape if it came to that. He was between me and the door, so any escapes would have to be made through the backyard. I hoped the plan was unnecessary. It wasn't a very good one. Through the backyard there would be little hope of someone seeing him chasing me, so I'd have to be faster. And I'd have to get through the gate before he caught up with me. When I didn't reply, Vlad continued, oblivious. He was looking at me, but only in the casual way of indicating that he was speaking to me, not as if he were watching to see if I'd try to run.

"I took care of the aristocracy as well. I invited them to a banquet, like the chivalrous ruler I am." He snickered. "To get to know them better, I inquired as to how many princes they'd seen in their lifetimes. They'd seen 20, 30, 40. Their lack of loyalty was clear. Had I not known already, I would have been outraged. As it was, I simply had many of them impaled and enslaved the rest."

"I-impaled?" I said weakly, before I could stop myself. I had asked in disbelief, but he took it as a request for more information.

"To impale a person is to insert a stick or pole through their body, going in through the bottom of their body and exiting through the top, such as from their mouth or shoulders. I preferred to use poles that were not too sharp, to ensure that death would not come too quickly. The most useful practice, I found, was to stick the pole into the ground to properly allow others to view the slow death. I have had my fair share of potential enemies, including Ottoman Sultan Mehmed II, turn and run when they saw my victims in such a state. In the sultan's defense, there were 20,000 people impaled outside the city when he saw it. It was extremely effective."

It had been awhile since I'd felt like I was about to faint, but I wondered if the familiar feeling was returning. I felt an empty nausea in my stomach and cold sweat breaking out across my forehead. I closed my eyes and took deep breaths. It was fine. It was just a story. Time travel wasn't even real. Wait, then Gannicus wasn't who he said he was, and our whole quasi-relationship was a lie. I couldn't have that. Just picturing Gannicus was a small source of comfort for me in this moment, and I wasn't about to let that go. Well, here was something. This all happened like, hundreds of years ago. It was long over. I knew horrible things had happened in history. Did it make it any more horrible that I was sitting across from the person who did it? Yes. It made it much more horrible. This wasn't helping. I wasn't sure I was capable of helping this situation. Vlad just kept going.

"My reputation has spread far and wide, my memory preserved in many a historical account. It is said that the vampire Dracula is based on my legacy. I believe this Dracula character was lacking. He never skinned a woman and sliced her body down the middle. It seems to me that he would have been a more formidable character had the writer used more of my exploits." Vlad calmly adjusted one of the buttons on his coat as if we were having a typical literary discussion. This was nothing more than an opportunity for him to brag.

My dizziness was only getting worse. I had to get out of there. Before I fainted. I muttered something about being right back as I stood up from my chair and stumbled to the bathroom. I stared at my panicked eyes in the mirror as I splashed water on my face and the back of my neck. *You can do this. You've seen worse on TV. Just because this is real makes no difference.* That line wasn't any more true than it was a minute ago, but I didn't have any idea what else to say to make myself feel better. I just had to keep myself upright; that was all. I dried off my face, focusing only on the slightly rough but warm towel as it rubbed on my skin.

Ok, back in there. It was just a story! I was an adult woman in the 21st century. I had social media. I knew what kind of horrible things existed in the world, and this being a shock to me just wasn't reasonable. It was time to grow up and get back in there. And tell Vlad to leave? I shuddered at the thought. No, there was no way I was brave enough to start some kind of altercation with that person sitting at the table. He'd tortured people for wanting to observe the dress standards of their religion, and who knew for what else. I refused to consider what he'd do to someone that tried to kick him out of their house. No, I was just going to have to stick it out for the rest of the hour, and write a strongly worded review on the app after he left. But what if he saw it? He knew where I lived! Alright, I'd go back in there and get through the hour. Then I'd decide what to do after that.

I went back into the dining room, prepared to face Vlad and hear more of whatever horror he decided to share with me. When I got there, though, I realized no one was there.

Vlad was gone.

The breeze rustled my hair before I turned and saw what it meant. The front door was wide open.

Chapter 11

Shit. No big deal, I'd just let a cold-blooded sadistic murderer be unleashed on Tucson. For a brief moment, I allowed myself the luxury of pretending that maybe he was just taking a walk, or that he thought our meeting was over, or that he had any sort of positive or neutral intentions. His description of what it meant to impale someone rang in my ears.

Well, I had to do something. There was only one person in this century who knew Vlad had escaped. I was less than thrilled that that someone was me, but there was nothing for it.

Partially stalling, I turned from the open door and went into the kitchen. I'd need a weapon. Hopefully it wouldn't come down to a physical fight, but I wasn't counting on that. Whether I liked it or not, I had to be prepared. We had a big butcher knife that my parents occasionally used on fancy meals—that would be a decent tool if I had to defend myself.

My breath caught. It wasn't in its spot. Where it should've been, if no one was using it. I hoped it was just in the dishwasher. I grabbed the next biggest one and ran after Vlad.

I was wary of running as fast as I could with a knife. I remembered years of being told not to run with scissors, and this was certainly worse. Still, what choice did I have? I didn't know how long his head start was, or even really how long I'd been in the bathroom. I'd been too preoccupied with calming myself down. Now all I knew was that he was running - or walking, he didn't have anyone to chase-down the sidewalk, away from the cul-de-sac, and I didn't see him in front of me. That meant he had some distance to work with. I'd have to be faster. When I got to the end of my street, I had to make a choice. Did I think he went left, or right? I didn't have time to pause and consider the options. Even if I did, how would I know? I didn't even know which direction *I'd* choose, and I'd grown up on this block. Either way led through more neighborhoods. I hit the corner and just picked a direction.

I chose the right, and was rewarded with a glimpse of a red coat turning down a side street. Pure beautiful luck.

My lungs were beginning to protest as I pursued him. I'd thought I was in decent shape, but apparently the only thing that prepared you for running was running. I'd have to consider adding that to my workout routine, if I managed to catch Vlad and make it through this experience. Ok, this was getting really hard. The more I ran, the more my legs felt like cement. I thought of Vlad's stories, of the mental image of what it meant to impale people, *of the fact that he had a strategy for it,* and kept myself pushing forward. How much longer could I keep running, if he didn't stop? What exactly was my plan, anyway? Was I going to tackle him? My fire died out at the thought, and I stopped running. This wasn't going to work. I had a knife, but I didn't really know how to use it. I certainly wasn't going to stab him in the back. No, I wasn't going to tackle him either. Sometimes moving forward blindly wasn't the best plan. I needed help.

Maybe my exhaustion was talking me into stopping, but if it was it was making good points. This wasn't a decathlon. All of this effort wasn't worth a thing if I didn't come out of it with Vlad taken off the streets. I took out my phone and called someone that I knew would be able to help me. Someone who was oddly well-versed in history and battle strategy, and was familiar with the app.

"Hello?" Levi answered.

I tried to think of a way to explain what had happened, to start the story in a reasonable place. My brain was frozen. All I could think was *He's getting away, he's getting away.* That wouldn't be helpful. If there was ever a time I needed to take a deep breath and think about what to say next, it was now. Unfortunately, I didn't have time for a breath. There was a maniac on the loose, and somehow I was the only one in the area to stop him.

"Levi!" I gasped. "I screwed up. Vlad got away."

"Vlad? As in Vlad the Impaler?" he said, giving a quick, humorless laugh of disbelief. "What happened?"

I told him the story quickly, anxiously swaying from one foot to the other as I wondered how far the killer would get before I could find a way to stop him.

"Well, you have to go get him," Levi said when I finished. "The app can track your location, so you just have to call Customer Service and tell them what happened. Once you find him they can come pick him up."

Oh, go get him! I didn't even think of that idea! My sigh of exasperation came out more as a desperate gasp for breath. I'd already thought of going after him, that's why I was standing by myself on the sidewalk in my bare feet struggling to breathe. I'd been through this with myself already. Me going after him alone wasn't going to work. And why should I have to? This wasn't a random man I'd encountered on the street and invited into my house. This was some kind of contractor or employee for an app, a business. They knew who he was. If he was dangerous, they should have had some method of keeping track of him. Yeah! Didn't they have a tracking system or something? I closed my eyes, willing myself to be relieved by this new idea even as I somehow knew there wasn't anything to it.

"Why can't they just track him?" I asked. Levi sighed. I was expecting a reaction like that, but a twinge of horror and disappointment still hit me as a replacement of the feeble hope I didn't know I'd actually had.

"They don't have a tracking device on him. He uses a phone for the app but it only works with WiFi and he has to leave it in his room when he goes out. You would think they'd have a tracking device on him, but fortunately they don't. I mean, unfortunately. It's fortunate for him." I'd been right about one thing. Levi had been a good person to call. Somehow he knew these details about the app that were definitely not widely advertised. I wondered if something like this had happened to him before. Maybe with Genghis Khan or someone. Whoever it was, I seriously doubted they were as creepy as Vlad.

"Will you come help me?" Waiting for Levi to get here from Marana would take about a half hour, but it seemed better than finding Vlad on my own. "I don't think I can find him alone."

Levi was quiet for what felt like a long time. He started to speak more than once, but stopped. I opened my mouth to say something instead, but realized I didn't have a thing to say. I needed him to agree, and I'd already made just about the best case I could for that. "Killer on the loose" was a short argument, but effective. Instead, I waited. Finally, he spoke.

"No, I can't. I'm sorry Lane. I have to go to work." I thought he had today off, based on past conversations about his schedule with Tamryn. I guessed I was wrong. It wasn't like I kept a calendar of his work schedule. Ok, so not wanting to miss work didn't really seem like a valid reason not to help me catch this man who pounded nails into people's skulls, but I hesitated to call him out on it.

"Ok, that's ok," I said, keeping my voice calm and strong, like someone who was prepared to go catch a criminal. I dragged my finger across the smooth part of the knife in my hand, familiarizing myself with my weapon. "I better go and do it then."

I hung up and immediately searched for the Customer Service number. There was no point in dwelling on Levi. There was no time. I had a task, and all I had to do was get it done. As I waited for them to answer, I felt my heart beating firmly in my throat.

"Hi, I lost your guy," I said when they answered. I didn't wait for a reply, but pressed on. "I was with Vlad the Impaler and I left the room and he was gone when I came back and now he's out on the streets and I don't know where to find him or what to do now." I swallowed big gulps of air when I finished, making up for the oxygen I'd sacrificed blurting out the story.

"I understand," said a calm male voice. "At this point, we need you to locate the instructor and call this number with the extension '911' when you find him. Keep your phone on. Please do not call the police." Levi was right. They really expected me to find him for them, to hand deliver him. They were no help at all. I slammed my finger onto the "end call" symbol and shoved my phone back into my pocket.

It looked like it was all up to me then.

With two phone calls, I had given Vlad an even bigger lead. I shoved my phone back into my pocket and took off running again, my feet slapping the sidewalk. Where in the modern world would a human vampire go? He was obviously making a break for it, so wherever he went would be a long-term destination. If he were attempting to get away from the app entirely, he'd have to make it to the main road. That was far enough away that if I ran fast enough and he was just walking, I might just catch up with him before he got there. Assuming he was walking. Assuming he was headed towards the main road—or even knew where it was. I didn't like to rely on assumptions. In a situation like this, I wanted concrete information.

My lungs protested, but I pushed myself further and faster despite their warning, past houses I'd seen a million times, one-story family houses with lawns made of decorative rocks. The neighborhood was typical Tucson fare, but it was anything but ordinary today. If anything happened, it was on me. I was the one who let him go. Then again, didn't IEducator hold some responsibility for this? They were unleashing a dangerous psychopath onto the world, and didn't even keep guard on him. Was going to the bathroom against the user rules of the app? I thought not. That suggested it was their fault for putting me in this position in the first place. The internal debate distracted me some from the pain of sprinting, but it didn't get me closer to finding Vlad.

Slowing as little as possible, I tried to reduce my sound and listen. I could hear sprinklers running and dogs barking, but nothing else. Wait, what were the dogs barking at? I knew from my few (very few) times going jogging that dogs were likely to respond to someone running past. When I had to choose a turn, I went towards the sound of the dogs.

Though I could hear more dogs barking further on, I still didn't see Vlad. The street was long and empty, and there was no reason I shouldn't see him by now. I kept going anyway.

"I will warn you once to stop following, woman," said a vampiric voice I recognized. My stomach dropped. I still didn't see him, but I could hear that he was somewhere in front of me, close. Too close. He could have been hiding behind a fence, or around one of the half dozen cars parked along the street.

All of my muscles tensed in a plea to turn around and give up, but I couldn't let a killer go free. I pulled out my phone and called Customer Service from my call history. My task had been to find him and alert them, so I did that. There was no reason for me to try to confront him now. If I could avoid any further interaction with him, in fact, that would be ideal. I backed up slowly, as if I was planning to leave him alone. I heard a voice on the phone, but I didn't answer. I didn't want him to wonder who was trying to talk to me. Instead I kept the call going and carefully slid my phone into my pocket, watching to make sure that I didn't accidentally cancel it.

My heart slammed in my chest when I looked up again. A red coat flapped against his body as Vlad came charging in my direction.

Chapter 12

Abandoning my well-intentioned plan in an instant, I turned on my heels and ran for my life. I tried to steady my breathing to prevent the gasping sobs that were attempting to disarm me, but calming down would have been hard enough if I were standing still. Now that I was running again, and a whole hell of a lot faster now, it was impossible.

"Help!" I screamed, turning around to see him much closer now. "Fire! Rape! Kidnapping!" I'd heard that yelling "help" wasn't conducive to getting people to actually respond. None of my three choices appeared to be much help either. Wasn't everyone in their houses these days? Why couldn't anyone hea-

My thoughts were interrupted when a heavy body crashed into me, slamming me to the ground. I felt a sting as my hands slapped the ground, followed too quickly by my chest. I gasped for air. I'd only felt this breathless feeling once before, when I was pushed on the asphalt in elementary school. The fall had knocked the wind out of me. My body screamed that my lungs had burst and I *was going to die.*

I kept gasping for air. As I did, I saw my knife lying in the grass of a lawn, about five feet away. So close. I turned around and tried to scramble for it, using my knees to try to push The Impaler off of me. I might as well have been a kitten for all the damage I did to him.

Unfortunately, Vlad caught sight of what I was reaching for, and shoved me to the ground. My head slammed against the cement, the sharp pain of impact slowly turning to a dull protest that hurt no less.

"Ah thank you, you brought a knife," he said as he stood up and retrieved it off the lawn. This was my chance. He was off of me, if only for a minute. I had to run for my life now, and not slow down again, and not get tackled again. If I didn't get up and run now, I didn't even want to think about what could happen. When I sat up, though, my vision filled with gray clouds and my head swam.

Some combination of panic and hitting my head on the sidewalk was clearly having an effect on me. I tried to run in spite of it, but I collapsed on a lawn one house over. My window for escape narrowed and disappeared altogether as Vlad came over me with the knife.

I had the vaguest recollection that carrying a knife could actually benefit one's attacker, but I didn't understand until now. Now it was too late.

"I detest the idea of killing a student of mine," he said, leaning so close to my face that I could feel his hot breath. "I even granted you a warning. Something my other enemies were not so lucky to receive. You pursued me regardless, going so far as to call my captors."

Captors? What was he talking about?

"I was just-" I tried to say, but he shoved his hand over my mouth and nose. Panic shot through me as the breath was caught in my lungs, and I jerked my head enough to expose my nose to the air. He didn't seem to have a problem with my newfound ability to breathe, or else he was too distracted to notice. While I desperately wracked my mind for an idea, he was patting me down. I didn't know why until he pulled my phone out of my pocket and squeezed the side button, watching with satisfaction as it shut off. He tossed it on the sidewalk behind him, where it landed face up.

"I don't have my usual tools at my disposal, but I did learn a delightful expression from your time. 'Death by a thousand cuts.' Let's see if that works, shall we?"

I bit at his hand as hard as I could, my blood chilling in response to his threat. I didn't know how long it would take to bleed out, especially knowing how he felt about taking his time with torturous deaths, and I refused to think about it. I wasn't going to find out. I was going to escape. Or not. He managed to pull his hand away in time, and my teeth banged together, empty. With the tenacity of a man enthusiastic about the opportunity to cause pain, he touched the cold edge of the knife to my arm, piercing the skin and making a small gash.

"One," he said. There was a second of shock before the pain set in, stinging like he had set it on fire. I watched beads of blood come to the surface and roll down my arm. I kicked and struggled against his weight, but held back, afraid to help the knife to a new target.

"Somebody *help!*" I screamed as loudly as I could, desperate that someone would hear me. Someone had to hear me. This wasn't the kind of thing that could happen. This wasn't happening. It wasn't. Someone would come. He started on a second cut, just under my collar bone. The pain of the cut was the same as the last, but compounded by the pain in my arm. He counted that too, and the one after that.

Tears rolled down my face, hot and futile. What was I supposed to do? Just lie here and suffer and die? I hated everyone in this neighborhood. I hated Levi for not helping me. I hated Tamryn for even suggesting this app. I hated the app. I hated myself. No, I didn't want my last thoughts to be about hate. I didn't hate them. Except Vlad, I hated him. I had to find a way to beat him. Another small slash with the knife caused me to scream again, emptying my mind of productive thoughts and leaving an opening for blind misery and panic.

Suddenly he stopped, looking up.

It was only then that I heard the hum of a car rolling down the street towards us. It was an old, white Toyota sedan. I had never seen anything so beautiful. Thank God. Thank God.

The honk of a horn broke Vlad's silence as the car halted. He thrust himself off of me, the push digging my back into the wet grass. I watched in silence as he looked at the car in frustration and took off running again. He was leaving, and I was alive. The car door slammed shut and someone came running towards me. I didn't see who it was, because I had sunk to the grass and closed my eyes, listening to the sound of my sobs.

"Are you ok?" a young woman asked. I opened my eyes when her shadow blocked the sun over me. She looked about 16 with long black hair hanging past her shoulders. "We should call the police!"

Of course we should've called the police. That was the only logical choice. Vlad needed to be stopped. But. But. The calm voice on the phone rang in my ears. Customer Service had told me not to call the police. They had no right to tell me that, obviously. They were criminally negligent at this point, and I'd be justified to call the authorities just to report them. What could they do about me calling the police on them? Well, there was just the one thing. They could block me from the app, keeping me from ever talking to Gannicus again. I didn't have a personal number for him, if he had one. I doubted he'd thought to memorize my phone number in case I called the police and got kicked off the app. No, if they decided to retaliate against me by cutting me off, I'd never have another meeting with Gannicus.

I remembered my phone, lying on the sidewalk. Instead of a black screen, I saw that it was lit up with an ongoing call. Was someone still waiting on the other end?

"Hello?" I called, wiping my nose. "Is anyone there?"

No one answered, but I could hear a steady hum in the background. I hoped they'd stayed connected and were on their way. I mopped the blood off my arms as well as I could with my shirt. It was one of my favorites, pink and off-the-shoulder. It would probably be stained with my blood. At least I could even think of something so trivial now. At this point, that was a definite blessing.

"No, let's not call the police," I told the girl who was still waiting for my reply, her car idling in the middle of the street. "That was... my boyfriend. He's harmless."

The lie made my face burn. I knew she was wondering what was wrong with me to make such a choice, but I couldn't defend myself. If I were her, I would want to slap some sense into me for saying something like that. Actually, I did want to slap some sense into myself for that. There were like a thousand other things I could've said that wouldn't sound as dumb. But I just needed to wait until a black SUV came to pick up Vlad. They could search the streets for him now. They might say I was responsible for finding him but I would say they could shut the hell up. The girl looked at me in disbelief and uncertainty, evidently wondering whether or not to honor my request.

"I'm ok now. But thank you so much for stopping. You have no idea," I told her with emotion, though I knew she would never understand what she had done for me. I couldn't even tell her, because then she'd call the police for sure. She gave me a small, polite smile that was more like an uncomfortable grimace and walked away.

I watched her get back into her car and drive off, my stomach clenching as I wondered if I'd made a mistake letting her go. What if Vlad was nearby? I picked up the knife he'd left on the ground in his haste and wiped my blood off of it onto the grass. I didn't know if I was qualified to use it for defense after what had just happened, but what choice did I have? Leaving it on the ground for him to find later was a worse idea.

Unsure of what else to do, and too tired to think of anything, I sat on the sidewalk and hugged my knees to my chest. All I could do was sit, absorbing the fact that I was alive and waiting for people who should have gone after Vlad themselves in the first place. It felt like a long time that I waited there, watching the street in front of me with tense muscles, waiting to see if Vlad would return. I didn't know what I'd do if he did.

He didn't, but the black SUV eventually rolled up. A woman in a pantsuit exited the passenger side door and came over to me. She had brown eyes and natural black hair, and might have been about 40.

"Where is he?" she demanded cooly, not noticing or choosing not to notice my cuts or the knife in my hand. Her question filled me with rage.

"He's gone! He tried to cut me up but he got scared by a car and ran! I could be DEAD!" I breathed heavily as I waited for her to apologize. She did not.

"We advise users not to allow the instructors out of their sight. He has not harmed anyone before because he knew we would find out and there would be consequences. Once you got in the way of his escape, though, that must have been another story. It's inadvisable for these people to roam freely." Tears gathered in my eyes at her audacity. *This doesn't happen to other people, this is your fault because you're reckless.* That was basically what she was saying to me right now.

"This is your fault. If he's not safe you should've let him rot in his own time! You need to go catch him!"

"We'll be sending a form to your email. We ask that you sign it as an agreement not to take legal action against us," she said, starting to walk back to the SUV.

"There is no way in hell that I am doing that," I spat. She didn't even turn around.

"If you don't, unfortunately we'll have to blackball you from further use of the app."

There was no way that argument should have been compelling. Their app was an awesome way to almost get tortured to death by the most evil person who had ever lived, and then get chastised for it. They should blackball the entire world from using it, and keep us all safer. Each and every person running it should be sued for every dime they'd ever owned for creating such an outrageously dangerous nightmare machine. They could take their app and shove it. Except.

Except then I wouldn't be able to contact Gannicus. He'd never know why I shut him out. I wasn't ready to give him up.

Fine. I thought. *I'll sign the form. But I'm not telling her that.*

I kept quiet, my mouth a thin line as she got back into the car and closed the door. When the car drove away, I sat back on the cement and bawled my eyes out.

Chapter 13

Finally, I stood up and started walking home. Though my bare feet were sensitive from running this far, the ground was warm in the sunshine and it was soothing. My head ached and the wounds stung, but they would heal. I couldn't know for sure if the app security had caught up with Vlad, but I was fairly certain that he wouldn't risk his freedom again by returning for me. Still, I checked to make sure I wasn't being followed, looking into the reflections off parked cars to subtly watch my back.

Even as I walked up the driveway, my muscles tensed, begging me to sprint into the house before Vlad could take advantage of this last chance to catch up to me. I reached for the door handle. Wait.

I couldn't go inside and be seen by my parents. They'd want to ensure that I called the police, and insist on following up on the case. I didn't need the police or my parents asking too many questions, so I couldn't let that happen. I peeked through the open window and didn't see anyone in the living room. I would be safe to dash upstairs without being seen.

By dash, it turned out that I meant amble at a careful pace, because any movement that was too fast made my head throb. I pressed my hand to the back of my head where I'd hit it on the ground, and discovered a lump already there. Holding the bump delicately, I kept an eye downstairs to make sure my parents weren't coming into the room.

I took a long shower, watching the dried blood run off my wounds. One on either side of my collarbone and one on my arm were the longest. They stung when the water hit them, and worse when I used soap. All things considered they didn't seem so bad, but I was afraid to risk it. It seemed like a good sign that they weren't really bleeding anymore. I watched blood swirl with the moving water and slide down the drain.

After I stepped out of the shower and wrapped myself in a towel, I noticed I had a missed call from Levi.

"Did you get him?" he said immediately when I called him back.

"I need a paramedic," I said instead of answering his question. Realistically I was probably fine, but the constant throb in my head demanded I get checked for a concussion. "No I didn't get him but he got me." Levi's breath caught.

"What happened?" he demanded.

"He was upset that I was following him so he attacked me. I hit my head pretty hard on the sidewalk. He also cut me in a few places, but he ran away when a car came by."

"How did he get a knife?" I realized this was an important question, one Levi would need to ask. It said a lot about the safety of the app. That didn't make it feel any less insulting.

"I brought it with me because I had to solve this problem *on my own*. He got it away from me."

For a moment, Levi was quiet. Finally he took a deep breath.

"I should have been there, Lane. I'm sorry. I'm on my way."

"I thought you had to work -" I started to say, but realized he'd already hung up.

I went to my room and got dressed. I was ready by the time he got there, wearing a strappy tank top to make my injuries more visible. My mother must have heard the doorbell too, because I ran into her at the bottom of the stairs. She just smiled and greeted me. It looked like I'd gotten lucky and she hadn't noticed them, but I covered the angry red gashes with my hair anyway.

"It's Levi," I said. "He said he was in the area so I said he should come by."

"Well, please tell him I said hello." Apparently thinking better than to let me convey her greeting, she waited until I opened the door and welcomed him. She left soon after, though, apparently busy with something else I was way too preoccupied to be concerned about. I took Levi outside where we could talk privately and I could sit in the back of the ambulance. When I walked out, though, I realized the ambulance wasn't with him. Had he actually been on a shift, he certainly would've had it. He followed my gaze, giving a small nod to himself.

"Lane, we need to talk," he said, motioning for me to sit on the wooden bench just outside the front door. He took out a flashlight from a small red medical kit he'd brought with him, examining my eyes and directing me different directions to look. "It doesn't look like you have a concussion." I sighed in relief.

He took out antiseptic and set to work on my cuts, declaring that they wouldn't need stitches but I should let him know if they got worse. I flinched at the cold sting, but I was relieved to hear the cuts weren't as deep as they seemed.

"I didn't have work today." Oh, ok. He didn't have work today. That meant he'd lied to me when I was in one of the most desperate moments of my life, and was pleading for his help. He'd just decided to say "no thanks" and do something else with his time. No, that wasn't fair. There must be a reason why he'd told me he had to work when he didn't.

Though my heart sank when he said it, I tried to keep a straight face and hear the rest of the story. "I just couldn't afford to be there when they came to pick Vlad up. If I had known he was gonna give you any trouble, I would've been there despite any risk. I just underestimated him. That could have been a fatal mistake. I'm so sorry."

Levi wasn't an extremely emotive person, but I could see the agony of failure in his blue eyes. He was a man of principles, and had failed his. Wait, there was something in his statement that I'd almost missed.

"Why couldn't you be there when they picked him up?" I asked, my heart rate quickening as I picked up on what was really the key part of his confession.

"Because I used to be a, uh, an instructor. On the app."

Ok. Ok. Hold on. I took a deep breath, putting my head in my hands when the shock of his words made my head throb. An instructor on the app. That explained how he knew so much about it, and so much about history for that matter. But instructors on the app were more than just teachers. That was how it worked. Being an instructor didn't mean that you'd done a lot of research into a particular time period. It meant that you'd lived in it.

"Where - when are you from?" I asked. I was surprised at how calm my voice sounded. I supposed I was exhausted from the day. It was hard enough to decide how I felt inside; there was nothing left in me to express it outwardly.

"The American Revolution. Lieutenant Colonel Levi Smith at your service. I was born in 1734." A small, hesitant smile crept across his features at the introduction. When I just stared back at him, it disappeared.

Every game night, every late IHOP dinner, every summer day spent in the pool flashed through my head. All this time I'd known Levi, all I'd told him about myself, all the private details of my family that he'd seen and learned, and he'd never once mentioned. Here I'd thought that we knew each other. Tamryn and Levi were my best friends. How could they go this long, spend time with me, *get married,* and lie to me all this time? I felt like I got kicked in the stomach.

"Does Tamryn - Tamryn has to know. She knows," I said more than asked. Levi only nodded. Even though I didn't even need him to nod, because I already knew, somehow the confirmation sent a fresh wash of pain over me. It hurt worse than the cuts.

Tamryn and I would never lie to each other. We told each other everything. We talked everyday. She had had every opportunity to tell me that her husband was around before our state was even owned by the US. Before the US even existed. She chose not to tell me. Why? Because she wanted to have some special little secret with him? Because she didn't trust me with information that big? It just didn't even seem possible. This was nonsense. I shook my head lethargically, forcing a gesture of disbelief through a feeling of fogginess. This was too much at once.

"We were always gonna tell you," Levi said, packing up his medical equipment and zipping up the bag. "Tamryn just didn't want to put the moral burden on you. She knew it would haunt you like it does her." Despite the apprehension that "moral burden" invited, I felt a tiny spark of hope. Tamryn didn't want to keep secrets from me. She was doing it out of some sense of duty towards me, to protect me. Maybe we were alright after all.

"What moral burden?" I asked, even though I didn't want to. "Wait." Levi raised his eyebrows and closed his mouth before he could start his answer. "If Tamryn didn't want me to know then I don't want to know." If she kept a secret like this from me, I knew she had a good reason. Levi's news had been an earth-shattering revelation, but I would not give up the trust I had with Tamryn. I wouldn't - couldn't - lose that.

"Lane, I just want you to know, I'm so sorry. I'm so sorry," he said, picking up his bag in a sign that he was ready to leave.

"It's ok," I said, even though I didn't know if it was. I needed to think. "I'm sure you guys had your reasons."

He nodded stiffly and said goodbye, looking back once or twice on his way back to his truck, guilt and concern obvious in the set of his brow. I waved and did my best to smile, but it was probably so unconvincing that it was worse than not smiling at all. When his truck was gone, I stood up and went back into the house. My heart was heavy, but no tears came.

All I wanted to do was talk to Gannicus. I needed to talk to Tamryn, but I wasn't ready. I knew she'd be crushed that she'd hurt me, and I wasn't ready to have the conversation. It had been a horrible day, and all I wanted to do was lay my head on Gannicus's shoulder and listen to his voice. As if he was summoned, my vibrating phone indicated that he was calling me. It must have been the end of his hour.

"Hello, beautiful," he said when I answered, smiling broadly. His smile deflated when he saw my face.

"How was your-" I started to say, but my traitorous voice wobbled.

"What is the matter?" he asked. It was the question, the concern in his voice, that made me fall apart. I burst into tears, unable to stop even though I could see he was stressed that he couldn't help. He watched me helplessly for awhile, letting me cry until I was ready to tell him. I finally calmed down and dried my eyes with the bottom of my shirt.

"I was attacked by Vlad the Impaler." I sighed, deciding it was better to just get the whole story out. "He tried to kill me. And then I found out that my sister and her husband have been lying to me for their entire relationship. And they still have some horrible secret they're not telling me and I don't even know if I want to know." I took a shaky breath and wiped quickly at my eyes.

He stared at me for a minute, likely trying to think of what to say. I should have been embarrassed about unloading all of this on him, or taken stock of the fact that this was the first time he'd seen me cry, but I didn't. Talking to Gannicus felt better. A small ray of sunshine was starting to poke through my clouds just knowing he was concerned, that he was listening. I let him digest everything I'd said, allowing myself to relax in the fact that he was there. Finally he asked me what happened with Vlad, where he was now. I told him every detail, cringing at the parts where I'd thought I might die. His eyes shone with dangerous fury. I finished by telling him about Levi, and how Tamryn had never told me.

He wasn't surprised by that part. I had expected shock or outrage on my behalf, but instead he looked down awkwardly and agreed that it was "terrible." The reaction didn't sit right with me.

"You knew," I said when he didn't say anything else. He nodded.

"It was never my place to tell you. But yes. One of the last times I saw Tamryn, she gave me an envelope, said it was from Levi. It contained forgeries of identification documents for me. If I ever left the app."

Part of me wanted to be angry, to unleash some of the pain and shock I'd felt all through this miserable day, but I couldn't do it. I couldn't really fault him for not telling me. My own sister had kept it from me. Pushing that outrage onto Gannicus didn't feel right. That didn't mean I knew what to say, though. I was feeling the same information overload that I'd felt when I began to realize Gannicus was from the past; it was the same helpless feeling of not knowing what reality I could trust anymore. The constant facts that I'd relied on without even thinking about were looking shaky at best; some of them were close to shattering apart. Instead of making it worse by going deeper, I changed the subject. After what had happened with Vlad, I didn't want to think so hard.

"Tell me about your meeting," I said. It doubled as a distraction and as an investigation into someone I really did want to know about. Another woman talking to my man was such a silly thing to worry about by comparison to what I'd been through. Maybe that was exactly why I latched onto it. "What was she like?"

His eyes sparkled when I asked, and he suppressed a laugh. Did I sound too jealous?

"She was in her early 20's, mid-height, blonde, with big blue eyes. She made me laugh." That wasn't the answer I'd been hoping for. She sounded like competition. The whole point of the questioning was to take away from my stress, not add to it! I supposed it was better to hear this right now, though, when it was put into perspective. It hurt to hear him talk about a girl that he seemed to have feelings for, but at least I wasn't dead. That didn't help much, but it helped a bit.

"Oh, that's good," I said, looking down to hide my inner turmoil. Wait. Was he *laughing?*

"Lane, you are the woman I described. The woman I met today was perfectly friendly. I enjoyed telling her about myself. But all I could think about was how much I wanted to be with you. I think about that quite a lot, actually." Now that was the win I needed right now. My face broke into a grin, but I didn't know how to respond.

"Me too," I said quietly, painfully aware that it was inadequate. He smiled, though, like maybe it was enough for him. "I'm excited to see you tomorrow."

"I count the minutes," he said. He put my meager expressions of affection to shame.

Though losing myself in Gannicus's voice had helped, I suddenly felt my exhaustion when we hung up. I collapsed on the couch, falling quickly into a deep sleep.

I found myself in a conference room, which was broken in half by a long table. Sunlight shone through the windows behind it, windows almost big enough to consume the entire back wall. I was standing in front of a panel of three professionals, one woman and two men. I wiped my sweating palms on my slacks, swallowing hard to get past my dry throat.

"That's why," I choked, "I think I would be a good candidate for the position." I gestured to a screen on my right, where I'd projected a graph depicting my potential "financial contributions."

The woman stared at me, her disapproving eyes burning through me. I looked away out the windows, where I could see a full city beneath us, teeming with life. I wanted to be down there, experiencing the world.

"We're looking for someone with passion for the company," one of the men said, adjusting his glasses as he looked at a paper in front of him. "Do you think you exemplify that?"

I wracked my brain, fiercely searching for some evidence that I felt anything in my heart for this company. My stomach tightened as I realized I didn't even know the name of it, much less what the employees did for a living. All I knew was I was here, trying to get a job already and make money. I was 35 and had never done anything with my life; I was still living with my parents. I had long ago given up on my dreams of reaching my potential, moving from one entry-level job to the next.

"Yes," I said, breathing deeply and reaching for my water bottle to give myself time to think. "I want to use my stellar communication skills to further enhance the already impressive reputation of this organization. Thinking of the impact that I believe I could make here thrills me." I didn't say it sarcastically; I really tried to mean it.

"Well thank you, Ms... Reid," the man said, checking his paper to remind himself of my name. The other two interviewers finished what they were writing on their own papers and looked up at me, their faces a matching stony neutral.

"Thank you for your time," I said, pasting on a gracious smile despite the rising lump in my throat.

I had no chance. It was a miracle I'd gotten the interview in the first place, given my general lack of applicable experience. Now that they'd heard from me, I knew I could expect to add this job to the long list of ones that had politely rejected me. For the time I'd spent filling out the application, writing the cover letter, and preparing for this interview, I'd receive nothing more than a copy and pasted rejection email encouraging me to try again in the future.

There really was no future. I'd long since given up on myself.

I didn't know what to do when I woke up and realized that it was just a hellish dream. It wasn't real. I was young. I had time. I peeled my face off the leather couch just to lie back down again, contemplating the dream. The best you can tell yourself after a bad dream is that it wasn't real. This dream *wasn't* real. But it could be, someday.

What was there to stop me from being 35 with no job, no family of my own, and no reason to get through the day? The foundations I was building for my future career? What exactly were those? They didn't exist. If I wasn't moving forward now, why should I expect the future to be any different than the present? No, that wasn't helpful. Before I could spiral out of control with my existential dread, I forced myself to look at the issue for its true face, not the monster mask I was attempting to give it.

I had applied for jobs, merely days ago. There was at least some decent likelihood that I'd hear from a few of them. I was loath to rely on a man in the 21st century, but since I was interested in having a family, I did have to recognize that I was forming a relationship with a man I truly cared about. Worst case scenario, I'd accept a shitty job that paid enough for me to get my own place.

Even though I didn't feel any better, I got up and went into the kitchen to make myself lunch anyway. Now that I'd given the issue thought, I was allowed to forget about it, wasn't I? I gave the dream an execution- death by macaroni and cheese distraction- and buried it away.

Chapter 14

When I heard the knock on my door the next day, the dream had long since disappeared from my mind. My mind was beginning a chant, made up only of the word *Gannicus* on repeat.

Gannicus, Gannicus, Gannicus

"Hi!" I said, whipping open the door like it was the one escape route from a burning building. Before he could even register my arrival at the door, I leapt at him, standing on my toes to try to wrap my arms around his neck. Though I managed that, I needed him to lean down so I could reach his lips. He wordlessly obliged, smiling into the kiss.

"It has been ages. Too long," he joked. At least, I assumed it was a joke. It had only been two days since we'd seen each other, and we'd talked on the phone just yesterday. By all reasonable accounts, it hadn't been long at all. Then again, it felt pretty long to me. After everything that had happened in those two days, I needed to reconnect. Was it crazy to think he felt the same? The intensity in his eyes spoke otherwise. I looked past him and saw that the black SUV was still parked in front of the house, making no move to leave. My heart thumped. I wondered if they were going to try to act like I was in some kind of trouble for what happened. When Vlad attacked me. I forced myself to think about it clearly, instead of hiding it behind phrases like "what happened." The more I faced it, the better off I'd be. Eventually. I hoped. For now, I pressed myself closer to Gannicus.

They'd be pretty bold to come here and try to chew me out after I did them the enormous favor of not calling the police or filing a lawsuit. I was the victim here, obviously. The image of the stern woman in the pantsuit popped into my head, though, and I realized that at least one of their employees thought I was entirely to blame for what happened to Vlad. It still infuriated me to think about it. Despite her personal feelings, though, surely the company would realize it wasn't good PR to yell at customers. Maybe they had news for me about Vlad's whereabouts. That thought wasn't any more comforting. Even if they'd caught him, what happened next? Did they have their own super secret jail where they stored employees that broke the law? I doubted they'd have him arrested after they demanded I not call the police. Whatever they were here to tell me, Gannicus either thought it was good news or didn't know what it was about, because his eyes were lit up. I was so lost in my own analysis that I almost didn't notice his explanation.

"Would you like to come see where I live?" Gannicus asked, following my line of sight. I stared up at him quickly, reading his face for any sign of teasing. His facial expression was sincere, patiently waiting to see what I would say. I felt a grin to match his spread across my lips. That hadn't been on my list of expectations, but to say it was a pleasant surprise would have been an understatement.

"Uh, hell yeah! Since when is that part of the package?"

"Since you got maimed by one of the instructors. They must try to get back in your good graces. With so few customers so early, they cannot afford to lose any positive recommendations." Now *this* was the treatment I expected from customer service. And it just made sense. After the horrors of the day before, I deserved this.

This was going to be fun. Just because Gannicus probably lived very near to where Vlad lived didn't mean I needed to worry. It wouldn't be a very good "sorry we almost got you killed" gift if they let Vlad come after me and kill me again. A small voice in the back of my mind suggested that Vlad might not be the only one on the app who was dangerous. They could have Attila the Hun or H. H. Holmes or maybe even Satan himself, who the hell knew? I took a deep breath.

After I'd retrieved my purse and keys, I reached for Gannicus's hand as we turned towards the car. I gripped his hand harder the closer we got, until I felt him uncomfortably adjust his grip and lean in to look at my face. He squeezed my hand briefly. I tried to accept the encouragement. I might have had a bad experience the last time I tried something new with the app, but this was different. I wasn't alone this time. Gannicus was here. He would protect me from any rogue historical figures that might try to come out of the woodwork and attack me.

I didn't say anything to the driver or passenger of the car as I waited for Gannicus to open the door and usher me in. It wasn't until I slid across the leather seat, goosebumps rising on my arms from the blasting air conditioning, that I thought it would be impolite not to speak.

"Thank you for giving us a ride," I said, pretending I was in middle school accepting a ride from a friend's parent instead of the people who let me get shanked by a wanna-be vampire. Before I could reach for it, Gannicus's hand was wrapped around mine again. I watched him carefully as we pulled out of the neighborhood, his serious expression only changing when he turned to meet my eyes. When our eyes met, he raised his eyebrows and smiled. A little thrill went through me in response.

No one spoke, so I didn't either. Instead, I listened to the intense blowing of the air conditioner and the radio almost inaudibly playing today's pop music. The longer we drove, though, the more I regretted not starting a conversation sooner. Now the silence seemed too thick to break, as if the two people in the front of the car would shatter if I spoke too loudly. Every time I shifted in the leather seat, I was sure everyone in the car was listening. I wasn't particularly comfortable, but I tried to stay still to avoid drawing undue attention.

After two hours that was actually just twenty long minutes, the car finally rolled to a stop at our destination.

"When do you need to be back?" the driver asked me.

"I'll let you know," Gannicus said, staring confidently back at him. The woman in the passenger seat turned around and just barely glared at him, her lips pursed. I wondered if she didn't appreciate him answering the question instead of me. I hesitated, wondering if it would be undermining Gannicus somehow to answer the question instead. When no one moved, I decided there was no choice but to just answer and hope Gannicus would blame her for ignoring him instead of me for going along with it.

"Uh, yeah, I'll let you know," I repeated. The woman nodded and turned back around in her seat. "Thank you." She just nodded curtly.

No one said anything else as we climbed out of the car, the warmth of the day wrapping around me as a welcome replacement to the icy interior of the car.

Only once I'd gotten out of the car did I really take it all in. I'd noticed it driving up, as much as necessary to watch the route we took there, wondering how this place could've existed in Tucson all this time without me noticing it. Only now did I really look. We had pulled through a gate, admitted by a guard when the driver flashed his ID.

It looked like a military base. I'd had a long distance relationship with a soldier at the beginning of college, and this looked just like the base he'd lived on. There were rows of large apartment-like buildings, all sand-colored. The parking lot we stood in was vast, though there were only two long rows of identical black SUV's. The rest was empty. I listened for voices or movement, but all I could hear was the whistling of a light breeze.

"This is home," Gannicus said satirically as I took it all in.

"It's lovely," I lied. It wasn't that it was ugly, just that it looked vaguely like a prison made only for giving people somewhere to live, rather than creating any sense of appealing aesthetic. Ok, maybe it was ugly. Gannicus just laughed.

"Thank you for lying, *melculum*." *Melculum*. I didn't know what it meant, but my heart beat faster at the word.

"Does Neil Davidson come by here much?" I asked, feeling uncharacteristically shy and eager to change the subject.

"He has, but not too often. He lives in a valley." I raised my eyebrows.

"What valley?"

"Sin-con Valley? I fail to remember the name." I tried not to laugh but failed.

"You mean Silicon Valley?" At the suggestion, Gannicus laughed too and confirmed.

The silence that followed was comfortable, until I realized I didn't know where to go next. It was just the two of us now. Well, this was Gannicus's place, so I decided it would be on him to decide what we'd do with our time here. I gestured for him to lead the way to his room, still smiling. Taking my cue easily, he stepped forward and led the way down the sidewalk, past beds of rocks that I assumed had been put there to create some kind of decoration. It wasn't unusual to see rocks as decoration in Tucson, but the mismatched gray and white heaps here weren't doing a great job.

We walked past outdoor stone staircases and doors that made up the first floor bedrooms, but he didn't slow down. All the doors were closed and quiet, with no windows that I could see. I groaned internally when we kept going, passing one bland building after the next. Even though I'd said I'd let the woman from the app know when I was ready to leave, I was still conscious that we didn't really know how much time we had. I didn't know how long the app's generosity in allowing my visit would last, and I didn't want to waste it walking past buildings.

Gannicus was oblivious to my impatience as he hiked up one of the staircases, me trailing behind. I tried to keep up, but his legs were longer and stronger than mine. His butt in black jeans provided the motivation I needed to keep going. Once I realized that, I kept pace a little bit better. That was the power of positive thinking. His speed was still better, effortless as it was, but at least I had renewed energy. I was starting to realize that I was here, spending time with someone I couldn't get enough of. I'd run marathons up these stairs as long as he was in front of me for it. He turned at the second floor and kept going, continuing up the staircase. By the time we neared the third floor, I gathered up the courage to speed up and smack him on the ass.

I didn't care that I was blushing when he turned around, his mouth agape in mock outrage. Suddenly my face was set on fire, though, when I heard a jolting roar of laughter above me on the third floor. Ok, that action was not meant for an audience. I was barely comfortable that *I'd* seen me do that. Who was laughing? We both turned up at the sound. My horror was written all over my face, but Gannicus lit up with recognition.

"Lewis!" he greeted, reaching back to grab my hand and pull me up to him, where I could see the man he was addressing. The man was wearing a white turtleneck, despite the 80 degree weather. It was better than Vlad's red coat- at least it was modern, if inappropriate- but I marveled at the fact that Gannicus seemed to be the only one of them who cared to really adopt the wardrobe of the time. "This is my Lane."

My Lane. I circled around the phrase, over and over again. I was interrupted by the response of my new acquaintance.

"Hello, Miss. My name is Meriwether Lewis. I was one of the leaders of-"

"I know who you are!" I gasped. "I did a play about you in fifth grade. My sister played Clark."

Lewis chuckled, coming over to the top of the stairs to shake my hand.

"Did that make you the Lewis?" he asked.

"No," I said, staring at the ground in mock bitterness. "I was the lead of the play but it was a character they made up so Tamryn gets all the credit for playing a lead." I broke character to smile up at him. If Gannicus wanted us to just knock on doors all day, I'd be ok with that too. If a lot of the instructors on the app lived here, this place would be better than Disneyland. Assuming they were all the good guys, like Lewis. I shook away the thought of another figure I'd met who'd been less friendly.

"It's always good to run into you, Lewis. But right now, Lane has somewhere to be. Somewhere private." Actually, it was starting to sound like Gannicus's idea might be better. It would be hard to stand here and talk to Lewis or anyone else when I was starting to get weak at the knees. My heart climbed into my throat when Gannicus leaned down and whispered, "Let's go." His warm breath in my ear gave me chills.

I weakly waved goodbye to Lewis and followed Gannicus down the outdoor hall to his door. I stared at the number on the door, 33. My lucky number.

The click of the door locking took away the casual friendliness he'd had towards Lewis completely. Every vein in my body hummed when I saw the possessive look in Gannicus's eyes. His huge form swallowed the studio apartment room until I felt like there wasn't enough air. I took a deep breath, then sucked in another. Why was this so different from all the other times I'd been alone with him? Surely we'd been alone plenty of times before. This time was the exact same, wasn't it?

Though it was a few feet away from me yet, I imagined I could feel the full bed behind me giving off an energy of its own. Oh yeah. That was it. As much time as we wanted, completely alone, with nothing to do but whatever we could think to do on that bed. I swallowed and tried to take in the other end of the room, the false classroom I'd seen in video chat, to distract myself. It reminded me of the first time I'd seen Gannicus, when all I could think was how much I wanted to *talk* to a guy who looked like that. Well, it looked like I got my wish here. And more. I swallowed.

"Lewis seemed pretty cool," I said, even though I knew it wasn't what either one of us wanted to talk about. Gannicus mostly ignored the remark, only nodding briefly as he crossed the few feet of room between us to meet me. He trailed a finger across my lip, looking at me with a tenderness I might not have been able to read if I hadn't felt the same way towards him.

I tilted my chin up in an invitation he accepted, leaning down to kiss me. His lips were warm as they wrapped around mine. He claimed my mouth with his tongue.

I need to tell him I won't have sex with him. It's only going to be harder to tell him the longer I wait. Now was an excellent time to go ahead and just say it. Just, "hey buddy, pal. My guy. This isn't going to happen tonight, unfortunately." Nothing of the sort came out of my mouth. Just breathing that was a little heavier than before I'd come into the room. That was actually the opposite of the message I needed to be sending.

I lost my good intentions for a moment when he lifted me up. I wrapped my legs around his waist and lightly sucked on his neck. He moaned quietly, an encouragement. This beautiful man wanted me. Why shouldn't he? I was pretty sexy myself. And right now, I definitely knew it. I kept going, kissing down his neck until I got to his shoulder. I nipped his shoulder, smiling playfully against his skin.

He threw me on the bed from high enough that I bounced when I hit the cool sheets. He gave me a beast-like grin before he followed, crawling on top of me. There was so much of him. I knew he was tall and muscular, but it was a lot easier to notice this way. I didn't mind the new perspective at all. Unfortunately, this was heading in a direction that was too far. As much as I was flattered, and ok, excited, about his implied plans, they happened to be against my personal beliefs.

"I have to tell you something," I said, my voice coming out in nothing more than a whisper. *Come on, Lane. You've had this conversation a million times. Ok, more like 5 times. But still, that was a lot.*

"Mm hmm," he muttered, running his warm hands under my shirt. He traced his fingers over the plane of my stomach.

"I'm a virgin," I said. Yes, this was hardly my first time having this conversation with a man, but this time was important. I actually cared if it was a dealbreaker for him. I shouldn't have waited to tell him. Why did I wait until now?

"I certainly do not mind," he said, leaning down to kiss my hip bones.

"I'm sure you don't. But I can't have sex with you." That got his attention. He looked up from my hips.

"No?" He wouldn't meet my eyes as he lowered my shirt and sat up. If I didn't know any better, I might have thought that was a blush that colored his cheeks. "I must have misread the situation." I laughed lightly, taking his hand and interlocking my fingers with his.

"No, trust me, I do *want* to." I took a breath to explain, but the energy that had deflated from him just a moment before was back with a vengeance.

"Alright, then," he said, his voice lower than usual. "Shh." The small hush he delivered into my ear, sending chills through my body. I closed my eyes as he kissed me intensely, stopping only to nibble on my bottom lip.

Wait, this wasn't going right.

I put my hand up on his chest, gently pushing him away. He gave a small growl of frustration that some part of my mind recognized as potentially extremely hot, but I didn't like what it meant right now. Did gladiators not hear the word "no" very often?

"I want to, but I can't," I said, sitting up.

"I do not understand," he said, resting on his arm and looking up at me with what I thought was a hint of irritation. I hoped I was just imagining things, but I had to admit I had waited an unfair amount of time to tell him this. Maybe he had a right to be a little annoyed.

"It's against my religion. I don't believe in having sex before marriage." I wracked my brain for a more specific way to explain. He probably didn't know too much about Christianity, having lived 70 years before Jesus Christ was born. Damn, and I'd thought this conversation had been hard to have with men from my own century. I just kept trying to think of more to say and coming up empty. Gannicus was shaking his head.

"That's nonsense," he said shortly, as if it were a simple fact. Ouch. The words settled like a rock in my stomach.

He just didn't understand. If he understood what I was saying, he'd be accepting of it. He'd get it. Sex was sacred to me; it meant something. It was more than just a physical interaction. I believed it was the connection of two souls. If I just told him that, he'd have to say that that was ok, that we could just kiss and talk instead. Just telling him that would be the reasonable thing to do. Except right now my face was getting hot, and I was having a hard time thinking of something practical to say.

"No it's not," I said instead, my jaw clenched.

"Sex is nature. Surely the religion of your day espouses the beauty of nature." As if to illustrate his point, Gannicus ran a finger lightly across my thigh. I flinched.

"Nature is fine," I said slowly, trying to think of a way to go back in time and decide to spend the day with him at my house, where it was safe. "But there's more to it than that. Just because humans have certain, um, instincts, doesn't mean we have to act on them blindly like animals."

Something about this conversation was making my heart beat loudly in my ears, and not in a good way. I wasn't a fan of confrontation, especially when I'd had such high hopes that we'd have a good time today. How did I not see this coming in the first place? Gannicus didn't seem to have the same issues with the conversation.

"Like animals?" he murmured, raising his eyebrows and crawling closer to me.

"No," I said, trying to laugh it off. It came out strained. I tried to get us back on track. "In my religion, God made sex as a way to unite couples that are married. For life."

"Why should your God care what you and I do?" he responded, leaning in to kiss me on the cheek. It was a fairly chaste gesture of affection. In that moment, though, it was exactly the wrong thing for me.

"Stop," I snapped, moving around him to climb off the bed. He reeled back slightly in surprise. I ignored it. "I don't want to, alright?"

To my horror, my lip quivered on the words. Great, I was really selling the logic of my ideas here. The worst part was, I could be convincing about it in any other situation. I had arguments, statistics, explanations. Right now, though, I didn't want to debate. I wanted him to accept what was important to me and respect it.

"Lane," he said quietly, eyebrows furrowed. He looked completely baffled, like he was doing the math and all this just wasn't adding up. "Please come back. This is silly. I can show you."

Show me? Was he listening at all? I got that consent probably wasn't a big topic of conversation in his time, but surely he cared how I felt about this. I swallowed thickly, desperately searching for a way to get back on track. This was not that big of a deal. It was just a miscommunication. I just needed to take a deep breath, regroup, and explain what I was feeling. I didn't get a chance.

My contemplations were interrupted by a knock on the door.

For a moment, neither Gannicus nor I moved. Then, on some silent cue, we both snapped back into action. I stepped back and out of the way while he moved to the door to open it. On purpose or not, he didn't look at me as he walked past. My stomach was a storm of misery as I watched his back, wishing I had done better at this entire conversation.

"It's time for us to take Miss Reid home," a voice said. I moved towards the door and saw the woman who'd responded to my call about Vlad. Just seeing her face made me feverish with frustration and rage all over again. I was appalled at her gall to come back here and fetch me herself instead of having anyone else do it. This was the last thing I needed right now.

Before I could think of a biting remark to make, I looked at Gannicus standing at the door. He wasn't looking at me. There was nothing I could say to this horrible woman in front of us. I had no right to stir up more turmoil for him. Besides, I wasn't sure I really wanted to be with him at the moment anyway. No sense staging a revolution against this woman if I was just going to walk out the door anyway. So instead of telling the woman what I thought of her, I grabbed my purse and headed for the door.

"We said we would tell you when she was ready to go," Gannicus said, irritation just barely perceptible in his voice.

"You don't get to make that decision," she said simply, stepping back to allow me to exit the room. "Say your good-byes."

Right, goodbyes. I tried not to seem stiff or awkward as I turned and kissed Gannicus quickly. We hadn't even gotten a chance to talk about what had happened. Before I could walk away, he lightly grabbed my wrist to stop me. His eyes were concerned yet guarded, like he didn't know how to act either.

"Are you still upset?" he said, looking into my eyes.

I thought about my answer. It was definitely yes, but that didn't mean I was right to be. I honestly didn't know what I should feel.

So instead of trying to hash it all out while the evil app woman was waiting for me, I just shook my head and tried to give a sincere smile.

"No," I said. "I'll see you later."

The car ride back was even more excruciating than the way there, considering my crushed plans for the day and my old friend sitting there in the passenger seat. I refused to say a word, hoping that the cloud of awkward silence would suffocate her too. It seemed unlikely, considering she didn't appear to have any feelings at all.

When we got back to my house I thanked the driver pointedly, ensuring that the phrase "Thank you for *driving me*" couldn't apply to the other party in the car.

I felt a sense of foreboding as I walked into the house. I'd thought things were rough after my run-in with Vlad yesterday, but now they were worse. The ghost of Vlad was still circling around in my head as I walked through the quiet house, but this time I didn't even have the comforting thought of Gannicus to help. Whenever I tried to think of Gannicus, I was washed in a confusing mix of guilt and irritation.

What the hell had actually happened back there? I tried to be mature, and to consider his side too. The phrases "I can show you" and "that's nonsense" were digging under my skin like mites, but I tried not to let it get the best of my reason. I'd definitely waited longer to tell Gannicus about my sexual limits than I should have. It was only natural that he'd get his hopes up based on the direction things were going and be surprised and disappointed when I suddenly shifted the conversation so completely. What I should have done was tell him in a more neutral setting, during an actual conversation. I'd been too afraid to ruin a different moment, though, so instead I'd destroyed this one. That was immature. Strike one for me.

On the other hand, I was inclined to think it also didn't matter when I told him I wasn't interested in having sex with him. I was well within my rights to change my mind at any point, and he had to take that answer whenever it came. Acting irritated and entitled to sex was not a good look on anyone. Strike one for Gannicus. I also definitely didn't like how flippant he was about my religious beliefs. They may not have had cell phones back in his time, but I was pretty damn sure they had religion. So I couldn't see that he had much excuse for dismissing mine. I was calling that strike two for Gannicus.

Then again, why had I basically *initiated* the encounter? Kissing his neck and all that nonsense? Sure, that was fine if he knew what the expectations were going in. But he didn't know. I never told him. Besides, he wasn't from my time. I was working with a completely different cultural understanding of sex and religion and *everything*, and I hadn't given that a shred of thought before I'd sprung the information on him at the last minute. Strike two for me. Then again, if our cultures were so different that we couldn't listen and understand where the other person was coming from, what chance did we have?

Whatever game the strikes were part of, there was no winner. I couldn't shake the sick feeling I got whenever I thought about all of it.

Somehow, we'd have to find a way to move past this. I just wanted to get back to the way things were before. I hated to admit it, but I already missed him.

Chapter 15

"I'm having boy problems."

To her credit, Valerie didn't squeal or laugh when I started the video chat so ominously. Most of my other friends would've been so excited about hearing the drama they might have missed how serious I was. As much as I loved them, and could be exactly the same way, I'd chosen to tell my problems to Valerie for a reason. I'd tell Tamryn too, but I had more important things to talk to her about. It felt like ages, but it had only been a day since I'd found out she'd been lying to me for her entire relationship. Somehow it didn't feel like a good time to bring my Gannicus conflict to her. But I had to talk to someone about it, because it was still making my stomach turn.

"What's going on?" Valerie asked, her lips turned down just enough to demonstrate concern. She wasn't particularly emotive, but that definitely didn't mean she didn't care.

Only once I opened my mouth to begin the story did I start to doubt my decision to bring my issues to one of my friends. Only now did I count the parts of my story that I couldn't tell her. Gannicus and I went to the apartment complex where his employer housed him because they didn't teach you how to rent an apartment in 71 B.C. He didn't understand Christian values because he'd lived before Christianity had even existed. We didn't get a chance to finish our conversation because we were only allotted so much time together as some kind of special promotion by the app to apologize for me almost getting killed by a psycho former ruler. I'd have to write a script to get around that minefield without saying anything that would blow my secrets!

"Well," I hedged. I sat on my bed, mindlessly tracing shapes on my pillow with my finger. "I was with this guy that I've been seeing."

"Adam?"

"No-" Oh shit, yeah, I did say his name was Adam. "I mean, yeah. I forgot I told you about him. Yeah, I was with Adam." Apparently my response hadn't been as suspicious as it seemed to me, because I could see Valerie in the camera just like she'd been before, nonjudgmentally waiting to hear what had happened. "I was alone with Adam."

She raised her eyebrows, but didn't say anything. Oh yeah, Valerie had definitely been the right friend to come to with this. I could take my time and think this through, say the right things.

"Things got..." There was no way to finish that sentence without sounding like a 50 year old housewife. I changed courses. "We were making out and whatever, obviously, but I hadn't told him I'm waiting to have sex, so I had to tell him then."

Valerie grimaced.

"And he didn't take it well?" she asked.

"Well I mean-" I tried to think of a way to make him sound better, to say that he took it great and we were getting married in a year and it was all perfect. Except if that had actually happened, we wouldn't be having this conversation in the first place. "He didn't get it. He thought the religious reason was stupid."

Valerie wasn't particularly religious herself, so I knew she wouldn't be defensive of my decisions on those grounds alone. It was safe to tell her what had happened without her judging Gannicus too harshly. She'd probably understand where he was coming from, on some level.

"Wow, what a douchebag," she said when I paused. Oops. Ok, I'd definitely called that one wrong. "Like he has any right to attack your beliefs like that."

Valerie was being protective of me, and completely taking my side. That should've been exactly what I wanted. Except, it wasn't. Besides the fact that I wanted her to still like Gannicus if he and I managed to move past this little disagreement, I couldn't help but feel like it wasn't fair. She didn't know that his perspective was a bit hindered by his past. He didn't really know all the facts like we did.

"I mean, true," I said, giving a small conciliatory laugh. "But he's from a different, uh, culture. So I don't think he really understands. I don't think he realized I'd be offended by him saying that he disagreed with my religion. He didn't mean for it to come out that way, I don't think."

I wasn't sure whether Valerie would accept that mitigating evidence or not, but she didn't give me any clues. She was too busy doing what I'd hoped she wouldn't do - asking for more information.

"From a different culture? What does that mean? Where is he from?"

Yikes. Yikes. I didn't know anywhere in the world that didn't know about Christianity, except maybe some secluded civilizations that didn't interact with the rest of the world. I didn't know where those civilizations were, either. No, I could do this. I could think my way out of this.

"He's from, you know, more east than here." I had to admit "you know" was a pretty bold filler phrase to put in that sentence, considering I didn't even know where I was talking about, so she certainly couldn't either. It was certainly vague enough to keep from exposing me, though. I could've meant anywhere from Pennsylvania to Russia or something. *Oh, please don't ask where I mean. Don't ask where I mean.*

"Oh ok. Well anyway, I still think it's none of his business what your reason is. You didn't ask him for his opinion. He's just some random guy who you didn't want to sleep with."

In a way, she was right, of course. I didn't ask Gannicus for his opinion about it. He'd just volunteered that he thought it was nonsense, as if we were about to take a vote on the issue. On the other hand, he wasn't just some random guy. We'd become comfortable sharing our thoughts with each other, and I didn't want to start saying I didn't care about his point of view. I did care. That was why the whole thing felt so much like I'd been kicked in the stomach.

"Well, he's not a random guy. We've actually been seeing each other for what feels like awhile now, even though it's been a few weeks, and I really do care about him."

"That makes it even worse then, because he should've been more considerate of your feelings if he really cared about you."

Right again. Valerie should've been a lawyer. But of course, it wasn't that simple. What about me being considerate of his feelings? I'd known that being alone together was going to head in a direction that it shouldn't, and I hadn't said a word. I could see that it hurt his feelings when he thought I didn't want to be with him, so I should've expected a little pushback. It didn't mean he was some kind of trashy guy that wanted to use me; he was just reacting emotionally to a surprise. I could certainly acknowledge his side of things without giving up my own convictions on the matter.

"Maybe," I said quietly, still thinking it through. I hated to be the kind of person who called and asked for advice just to do the exact opposite, but feeling defensive of Gannicus was starting to make me see that my side wasn't the only one in this story.

I still thought he was wrong to have an attitude with me about something that was my decision to make, but I felt a lot more compassion for him than I had even an hour ago when I'd left him today. So when I thanked Valerie for her help, I really meant it.

Then I hung up with her, because there was someone else I needed to call next.

"Hello, Lane," Gannicus said when the video call connected. I could see from the background that he was sitting on the bed. That bed that was the cause of our current problems. I focused on his face instead.

His greeting had been a little hesitant, a little stilted. If I looked closely I could see a slight tension in his face. Despite his attempt to sound normal, he was nervous about my call. I imagined he didn't like the way we'd left things any better than I did.

I tried to think of what I'd called to say. Maybe I should've written a script. Talking from the heart was overrated. My heart didn't know how to handle a situation like this either. Instead of letting myself get overly attached to the details, though, I took a deep breath and remembered my conversation with Valerie. I was calling because I'd realized there were two perspectives in this conflict, and I was genuinely open to the other one.

"I just wanted to talk about earlier today," I said quickly, expelling the words from my mouth as if they'd just come out of the oven and were too hot to have taken a bite of. I was known to talk too fast when I was nervous, and this time was even worse because I had something specific I needed to say. When Gannicus opened his mouth to speak, it was an act of enormous strength for me to close mine and see what he had to say.

"I still cannot see why you were so upset," he said. That wasn't the apology I'd been waiting for, and I felt my stomach drop slightly in surprise.

No, no, this was good. The whole point of this was to see his perspective! He was telling me how he felt. All I could do in response was to try to do the same thing.

"Well," I said, swallowing. What did I feel? "I take my religion pretty- very- seriously, and I kind of felt like you were mocking it. Which I didn't think you had a right to do, since you don't even know anything about it and it's important to me. And anyway-" I stopped my rambling when I realized his face had completely changed during my little speech. He's gone from bewilderment to what I thought looked a lot like contrition.

"I see," he said, running a hand through his long hair. "I never meant to disrespect your beliefs. I only sought to explain why you should consider changing your mind."

Alright, well, that was a start. Maybe I'd call that phase one. He understood why I didn't like him criticizing my religion, at least. Unfortunately he still seemed to think the issue was up for debate, which it wasn't now and wouldn't be in the future either.

"Oh ok, well... don't." I laughed quietly, acknowledging the ridiculous simplicity of the response. He smiled slightly, but furrowed his brows in confusion. I pushed on. "It's not really something that I'm looking to have a discussion about. If I say I don't want to have sex, I don't mean that I'm not sure or I could use advice about it. I mean I don't want to and I need you to respect that."

I rubbed the back of my neck as I waited for his response, hoping I'd managed to get the message across somehow. I'd never had to explain this part before, because in 2020 everyone was more or less on the same page about this being a personal choice.

"Alright," he said, taking his time with the word as if he were still digesting the idea. "No discussion needed."

Well yes, but also no. I didn't want him to think we couldn't talk about things at all. This sucked.

"Right but like, just in this very specific case. We can still talk about our thoughts and our opinions, I just don't want you to try to change my mind about sex because I already decided. But that doesn't mean that we can't ever talk about anything, just that-" I stopped. I was rambling again. Gannicus confirmed my rambling diagnosis when he jumped in as soon as I stopped talking.

"May I still kiss you?" He asked, his easy smile returning. I'd missed it.

"Yes."

"Then I accept your conditions."

Relief washed over me and I relaxed the tension in my shoulders. See, that wasn't so bad. And maybe we didn't understand everything about each other right now, but we understood the important things.

Chapter 16

I spent the next week or two alternating between spending time with Gannicus and my parents. Though I still struggled with tension whenever I thought too much about what had happened with Vlad, it helped to know he was no longer on the loose. Unless he got away from someone else, that was. That concern was why I preferred not to be alone.

Whenever I made the mistake of allowing myself, I'd wonder what would have happened if that girl hadn't driven up. Would Customer Service have gotten there in time? How many cuts would Vlad have managed to add? It didn't sit right with me that there could be an app that exposed customers to such dangerous men. What if someone opened a zoo where you were just advised to be careful of the tigers when you welcomed them into your house?

Anyway, why didn't Vlad just quit if he wanted to leave? Were they keeping him now as a prisoner for his dangerous actions? I'd briefly discussed the issue with Tamryn when I'd called her over a week ago to talk about Levi.

"So, Levi," I'd said immediately when she answered the video call. She was brushing her hair, absentmindedly pulling it harder than was probably comfortable.

"Yes. I'm so sorry I didn't tell you. I really thought it was the right thing to do." She put down the hairbrush, only to look down for a minute and pick it up again.

"Why?" I wanted to believe her that the secret was for my own interest, but I needed to hear her say it.

"Because then you'd have more questions. It leads down a road of too much information. You don't want to know where that goes. Just trust me, ok?"

I rubbed my face, not sure what to say. She asked me to trust her, though, so I decided to do that, as much as I could. I changed the subject, telling her about Vlad. I asked her my questions about why he hadn't just left before. The discussion was intended to divert from an uncomfortable issue she didn't want to tell me, but somehow I guessed it had the opposite effect.

"I don't know. That is a good point," she said, her voice higher and faster than usual. I raised my eyebrows silently, wordlessly urging her to explain why she sounded so weird. She didn't.

I just felt tired as I changed the subject again, this time asking her about her finals instead. Her shoulders relaxed when I asked, and she answered easily. I was listening to her stories about school (I really was listening), but every so often my mind tried to work over the puzzle of what was going on here. If Tamryn didn't want to tell me then I wouldn't ask. Maybe, though, I could get more information from Gannicus.

When Gannicus arrived the next day, I momentarily forgot about the Vlad enigma. I was too busy appreciating the way his tank top showed off his broad shoulders. Almost involuntarily, I grabbed those shoulders as I kissed him, running my hands down his muscular arms. I spent so much time planning what I'd do when I was with him, but as soon as I finally got around him, all I wanted to do was soak it in.

"Have you ever heard of Zumba?" I asked, bouncing on the balls of my feet. I hoped so much that he hadn't, that I had the element of surprise on my side. He looked like the type of guy who enjoyed working out, but I wasn't sure if a dance workout would be his style.

"Zumba... I cannot say that I have. Is it food?" I laughed at the question, shaking my head but inviting him to follow me to the kitchen. It would be smart to feed him before I asked him to try something that was almost certainly out of his element. As soon as he'd gotten a snack, I set to work. I set up YouTube on my TV and pulled up the necessary video.

"Ok, here's what you have to do," I said. He leaned in to stare directly into my eyes in mock concentration. "You just have to do the dance moves as she does them."

Though the first song involved a lot of running into each other and flailing around, I was shocked at how quickly he caught up. I found myself forgetting to follow the instructor as I watched him. He chuckled a lot, maintaining an expression on his face put there to remind me that he wasn't taking this seriously. His ability spoke otherwise. For someone so large, his dancing was remarkably lithe.

My heart swelled as I tried to follow along again, laughter of pure joy escaping the whole time.

I love you. I mouthed the words at him when his head was turned. I knew it was so early that no one would believe I really felt it. But nobody had to believe me. I didn't plan to tell them. It was my secret. It was enough that I knew it was true.

"Oh nooo," he said, pretending to lose his balance. He barrelled into me, tackling me in an absurd imitation of falling on accident that took us both all the way onto the floor. We both laughed as I shoved at him and he refused to get off of me. The mood took a slight turn as we became conscious of the length of our eye contact. He kissed me with intention, like he was trying to communicate by it. I felt like I might have known what he meant.

"I have to ask you something," he said, apparently feigning solemnity as his lips just barely quirked up at the corners.

"Ok," I said breathlessly.

"Are you ticklish?"

I didn't have time to react before he decided to find out for himself. I shrieked in protest, uselessly attempting to fight off his advance. The scientific experiment gave the result that I was, in fact, ticklish.

I was still laughing when I noticed his expression had sobered. He was looking intently at the cut on my arm, which by now was mostly healed.

He didn't have to say a word for me to understand what he was thinking. The cuts were a reminder of an event we'd both rather forget, something that never should have happened in the first place. I didn't need the cuts to remind me, either. The nightmares I still had sometimes were enough to keep it fresh in my mind, the way I'd been helpless as the knife stung and drew blood. When I was awake I tried not to think about it, and mostly did a decent job focusing on other things. It wasn't always easy to do, though. It wasn't easy for Gannicus, either.

"It's fine," I told him, putting my hand on his chest in a plea for him to refocus. It was the middle of the day, we were together, we were safe and inside the house. There was no Vlad hiding in the closet. It was all behind us now. "It's almost healed." He paid no attention to my arguments as he squeezed me protectively into his chest.

"Don't ever go to battle without me again," he urged seriously. It wasn't quite a battle with the Roman army, but I didn't argue with his word choice. What had happened with Vlad mattered to me too.

"I've been meaning to ask," I said, now that Vlad had already invaded this moment. I'd been avoiding it thus far, changing the subject when Vlad happened to come up. He wasn't my favorite topic, and there were plenty of things I did enjoy talking to Gannicus about. Now that the topic was already broached, though, maybe it was time to take advantage of it to make sense of a question that had been lingering on my mind. "If he wanted to escape, why didn't he just quit the app?"

"Lane, if he had to escape, why did he not just quit?" I furrowed my eyebrows. I wondered if he'd understood me.

"I just asked you that."

"No, consider it. If quitting was an option, why did he have to escape?"

My stomach turned when I grasped his meaning. I was too busy connecting dots to answer the question, so I just shrugged and let him tell me straight out.

"Vlad couldn't leave because he's not really an employee. None of us are. He is a slave."

There was a moment of silence between us.

I tensed as I forgot about Vlad. Gannicus had said "he" in reference to Vlad, but it was pretty clear who else he was referring to. The word "us" made that hideously clear. Us. Slave. The words cut deeper than the slice of Vlad's knife. I tried to push them away, but they were relentless. Pain spread through me like poison in my veins as I thought about all this time, all these meetings, all that I'd misunderstood.

I wasn't Gannicus's girlfriend. I was just another slave owner.

Either he didn't notice my eyes were filled with tears, or he thought it was a reasonable reaction to what he'd just said, but Gannicus kept talking. I stared at his moving lips in horror, every word that left them another stab in my chest.

"You know I was taken from my own time, deprived of my rightful death in battle. When I found myself in this new world, I thought I would wait until I discovered how to get back home. Not much time passed before I determined that was not going to happen easily. Along with our history training, we were informed that any of us that tried to escape would be killed outright. As soon as we started to risk talking amongst ourselves, we started to risk forming a plan. Like my time as a gladiator, the answer to freedom would require the strength of numbers. When Levi met Tamryn, he began to prepare his escape. Alone. Those of us who knew of his plan tried to discourage him. We had - have- a plan, and it relies on us all working together."

I didn't want to hear about Levi. I didn't want to realize how Tamryn had known I would be participating in the enslavement of innocent people and *encouraged* me to try the app. I didn't want to hear anything. His words cut through the roaring in my ears anyway.

"Somehow he managed it. Though I was glad to hear of his success, I knew more responsibility fell on my shoulders than would allow me to follow. I remain determined to help the others out. Still, when I saw you for the first time, I mistook you for Tamryn, visiting me to offer me the same way out that Levi had taken."

A way out. He'd seen me as a means of escape. A life preserver. I'd let him drown instead, playing in the pool with him and feeding him snacks like a pet. I was going to vomit.

"I still plan to escape," he said quietly, as an afterthought.

All I could see were the colors of his form through the blur of my tears. I didn't even want to see that.

Pain registered in his face as he took in my misery at the news. He lifted his arm around me, but I shrank away from him. The fact that *he* was trying to comfort *me* in this moment was a fresh stab of pain. I wanted to stand up and run away, to cover my ears and not hear another word of this. But I wouldn't be able to stop my mind from connecting the dots. Anyway, I was frozen to the spot.

"I was always planning to leave at some point. I had some semblance of a plan, to break free and gather weapons to return with for the others. That might have been the moral choice, but I could not leave without telling you the truth. Besides, I was afraid I might never see you again if I did."

Ouch. It was really my fault. He was the brave hero he'd always been, the one that was here in my time because he was remembered through thousands of years for his willingness to die for his own freedom and the freedom of others. He'd been willing to fight for that freedom once again, at insurmountable disadvantage, because it was what he believed in. He'd felt obligated to not leave me behind, though, so he'd given up his plan.

I shook my head and swallowed back my tears. I hadn't known. He hadn't given me the chance to be a part of this nightmare knowingly. It wasn't fair to put it on me that he'd turned back for me.

"You should've," I said, even though I didn't really know what I thought. Anger was a lot easier to swallow than guilt. It *was* his fault I felt this way. "You should've left. You should leave now."

"Lane -" he protested, turning to look into my eyes. I looked away. "You have no idea how I feel about you. I would never want to leave you now."

That was how I felt about him, but I had made my decisions to see him of my own volition. I could have done anything with my time; I *chose* to be with him. Any emotions he thought he had towards me could be nothing more than Stockholm Syndrome, coerced out of him from a little bit of kindness in his situation. As much as my torn heart begged, I couldn't accept his words as the truth.

"Get out. Please, go. Now's your chance to escape," I said, standing up and wiping my eyes. He reached for my hand, but I stepped back out of reach.

My prison of misery compelled me to turn away when he stood up and tried to argue; I felt as if I were watching somebody else instead of experiencing this myself. Just because I felt like I was running towards my own execution didn't mean that I was wrong. This was the right thing - the only thing - I could do. I'd been blind and selfish long enough.

He just stood there, staring at me helplessly.

"Get out!" I sobbed, taking one heart-wrenching look at him before I turned and left the room, walking slowly but deliberately up the stairs. Some time later, I heard the front door close quietly behind him, like it had so many times before. It was a punch in the stomach to realize this would be the last time.

By the time the door closed, I was lying on my bedroom floor. I spent the next hour lying there, alternating between staring at the wall and curling into body-wracking sobs. Had I just lost a relationship with a man I loved, I could've dealt with that. The slavery aspect was inconceivable. The combination was intolerable.

Chapter 17

I was still on the floor when I heard the doorbell ring. My heart leaped into my throat. Could he be back? I knew I had no right to hope for it, but I did. I dashed down the stairs and threw open the door, only to be greeted by a man about my parents' age wearing a suit.

"Hello, Miss Reid," he said, adjusting his jacket. "We're looking for," he checked the clipboard in his hands. "Gannicus."

"You won't find him here," I said, the disappointment of finding this strange man at my door sapping my energy. I registered somewhere in my mind that maybe I should have a story for where he was, but there wasn't an explanation that would get this man to go away without Gannicus going with him. I gave up and muttered some version of the truth. "I got upset and went upstairs. I guess he left."

The man looked down at his clipboard, apparently unsure what to do now. I wondered if this was his first time seeking an instructor-*slave* - that didn't come to the door.

"Well if he comes back, please call me here." He handed me a classic white business card. I took it, clutching it in my hand carefully as if I ever planned to use it. I nodded and closed the door. In the back of my mind I wondered if I should yell at this man, demand to know why he participated in this kind of evil. I didn't have the strength. Anyway, who was I to ask anyone why they were participating? Gannicus had been at my house this very same hour, as part of the very same program. I wiped my eyes on my shirt, my face raw from scrubbing away so many tears.

My heart ached that the interruption hadn't been Gannicus, even as I told myself I had no right to feel that way. No, if I had any heart at all, any semblance of decency, I would be happy for him that he'd finally managed to get out on his own. The right thing was exactly what was happening now. The best I could do was to accept my own misery though, and not try to change it or get him back. That would have to be enough for now. I stumbled back into my room and laid on my bed, falling in and out of sleep.

My fitful nap was eventually interrupted by a light knock on the door, followed by my mother letting me know she had dinner ready. I pushed against the disorienting fogginess of waking up in the middle of the day. It was likely my mother had heard me crying earlier, but I knew she wouldn't say a word even if she had.

"Coming," I mumbled, my voice thick as I tried to shake off my sleep. That was enough. A short period of mourning was appropriate, but it was time to pull myself together. This wasn't about me. There were real people that had suffered because of the app that I'd participated in, and I wasn't going to use them as an excuse to wallow. I could cry in the shower like an adult.

I didn't say much at dinner. Instead, I pushed my pasta around the plate and thought about how a person could make up for something like this. I kept going back and forth on the mitigating aspect of ignorance. Sure, no one had told me this was going on. Then again, why hadn't I wondered? When Vlad ran away, I should've asked myself sooner why he would have to escape unless he were a prisoner. Had I been willfully blind, or just blind? What was I supposed to do about it now?

"Have you talked to Tamryn?" my father asked, giving a friendly smile with what he assumed was a casual question. Unfortunately, he was incorrect.

My stomach twisted when I thought of Tamryn. My trust in her had been absolute for my entire life. It was more than trusting her to tell me the truth, or believing that she had my best interest in mind. I'd always known, with an unshakable certainty, that her sense of morality was steadfast, inflexible. Her judgment was something I could fall back on when I wasn't sure what to do myself. To learn that she'd enthusiastically invited me into this affront to human decency was beyond my comprehension. I didn't know what to believe anymore.

"No," I said, scowling. When my dad gave my mom a side glance, though, I realized it wasn't fair to show signs of a reaction to an event I refused to tell them about. It wasn't their fault. I tried to adopt a neutral facial expression, as if I wasn't falling apart. "I mean, not since a couple days ago. She's just working on her finals."

My attempt to assuage him worked; my parents struck up a conversation about Tamryn graduating online in a week or so. I chimed in when necessary, offering my opinions about how different Tamryn's virtual graduation would be from mine, which had been in person. Though I spoke warmly about her accomplishment, the very thought of Tamryn right now turned my blood to ice.

What, exactly, had been her plan? She knew that Levi had escaped, which meant there was no dodging the truth that she knew about the enslavement. I thought I knew her too well to assume that she had become comfortable with human beings in captivity, but I also would have thought I'd known her too well for any of this.

I had to call her. I had to confront her and ask these questions, if only to grasp some small semblance of understanding. No, actually, I wasn't going to call her.

As soon as I'd managed to swallow some of my food, I grabbed my purse and stormed out of the house, telling my parents I'd be back soon.

The drive to Marana was usually peaceful, with Saguaro cacti greeting me as I listened to the same twenty songs on my phone. This time I drove in silence, not even noticing the Arizona landscape that I always appreciated as an integral part of my soul. My heart thumped its own beat for me to listen to, warning me that a formidable confrontation was coming. I didn't need its warning. I was well aware of where I was going.

Where to go was the easy part. I'd made this drive more times than I could count since Tamryn and Levi had moved out to an apartment on the outskirts of Tucson. The apartment had become a second home to me, a place that formed only safe, happy memories. I was reluctant to change that. But it wasn't my doing. I hadn't been the one to suggest the app. I hadn't been the one who encouraged me to get to know Gannicus, who cheered on the relationship as if it were a normal, healthy situation. I knew Tamryn too well to think that her involvement was any kind of sinister, but that just enhanced my confusion. How could she have possibly rationalized any of this? I wasn't looking forward to the confrontation, but I had no choice but to get answers to these questions.

When I got to my sister's apartment, I slammed my fist on the door. It was unnecessary to be so aggressive, but the door was a willing outlet for my frustration, and I took advantage. My stomach was turning painfully, and I needed her to let me in immediately so I could get this over with. No matter what explanation she offered, it couldn't make me feel any worse than I did now.

Tamryn opened the door, a smile lighting up her face when she saw I'd come to visit her. Of course she was happy to see me. She was my best friend, and I was hers. That was enough to break me down all over again. I fought tears as I walked in, telling her that we needed to talk.

"How could you do this to me?" I asked immediately, a tactic I knew was ineffective. I hadn't even told her what I was talking about. The situation was suddenly made much worse when I saw her stricken expression and realized I didn't have to tell her anything. She already knew exactly what I was talking about. She'd been waiting for this.

"Why don't we sit down?" she said slowly, making a visible effort to maintain a sense of order in the conversation. What else could I do? I didn't know how else to respond, so I complied. I sat in a plush chair in the little living room, staring blankly at the upholstery as if I could hide from my own words.

"You knew. I just don't understand. Please help explain it to me because I don't understand how you could suggest the app like it was something fun, and let me talk about him like he was just any other guy and everything was fine. Like it was fine that he was some sort of toy. Or is that how you saw Levi too? Just a captive audience to play with?" I felt a pang of regret when she reeled back like I'd struck her.

"Of *course* not. You know that. I know you're upset, but I can't talk to you unless you try to be reasonable." Her level-headedness felt like an attack. I was trying to pull myself together, but this was anything but a reasonable situation.

"You made me a *slave owner* and you're asking me to be *reasonable*?" I was appalled by the ridiculousness of the request. This wasn't your typical sibling fight. She wasn't going to win any points by acting like this was a purely academic debate. When I saw her swallow past a lump in her throat and quickly swipe at her eyes, though, the fight faded out of me.

"I care about Gannicus," she said. "I never intended to tell you anything about the app, but when I heard that you were looking for something to do with your time, I wondered if there might be more that I could do for him than the documents Levi had given him. I wondered if I could help him get freedom and love like Levi had."

I stared pointedly at the carpet, digesting the explanation.

"I knew you'd love him," she said, causing me to look at her despite myself.

"I didn't say I loved him," I protested.

"I know you didn't," she said, giving me a short, knowing grin. The smile faded as quickly as it had come as she continued her story. "I thought I'd let the relationship build, and when the time was right he'd tell you the truth. You would probably have had to help him find a place to live like we did, maybe even get married eventually if you wanted to."

Hearing her explanation was disorienting, like accidentally walking into the wrong movie at the theater. Somehow we'd gone from horror to fairytale. Find him a place to live? Get married? What world was she living in?

"What are you talking about?" I said, interrupting her musings. "He doesn't love me. He's a slave."

"Levi was a slave too. We got him out together. I *never* forced him to love me. It's just what happened."

That was all well and good for them, I thought, but it didn't prove anything for me. I remembered their relationship lasting a year before they got married, though I didn't know how that fit in with her story. Frankly, I didn't care. Gannicus and I had been together - no, *had interacted* - for less than three months. I didn't see how it could go any further now.

"You told me about the app so I could rescue Gannicus. Then why didn't you tell me the truth?" I asked, overwhelmed by the disaster that was becoming my life. I tried to get things back on track.

"I... I don't know. I thought it would be better if he told you. And if you knew too early, you might try to get them all sent back to their own times."

I thought about what Gannicus had said, about having a responsibility to help the others. Was that what he'd meant? Not only did I agree with him, I was a little shocked that Tamryn didn't. It was all well and good to help Levi because she loved him, but what about the others? She was right. I would have wanted to save them all.

"That would be the right thing to do," I said.

"Yeah, I guess so. But I'm not willing to do it. Because if we reported it, any organization that did a basic inventory of everyone collected out of time would realize that Levi was missing. Once they found us, and that couldn't take too long, what if they didn't believe that he really wanted to be with me? What if they thought I was taking advantage of his circumstances, and he only *thought* he wanted me? Like -" she stopped, stuck on a word.

"Like Stockholm Syndrome," I said blandly. She just cringed and nodded.

"You might think I'm selfish for choosing Levi over any of the others." I did sort of think that, but I wouldn't say something so cruel to her now that I'd calmed down. Not when I knew it wouldn't make any difference. "If the whole world had to burn for me to have him, I guess I'd pour the gasoline."

I might have felt that way about Gannicus if burning the world down would mean that he wanted me back. Not when I didn't know if he *really* wanted me. For all I knew, I had been nothing more than a potential vehicle to freedom. Or worse, a minor bright side to slavery.

I stayed at Tamryn's and told her everything that had happened with Gannicus. She pleaded with me to not be so rigid, to find him and tell him how I felt. That was easy for her to say, and I told her that. I felt a bit better as I left, though, appreciating the slight relief of no longer suffering alone. A hidden corner of my heart lightened to have Tamryn's approval of its idea: to find Gannicus and take him back. I pointedly ignored it.

My soul cried out for Gannicus when I climbed into bed well past midnight each night, and begged for him when I opened my eyes in the morning. Every so often my heart would skip when he came into my mind, only to usher in a sinking feeling when I remembered he was no longer mine.

Every other day, a calendar of its own, I'd find a pink rose on the deck chair where he'd sat in my backyard. My heart swelled every time, though I tried to tell myself that there was a reason I'd told him to leave in the first place. "If you love something, set it free," I'd always heard. I tried not to let myself finish the expression. Sooner or later he'd either stop sending the roses, or he'd approach me. But I couldn't make a move, or else I'd never know for sure how he would've chosen to end things. That did nothing to stop me from adding each new rose to a vase I kept in my room.

There was also the problem of the slavery. I couldn't allow that to go on, but what choice did I have? I would never dream of hurting Tamryn by reporting the app and risking the loss of Levi. Even thinking of Tamryn heartbroken hurt me. The idea that it could be my fault was unbearable. I could judge her for not doing the right thing for his sake, but was I any better for choosing not to do it for hers?

Chapter 18

I forced myself to focus on my old life, which had once again become my new reality. My familiar problems had only been concealed by the glow of Gannicus. Without him, they returned with a vengeance. When I wasn't missing Gannicus, I was lying in bed wondering what I was going to do with my life. Losing him just solidified my fears that I had nothing real going for me.

My life stalemate was beginning to appear as if it might suffocate me when I answered an incoming call from a number I didn't recognize.

"Hello, this is Lane Reid," I answered, in the professional way strangers on Twitter had recommended. Just because every other call had been a spam call warning me about my car's warranty expiring didn't mean that this time wouldn't be something important. I was instantly glad I made that decision.

"Hello, Lane," said a warm, cheerful woman's voice. "My name is Mariah Hernandez. I'm calling from the National Alliance Against Human Trafficking. I was wondering if you were still interested in the Junior Investigator position?"

A job! My first reaction was one of excitement and relief. Maybe things were on the right track after all. Then I was stopped before I could answer her by a realization I wished I could return to the recesses of my mind. I felt a cold sweat break out on the back of my neck. Though I had a twinge of joy at the opportunity she was discussing, another detail she'd mentioned was actually far more pressing. Human trafficking. Hadn't I just been a part of such a thing? Would that ever come to light if I accepted this job? The only smart choice would be to run far, far away. I had enough problems to solve as it was.

"Yes," I said, widening my eyes at my own answer. Was I *crazy?* "I am still interested."

"That's great. We would love to set up a virtual interview. What time works for you next week?"

My head swam with a potent combination of excitement and apprehension.

"I can do Tuesday or Thursday?" I replied. Actually, I could do any time, any day of the week. I wasn't sure if my wide-open schedule would be seen as a negative, though. I let myself move on from thinking about strategies and drawbacks. The last thing I wanted was to let this be a bad thing. I so desperately needed a win. Who said this had to be related to Gannicus and the app at all? I could have a job and free everyone who worked for the app at the same time, if I worked at it.

"Let's make it Tuesday. How does 1 o'clock sound?"

I was buzzing by now. I was sure I could power a clock with the electricity that was coursing through me. As calmly and coherently as I could, I told her that that would be wonderful and thanked her heartily. With what little tranquility I had left, I made a note of it in my phone's calendar. Wouldn't want to forget my interview time. Then I lost my mind.

Screaming and whooping, I danced around the room. A pang of concern tried to break through and remind me that I'd probably have to end up investigating myself, but I brushed it aside easily. What a job! I could really help people. I could wake up every morning and know that my time *meant* something.

By the time I decided to tell my parents, I'd managed to calm down. Not only did I not have the job yet, I knew very little about it. Just because it sounded like something I wanted didn't mean I should call the newspapers yet. When I rushed into the living room to tell them the news, I did my best to temper it with logic and drawbacks so they wouldn't be disappointed when they started asking questions about it. It would be embarrassing for everyone if I oversold the news only to reveal that it wasn't as great as I'd made it out to be. I didn't need to worry about that, though. My parents were just as thrilled as I was, despite my efforts to conserve my joy.

My mom ushered my dad and me into the kitchen, getting down the champagne glasses we almost never used. Considering we never used the glasses, we also didn't have champagne. We settled for regular white wine.

"To Lane," she said, holding up her glass. "Let the adventure begin."

It was certainly an overreaction to a job interview. In fact, it was borderline insulting that my even being considered for a job felt like such a momentous occasion. The truth was, though, that it *was* a big deal. So I refused to tether my celebration as I tapped my glass with theirs, beaming.

I felt a familiar sinking in my stomach as I realized my first instinct was to call Gannicus and tell him the news. I brushed it off, taking a longer sip from my glass.

Pink flowers were beginning to overcrowd my vase. Even after pressing the older ones into my Bible, I was left with a staggering image of just how much time had passed since I'd last seen Gannicus. As if I wasn't counting the days already, wondering how long was too long to expect him to come back for me.

By all reasonable accounts, it seemed like too much time had passed to recover from a couple's first fight. Well, calling it a fight was disingenuous. I'd discovered that he had never really been mine all along. The roses left behind suggested that maybe I still had a piece of his heart, but I couldn't know what that truly meant. It was just as believable that he was working through his complicated emotions following his freedom from slavery. He'd already told me at the house that he cared about me and wanted to be with me, and that his feelings hadn't changed since he'd tried to escape. It didn't mean he really knew how he felt. He'd had to *escape* in the first place! That wasn't a fairytale in the making. No, the most I could do was look back on the time we'd had and try to be glad that I'd had that at all.

I put the day's fresh rose into the vase, taking the time to appreciate the silkiness of the petals. This was a gift from Gannicus, and its frequency couldn't make me take it for granted. Pain squeezed my heart as I turned away from the vase, wondering if they could mean anything, or if he just didn't know anyone else. Wondering if he'd ever really love me.

Since it was the only distraction I had during quarantine, and because it was my chance to make something of myself, I threw myself into preparing for my job interview. By now I only had two days left, but I'd managed to learn that my position would give me face-to-face interaction with human trafficking victims. I'd shadow senior investigators as they built a case against the perpetrators. One day I'd be ready to take on investigations on my own.

If I got the job. If no one discovered that I was currently aware of a human trafficking plot myself. Though I hadn't given up on finding a solution, I was as in the dark as ever. It grated on my conscience, but I understood why Tamryn had felt frozen in inaction. It was one thing to know what to do and to be afraid to do it. It was something else entirely when you had no idea what the right thing was, but you had to figure something out anyway.

Unsure of what else to do to ease the weight of responsibility, I dug out a notebook from under my bed, turning past old calculus notes until I found an empty page. All I could find was a purple pen, but it would have to do. I began to write.

I, Lane Elizabeth Reid, promise that I will stop the enslavement of historical figures-

I crossed that out.

will stop the enslavement of people *by Neil Davidson and the producers of the IEducator app. I will not make excuses to put off this task indefinitely, but instead I will take action. Until I find a way, I will consider the issue ceaselessly. I will* put a stop to it. I promise.

Lane Reid

It wasn't a solution, but I took promises seriously. The written contract burned in my hand. Now it was up to me to solve this problem. Just writing the note and shoving it back under my bed wasn't enough, though. There was someone else that needed to know I understood my role. I ripped the note out of the book and folded it in half, putting it on my dresser next to the vase.

I'd set it out tomorrow night on the deck chair after my parents went to sleep, where he'd find it whenever he came the next day.

I dipped my foot in and out of my heel as I sat at the dining room table, listening to the slight rustle of my pantyhose on the shoe's interior every time I did it. All I was doing was sitting in my own house, familiar territory, alone, with a computer in front of me. I was not a gazelle being chased through the savannah by a hungry lion. So why did my heart constrict painfully in my chest? Why did I have to keep taking deep breaths and reminding myself to smile and act calm? It turned out that even virtual job interviews were hell on earth.

Even though they were only seeing the top half of me, I'd worn a suit and heels in case I had to stand up for some reason and walk away from the camera. I had some bizarre fear that they'd demand that I show them my whole outfit to make sure I wasn't just wearing pajamas, like someone who was lazy and didn't fully dress for the job interview. Obviously they wouldn't care about something so absurd as that. Obviously. And yet. I was relieved to be wearing my uncomfortable pencil skirt and slick black heels.

My stomach protested with a continuous dull ache as the screen changed, going from a black screen to the neutral colors of an office conference room. Though it couldn't be the same, the room did look too much like my old nightmare for comfort. There was a long table like before, and large windows taking up the back wall. This time, though, I only had one interviewer. The camera was pointed in the middle of the room, even though she was on the left side of the table. She was close enough that I could make out her facial expressions, though, and that was the important thing. She didn't look cruelly neutral, or like she was just waiting to judge that I wasn't good enough. My dream hadn't been any kind of omen; it was nothing more than a stress dream. I was young and capable, and this was my job to take.

The interviewer was younger than I'd expected, probably in her 30's. She introduced herself as Mariah Hernandez from the phone call, and gave me an encouraging smile that contrasted sharply with the female interviewer in my dream. I returned her smile, holding a paper copy of my resume firmly just off camera, in case there were any specific questions I'd need it to answer. I set it on the table next to the laptop when I noticed the slight flapping sound it was making from being in my shaky hands.

"Are you nervous?" she asked, to my chagrin. I hated it when interviewers asked that. Of course I was nervous. It was only my future that was hanging in the balance here. My irritation was extinguished, though, when I saw in her sympathetic eyes that she asked as a friend.

"A bit," I admitted. "Truthfully, this job means a lot to me. It's important that I show you I'm the right person for it." I thought that was a pretty good answer.

All things considered, the interview was a success from there. We had a strong conversation that happened to include my qualifications and experiences, rather than a bland question-and-answer session.

When she gave me a chance to ask questions of my own, I discovered that the culture of the organization was cooperative and close-knit. It seemed like the right place for me. Not that I hadn't already made up my mind about wanting the job before I'd asked any questions, but she didn't need to know that. I thanked her at the end, and my hand hovered above the "end call" button on the screen.

Then I stopped.

I couldn't just leave. Finding a job was important to me, obviously. But there was something more important involved here. This woman across from me had experience in saving people that were enslaved, locked in hopeless situations like the one I'd stumbled across. How could I close out of this call with a smile on my face like this was just another conversation? Like it was all about me? It wasn't about me. Not anymore. It was about them. And him. It had been since I'd answered that first video call. There was a chance, maybe even a big one, that whatever question I asked would ruin the progress I thought I'd made in my interview, convincing her I had something to hide. And didn't I? But I'd already made up my mind.

"What do you guys do in a trafficking situation where you don't want to involve the police? Where some of the people don't want to be forced to, uh, go home?" That was the closest I could get to my situation without divulging anything. It wasn't self-preservation that kept me from going into too much detail. Instead, I was conscious of the fact that whatever I said couldn't be taken back. If I said definitively that there were people that needed help, there was a good chance she'd feel compelled to try to help them. My situation was just too complex to bring in a stranger.

She didn't respond right away, but instead sat thoughtfully for a moment. Her eyes studied me. I wondered what part of my question she was dissecting, and what conclusions she was coming to.

"Well, you'd be surprised how often that's the case. Many human trafficking victims don't want to get the police involved because of immigration status, and many others come from unhealthy home situations. It depends on the situation you're looking at, but for us, in many cases, it's enough to bring down the person or organization that's trafficking, and see what individual help the victims say they want after that. We treat it on a case-by-case basis."

I nodded and thanked her again, mulling over the advice she'd given me. Was that something I could use? I definitely liked the idea of leaving certain people out of it if they didn't want to get involved or sent back. My big problem was the risk of sending Levi back, and I'd be lying if I said I didn't have the same concerns about Gannicus. A solution that meant destroying Neil Davidson's operation without losing the man I loved sounded like one I'd better consider.

The suggestion kept buzzing through my mind as I made my way up to my room, kicking my heels across the floor and peeling off my suit. It was a relief to be out of the tension of the fabric, both physical and psychological.

I took a long shower, singing a concoction of whatever love song lyrics popped into my head. Now that I had the seeds of a plan forming in my mind, I allowed myself to consider the possibility of seeing Gannicus again when I brought down the app. Certainly he'd at least want to thank me, right? It ached like a deep wound to imagine it, but I decided I'd rather be his friend than nothing at all. If all he wanted after all of this was to shake hands and part on good terms, I would have to take that. If he wanted less than that? Well, that was his choice. But I was going to do the right thing for him and the others regardless, if I could manage it.

What now?

Compelled by the promise I'd made not to put it off, I found a notebook and pen on the nightstand and started writing down the conceptions of a plan as soon as I got out of the shower.

What brought down a company? I thought about my trip to Gannicus's dorm, about how the company had been so eager to gain my forgiveness after what happened with Vlad. Bad press could be lethal for a budding company. If the public learned the horrors that the app was responsible for, the app would have no chance of surviving. All I had to do was gather some information and pass it on to the news outlets so they could report on it. Actually, I could do even better than that. I knew how to write an article. My communications major had put me in my share of journalism courses. If I wrote an article myself, the news could have it in the paper and online in a day.

What I needed was an interview with the app's creator, the main enemy himself, Neil Davidson. I was sure it was ordinarily impossible to get an interview with a CEO and company creator as a nobody, but I knew Davidson would be eager for the publicity. Gannicus had said that the plan for the app was to widen its influence to other parts of the country. Surely Davidson would be interested in any opportunity to get his name and product out there. That was just good PR. It was certainly worth a try. Besides, I could make up an identity. All's fair in love and war, right? This was certainly war. I thought of Gannicus. Maybe it was love, too.

Now was as good a time as any to make my first attack. It was easy enough to find the app creator's contact information online, easier than it should have been. I opened an email to him on my phone, stretching my legs out on the carpet as I thought about what I'd say.

Dear Dr. Neil Davidson,

Hello, my name is Lane Randolph. I am the Editor in Chief at *The Daily Wildcat*, the University of Arizona's student newspaper. I am currently writing an article on the best ways for students to prepare for next semester's classes, and I believe the IEducator app is the most effective means. It would be an honor if you would allow me to interview you for the story. Thank you very much for your time, and I hope to hear back from you soon.

Sincerely,
Lane Randolph
Editor in Chief
The Daily Wildcat

I finished the email, my hands just barely shaking as I hit "send." There. It was out there for him to agree to or not. He could easily consult the student newspaper's website and see that I wasn't really the Editor in Chief, but I didn't want to change my first name because if he referred to me by a fake name in person it would throw me off. Nobody ever read those news staff bios anyway.

My cover wasn't a total lie. I had spent a semester writing for the paper, though I'd written for the Opinions section and was never an editor. Also, I didn't go to school there anymore. Alright, it was a total lie. I had already given myself permission to be dishonest, though, in pursuit of justice, and there was no use questioning it now.

And what was there to question, really? My heart glowed with a sense of accomplishment, and with the lifting of the guilt I'd felt ignoring the app all this time. Now I was finally making an effort to put a stop to the slavery, and I could begin to forgive myself for all of the time I spent contributing to it. I wondered if Gannicus would be proud of me for taking a stand. I liked to think that he would be.

As I lay in bed that night, staring at the empty bunk above me, I speculated about what Gannicus was up to these days. Where was he living? How was he supporting himself? I physically shut my eyes against the doubts that filled my mind about how I'd reacted to what he told me, but they played behind my eyelids. Maybe I should have insisted he stay at my house since he had nowhere else to go. What did he know about finding a job or renting an apartment? Then again, they'd have had an easy time tracking him down if he'd stayed. Even if they didn't, keeping him in my house would just be making him into a pet, a thought I abhorred. At least this way he was finally making his own choices.

I continued to debate with myself, not noticing when I slowly started to drift to sleep.

Chapter 19

"Tell us everything about it," my mother said as soon as I came down for breakfast the next day.

"I already did!" I laughed, nodding when my dad asked if I wanted a waffle. I had in fact told my parents about the interview right after my shower, in as many details as I could possibly remember. In fact, I was pretty sure we'd gone over every question and answer, and every reaction of the interviewer to try to guess her thoughts.

"We want to hear it again."

I dutifully told the story of my job interview all over again. They grinned at all of the appropriate points, and their enthusiasm was contagious. Every smile was a confirmation that I'd done as well as I'd thought at the interview. I was starting to feel like maybe my chances of getting the job were pretty good. Then I remembered my final question to the interviewer. That one was complicated. Obviously I didn't regret it, because I'd needed the answer to form a plan to help Gannicus. Just because I'd do it again didn't mean it might not have a negative consequence for me, though. I left that part out even now as I retold my parents the story, like I had the first time I told them about the interview. I had no way of explaining to them where such a concern about handling human trafficking had come from. I wished I could ask them, though, if they thought the question might ruin my chances.

As soon as I'd appeased them with my story, I finally let myself attend to a detail that had been playing through my mind since I woke up. I'd checked yesterday and hadn't seen a rose, so that meant today I must have one. I speed-walked as casually as I possibly could to the backyard. Whether or not Gannicus had left a rose didn't mean anything. Just because he left them regularly didn't mean he'd keep leaving them regularly. Someday he'd have to reduce the frequency, and then one day they would stop coming altogether. I tried to tell myself that that was just fine, but it was a waste of mental words. Getting a rose from Gannicus was the closest I came to seeing him these days, and I was starving for any crumb that I could get.

My heart sank. There was no pink rose on the deck chair. Well, that was okay. So he missed a morning. That was not a reason for my heart to sink.

"I put your rose in the vase for you," she said simply. She didn't ask about the source of the roses, or how long I expected them to keep coming. It was a gesture of pure consideration with no ulterior motives. Wow. That was really nice of her.

"Thank you, Mom," I said, going back into the house.

So he had left a rose today. I couldn't keep the smile off my face. Yes, it was still true that one day he'd have to stop bringing them. I'd been right when I'd said it was time to stop expecting them, that I needed to let him move on and be happy when that time finally came. I truly did want what was best for him, and maybe sticking around and leaving me messages of love wasn't that. Still, was it so evil to enjoy it while it lasted?

A few days passed uneventfully before I got a notification on my phone of a new email. I gasped when I saw the sender- Neil Davidson, CEO.

Dear Lane,

It would be an honor to have you. I'm available next Wednesday at one for the interview. I have attached the address with a map of the building so you can conveniently find my office. Please let me know if this works for you. Thank you very much for your interest.

Best,

Neil Davidson

CEO

IEducator

Besides the fact that he'd referred to me by my first name, an email habit I'd never understood from perfect strangers, I had an uncomfortable feeling of actually liking Davidson. He seemed humble and accommodating. Here I was, only a fake editor at a university newspaper, and he was willing to meet with me and give me an interview. He also expected me to hop in my car and interview him in California, which was an unexpected twist. My first instinct was to reply that I would prefer a virtual interview, blaming it on the pandemic rather than my wariness of traveling to California alone, but I wondered if I'd learn more about my enemy by seeing him face-to-face.

I'd just have to suck it up and buy my first plane ticket.

It wasn't that I was afraid to fly, I was simply afraid of having a medical emergency on the plane and being left to die without access to a hospital, or falling out of the sky to my death. Simple considerations. No, this wouldn't work. I pictured myself squeezed into a tube in the sky, trapped inside until it finally touched down in California. My heart was pounding faster than I was comfortable with. I'd have to tell Davidson we couldn't do an interview in person. If he insisted on doing it in person then maybe this wasn't the right plan after all. There were other ways to bring down the app. Why would flying in an airplane be a requirement for any good plan? It wasn't. I'd gotten this far in life without flying. I'd enjoyed my life so far, and I wasn't ready to risk it.

Of course I didn't let myself cancel. Gannicus was always on my mind, and right now he was at the forefront. He'd been uprooted from his own *century* and he'd survived. I could handle leaving the ground for two hours.

Alright, so I'd get on a plane. Unfortunately, that wasn't the last terrifying consideration to get this plan into action.

This time, I had to tell my parents something about the app. I couldn't think of any more viable excuses for not telling them about something so important that it might completely change my life. I didn't have to tell them all of the details, nor did I plan to, but they'd want to know what was bringing me to fly on a plane for the first time. Taking a deep breath, I walked through the house until I found them sitting in the living room. My mom was in her usual chair and my dad was sprawled on the couch, both of them on their phones while a movie I didn't recognize played on the screen.

"Hey," I said quietly, too quietly. It didn't count as telling them if they didn't hear me. I cleared my throat. "I'm going to California." No one could accuse me of burying the lead. My journalism professor would be proud. My parents weren't as thrilled.

"What?" my mom asked, setting her phone down on the arm of the couch with mild force. She didn't return my smile, but pushed her glasses up and stared at me.

"I'm writing this story, sort of a freelance thing. It's about that history app, I think I told you. Anyway I'm interviewing this dude, and, uh, I have to. . . Go to California. To talk to him." I took a deep breath. Yeah, that was good. The message was out there. It was a little short on details, but I was saving my verbal skills for the article.

My parents exchanged silent glances, raising their eyebrows. My dad shrugged, and my mom widened her eyes, shaking her head. There was a whole conversation going on there, but I was ok with not hearing it.

"I think that's great," my dad finally said, though he drew the words out and watched my mom as he said it. She glared at him, but he went on. "You are an *adult,* after all, and you're making an effort professionally. That's what we've been wanting from you." His eyes never left my mom, and I kept my mouth shut. He was going to do a much better job of smoothing this over than I could, and I was not interested in ruining that.

After a never ending moment, my mom nodded too.

"That's wonderful, Lane. Do you need help booking a flight?"

Now that Davidson and I had agreed on a time for our interview and I'd bought a plane ticket, there was no going back. I hoped flying would be exciting, but I resolved to toss a bottle of Malibu rum in my purse just in case it went right past exciting into awful.

Most of my plan involved seeing what questions popped into my head when I faced Davidson, because I imagined our conversation would lead to plenty that I wanted to know from him. I thought I remembered learning in one of my journalism courses that a genuine conversation was a better way to get information than sticking solely to written questions. Reporters could fall into the trap of reading question after question, rather than thinking about the other person's answers and responding with relevant follow-up questions. The last thing I wanted was to leave the interview and realize he'd said something important that I should've followed up on.

Still, it would be ill-advised to go in completely blind. I researched his name and organization, but I only found a few vague articles describing the release of his new app. The other articles I found were about his other work. There was only one article on the time travel element, from a news organization I'd never heard of before. It was an introduction to the app and the way it worked, with no mention of how the time travelers were ripped from their times against their will.

My article would be ground-breaking then. I hadn't been completely dishonest when I'd told my parents I was writing a freelance article. I really did plan to sell - or even give, it didn't matter - my article to a news organization that would spread the story.

Nervousness burned through me like a fever as I made my way into the airport the day before the interview. My parents had given me a bag of snacks for the plane and a plethora of traveling advice on the drive there, most of which I'd forgotten. It was some consolation to them that my plane ticket had been dirt cheap as a result of the virus, but I knew they secretly worried that I'd bring it back with me. I appreciated that they didn't discourage me anyway as they said goodbye from the car.

The Tucson International Airport had more bustle than I'd imagined in a time like this, though I was sure it was far less than the airport usually saw. Everyone was wearing masks over their noses and mouths as they pulled their suitcases across the linoleum floor. Each airline had rows of stations where lines of travelers waited to check in their baggage. I found mine and waited at the end, forcing the idea of the flight out of my head. If I didn't think about it then I couldn't be nervous about it, right? Wrong. My stomach remembered even when my brain focused on something else.

I knew my suitcase was under the weight limit, but my muscles tensed when the airline employee lifted it onto the scale anyway. The electronic scale approved me, so I waited awkwardly while she loaded my bag onto the conveyor belt and turned to me expectantly.

"Your ID?" she said, in a tone that suggested she had already asked for it. My hands shook slightly as I scrambled to pull my wallet out of my purse and slide the ID out of it. I tried not to gasp in frustration when I dropped it on the ground. When I handed it to her the second time, I held it in a claw-like grip. I shoved it and the boarding pass she gave me haphazardly into my wallet and dashed away, making room for the next stressed traveler.

My trip through security was easier, until I saw a large man with long blondish hair waiting in one of the lines ahead of me. My heart thumped faster until he turned his head to reveal a profile I didn't recognize. It wasn't Gannicus. I knew it was stupid, but my heart sank anyway.

By the time I slid into my seat on the plane, I was just relieved the airport experience was over for now. I looked out the window I'd made sure I sat next to and tried not to think about how the air felt less clear in this giant tin can than it did outside. My attempt to distract myself by looking at the safety instructions was thwarted when I grabbed the laminated brochure and found that it was sticky. I shoved it further into the back of the seat in front of me and closed my eyes.

I had the whole row to myself, thanks to the fact that fewer were traveling these days. I stared out the window for the whole two hours, enchanted by a sky view of the world. Fluffy white clouds created their own world, obscuring the ground in a backdrop of blue sky. I quietly sipped an apple juice I'd requested from the flight attendant as we sailed through the heavens.

Flying was far too magical to be scary. I wished Gannicus could've been there to see it.

Chapter 20

"I'm here to see Neil Davidson," I said when I arrived for the interview. I'd rehearsed this simple line in my head a lot in the elevator on the way up, so my nerves barely came out in my voice. I was happy with those results. The receptionist nodded and smiled at me briefly before returning to whatever she was rapidly typing on her computer. Was I supposed to stand here and wait, or sit down? I glanced at the waiting area to my right, which had a few thick plush chairs arranged next to small coffee tables. I could have sat there, if I was supposed to. Instead, I just fidgeted with my hands and hoped the receptionist would tell me what to do.

"You can have a seat right over there," she finally said, a slightly raised eyebrow suggesting she didn't think she'd needed to give me those directions. Well, she'd been wrong. It was a little irrational, but I was afraid I'd somehow miss my interview if I wasn't exactly where I was supposed to be. Considering this interview was my only idea to save Gannicus, I couldn't afford to miss it. I wasn't giving Davidson any excuses to blow me off, either.

Now that I knew I was safe to, I settled into one of the chairs and prepared to wait. I glanced down at my notes, because maybe it would be a good idea to study what few notes I'd written in preparation for this. Davidson's responses would give me all the inspiration I needed for follow-up questions, but I started to read the bullet points of topics I'd want to address with him for the millionth time anyway. I barely made it to the second bullet before I closed my notebook. My stomach hurt too much to focus, and my heart was beating in my throat. Instead of thinking about the upcoming confrontation, I forced myself to look at the strange art piece in the middle of the waiting area.

It was made of curving black tubes in no discernible shape. I leaned forward to see a small silver plaque on the base of the statute.

It read "Harmony." As far as I was concerned, the statue evoked the image of snakes more than any positive value like harmony, but maybe I was biased. The person I was waiting to talk to evoked the image of snakes more than anything else too.

There was a tapping sound on the linoleum floor. It took a second before I even realized it was me, clicking my heels against the floor. I glanced up at the receptionist. She was already looking at me. The sound of my heels had broken the pristine, corporate quiet. Yikes. I crossed my ankles under my chair, forcing myself to be still. This was fine. Even if the conversation with Davidson went absolutely horribly, and he slapped me or I threw up or something—actually that wasn't making me feel any better. I skipped to the end of the sentiment. The interview couldn't last forever. That was a small comfort, but it was one.

"Miss Randolph?" the receptionist said in an even tone. I jumped anyway. "I can show you to Mr. Davidson's office now."

Oh shit. It was time.

Wordlessly, I stood up and made my way over to her. I followed as she walked five steps past her desk, gesturing for me to continue forward towards an open office door. A man was standing in the doorway. Ok, this was it. He held out his hand and I took it, focusing on holding it firmly enough to convey confidence, but not so tightly that he might read insecurity into it.

"You must be Lane Randolph," he said. He was wearing a dark blue polo shirt that managed to send the paradoxical message that he was professional, but this was his office and he could dress as casually as he wanted. He was shorter than I thought he'd be. "I'm Neil Davidson."

"I know," I said, too busy wondering if I thought curly hair was a good look on him or not to prepare a more polite response. I shook my head, laughing nervously. "I mean, it's nice to meet you."

I thought he might have smiled in response, but I turned away too fast to say for sure. I walked through the open door, taking in the sight of his office. In my humble opinion, it was too big to be practical. I could tell he didn't have to clean the hardwood floors himself, or else he might have opted for an office that didn't look like it could fit 5 cubicles. The space was interrupted by a glass table halfway through the room, then the empty floor led the way to his desk. I tried not to focus on the clicking of my heels as I approached the chairs in front of the desk.

Sitting down, I noticed how much Davidson's chair towered behind the desk over the chairs he left out for his guests. Interesting that he would make that design choice. Did he invite a lot of people into his office who needed to be subconsciously reminded that he was in charge? Whatever. He could roll in a lifeguard tower for all I cared; I didn't come here to be intimidated.

My composure was almost shattered as I finally paid attention to the wall decor. In large bronze painted frames, portraits of people in various dress lined the office. My stomach turned when I saw that one picture showed a familiar man in a red coat and black hair. Vlad the Impaler. Just seeing the face of my attacker made it hard to breathe. It was just a painting. It wasn't real. He wasn't here. And neither was anyone else that I might see on the walls. I forgot about Davidson completely as I scanned the walls desperately, seeking a different face.

There he was. Gannicus. Bare chested and scarred as I'd seen him on my couch, when he'd tried to prove to me that he was real. When he'd probably been silently begging me to save him. I'd done nothing then. But I was here now, trying to make up for the past. That had to count for something, didn't it? The sudden ache in my stomach didn't seem convinced. It was actually a relief when Davidson broke my concentration.

"So, Lane," he said, settling into his own chair and pushing a stack of papers to the side. "What questions do you have for me?"

Deep breath. This was what I was there for. I could ask a few questions, stay in character, and get the information I needed to destroy this app. Maybe I could even do it without throwing up. I reached for my water bottle, taking a long sip as I reminded myself of my key points. I needed to get him to admit that his "employees" were forced to work somehow. It would be ideal to leave with an idea of what threats Gannicus faced, and if the others who were still held at the base were in any kind of danger themselves. I wasn't holding my breath on finding an easy way to ask how they might escape, though. Some answers just didn't have questions that I could reasonably ask him. The main goal here was to get him to confirm that there was human trafficking going on here. Unfortunately, I didn't think he'd be too eager to admit that either. But there was only one way to find out.

"Do you mind if I record this interview?" I asked, sliding my phone out of my purse and balancing it casually on one of my legs. I opened the recording app without looking at him. "It just makes it easier than having to take notes-"

"You know, Lane," he said quickly, almost before I'd finished. "I'd rather not have any recordings in here. You understand."

Actually, I didn't understand. In fact, I found it pretty irritating. How was he going to tell a student journalist to make her job harder, when all she wanted to do was write an article on him for her school newspaper? Just because that was just my cover story didn't mean I wasn't right. In principle. I nodded anyway, closing out the app and dropping my phone into my purse.

I hesitated. Should I not give up so easily? Could I have gotten away with hitting record anyway, and slipping the phone into my purse? If the news organizations asked me for proof and I couldn't deliver any, what good would any of this do? No, I was doing the right thing. It was illegal to record someone without their permission in this state, and I felt pretty sure a guy like this would have a lawyer or two to tell him that if the recordings ever came out. Besides, not every journalist used recordings. I'd just have to keep faithful notes. I pulled out a new notebook and pen instead, raising the pen in acknowledgement of his request. He flashed a saccharine smile in response. I tried to remember that as far as he was concerned, I didn't hate him. I didn't even mind having to take notes if it made him more comfortable. I returned the smile.

"What gave you the idea to start iEducator?" I asked. It was an easy place to start for both of us.

"The same way any successful person gets their start. With an inspiring teacher." He waited while I pretended to write that down.

"And who was that?" I prompted, giving him time to get this filler nonsense out before I got down to the important details.

"Her name was Ms. Whitemore. She was my sophomore year history teacher. She made me realize that education could be lasting when it was fun. I was always more interested in math and science, but she showed me that history could be fun too, when you really got to know the people of the past." It was apparently not the first time he'd been asked. His eyes drifted as he spoke, settling on a large cabinet coming out of the wall on my right side of the room. The door was only slightly open, but he was narrowing his eyes at it as if that tiny bit of imperfection in the room was more than he could stand. His voice faded out.

"That's interesting," I said, pausing to let him continue. He didn't. "How did that lead to the idea for the app?"

"Well, it—hang on." He stood up and closed the cabinet all the way. I suppressed my slight irritation at his decision to do that. Was he really so much of a control freak that he couldn't just leave one thing slightly out of place for an hour? When he continued, I let it go and focused on his response. "Anyway, I started experimenting with time travel in college. I worked under a professor who was doing some groundbreaking research. A few years later I was looking back on old times and remembered Ms. Whitemore. And it all just came to me in a sort of vision for the future."

"A vision," I repeated, drawing a symbol on my paper that was my own shorthand for "what the hell?" A vision? Please. What a pretentious description. "What did that future look like?"

"A collaboration," he said simply, a slight smile lifting his lips.

"A collaboration?" I repeated.

"Yes. A collaboration between the people of today and the people of yesterday. All of humanity could come together for the betterment of the world. Can you imagine anything more meaningful than that?"

"Freedom," I muttered, but I quickly coughed to cover it. I wasn't here to challenge him on what he did. That wouldn't help anyone. I changed course. "That certainly does sound enlightening. How do you recruit for the app?"

The pause before his answer was so short it might have been a breath. Any other interviewer would've thought nothing of it. I'd asked the question knowing the answer, though, and I was gratified to see it give him pause. Making him pause to think about his next move was acres away from what I wanted to do to him, but it was a start.

"Well, Lane, that's a good question." Was he stalling? Before he could give a quick answer I might be able to catch him in, though, his phone rang. He didn't seem either annoyed or relieved when he picked it up to answer it, mouthing an apology to me.

"Elle, I'm in a meeting. Now isn't a—alright, hold on. I'm coming out." He stood up and set the phone down. "I'm sorry, Lane.

I need to approve a quick shipment before it goes out in a few minutes."

He left the room quickly, leaving the door open behind him. Maybe it was a good time for me to take a look at the portraits and try to catalog just how many people he was keeping. Only, my eyes fell on the cabinet instead.

Why had he been so weird about that cabinet being open? It was probably because he was used to having everything exactly the way he wanted it every second. But. Wasn't there also a possibility that he didn't want anyone to see what was inside? I glanced at the door behind me to make sure he wasn't coming in, then jogged on the balls of my feet so he wouldn't hear my heels as I made my way over to the cabinet as quickly as I could.

I felt my heart skip a beat down to my toes when a small noise broke the silence. As far as I could tell, though, he wasn't coming back yet. If I strained, I thought I could hear him talking to someone outside the room. Still, he had to come back soon. My time was limited. I pushed open the door as quietly and quickly as I could, taking the best mental picture of the interior as I could.

It didn't look like much. The inside of the door had a colorless spreadsheet, and the shelves had a few decorative bottles with gray dust in them. I was about to turn away in disappointment when my eyes caught a name on the spreadsheet: Gannicus. There was a date next to his name: the day he left. The box next to it was blank.

I shouldn't have been surprised that Davidson was keeping track of who left. It was a risky choice to escape for a reason. Still, seeing Gannicus's name in cold black and white reinforced a fact that I'd been trying to avoid: he was still very much in danger. Davidson, a man with more than enough resources to find Gannicus and recapture him, had apparently not forgotten about him.

I tore my eyes away from his name when I realized there were some on the list that had been crossed out.

Napoleon was the first name I saw. What did getting crossed out mean? Did that mean the person wasn't able to be captured and brought to our time? If that was the case, maybe Napoleon had gotten lucky.

Wait. My breath caught when I finally found a name I recognized from more than just a history class. Vlad Dracula. Next to his name was a date, just like Gannicus. I recognized the day he came to my house. I hadn't meant to memorize the day, but somehow it had stuck with me. The date was written twice, in the same place that Gannicus's column was empty. The column was labeled "Seized." I remembered that day. I'd called to report him. They must have caught him soon after. And done what?

I looked at the little gray jars of dust. For a moment too long, I wondered what was in there. I only had one theory, and it made my stomach turn over.

I needed to go sit back down. Davidson could get back any minute, and I didn't want him to know what I'd seen.

I pushed the cabinet closed with a shaky hand.

Instead of analyzing the spreadsheet, I forced myself over to my seat as quietly as I could manage. The only thing I needed to worry about right now was whether Davidson saw my little investigation. Judging from the lack of yelling or running feet coming towards the room, I guessed he didn't have a clue. I should have been relieved. I was relieved. *I was relieved.* I wasn't panicking. I could breathe. I didn't know what happened to Vlad. I didn't know what a name being crossed out meant. I didn't know what was in the jars. I didn't know what would happen to Gannicus if he got caught. I didn't know. I needed to focus on Davidson. I needed to relax right now.

He came in a moment or so later, smiling casually as he moved his lips as if he were talking to me. I shook my head. That didn't make sense. He *was* talking to me. I felt too light, dizzy, as if I were floating out of my chair.

He killed them. They escaped and if he caught them he killed them.

"Lane?" Davidson asked, sitting back in his chair and waving a hand in my direction. "You still with me?"

I sucked in a breath. What was I supposed to do now? Maybe this plan to sneak in here and steal information from him wasn't enough. He was a murderer. What were you supposed to do in the same room as a murderer? Kill him first? I almost laughed at myself. "Kill him first?" I seriously needed to get a grip.

"Yes," I said weakly, even as I willed myself to sound confident. "I was just wondering what happens if someone from the app doesn't want to work for you anymore."

His eyebrows furrowed in a look of such utter confusion that I didn't know what to think myself. Did the question not come out of my mouth? I was pretty sure I'd really said it.

"What?" he asked.

"If they want to leave. If they try to leave. What do you do to—what happens?" I choked out the words.

He cocked his head to the side, cartoonishly confused by some part of what I'd asked. I didn't know why. It seemed like a simple question to me.

"Well, let me just start by saying that doesn't happen very often. This is a rare opportunity that most people would pay every cent they had for—the chance to cheat death and be reborn into a new life." He gave a small laugh, as if it were absurd to think anything else. His smile faded soon after into a more serious expression. "But it has happened once or twice. In that case I had to send them back."

Send them back? What kind of idiot did he think I was?

Except, that sort of made sense. I let the idea sink in. All I saw were some names crossed off of a list. I didn't see pictures of their grave stones. Why would he want to kill them in the first place? Would he hire hitmen or would he do it himself? He didn't seem like much of the assassin type. My face burned. Was I being completely insane? Davidson must have misunderstood the look on my face, because he grimaced and continued haltingly.

"I know that... must sound harsh. Because if they go back to their own times then we're no longer... saving them from their fate. But I've worked with a team of nationally recognized mental health professionals who advised me that for some it might be worse to be taken from their own time than to face their own fate. So we do the best we can to reach a solution that makes everyone happy."

This wasn't what I expected. I'd been somewhat prepared for him to cackle like a villain and say that he kept people locked in his basement, or to demand that I leave at the first difficult question. I'd imagined that maybe he'd deny everything and say that the historical people were really just super dedicated actors. I sure wasn't ready to confront the fact that maybe he thought this was a favor to them.

But it wasn't so absurd, was it? He took Gannicus away at the battle where he was about to die, so wasn't that like saving his life? If he did that with everyone, which I imagined he would have to in order to not change history, then he saved their lives. They were given a place to stay, a job, a way to adapt to this new time that they found themselves in. Just because there was more to it than that, that it was holding them back from being free, didn't mean he was being malicious. Maybe Gannicus and the others had jumped to conclusions, assumed that he meant to do this to them. I didn't know.

"Do you think they like being a part of the app?" I asked carefully. I wasn't sure it was time to completely reveal my true reasons for being here, or my connections to the app, so I tried to maintain a neutral expression. I dangled my pen over my notebook, waiting for his answer.

"Of course," he said quickly, at peace with a question that he apparently thought was an easy one. "This is a great opportunity for everyone involved."

Alright, he'd already said that. He was under the impression that this was an interview for a school newspaper, though, so it wasn't unreasonable for him to want to get his talking points in. I just needed to steer him back on course.

"Don't you worry about taking away their freedom of choice?"

"What choice?" he said, his smile slipping. "Death or new life? It doesn't seem like a very tough one, Lane."

I paused. When you looked at it that way, it did seem simple. What he needed was to actually know how his victims felt, not hypothesize about how they should feel. There was no way he could imagine what this would be like for them, being pulled from a completely different world and feeling like they couldn't leave. If I wanted to give him that chance, I'd have to reveal myself. Give up the character I was playing and speak up for Gannicus and Levi, and for so many others I didn't even have the chance to know yet. I sighed.

"You don't understand," I said, aiming for gentleness. He only stared at me, waiting for what I would stay next. "They don't feel like it's their choice. I know them. I knew Gannicus." Why did I say "knew"? Did I really think our relationship was done for good? I tried to refocus. That wasn't important right now.

"Gannicus?" He stood up. For a half a second - or maybe an hour, it was hard to tell- we were silent as I digested his reaction. It wasn't joy at the delight of discovering that we had mutual friends. "What's going on here?"

This wasn't going well. It was out there now, though, so there was nothing to do but keep going.

"My real name is Lane Reid. I was actually a user of your app, before I actually got to know the people involved. They don't want to be there. I was almost killed by Vlad-"

"Vlad the Impaler. That was you." He ran a hand down his face as if he could wipe away its exhausted expression. When his hand fell to his side, his expression had turned unreadable. That was too bad, because I really needed a clue of just what was going on in his head right now. Was he betrayed that I'd lied about my intentions here? Did he think I was wrong about Vlad and the others wanting to escape? Unsure of what else to do, I kept talking.

"Vlad was—is—horrible and evil, but part of the reason for what happened is that he was trying to escape you. I mean, the app. Gannicus didn't want to be there either. He would've preferred to be in his own time. Did they really never tell you that?" I'd already said as much as I could think to say, but he wasn't responding. He was just standing there behind his desk, staring at me. I'd never been very good at allowing silence, so I kept going, hoping for the magic words to break the tension. "They believe that you'll kill... they believe that something bad will happen to them if they even try to leave. You don't understand."

I faded out. For an agonizing moment, no one said anything. The only sound was the slight whir of the ceiling fan above us.

"You know, Lane, I appreciate this."

My breath rushed out in a sigh. That sounded like a decent start. I was less tense as he continued.

"It can be hard to know what people are really feeling if we don't ask them ourselves. It's not easy for me to admit this, but I was making a lot of assumptions. I know how I would feel in their position, but that doesn't mean I know what they're feeling. I'll think on this, and get together with my employees to see how they're really doing with this experience."

My first, immediate thought was that he was laying it on a little thick. No, I was falling back on old judgments of him. I tried to listen to his words as he went on, and leave my own assumptions behind.

"Who knows? Maybe if you were in their shoes you might feel differently."

That was an attempt at agreement, wasn't it? He was trying to acknowledge that both sides of the argument had merit, but he was going to sit down with the people from the past and listen to their concerns. This was a positive.

But if it was positive, why did the look on his face make me feel like the room had suddenly gotten 10 degrees colder? Why did his comment about time travel sound less like an offer and more like a threat? Was I just being paranoid again?

Or had I been being naive since then?

I didn't know what to think. For the first time it really hit me that I had no idea what I was doing here, with this whole situation. Had I really thought I could stumble my way through until I found a solution to save Gannicus? Here I was, in front of Gannicus's employer or captor, and I wasn't even 100% sure which one he really was. I had to get out. The only thing I knew to do was decide on my very next move, and that move was to get the hell out of here.

"Well, you've given me a lot to think about," I said to Davidson. I tried not to flinch when he walked towards me and held out his hand.

"This was a very... unusual interview," he laughed as I took his hand and shook it. Hopefully he didn't notice my palm was starting to sweat. "I hope you consider that there are two sides to every story, and all we're trying to do here at iEducator is our very best. Thanks for coming in today, Lane Reid."

When he winked like my real name was an inside joke between us, I laughed along with him. I turned and left, walking out of his office and through the hallways in a sort of trance. All I could hear was the echo of my heels clicking on the floor, and a single refrain in my head: "What the hell just happened?"

Chapter 21

The drive to the hotel was a blur. It was some kind of miracle that I managed to get there at all, because if anyone asked me if I had actually been driving that whole time, I wouldn't have been sure. All I could think was that I didn't know what the hell to think.

This was a victory, wasn't it? Davidson was going to sit down with his captives from the past and discover how they really felt about the situation he'd put them in. They'd come to an agreement about how he could best make up for his mistakes, and everyone would go away happier and might even still get together for holidays to share a Thanksgiving turkey.

Ok, I knew that was crap.

If I forced myself to argue out the facts, I couldn't prove that Davidson had bad intentions. From the interaction we'd had, he'd been as reasonable as a person could be in this situation. He'd offered to hear out the other side. If it were that easy, though, why had this struggle been going on for years? Why did Levi and Gannicus have to escape? Did Davidson see people running away from him and assume there was nothing wrong there? That was unlikely. Were Levi and Gannicus paranoid nutcases who invented a captor out of someone who only wanted to help them? No. I knew that wasn't the case. All this was was me being confused by a talented manipulator. Davidson played dumb and I fell for it.

I didn't feel good about that. The more I thought about it, the more I realized that believing that Davidson didn't know the truth about his own app was me disbelieving Levi and Gannicus about what they'd been through. I liked to think that I knew Levi better than that, even if he hadn't been honest with me about being from the past. I might not have known Gannicus for long, but I did believe, deep enough to know it was true, that I knew who he was. If I was honest with myself, I'd wanted to believe that Davidson was oblivious because it would have made the whole thing a lot easier. We could've solved the problem with a little communication, and I could help all the others and be with Gannicus again, knowing he was entirely free and would never have to worry about being pursued. That did sound a lot nicer than the real situation. Unfortunately, it wasn't the real situation. In my gut, I knew that. So what was I going to do about the real situation?

Stick to the plan. I needed to spread the word about the app as far as I could. If Davidson wasn't willing to stop out of the decency of his humanity, then I'd just have to stop him instead.

I settled on the hotel bed, sliding my laptop over the comforter onto my lap and starting to type. I kept my notes next to me as a guide, but the truth was that I already remembered everything he'd said during the interview. More than that, though, I remembered my own experiences with the app, and the events that I'd seen. This was no time to be an objective reporter of the interview alone. My part of the story mattered too, because I was a witness to this injustice.

By the time I'd written the whole story, I was proud of my work. I'd crafted an attention-grabbing story that still told the truth without hyperbole. Now all I had to do was find a news organization that was willing to publish my story and tell the world what was going on.

"Hello, my name is Lane Reid. I have a breaking news story and I was wondering if your organization would be interested in covering it," I said to the first Tucson news station I'd called.

"Thank you for calling. What is it?" a cheerful male voice responded. I was encouraged by the fact that he was willing to listen right now. I'd half been expecting him to ask me to make an appointment for next week. This was definitely something I wanted to get done sooner rather than later. I told him the whole story as quickly as I could, hoping I wouldn't lose him in the time travel element. For a second I'd considered just reading him what I wrote, but I figured getting to the point was my better strategy.

"Neil Davidson? That's the tech guy, right?" That was a surprising part of the events to get stuck on, but I stayed with him. Getting the details right was important, so I was encouraged that he was at least taking an interest. Still, I was expecting something closer to shock as an initial reaction.

"Yes. Apparently he's done other work in Silicon Valley but I really think the historical slavery is the focal point."

There was a heavy pause. Instead of addressing my opinion, the man on the phone finally sighed deeply.

"Yeah, I don't know if we're interested in covering that just now."

The air deflated out of my lungs.

"You don't believe me? I can give you my notes from my interview. I wasn't allowed to record it but I bet I could get interviews-" I was cut off by his abrupt response.

"I'm sorry. We're going to have to say no." He hung up before I could give any more protest.

I just sat there, staring at the black screen of the hotel TV in disbelief. Was it my lack of concrete evidence? I *had* offered to find more. Were they afraid to cover a negative story on Davidson?

My attempts to call five more news outlets, three more in Arizona and two in California, were fruitless. None of them gave any particular reasons why they didn't want to cover the story, but they made it very clear that they were intractable on the issue anyway. I thanked them each for their time, determined not to burn any bridges, but I was astounded at their lack of journalistic drive. This was the kind of story that could make a real difference, and no one even wanted to get the details?

Now what was I going to do? If the news stations wouldn't take the story, how was I going to take down the app? It wouldn't do any good to storm in there and demand that Davidson put a stop to everything. I'd basically done that already. My only idea had seemed terrifying, but I'd really expected it to work.

I stood up and started repacking my suitcase, wallowing in disappointment and helplessness. As I gathered my belongings and got ready for the flight home, I was forced to face the truth: whatever I did to stop this app, I couldn't do it alone.

#

Weariness threatened to overpower me when I finally dragged my suitcase to my mom's car and slid inside after a long day flying home. My parents' curiosity radiated off of them, but they settled for a muttered, "they don't want the article" and let me fall asleep. Just before I closed my eyes I saw them make eye contact with each other. I'd flown all the way to California to write an article that the news didn't even want? I was sure they'd have more questions when I woke up, but I couldn't be bothered with that right now.

I woke up to the groan of the garage door opening when we reached the house. Being home again was a cruel reminder that despite the horrors I'd endured with Davidson, I was no closer to stopping him.

If Gannicus were here, what would he do? Would he have attacked Davidson if he had gotten my chance to be alone with him? What about Levi? These were both men who had fought in their respective wars for freedom. It had been arrogant of me to think I could single-handedly solve a problem they'd been grappling with for two years. I wondered what they'd think of my efforts. Would they be proud and appreciative that I'd tried? Or would it make their situation feel more hopeless, to know that I'd tried my only idea and failed? I didn't even want to think of that.

I called Tamryn about it, but she had little to add to solve the problem.

"No one will take the story. Davidson is out here killing people for escaping and..." I paused. I hadn't fully admitted to myself that I still thought that was what he was doing, despite his protests that he simply sent them back. What kind of punishment would it be, after all, to send them back when they didn't want to be taken from their own times in the first place? Surely he would have thought of that too. I remembered the jars of gray dust I found in the cabinets. People didn't keep jars of gray dust for decoration. As soon as the thought turned my stomach, I decided not to tell Tamryn the details.

"Killing them?" she gasped.

"I technically don't know that," I said, my voice coming out as more of a squeak than I intended. I really didn't know that. I didn't know anything. I just knew what my gut was telling me, and I honestly didn't know how reliable that was. "I just assumed that based on the fact that he catches them if they escape." I told her about the spreadsheet, but I chose not to mention the possible jars of ashes. As believably as I could, I emphasized the fact that Davidson insisted he sent them back to their own times.

"Yeah," she said with effort. "He just sends them back. That makes more sense."

I didn't know whether her words sounded stilted because she didn't believe what she was saying, or because she realized that Levi or Gannicus getting sent back to their own times would also be a tragedy, and that was the better of the two scenarios. No matter how you looked at it, if either of them were ever caught, the prognosis couldn't be tolerable.

"Not that they'd get caught," I said.

"No, they wouldn't," she agreed. "I really don't think they will."

I agreed, both because it was the only thing to say and because the idea of anything happening to either of them was simply too bad to be true. My brain refused to fully comprehend that possibility, and I wasn't going to force it. We hung up.

When she told Levi what I told her, how would he react? Would he be unsurprised, having known all along how evil Davidson truly was? Or would he be disappointed to hear that Davidson was a more formidable enemy than we'd even realized? After all, I'd taken the story to the news, and no one would touch it. How could you stop a villain when revealing his evil plan didn't even make a difference? On some level, I'd been hoping to call Tamryn and have her say that the whole news story idea was a great effort, but that she and Levi had worked it all out while I was in California. That they had the perfect plan to save everyone, put an end to the app, and keep both of the men close to us. Of course, she'd already had way more time than I had to come up with a solution by now, and she hadn't found anything yet. It wasn't very likely that she'd thought of something now.

This whole thing would have been a lot easier with Gannicus around. I was horrified when the thought entered my head that if he were still at the base at least we could work together, but living out in the free world away from me, he wasn't much help. I reminded myself that he didn't need to help. He had every right to be out there on his own, enjoying the freedom he'd never had before. He'd already fought in a war for it, then been grabbed from that war and shoved into a new form of captivity in this time period. Now that he was out, he deserved to live a normal life on his own terms. Maybe someday he'd come around and I could tell him the story of how I took down Davidson with the help of Tamryn and Levi, and that everyone was free like him. We'd have a chance to reconnect, and maybe I'd have made up for my part in the app by getting rid of it for good.

Just a few hours after I hung up with Tamryn, I got another phone call. It was Mariah Hernandez, offering me the Junior Investigator position. The joy that I'd always imagined I'd feel when I finally got an opportunity to start my life was there in me somewhere. I was able to thank her with genuine enthusiasm, and to celebrate with my parents. I was able to give real smiles and consider how it was all finally coming together, after all this time of stressing that I had no prospects. Under the shadow of the problem I'd yet to solve, though, the sweetness of the news was tinged with sour.

"Lane, can I speak with you?" my mother asked a few days later, opening my bedroom door. Luckily for her I was awake and just staring at social media, or I wouldn't have appreciated her waking me up in the morning. "I need you to tell me if you're on friendly terms with a gentleman outside or if I need to call the police."

This was one of those situations where the outcome could be very good or very bad. A man being at my house to see me could have been Davidson sending someone to silence me for getting involved in his business. If he did, what would I do? I grasped for a plan, but there wasn't much I could do. I could tell my parents that someone was trying to assassinate me, but I doubted an assassin would give enough warning for that. Besides, what if the hitman turned on them for trying to protect me?

No, that was ridiculous. I was just a regular girl who didn't approve of the app that Davidson made. What was that to him, a famous multimillionaire inventor? I was no match for him, and I was pretty sure we both knew it. Ruling that out made me feel better, in more ways than one. If it wasn't someone sent to make me regret reaching out to Davidson, then there was only one other man I could think of that might come to see me despite my mom not knowing him.

I tried to get the thought out of my head, and out of my heart. If I expected to see him standing out there and it wasn't him, it would reopen wounds that were barely closed to begin with. Letting myself get excited only to be disappointed was a drop from a height that I wouldn't handle well. The smart thing to do was to believe wholeheartedly that it wasn't him. It was probably some other man, who showed up to the wrong house by mistake. Despite my inner warnings not to get my hopes up, though, my heart took off in an erratic rhythm as I got out of bed and followed my mom down the stairs and through the kitchen. She gestured out the window to a man sitting on a deck chair in the backyard.

It wasn't just any man.

He was here.

Before I could think better of it, I threw open the backdoor and hurled myself at Gannicus, wrapping my arms around his neck. He held me in return, lifting me up as he stood from the chair. I closed my eyes as I took it all in: his warm smell, almost like vanilla; his hard muscles; his strong heartbeat. Once the moment was over, though, I had to face reality.

Things weren't normal between us. He'd left, escaped. I'd been unknowingly keeping him against his will, and he didn't even know that I'd flown to California and tried to make up for it. Or that that hadn't worked out the way I'd planned. What would make him come back now? I tried to think of what to say.

"What are you doing here?" I asked breathlessly, pulling back to look into his face. I could see that his smile was genuine, but there was a slight guardedness in his eyes. He was no doubt aware that this conversation was fraught with complications, given the way things had ended between us. Something was making him smile, though, and my heart dared to hope. Maybe seeing me gave him a fraction of the joy that seeing him gave to me. That would be enough.

"I'm here to prove to you that I am a worthy man for you. I have a job now, and a home of my own. Most of my coworkers are children and my house is not nearly as grand as yours, but I can do better if you give me the time." He looked earnestly at me, waiting for my approval. My heart cracked.

What? Worthy of *me*? The person he'd only gotten to know because of his enslavement? While I'd been spending weeks hoping he'd understand some day and choose to love me with his own free will, he'd thought I was waiting for him to prove himself as a man? That was sweet, I guessed, but mostly it was just devastating. All of that time wasted, both of us suffering. It was worse because he'd spent that time thinking that he somehow didn't measure up, and that that was why I'd sent him away. I had a hard time looking him in the eyes, so I spent most of the time giving my response to his eyebrows.

"Me telling you to leave wasn't because I didn't think you were good enough for me," I whispered in horror. I couldn't believe it. All this time that we'd been apart, he'd thought I just didn't want him. His eyebrows furrowed, like he couldn't understand this change of events.

"Why, then? Why tell me to leave?" My hands were wrapped in his; he absentmindedly tightened his grip. I watched him shake his head slightly, but then my eyes fell to our joined hands as I tried to think of a way to answer that question that could possibly repair this misunderstanding. I'd thought I was the one who needed to be proven good enough. Good enough to be loved with true consent and freedom- by someone who understood that he had a choice to say no. I didn't want him to be here loving me until he knew that that was what he really wanted too.

Now, here he was. That must have meant... Despite the tragedy of the misunderstanding, joy bubbled up inside me as I realized that he was on his own now, had his own life, and he still wanted me. He'd had every chance to find someone else, or just be on his own. He'd managed to arrange a life for himself. It seemed like he still wanted me to be a part of it.

"I wanted you to be free," I said, not sure whether to laugh or cry. "I didn't want you to be with me because you were a slave and you didn't know of any other option. I didn't know if your feelings for me were real, if you even knew what you felt." I kept talking, kept explaining, desperately trying to assuage all the pain and rejection we'd both felt in the past weeks. As I spoke, I regretted telling him to leave, and all the agony that had gone with it. I'd been too crushed by the news of the app to realize that I wasn't communicating to him what I'd actually felt. The only reason I might have a chance to make up for it was that despite this awful misunderstanding, he'd come back to me. I was getting tangled in my emotions.

He stopped my explanations with a definitive answer. He kissed me hard, like he'd been storing up his emotions for me and they were all concentrated there on his lips. The fireworks show at Disneyland had previously been my favorite experience of God's world, but this one made that show seem like a half-dead firefly. Not only were his lips just as strong and warm and safe as they'd always been, but now I knew what it was like to be without them. I understood that I'd choose them over water in the desert. Something in his intensity suggested that the feeling might just be mutual.

Our passionate reunion was interrupted by the soft closing of the backdoor. I turned and saw my mother, who had just come into the backyard.

Well, that was a change in mood. It wasn't everyday that my mom approached me passionately kissing the man I loved. It didn't help that she didn't even know who he was. My face burned as I stepped towards her, almost as if I could block him from her view until I was ready to have this conversation with her. Unfortunately, he was far too tall for that plan to have any chance of working. Maybe I should've told her the details sooner. Still, despite the embarrassing situation, my excitement at reuniting with Gannicus couldn't be diminished by it. There was nothing to do but go with the situation.

"Uh, Mom, this is Gannicus," I said simply, knowing she'd want a far longer explanation yet too aware she couldn't have it. We'd get to that eventually. It might have been silly given the fact that he and I hadn't been together that long, but I was so proud to introduce him as mine. She smiled warmly at him, taking his outstretched hand in both of hers.

"That's a very unique name, Gannicus," she said, raising an eyebrow. She was a historian, after all. "It's very nice to meet you."

To my enormous relief, she went back inside after the introductions. I was thrilled to have her see the man who had my heart, but I wanted him all to myself now. Gannicus and I were left alone to catch up on the time we'd each spent with half a heart.

"You have to tell me," I said, following him back to the deck chairs. He dragged one over right across from his so I could sit as close as possible. A light, warm breeze stirred the hair hanging onto his shoulder. I couldn't take my eyes off of him as I settled into the chair. It felt like we had years to catch up on, when it had only been weeks. After everything I'd been through with Davidson and the job interview, I felt like my entire perception on our situation had changed. I was dying to know what he'd been up to since we'd said goodbye. I started at the beginning. "What's your job?"

"I am a delivery driver for pizzas," he said, breaking eye contact to look down at his hands. "Your time doesn't have many openings for warriors."

He was incredible. Here he was, thrust into a completely new time period, with no rulebook on how to make a life for himself. He had every right to complain and feel sorry for himself about what had happened, and languish away in our time. Instead, he'd ventured out to make something of himself. He was so brave, and so inspiring. My throat tightened with the sting of seeing in his body language that he was somehow embarrassed about where he'd ended up. The only thing he should have been feeling was pride.

"That's wonderful," I said honestly, reaching out to grab his hand. "I'm so impressed that you've managed to get a job and support yourself when this isn't even your century. You should be so proud of yourself."

He looked up and gave me a small smile. He sat up straighter as he told me about his new place. It was heartening to see the effect of my words, for more reasons than one. Knowing that he might have seen the truth in them and realized how amazing he really was was the best part. I had to admit, though, that it was nice to see that my opinion meant something to him.

"I live over there," he said, pointing behind my backyard. There was an apartment complex nearby in that direction, so it wasn't hard to gather where he meant. "I wanted to be close."

I wanted to be close. I beamed. He could never be close enough. He could sleep in my room every night and he still wouldn't be close enough. I couldn't stop smiling as I watched him tell me about his apartment. It was a one bedroom place on the second floor with its own small balcony. He said the balcony reminded him of the arena, but in a good way. It reminded him how high he'd risen from his former captivity. I cataloged his grinning white teeth and shining eyes in a safe corner of my mind, for a future time when I'd need a happy place to go.

Chapter 22

My joy faltered when I considered what he'd risked to get the apartment he was so thrilled to tell me about. I wondered if he'd had any idea what could have become of him if he'd failed. All it would've taken for him to be reduced to ash was the black SUV turning in the same direction he'd turned after leaving my house. It was pure luck that he was even alive. I didn't know much about what Davidson really did when someone got caught, but I knew it wasn't good. I had a strong feeling it was even worse than that. I regretted ruining a happy moment with these horrible thoughts, but they were our reality. I couldn't keep the direction of my thoughts from flashing across my face.

"What's wrong, *deliciae*?" he asked, lifting my chin with his finger. *Deliciae.* My brain didn't have to know what the word meant for my heart to react to it.

"I went to California." He raised an eyebrow but let me continue. "To Silicon Valley."

He clenched his jaw when he recognized the name, and then started to open his mouth. I held up my hand, silently asking him to just hear the whole story. He wasn't going to think it was any safer after he heard the story, but at least he'd have all the facts.

"Then I wrote the article about him to send to the newspapers. It didn't work. They wouldn't take it," I finished. I looked down at my bare feet, defeated. I'd really wanted to come back to him with good news.

"Newspapers? Why would you do that?" I hadn't expected the confusion in his tone, or the way his frown reached deep into his eyes, as if he couldn't possibly understand why I'd thought that was a good idea.

I was momentarily stumped by the question. I'd have thought my reasoning would be obvious. Then again, he didn't know what

I'd learned about human trafficking, and how getting authorities involved can sometimes go against the wishes of the people involved. I explained the intent to shut down the app through public outrage, where we could tell our story on our own terms, and make it clear that Gannicus and Levi had made lives for themselves here already.

"You failed to think it all through," he sighed.

I recoiled, instantly hurt by his reaction. What didn't I think through? That the news organizations wouldn't want the story? That Davidson wouldn't admit to anything? Maybe I hadn't exactly thought those things through, but I'd been trying to help. I didn't need a parade or anything, but I would've appreciated some gratitude. I'd been through a lot trying to make the plan work.

"What didn't I think through?" I demanded. He blinked in surprise at my tone, but continued without acknowledging it. Honestly, I did not like that.

"Where would they go?" he asked. I was too busy wondering why he wasn't picking up on my irritation to really focus on his question. His facial expression had turned matter-of-fact as he asked, and that was a less helpful expression to me than the one I was looking for, which was remorse at having insulted me. He was waiting for an answer though, to a question I'd barely understood.

"Who?" I asked, introducing a stony expression to conceal my conflicting anger and confusion.

"All of the others, especially the older ones. Benjamin Franklin, Wyatt Earp? Would you have them sent to the streets of the year 2020 to try to support themselves?"

Oh shit. I actually hadn't thought of that. That would be a problem. Maybe they'd like our time, though! They could move to Florida and have a nice retirement. With what money I didn't know because I hadn't thought this all through yet. He still wasn't getting it, though. I went out and tried to help him and others like him, and he had yet to thank me for it. It was easy to be critical when you were the one standing back and analyzing other people's ideas.

"I guess not," I mumbled, staring down at his knees so I wouldn't have to look at his face. He nudged my foot with his, but I pretended not to notice.

"You tried," he said. Ok, now we were getting somewhere. I glanced up to see him staring at me intently. "You were so brave to go there alone and take him on." Well, that was more of the reaction I was looking for. It didn't feel as good as I'd expected it to. I shrugged, uncomfortable with this consolatory remark that I didn't deserve, especially since I'd basically forced him to say it. Still, I didn't shy away when he leaned down to kiss me on the cheek. "I must ask."

"What?"

"Did you really think I wasn't planning to go back for all of them?"

My head snapped up. Did this mean he had a plan, or that he was just going to storm the base and go down swinging? I didn't like the second option.

"I would never leave another behind. I escaped with every intention of returning stronger, to send them back where they belong."

"Ok," I said slowly, waiting for his plan to become clear to me without him having to say. It continued to not make sense. There was no common sense plan at this point. I'd thought through everything and hadn't come up with a solution that didn't raise more problems than it solved. "What are you planning to do?"

"Come with me tonight and you'll see."

Even though Gannicus had given me a brief explanation, I still wasn't comfortable with the plan. Sneaking on to the base that he'd managed to escape from? Staying there, unprotected, long enough to conduct what was essentially a town hall meeting?

Talk about not thinking things through. At least my plan hadn't involved breaking and entering.

I pulled on my black jeans and black t-shirt anyway, deciding to wear all black to better blend with the night. Besides, that was what you were supposed to wear on secret missions like this, right? I wanted to get into the mindset that this was an exciting adventure with my boyfriend, and that we were fighting a just cause. My stomach didn't think it sounded all that fun, though, and seemed like it was trying to twist itself inside out so that I'd have to go to the hospital instead. I emerged from my room to find Gannicus waiting downstairs on the couch. He was just sitting there, leaning back against the cushions like he didn't even care that he might be risking his liberty along with his life. I supposed this wasn't his first battle, so it wasn't that big of a deal to him. Well, it was to me. Just because I wasn't carrying a weapon didn't mean I wasn't going to war.

"I'm ready," I said, lifting my lips into something of a smile. I bared my teeth, at least.

"You look stunning and courageous," he said, standing up and motioning for me to lead the way to the car.

This time it wasn't as difficult to smile.

I managed to make it halfway down the driveway before I asked him to go over the plan again. To his credit, he didn't sigh or seem put off that I wasn't sure. He just added more details.

"We've been spreading the word about discussing an escape plan gradually. No one has given the time or date to anyone else without express approval from the chosen meeting leader. If anyone shows tonight who supports Davidson more than us, we're lost."

"Lost?" I asked as I climbed into my car, absentmindedly pushing him towards the passenger side when he looked like he might be trying to sit in the driver's seat. I adored him very much, but this was *my* car.

The idea of someone infiltrating this little mutiny seemed highly possible, considering there were other people who worked on the base that weren't historical figures- security guards, cleaning crews, and whoever else Davidson was actually paying to work by choice, as opposed to forcing. What if one of them came in when Gannicus was standing there? Would they know he was a fugitive? Would it even matter? At that point all of us would be caught discussing how to destroy Davidson's livelihood, so we'd all be in danger. Gannicus was less concerned about that than I thought he should've been.

"No one enters the recreation room. Only those of us with a purpose will be there."

I gave a halfhearted nod and drove in silence, following the directions he gave me, turn by turn. His sense of direction wasn't half bad, considering he'd never been the one actually driving to or from the base. I guessed that was a skill that was more common in his time than mine.

Instead of asking more questions, I stewed in my apprehension by myself. Why didn't people use the recreation room? It sounded like a room that would be popular. It seemed pretty reasonable to me that someone might go in there for a quick game of air hockey, just to discover a whole group of people that Davidson might benefit from murdering. Even if no one came in tonight, what about the execution of this plan? Gannicus was refusing to tell me what his solution was until I saw for myself how much the others were on board, but he was wrong if he thought a group consensus would be enough to calm my fears. Given Gannicus's history, I was afraid to imagine a plan involving all out warfare, but I had a hunch that it was a decent guess.

"Turn in here," he said, yanking me out of my thoughts. My sense of direction was admittedly not the best, but I could tell that we weren't at the base yet. Instead, he was directing me down a dirt road. Oh yes. The breaking and entering part. My favorite.

I complied anyway, turning down the road and watching clouds of dust rise in the shine of my headlights. Desert plant life bookended the road to the left and right, and I tried to take some comfort from its silent stoicism. Instead, I was finding it a little hard to breathe.

"Aren't the headlights going to give us away?" I said, unnerved by the way my voice broke the quiet. Gannicus reached over and squeezed my hand.

"Do you want to turn back?" he asked. I glanced over to see a mix of guilt and sympathy. I wondered if he was regretting his decision to insist on my coming tonight.

Did I want to turn back? It was clear from the fact that he hadn't stopped my continuous driving that he wasn't concerned about them seeing the headlights. He was only asking because I was clearly freaked out, and maybe not ready for this kind of adventure. Would he be right about that? Was I not ready? I considered a conversation we'd had earlier and wondered if I'd been too quick to dismiss his idea of inviting Levi. After all, I wouldn't have minded an extra bodyguard or two right now. There was a reason I'd refused, though. I knew Tamryn was close to giving in and helping us, but I needed to come to her with a solid plan. She wasn't going to want to risk Levi on a martyr's plan, and I didn't blame her. Since my boyfriend was the one who might have the martyr's plan, though, I had to be here. I figured I might as well hear it out and see if it was something Tamryn might be willing to work with. I reminded myself that I was only there to listen and consider, and if Gannicus's plan was completely stupid, it was my job to tell him.

I returned my thoughts to his question. Did I want to turn back? Was I ready to risk getting caught attending this meeting? Was I ready to keep an open mind about this fledgling plan? Maybe I was ready or maybe I wasn't. Hell, I probably wasn't. It didn't sound like my idea of a great time, to be perfectly honest. But instead of thinking about my own apprehension, I thought about the others that would be there tonight. They had a basic right to freedom. If I had to hear them out tonight, and even take some risks to myself, then I would. This was what I had to do, and that was the only thing he needed to know. So I shook my head and kept driving until he held up a hand and told me we'd gone far enough.

Chapter 23

I could barely see the chain link border of the base just beyond us in the distance. We slid out of the car, softly closing our doors behind us. Gannicus walked over to me, the sound of his feet brushing against the dirt breaking the eerie silence of the night. He grabbed my hand and squeezed it.

"One more thing," he whispered as we started creeping towards the gate. I was beginning to notice the outline of razor wire at the top, and that, frankly, made me feel a little less enthusiastic about our grand entrance into this place. I held Gannicus's hand more firmly.

"Another thing?" I asked, suppressing a sigh. This was no time for last minute notes. That time was in the car. Now we were here, approaching Gannicus's former prison. A prison that might be the last place we ever saw each other, if this went badly. I tried to focus on my breathing.

"You are aware I love you?" he said, stopping to look into my eyes for just a moment.

So much for focusing on my breathing. That skill had completely escaped me. He loved me. He loved me. *Gannicus* loved *me!* It took a lot to make me forget about prison and razor wire and risk to life and limb, but this was a lot. I'd hoped he felt that way, even guessed that he did, but that was nothing compared to hearing it. There was only one thing better than hearing it. Now I got to say it back.

The words settled into me, his words and the words I was about to say back, like they belonged there. I'd always thought saying "I love you" would be a scary thing, a dramatic moment with baited breath and the potential for regrets. Now that we were here, though, it seemed simple. When we came back to each other after our devastating separation, it was like two halves were made whole again. If I knew him at all, I knew that he loved me. And I knew that I loved him too. So I told him.

"I love you, too."

He stalked towards me, silently closing the small distance between us to hold my face in his hands. He bent down to kiss me; it was a soft, quick kiss that lacked nothing despite its brevity. For a moment, I let myself close my eyes and focus on my feelings. That moment was shorter than I would've liked, though. As soon as he pulled away, apprehension soon took its place at the forefront of my mind. We were a few steps away from reaching the fence, and as far as I could tell, there was no gate on this side for us to casually stroll through. Did he think we'd be going over? Over the razor wire? If so, he might have had to rethink that "I love you," because he didn't know me at all. Crawling over stabby metal wasn't something I did. Before I could panic, though, he knelt down and pulled at the bottom of the fence to reveal a small opening torn at the bottom. It looked like it was just barely big enough for him to slide under, so I would be able to fit under fairly easily.

"Why doesn't everyone just escape under this fence?" I whispered.

Gannicus leaned down until his lips were practically in my ear. It was a practical choice so he'd be able to barely whisper and I'd hear every word, but its practicality didn't stop it from sending shivers all over my body.

"First, shh. Second, no time machine out here. Third..." he pulled away just enough to kiss me on the cheek. I liked his third point the best. I did understand the other two points, though. I *was* capable of halfway focusing on the plan.

He held up the edge of the fence, so I guessed it was time for me to climb under there. Just... climb under there. A quick slide under there. I could do that. I switched my weight back and forth between my feet, visualizing the fence. This was something I could do. I could just creep under there. Right now.

"Lane," he whispered, tilting his head towards the hole in the fence.

Right. It was time for me to slide under the fence and stop thinking about sliding under the fence. Well, no time like the present. I crouched down to my knees, crawling towards the fence. Gannicus tried to lift it a little higher, but it was such a small opening that I'd have to pull myself through on my stomach. With as much grace as I could have expected in this situation, which was to say none at all, I managed to shove myself to the other side. I stood up and brushed the dirt off my clothes, trying with all my might not to wonder if there were scorpions clinging to me where I couldn't see them. Now it was my turn to hold the fence for him, which was much easier than my first task. Mostly. I cringed when the bottom edges of the fence tore a small hole in his shirt, but I'd already lifted the fence as high as it could go. That was what he got for being muscular, I supposed.

When he stood up, we both turned towards the rows of buildings about a football field length away from us. After all that, now it was time for the hard part.

We both took a deep breath and started forward. Gannicus stepped in front of me, protectively leading the way. That was extremely sweet, but I didn't know how to tell him that his back blocking my view of where we were going was only going to add to my terror. Instead of mentioning it, I stepped out to the side so I could see around him. The parking lot was just the parking lot, and the silent buildings were just the silent buildings. For now, it looked like there was nothing to be afraid of. We pressed on across the lot and past the first row of buildings before Gannicus took a turn. I followed.

I'd thought we were already walking carefully, but Gannicus's steps managed to get even softer as we brushed past walls and darted across walkways. Even if someone had been waiting for us, they wouldn't have known we were here. I tried to keep on my toes and match his silence.

A head tilt towards a door was my only indication that we'd made it to our destination. Gannicus glanced in both directions as he ushered me up to the door, stepping close behind me as I turned the knob.

The room was dimly lit, with one hanging lightbulb illuminating a battered pool table and throwing shadows on the faces around it. There were a lot of faces. The recreation room was filled to capacity, with people pressed against each other and the walls. Everyone turned and looked when we came in, but the woman who was speaking on the other side of the room didn't pause. As soon as her audience was satisfied that we weren't a threat, they turned back to look at her again. She finished her thought, which I was too nervous to remember as soon as she said it, and waved Gannicus over.

She was standing on a chair to be seen by the whole room. When she turned towards us, I realized that her face was one of the few in the room that was familiar to me from history class. Harriet Tubman.

Gannicus reached her and stood by the side of the chair, surveying the room. He didn't look surprised by the turnout or nervous about being caught; not a single emotion flashed across his face. Instead, he leaned closer to Harriett as she began to speak, keeping her eyes on me. Her words seemed to be meant only for Gannicus, but I guessed most of the people in the room were straining to hear what she said. I was, at least.

"She didn't think we..." were the words I managed to make out from her before she glanced at the crowd and lowered her voice even more. I had an uncomfortable feeling that "she" was referring to me. I felt at a bit of a disadvantage, only knowing that they were talking about me not thinking, and not even knowing what I hadn't thought about. Was coming here a bad choice? If it was, that was

Gannicus's fault, not mine! I considered turning and leaving, but my heart pounded at the thought. I wasn't exactly a welcome visitor on the rest of the base, and I didn't want to face the dark hallways outside alone.

Some of my apprehension must have shown on my face, because Gannicus gave a small smile of encouragement. Following his line of sight, Harriett turned to me and made a small expression of sympathy.

"Why don't you come over here, Lane?" she said kindly, holding a hand out towards me. I complied, walking slowly to allow the crowd to step out of my way as I made my way through. "I hear you went and met with Neil Davidson in person. Is that right?"

I glanced around nervously, hearing the question from the point of view of the others in the room who might not make the best assumptions about me.

"Yeah," I said quietly. I cleared my throat and spoke up. "I just thought maybe if I exposed him, then he'd have to do the right thing by you guys."

"You didn't think we could take care of things by ourselves?" a male voice said, speaking out from the crowd. My stomach dropped. I didn't look at him. I wanted to come back with some defense about how I was only trying to help, but my tongue felt stuck in my mouth. I just froze, marinating in the horror of the fact that I was a stranger in this room, and someone had already decided to try to call me out. This was starting to seem like the kind of situation that was only going to get worse.

"No," Gannicus warned, staring at my accuser. "Enough."

The other man didn't say anything. I turned to look in the direction his voice had come from, but it was hard now to tell who had said anything. Several people were avoiding eye contact with Gannicus, so it was hard to narrow it down to just one. I appreciated his sticking up for me, but it was only a small relief. Even if they were too scared to show it out loud again, the people in the room were prepared to judge me for whatever I said, or whatever anyone else said about me. They were on their guard, and I was an outsider. Not that I was trying to be understanding of the guy, because I kind of just wanted Gannicus to kick his ass. He didn't even know me and he wanted to have an attitude with me in front of all these people? I sighed and tried to get my thoughts back on track.

"He knows that you guys are trapped here against your will; it's not like he thinks he's doing you guys a favor or anything." I started to sweat when I heard someone scoff under their breath, and another person muttering. I should just stop talking. No, wait, maybe I should fix it. I tried to assuage the damage. "I mean, of course you guys know that. But he's willing to fight to keep you here. He even implied to me that if I tried to help you, he'd put me in the time machine and send me somewhere."

The room was silent. Was that good? Had I given them helpful information about the vengeful attitude of their enemy? Or were they silently contemplating the risk factors involved in beating me up?

"He said he'd take you to the time machine?" a woman to my right asked. She, like Gannicus, had adopted the clothes of our time, but the cut of her blonde bob hairstyle reminded me of the style of the 1920's. A few people stepped closer to hear my answer. "So you'd find out where it was."

Excited mutters filled the room.

"No!" Gannicus suddenly yelled, causing a few people in the front row to jump in surprise. "Do not even think of it."

Chapter 24

"Think of what?" I asked, my blood running cold. It sounded like they were looking for someone to go on a suicide run for them.

"Yes!" a man shouted. He looked familiar with his wide nose and arching brows, but I couldn't place from where I might recognize him. "You make an enemy of him, get caught on purpose, and he takes you to the time machine. Then you come back to this time and tell us where he keeps it. Any one of us would undertake the feat, but he wouldn't have any cause to show us." Some in the crowd nodded, and a few "Yeah!"'s could be heard scattered throughout the room.

Oh, so that was all. Just get kidnapped, tossed into a random point in the future, and somehow manage to stumble my way back into this lovely recreation room and tell all my new friends where exactly I was taken when I was kidnapped. Assuming I ever got back, that was. I wondered if anyone had even thought of that little issue. If it was so easy to get back to your own time, after all, why exactly were we having this meeting in the first place? Why didn't Mr. I-Wear-Pantyhose over there with his big black hat just go back to his own time then? Whenever that was.

It turned out I wasn't the only one who had issues with the proposed plan. People jumped out of the way when Gannicus hurled into the crowd, grabbing the man by the front of the lapels of his overcoat and shoving him against a wall. I yelped in surprise, and I wasn't the only one. Several people in the crowd were shocked at the turn the meeting had taken. Judging from the nervous murmuring and the way the space around Gannicus and his victim widened, I imagined no one else was very interested in getting involved at the moment.

"You think yourself so brave to send her as a sacrifice to save yourself?" Gannicus growled, throwing the man down. The man stayed sitting against the wall until Gannicus turned away, then shakily stood up and brushed himself off with dignity.

"It was just a proposal," he said proudly. "We didn't know she was more precious to you than freedom."

"I agree with Columbus," someone said, her voice shaky at first from growing in volume.

"Yeah!" another voice shouted towards the back of the room. "She said she wanted to help!"

Gannicus turned his head from person to person as the room broke out into cries of agreement in favor of the proposal suggested by, I gathered, Christopher Columbus. Judging from the glint of fury in his eyes, I thought Gannicus might be considering kicking the Nina, Pinta, and Santa Maria out of Columbus, and maybe even everyone else in the room. Even in his galant determination to defend me, I could see that Gannicus was struggling with what to do next, how to get the crowd to turn away from the idea.

"Enough!" he yelled, speed walking over to me and pulling me protectively against him. "This is not her fight. You will not sacrifice her."

Some in the crowd settled down at his words- mostly the ones within punching range. Some further out in the crowd, though, continued expressing their distaste for Gannicus's protests.

"Enough!" another voice shouted from the front, and this time most of the crowd fell quiet and listened. It was Harriett Tubman, who had resumed her position on top of the chair so that everyone could see her without difficulty. "Gannicus, you have to acknowledge that there is something to the idea."

The crowd started to cheer their agreement, encouraged by this group leader taking their side. My chest tightened. I didn't want to argue with Harriett Tubman about making sacrifices and fighting the good fight to end slavery, because I didn't know that I'd win that one. But I didn't think the plan was a very good one either, especially not for me. How was I supposed to come back? What if he didn't send me to the future? What if he sent me to the Jurassic Era to be eaten by Barney's ancestors?

As if in answer to my question, a woman next to me boldly spoke up and started explaining the plan in greater detail. She looked at Gannicus with a sympathy in her eyes that was frankly a little too personal for my taste. She reminded me of the girl in that Disney movie *Anastasia,* with her thick, dark hair.. Was it Duchess Anastasia? I realized when she started talking that I had more important things to worry about at the moment.

"If there is one thing we can say about Davidson, it's that he goes to great lengths to not disturb the future by altering the past. We know we were all taken right before we would have passed- or disappeared- anyway. So, he'd have to bring her to the future. Given that the time machine exists in this time, it's bound to exist in the future- and be a lot more common. All Lane would need to do would be to get to the time machine here, be taken to the future, and then find any time machine to travel back. She could tell us where Davidson keeps the one here, and then we could carry out our escape."

Alright, so there was that. What if there weren't time machines in the future? What if no one wanted them and they fell out of fashion before the time that Davidson sent me? I considered voicing that concern, but it didn't seem convincing even to me. In what universe would people know how to travel through time and decide that *wasn't* something every household would enjoy doing? I knew a winner of an invention when I heard one. Even if I wanted to protest the conversation, though, I was distracted by Gannicus's hand lifting up my chin to face him.

"Guard your ears from this," he said intensely, frustration etched in lines on his face. "This will not happen."

I nodded, only because I didn't know what else to do. Though there were a lot of people in the crowd coming to my defense and arguing that putting me in danger that way was wrong, there were too many on the other side that flatly disagreed. The more the people around me talked amongst themselves about the genius of this new idea, and how there was no way I could be allowed to pass it up, the angrier and more anxious I was getting. These people were really willing to throw me to Davidson like a juicy worm on a hook, weren't they? That scenario usually didn't end very well for the worm!

"I'm not a worm," I muttered to myself. Gannicus raised an eyebrow, but he didn't acknowledge my words. Instead, he acknowledged my sentiment with a flash of pain across his face.

"I never should have brought you here," he said, holding my hands in his carefully. "It's time for us to leave."

Just as I was about to consent to that plan, Harriett Tubman admonished the crowd.

"Enough bickering. This is Lane's decision. If any of you try to force her to put herself at risk, then you're no better than Davidson. You should be ashamed of yourselves. This may be a difficult situation, but I hope we'd never sink low enough to take away someone else's freedom like ours was taken from us."

I sighed in relief, and I even noticed Gannicus lose some of the tension in his shoulders. Good. We could get back to brainstorming a solution that didn't involve me being a human sacrifice.

"But we will ask," Harriett continued.

Shit. My heart pounded as she continued.

"We all have moments where we have to choose whether to take a risk to stand up for the right thing. None of us are free until all of us are free. Lane, you have every right to walk out of here, and none of us will hold it against you. If you did want to help us, though, this is the way."

I was sick to my stomach. I tried to pull in a deep breath, but my lungs felt like they were made of wood, and the relief of a deep breath evaded me. The room was quiet as hundreds of eyes ate into me.

I didn't want to do this. I didn't want to go out there and throw myself in front of Davidson's cannons for the good of the group. There was a chance I'd be lost from my family forever. Did my family deserve that? Of course not. The right thing to do would be to tell everyone good luck but no thanks, and that I'd help them with their next plan. That would even be pretty altruistic of me to go that far, considering they weren't exactly thinking of what was best for me here. That was the right choice. So why did the words burn in my throat like bile?

"Let's go," Gannicus said, nudging me towards the door. I was about to agree and leave, I really was. But right at that moment, something about the way the light hit his face reminded me of one of the first few times we'd met, when I'd told him that I wanted to do something important with my life- that I *would* do something important with my life. Was running away from the chance to help people the way I was going to do that? Columbus was right, really. The others couldn't do this for themselves. They needed an outsider to play this role, and as far as I could tell, I was the only one of those standing here.

I didn't know everyone in this room, or even most of them, but I did know that at least two of them had been willing to give their lives to the fight against slavery. One of them, the one I loved, who was trying so hard to steer me out the door right now, actually had given his life fighting that fight, as far as history was concerned. Harriett knew something about making the choice to risk yourself to rescue others herself, so she was hardly asking from a place of ignorance. What kind of person would I be if I looked at them and said I wouldn't do it? That I wouldn't perform this vital part of the plan that would lead to their freedom? A coward. And to be a coward was scarier than anything Davidson could do to me.

"I'm in," I said.

Chapter 25

The walk through the darkness back to the car had been silent, but that made sense given that we were trying to make it back without being caught. Once we got safely inside the car and I began to drive away, I could feel the silence resting its oppressive hands on my shoulders. Even the seatbelt across my chest was starting to feel constricting, and the cloth seat beneath me suddenly seemed like it was made of stone. I shifted. This should have been a time to discuss the next steps that had just been planned in the meeting. Surely as a soldier Gannicus would see the need for a debriefing of sorts after a meeting like the one we'd just experienced. I broke the silence myself.

"When do you think we should do it? Sooner rather than later, right?"

The low drone of the radio was the only sound for a moment, then Gannicus sucked in a breath.

"Never," he said. I turned to see him staring holes into me. I sighed. I didn't want to see him upset over this, or about anything for that matter. Especially if he was mad at *me*.

"I know," I said softly, turning back to watch the darkness of the road get sucked away by my headlights. "But they're right. I'm the only one who can do it."

I waited for a response, but I didn't get one. When I glanced over, Gannicus was staring out at the road, his jaw set.

This wasn't helpful. Making the decision to risk myself for people I didn't even know hadn't been a very easy decision in the first place. So much of me wanted to take it all back and agree that I couldn't, shouldn't, do it and just get back to the drawing board. If Gannicus continued to fight me on it, I'd be even more tempted to just give up the whole idea. I couldn't, though. I really believed that the plan was a good one. Davidson would probably just dump me in the future to get rid of me, and then I could find another time machine and ride it back home. It was a risk to assume the time machine would become more common in the future, but it was the pattern of technological advancement. First it might belong to only a tiny subsection of people, but at some point most people would have one. It happened that way with the car and the computer, and I had a feeling this would be no different. If someone came to my current time looking for a computer, they'd have no trouble finding one to borrow.

"I'm doing this for you," I said to Gannicus, as softly and non-reproachfully as I could. I understood where he was coming from, but he did have to acknowledge that I wasn't trying to hurt him by agreeing to try this. "For you and the others, so everyone can live normal lives again."

"What good will any of it do, Lane?" he said, the volume of his voice rising as he released the pent up anger he'd been avoiding before. "You can go and end up just like me, a slave to Davidson."

I considered that. Clearly it would be a similar situation. I'd be in a different time, with Davidson as the only person there who knew about the time I was from. Except, that wasn't necessarily true, was it? If these people in the future had time machines, they probably used them! So there'd be people there who understood the time travel thing, and would have the resources to help me. That was something. That was enough, in fact.

I explained to Gannicus, only getting a pouting grunt in response. I sighed. Was there a way to get him on my side? I thought it through, trying to figure out the right thing to say when you knew you might be leaving the person you loved behind, putting their happiness on the same table on which you were betting your own life. There wasn't much I could say, so I just let the silence sit. To my surprise, Gannicus was the one who broke it.

"You only support this idea because you believe it to be your obligation. You're not looking at it through objective eyes."

"Neither are you," I said, almost as soon as he'd finished the sentence.

"It looks as though we're at an impasse," he said, and a hint of a smile crossed his face for a moment before it was replaced by its former solemn expression. I wondered then if he thought highly of his chances of changing my mind. It was one to one, though. By that logic, my chances of changing his mind were equal. Yeah, this was an impasse.

Unless. Unless I could think of two people who would take Gannicus's side in the beginning, out of love for me. If I could change *their* minds, he'd have to realize that if they chose my side despite being biased towards protecting me, that this idea wasn't such a bad idea. Now where could I find those two people? People who understood the cause and everything that was at stake.

I changed my course, turning from the familiar route home to the almost equally familiar route to Marana.

"I don't like it," Tamryn said immediately, as soon as we'd walked through the door announcing that we had a plan to fight Davidson and the words "hear me out" had exited my lips. She crossed her arms, an impenetrable stony expression on her face. "I can tell that Gannicus doesn't like it and neither do I."

"You don't even know what it is!" I said, stepping in front of Gannicus in a futile attempt to block his silent persuasion. "This is the only thing that might actually work."

"*Might* is not a trustworthy friend," Gannicus broke in, in an almost bored tone. He was already getting complacent that he'd win, and we hadn't even started yet! Honestly, judging from the wince on Levi's face and the glare on Tamryn's, I thought he might have a good reason to think so. Maybe I'd overestimated my ability to get them all to focus on the big picture.

"They need someone to be caught by Davidson and brought to the time machine so they'll know where he hides it," I said quickly, not stopping out of fear that if I took a breath I'd be interrupted, "Davidson already threatened to send me to the future so I'm the perfect candidate. I'd just pop into the time machine, go to the future, and come back with the information we need. Then we'd send everyone back and the day would be saved. Quick, easy, and cheap."

To their credit, no one immediately said "no." Less to their credit, no one said anything. Immediately or otherwise. Tamryn just walked over to the little glass kitchen table by the front door, adjusting the flowers in a vase as if she could ignore what I'd said.

"So?" I prompted. I turned my head towards each of them, making eye contact in a silent demand for an answer. Did the idea sound so bad that they couldn't even respond to it? I started to doubt myself. Maybe Gannicus was right. Maybe the only reason I thought this would even work was that I didn't think I had any other choice, and I wanted to take action and get it over with already. What would I do once Davidson threw me into the future, after all? Just make a cardboard sign that said, "Will work for transportation back to 2020?" Actually, yeah, maybe. Or maybe they'd have public transport time machines and I could get a time machine bus ticket.

"I don't think it's that bad of an idea," Levi said, glancing at the others' reactions to see if he was the only one. He walked a few short steps into the small kitchen and put his hand on Tamryn's shoulder. "I'll go, of course. Not you. But other than that, it seems like the only way to solve a pretty tough problem."

"I accept," Gannicus said nobly, nodding his head at Levi. Levi raised a hand at him as if to say "See? We're agreed." Oh, so now we were agreed. How nice.

But that wasn't the plan! Levi couldn't go because Davidson probably wouldn't take him. He'd probably kill him and burn his body before anyone had time to wonder where he'd gone. Levi saying it was a smart plan didn't help if he insisted on going through with it himself. Wait. Actually, I could work with that. If it was such a great plan, then it didn't matter who went because it was going to work. Levi had already admitted he thought it was our only option, and Gannicus had agreed that he could go with it. They might not know each other that well, but Gannicus wouldn't let Levi go without a fight if he really thought it was a ridiculous plan that was bound to fail. No, they'd both exposed themselves as believing in the plan. That was all I needed.

"Alright," I said, hiding my smile. "So we all agree it's a good plan. Thank you guys. I will be going myself, because otherwise it won't work and you know it. But the vote of confidence has already been entered, and it's too late to draw it back."

Once again, everyone was quiet. I saw Gannicus open his mouth in what I assumed was about to be a protest, but he closed it again and rubbed his face with exhaustion instead. No one looked particularly happy, but what could they do? The truth was, this plan was as good as any. I might not be a warrior who had fought for freedom like Gannicus or Levi, but it looked like I was about to get some of my own experience in that department. Anyway, it wasn't like I was heading into an assassination attempt of Davidson. All I had to do was get caught. That couldn't be too hard.

I tried to believe that, and to feel triumphant that I'd managed to convince them. I tapped my foot on the tiled floor absently, picking up speed as I considered the implications of the conversation. I'd known I'd have to convince them of the merits of the plan, but if I was being honest with myself, I hadn't known whether or not I'd be successful. I did believe it was a decent plan, but there was no such thing as foolproof in a situation like this. Risks were inherent, and no one in the room wanted me to incur any risk. It was a testament to the severity of our situation that they all agreed.

With a terse nod or two, we settled on the couch and mismatched chairs in Tamryn and Levi's living room and started discussing the logistics. I clutched a small embroidered pillow to my chest and tried to absorb the energy from it: it had a stitched sheep with the words "I don't give a sheep." Yes. I didn't give a sheep about the danger. I could do this. I squeezed it harder.

In order for Davidson to catch me, he'd have to know that I was on base, interfering with his business. I had no doubt that he meant his threat, but I imagined he would prefer for it to just remain a threat. That meant I'd have to provoke him. What I'd also have to do, though, was make it seem like I wasn't out to get his attention at all. A plan that made the enemy suspicious wasn't a very good one. I was surprised when it was Tamryn who proposed the solution. I tended to forget that she was as familiar with the app as I was, despite the fact that we'd never talked about it before she'd suggested I download it not too long ago. For a second, a hint of bitterness hit me as I considered the time that had passed between her downloading the app, meeting Levi, marrying him, and then me finally getting around to knowing the truth. I shook it away, though. Now that I'd seen what a burden knowledge of the app could be, I couldn't fault her for trying to shield me from it. Not that I regretted being involved, but it was a perspective I could understand.

"The app tracks your location when you request a lesson, right?" Tamryn started, introducing her plan.

"And every other waking minute, I'm sure," I said.

"Yeah, probably. But I doubt they have people assigned to check every user every second. You'd have to prompt them to pay attention to your location. So, you'd have to request a lesson. Then they'd have to check where you were in order to send you someone. What if when you did, your location happened to be on the base? That would get their attention. That'd be something they'd report to Davidson."

That wasn't a bad plan. It would ensure that Davidson knew where I was without him thinking that I knew he was watching. I was less convinced, though, that he'd believe that I'd use the app voluntarily after our conversation. Tamryn had an answer to this too.

"As soon as you request the class, cancel it right away. That'll still send an alert, but they'll see that you tried to stop it. It'll look like you'd only opened a request on accident, and Davidson will think you have no idea that the request still went through."

"How do you know the request still *will* go through?" I asked. There was a pause. Tamryn picked at a loose stitch on the arm of the couch while we all waited for her answer.

"I assume it goes through immediately," she said, shrugging with a slightly apologetic look. It wasn't the level of confidence I wanted to see in the person proposing a battle plan, but it was good enough. After all, if the request didn't go through then I'd just go home. He wouldn't know I was on the base, and we'd just have to find a different way to set the trap. As far as potential ways the plan could go wrong, this one was probably one of my favorites. At least it didn't involve getting lost in the future.

"What if the unexpected occurs?" Gannicus broke in, somewhat randomly. He'd clearly been thinking of the things that could go wrong too, as if we'd gotten the idea from each other's brains.

"What's the unexpected?" I asked, hoping for a specific concern that we could work together to address. Vague worries weren't productive. The plan was happening and that was that.

"The nature of the unexpected is that we cannot know," he said, almost sharply. I sighed. His obvious irritation bit at me. I knew it came from a place of love and worry, though, so I tried to push it aside. I nudged his knee with my own, and he didn't pull away. I took that as a decent sign.

"We can only do our best to prepare for anything that comes," Levi said.

As true as his words were, they weren't a big help. Gannicus's displeasure at the current plan was simmering just below the surface, though it wasn't in his nature to hide what he was feeling entirely. In a way I wished he would. Knowing that he was so unhappy about me going forward against Davidson reminded me that he was worried, which forced me to consider that maybe he *should* be nervous. Maybe we all should be.

It was Friday night. I was outfitted in all black, as if I were intending to blend into the night instead of trying to get caught on purpose. I was back in the wild desert behind the base, where Gannicus and I had broken in for the meeting. Only this time, we weren't here just to talk.

My nervous shaking was almost closer to vibrating at this point.

What was that? My stomach dropped at the sound of rustling a few feet away. I flashed the light of my phone in that direction, but there was nothing there but sagebrush.

There was nothing else here. There was *no one* else here. Gannicus had dropped me off and driven away, despite his distaste for that part of the plan.

I was surprised I'd finally managed to convince him. He'd been adamant that he could hide in the desert and wait for me in case I needed protection. Levi, Tamryn, and I, however, had all been sure that his hiding would only put him at risk. After all, what was he going to do? Stop Davidson from capturing me? That would be a pretty counterproductive act of heroism, considering the plan relied on Davidson doing just that. Besides, if Davidson got any indication that I wasn't alone, he'd know he'd been set up. I was loath to pay a compliment to my enemy, but Davidson was obviously smart. To underestimate him at this point would be to waste all of the effort we'd put in so far.

So instead, I was standing in the dirt by myself, the dry warmth of a coming Arizona summer brushing my arms. I took a deep breath and looked at the millions of stars freckling the sky, trying desperately to focus on the beauty of nature instead of wondering if that tickle I just felt on my leg was a scorpion preparing to sting me. I gave up and glanced down. No, there was nothing there.

It wasn't rational, but the perils of the darkness and the desert were starting to seem worse than anything Davidson could dish out. With a shaky breath and a quick mantra of "Ok, I can do this I can do this I can do this," I slid under the fence and opened my phone to the random history class I'd chosen on the iEducator app. I tapped to request the class, then counted three breaths and canceled.

As if I thought Davidson would instantly teleport to me, I whipped my head around as soon as I'd done it. The night was as quiet as it had been before, the darkness unpolluted now by the light of my phone. I started making my way towards the buildings, slowing my walk every time I noticed my nerves were forcing me to pick up speed.

There was some comfort in reaching the line of the first buildings. I recognized the sort of decorative beds of stones at my feet, and the slight shadows of the buildings in the light of a few outdoor lamps scattered around the hallways. I'd just been here with Gannicus. I'd even met some of the people here. Without thinking, I found myself heading towards Gannicus's former dorm, as if he might be there to offer me some protection. But of course, he wouldn't. And the whole reason I was here was so that he and the others wouldn't be here for any reason, ever again. I carried that reminder around me like an old blanket as I crept around the base, wondering what I was supposed to do now.

Every breath of a breeze startled me. I thought I heard a stone shift, but that was impossible. If there was someone behind me, they'd be making more noise than that. I whipped my head around anyway, but my search came up empty. What if he didn't get the alert? What if it didn't go through? What if he did get it and he just didn't care? That one was possibly the worst option. If he didn't care that I was meddling, we'd have to start completely over with a new plan. There was a tiny part of me that hoped that would happen. Maybe the new plan would involve someone else creeping around in the night on behalf of the group. Maybe-

Maybe- *oww. Shit!* I automatically reached for my neck as I registered a sharp sting. My hand came away with a small yellow dart, tipped with the smallest hint of blood. My blood. My stomach rolled.

This was ok. The plan was working. My muscles started to feel weak, to collapse without my permission, without even my understanding. I'd been caught. My vision was starting to blur, and panic squeezed at my chest as I tried to lower myself safely to the ground before I completely lost consciousness. Despite my efforts, I saw the pavement come up to meet my face faster than I'd planned.

And then I didn't see anything at all.

Chapter 26

There was a rumbling vibration under and against me, the feeling of movement. I was in a car. I didn't remember falling asleep in the car. I didn't remember anything.

Oh! I jolted. The memories poured in, memories of traveling across the base in the dark, feeling a sting, the pavement coming up to meet my face. That explained the throbbing in my head, and the burning on my face. My lip felt somewhat numb in a paradoxically painful way, especially on the right side, which told me how I'd fallen. I still hadn't opened my eyes, as if I could shield myself from reality by refusing to look at it. If I couldn't see it, maybe it couldn't see me.

I hadn't just fallen and gotten knocked out. I'd been hit with some kind of tranquilizer, and was now in the process of being kidnapped. A rush of panic raced from my chest up to my throat, but I tried to quell it. Focus. This was part of the plan. Was Davidson here? Was I in his car?

"Is she awake?" a familiar female voice asked, disembodied by my still closed eyes. I tried to breathe evenly when a large meaty hand was pushed against my face. On some instinct, I decided to pretend to be asleep as long as I could. As scary as it was knowing I was in this situation—and I didn't want to understate how scary that was, because it was at least a 10 out of 10 on that scale—I thought that having to interact with my captors would be even worse. The longer I could make them believe that I was just a lump of unconscious person, the better.

"No, she's out, Amanda. Uh, ma'am," a deep male voice replied, apparently the owner of the hand that had pushed me.

I didn't recognize the man's voice. If I'd ever heard it before, I didn't remember it now. The woman's voice, though, I knew. I brought the voice to mind as I'd just heard it, playing it in my memory as clearly as I could. It was reminding me of Gannicus. Oh! Oh no. It was that horrible woman who'd blamed me for what happened with Vlad! Fantastic. As if I needed another reason to think she was the worst. Now I had a name for her, but it didn't do me much good. If our previous encounters were any indication, she was not going to be very sympathetic to my feelings on being the victim of a kidnapping. Not that I planned to ask for her help. As precarious as my situation might have seemed, I did have the upper hand. This was the plan going exactly as it was supposed to. I could have done without the possible concussion, but no plan was ever executed perfectly.

Carefully, exceedingly carefully, I peeked between my eyelashes to see where we were. I recognized the faded buildings of the bad parts of downtown Tucson. Many of the buildings we passed were dilapidated, abandoned by their former owners. My sense of direction was lacking, but I did my best to commit each turn of the car to memory. My getting sent to the future didn't do anyone any good if I failed to remember where the time machine was when I came back to this time.

Our surroundings kept getting worse as we ventured deeper downtown until the car rolled right onto the grass of an empty park. I had to admit, this wasn't where I'd imagined Davidson hiding his time machine. I'd expected somewhere creepy for sure, but more like a nice warehouse kind of creepy, or a big mansion with a bunch of barking rottweilers. This was a random part in a dangerous part of town, where I'd think Davidson would be uncomfortable leaving priceless technology alone. It was good news for me, though. If the machine was as unprotected as it seemed so far, then stealing it would be a lot easier than I'd thought.

I tried to stay still despite my urgency for a better look as we approached a cement block of a building at the end of the park. There was nothing but a chain link fence and the desert behind it.

The building looked like a run-down public restroom from the outside, but I assumed—and hoped, really—that that wasn't the case.

"Grab her," the horrible woman Amanda said when the SUV jolted to a stop, causing me to slide forward on the leather seats. I stayed limp, making no move to adjust my position.

I was suddenly scooped up by a pair of large, sweaty arms, and lifted out of the car. Though it sort of hurt my neck, I let my head dangle back to maintain the illusion that I was still unconscious. It wasn't obvious how long I'd be able to keep up the charade, but it seemed to be in my best interest to keep it going as long as I could.

Though I was lowered most of the way, I was finally cast like a heap of dirty clothes onto a cold, cement floor. My face landed safely on my arms, which I'd thrown in front of me during the fall.

"Wake her up." I barely had time to register Amanda's demand before I was kicked in the side harder than necessary by the toe of a leather boot. My gasp was real as I sat up and finally got a full look at my surroundings. I rubbed my injured side as I tried to notice every detail that I could.

The entire cement building was made up of one room, with a small open window near the top of each wall. The floor and walls were all made of plain cement, with no decoration. There was one door, a rusty metal thing that looked like someone had just shoved it into the wall. In one of the corners stood two tall cylinders with tube-shaped light bulbs wrapped around inside their glass covers. Looking around the room, there was no way I wasn't here to be murdered. Maybe Davidson has just used the threat of the future to sound more creative. Maybe he was really just going to shoot me and leave me in this rundown park where my death could be blamed on gang activity. A chill ran through me at the thought. Maybe Davidson wasn't coming. Maybe these two goons were all I'd ever see again. As if I'd spoken out loud, one of them broke the silence.

"Is he coming?" The man who asked was the only person in the room with Amanda and me. He was heavy-set, his bulk soft, unlike the muscles that made Gannicus huge. His hairline of dark brown was receding. Overall, he didn't seem like the threatening henchman I'd expected.

"He'll get here when he gets here. Then we'll take care of her," Amanda replied. I wondered who "he" was. My only guess was Davidson. I hoped I was right. Surely Davidson wouldn't bother showing up just to watch me get murdered.

"When he gets here" turned out to be less immediate than I'd guessed. Amanda and her subordinate just stood around, pretending I wasn't there. That suited me fine. I didn't even really notice they were there.

I was too busy thinking my way through the plan, which was starting to seem less and less concrete. Here I was, waiting for Davidson. Judging from the futuristic cylinders in the room, I knew he kept the time machine, and apparently another time machine, in Saguaro Community Park downtown. So now I had the information I needed to get everyone to a time machine once we broke them free. So... now what? I just waited for Davidson to attempt to psychologically torture me with his act of revenge? I sighed and tapped my fingers against the cold cement floor. It looked like that was exactly what had to happen next.

I wasn't sure how long we waited, but it was long enough for my butt to both hurt and get numb from sitting on the hard floor. I knew time went slowly when it came to waiting in tiny concrete rooms with creepy people, but my best guess was still that it was taking a couple of hours. I made a move at one point to stand up and walk off my stiffness, but when the large man who'd carried me in here made stony eye contact with me, I changed my mind. I decided maybe I'd just continue sitting and minding my business instead. I wondered what we were waiting for. Did Davidson actually fly here from California?

I'd been zoned out for some time when there was a small squelching outside, like the sound of feet on wet grass. Amanda's head turned towards the door at the same moment that mine did. Adrenaline coursed through me all over again as I rose to my feet and waited for the door to open. Finally, he was here. I shook out my legs and rubbed my back, as if preparing to attack him as soon as he came into the room. Of course I wasn't going to do that, though, because *he* was the one falling into *my* trap. Assuming it was him. For a horrible moment, my stomach twisted as I considered that maybe it wasn't Davidson we'd heard approaching. Maybe it was another one of his employees, sent to get rid of me for good.

Time seemed to freeze as we listened to the sound of a key twisting in the metal lock. *Ok, here we go.* The door slowly swung open, and Davidson's boyish face appeared. Some of the tension eased from my body. At least it was Davidson. When we made eye contact, though, the relief was washed away by a strange mix of anger and embarrassment. Why was I embarrassed? He was the one who was being caught out here, not me. Still, there was something about his look of disapproval that made my face get hot, as if I were getting in trouble at school. I didn't like it.

"Hello, Lane," Davidson said, crossing the small room to the cylinders that I'd already determined were time machines. They were about a foot taller than him, and at least twice as wide as him. Amanda was turning the dials on the first one. I watched carefully, in case I'd need to work one of them on my own. Her body was blocking most of the control panel, though, so it was hard to tell what she was actually doing. I considered asking her to please get her ass out of the way, but I didn't think it was in my best interest to draw excessive attention towards myself, and especially not towards the fact that I cared to learn how the machines worked.

"Not that one," he snapped, shoving her hand away from the dial. She and I both jumped at the sudden sharp words. "That's the new prototype." He turned the dials of the one next to it, which was almost identical except with slightly shorter light bulbs and fewer dials. He jerked his head towards me while keeping his eye on the machine. "Bring her here."

Alright, this was it. The whole plan was to get into that machine. This was working. So why did my chest tighten when the large henchman stomped his way over to me and grabbed my arm? His grip was tight, but not necessarily painful. Or maybe it was painful and I just didn't notice. I was too numb with terror to care about my current physical sensations.

"Do you know what this is?" Davidson asked me when I was brought right in front of him. My only response was to glare at him and try to steady my breath. Just because I was a little nervous didn't mean he needed to see it. "This is a time machine."

"It doesn't look like a time machine. It looks stupid," I blurted.

It wasn't my most cutting remark, but lashing out against his creation helped somewhat in taking my mind off of the fact that I'd soon be inside of it. I was claustrophobic just looking at it. I tried to focus on his response.

"I made that, Lane," he said, simpering. "You'll hurt my feelings."

Maybe we'd both do better in the real battle that loomed in our future than we were doing at this current battle of wits. I didn't have anything else to say to delay the inevitable any longer, so I just sneered at him.

No one spoke as Davidson dragged me to the machine, opening the glass window and shoving me inside. I could feel the tubular light bulbs against my back, and flinched reflexively as I wondered if they were hot enough to burn me. I didn't register heat, but I stepped forward until I wasn't touching anything anyway. Davidson shoved against me, pushing his way inside.

I didn't like this. It was too tight in here, and Davidson was too close. I could smell his cologne, which would have actually been a decent scent if the man wearing it didn't make me sick to my stomach. The fabric of his long sleeved shirt brushed against my arm, and I jerked away as much as I could given the lack of space.

He closed the door, flashing a sarcastic thumbs up at Amanda. She poked her finger at the machine, presumably pushing a button.

Everything went black.

Chapter 27

My stomach dropped out in that weightless feeling I'd felt a thousand times before on rollercoasters. It was hard to catch my breath, but I tried not to panic. I tried to go with the feeling. I tried to will away the stiffness in my limbs and take deep breaths. This would be over soon. It would be over soon. It would be—As soon as they had appeared, the strange feelings vanished, and my vision was restored. I looked out the glass walls of the machine, hungrily searching for information about my new surroundings.

Instead of the cement building, I was in what appeared to be a huge office building. An image of the time machine reflected off the linoleum floors. There were rows of cubicles, with people working quietly and apparently unaware of, or apathetic towards, my arrival. The walls were mostly windows, and I could make out the roofs and exteriors and other buildings outside, showing that we were on a high floor. My breath was stolen by shock when I heard a phone buzzing, only to see the phone emit a holographic image of a man in a business suit. The owner of the phone continued eating her ramen noodles as she conversed with the hologram.

Well, here we were. Toto, I didn't think we were in 2020 anymore.

The glass door swung open and Davidson stepped out. He held his hand out to me, offering to help me exit the machine. It was a kind of obscene gesture to me, so out of place given our relationship and circumstances. I'd been forced to be in close proximity with him to get here, but that didn't mean I wanted to extend my time touching him any more than I needed to. I pulled my arm away from his outstretched hand, and waited until he backed up before I exited. To his credit, he got the message pretty quickly and gave me some space to get out of the machine.

I didn't say a word as he led me through the building, passing cubicles of people to whom we might as well have been invisible. He didn't look at them, and they didn't look at him. I wondered if they talked bad about him when he wasn't there. When he left to visit the past, were they relieved? Or were they just as evil as him? Either way, we kept moving forward with no major interaction. There was no choice but to stop, though, when I saw one of the workers.

It was a dog. At a desk. Typing. My feet were frozen on the linoleum floor as I watched his paws move across the keys, as efficient as a set of fingers. The keys were larger on this keyboard, probably to accommodate paws that were wider than fingers.

"Yes, they train them better in the future," Davidson said impatiently, as if a labrador sending a memo was just part of the mundane work day. I supposed he must be used to the shocks of time travel by now.

I suddenly had the strange feeling that it might be rude to stare, so I walked faster to catch up with Davidson. Even as we walked, though, I couldn't help but take stock of the future. Much of the office looked like an ordinary office, though there were minor differences. Though some were still typing, many of the workers were speaking the words right out, watching their computer screens as the words appeared.

Was this how Gannicus felt when he came to my time? This sense that he was an alien in a place that didn't really exist? Gannicus. I wondered what he was thinking right now. Besides the fact that I'd time traveled to the future, time had passed the old fashioned way too. It had been, what? A full night so far? He'd know by now that I'd been taken. He wouldn't know where, or when I'd be back. *I* didn't even know those things. Was he afraid for me? Did he regret letting me go out to take this chance? I hoped not. I'd made this decision as carefully as I could, and the fact that I was actually here now, away from him and my family, didn't change a thing. I didn't know how he felt, but I couldn't let myself start to regret this. He'd worry and miss me, and I'd worry and miss him. It didn't change a thing. I tried to turn my attention back to the present. Or, the future. Whatever.

My clothes stood out in this place for being too plain. Each worker, man or woman, was wearing bright colors or startling patterns. More surprisingly, a lot of them were wearing clothing that covered far more of them than mine did, despite the warm temperature of the office. Had fashion taken a turn towards conservatism? I supposed it was the only way to be shocking at a certain point. Just what time was it here? It didn't seem like enough had changed for this to be centuries in the future, especially with how quickly technology already changed in my own time. Davidson didn't have to take me that far into the future, as long as it was foreign enough that I'd feel isolated and terrified. As much as I appreciated seeing a dog working in an office, it was safe to say that his plan was working. I'd already started avoiding looking too closely at the cubicles as we walked by, hoping I could manage to convince myself that I was still in the same time period that I'd always been in, and that time was just moving normally. I tried to take a deep breath, but it got stuck in my chest. No, I wasn't going to start getting anxious. I was here, and I had a job to do.

"What year is this?" I finally asked Davidson. I'd been avoiding talking to him, but sticking to my own thoughts wasn't making me feel as strong as I'd hoped.

"2106," he replied, checking his watch. I wondered if he did that just to be a jerk, or if he really had a watch that kept the year.

2106. 86 years in the future. That wasn't really that far ahead, when I thought about it. I probably wouldn't live to that time organically, but my kids would. If I ever made it back to my own time to have them, that was. I wondered what Gannicus thought about kids. We hadn't really talked about it yet. Things had been so serious for us, given our situation, but there were places in our relationship that we had yet to go. For a split second, I let myself imagine a little boy with blonde hair and big blue eyes held high up on Gannicus's shoulders. *That* was the future I was interested in. This was nothing more than a visit. When I got back to my own world, I'd make sure to ask Gannicus what the future looked like to him.

Oh no, more unknown technology. My sweet thoughts were torn away by the present.

My stomach rolled in apprehension when we approached a door in the hallway. It appeared to be an elevator, complete with buttons to went up or down. That was something I was used to, and calling it "technology" even seemed like a bit of a stretch. Considering this was the future, though, I was afraid to see what set it apart from the elevators of my time. Maybe futuristic elevators involved separating all of the atoms in your body and rejoining them on a new floor? Or taking you to a completely different part of the building? What had changed about elevators in the 8 decades that separated me from my real time?

Mostly, nothing. We stepped into the small compartment and faced the doors as they closed. Davidson pressed a button labeled "G," presumably for Ground Floor. I waited for the familiar swoop that meant the elevator was on its way. It never came. Instead, a second after Davidson pressed the button, the doors opened again. So elevators were instant in the future. Actually, that was an improvement I could get behind. The awkward tension of standing in an elevator with strangers made those 30 seconds of elevator riding feel like a lifetime of torture sometimes. I wouldn't mind skipping that part. Considering I was with Davidson right now, I especially appreciated the efficiency.

Warm Arizona air caressed me as we walked out the double doors of the building to the outside world. I hadn't really noticed how cold the office had been, but goosebumps had started to rise on my arms in the artificial air-conditioned chill. Stepping into the sunshine felt like a strong hug after a difficult day. The familiarity of the feeling brought me a small bit of comfort. The comfort was short-lived. Instead, in the next moment, I felt a disconcerting combination of disappointment and relief when I saw what greeted me outside the building. There were tall rows of apartment-like buildings. Though they were gray instead of sand-colored, they were the same type of buildings I'd been surrounded by when I was kidnapped. On one hand, at least I hadn't been confronted by a sea of giant colorful tubes, like the kind that decorate a hamster's cage, or some other absurd form of architecture that the future always seemed to have in cartoons. On the other hand, I hadn't liked these sterile buildings when I'd just been visiting with Gannicus. They weren't much better now that I was here alone. If my guess was right, one of these buildings would be my new home.

I followed Davidson wordlessly, surprised that he was taking me this far. Didn't being the boss mean that he had someone else to do such mundane tasks as this? He didn't even use this time to gloat about my new imprisonment, or pretend that this was a great adventure for me. He just kept walking authoritatively, like he was giving a campus tour to a horde of eager freshmen. It was starting to creep me out.

We made it up to a plain gray building just like all the others, and Davidson stated simply that this one was mine. I tried to think of this one as special, but it was just one in a collection. If I were taken back to the office building and had to find my way back here, I'd probably pick a different building and declare confidently that it was mine. There was no real difference, as far as I could tell. Still, this was the one. I wondered what floor I'd be on, stupidly contemplating how the first floor was the least safe because someone could come through the windows. What was the meaning of safe anymore? I was here because I'd been tranquilized and kidnapped. Davidson turned around a corner of the building and walked to another elevator. I followed.

A second later, we stepped onto the third floor. My hands were shaking as I wondered who else was here. It was doubtful that Davidson was running a one-act show with me, so there were other historical figures hidden behind these doors. Were there any of the same people from the time I'd just left? Or did he collect new people for this time? I tried to look at the door labeled "33," but I had to look away. It was too personal, the fact that that was Gannicus's door and I cared enough to want to see it. Maybe he'd guess anyway, but I didn't want Davidson to know I was thinking of Gannicus. It was none of his business.

My room, 35, was just like the one where I'd visited Gannicus. Even though the year was decades in the future, apparently Davidson saw little reason to stray from a working strategy. One half of my room was dedicated to a faux classroom, with a dry erase board. By this year, a dry erase board was probably meant to evoke nostalgia. The bedroom side was plain, with a white bedspread and white pillowcases barely standing out against the simple white wall. I wondered if I'd be allowed to put up a poster, or if Davidson had ever seen *The Shawshank Redemption*. There was no reason that being in this room was any worse than being taken to a new time in the first place, but my stomach turned anyway. Somehow this made it a lot more real. Worse than that, seeing my new "home" here made it feel like it was permanent.

I really had to hand it to Davidson. Forcing me into the same slavery I was trying so hard to stop was excellent revenge. If being sent here hadn't been part of my plan, I'd be crushed to be here.

Everything *was* going according to plan, and the situation was still managing to make me tense.

"This is for you," Davidson said, handing me a small tablet. It looked something like my phone, except bigger. It had a huge camera lens on the top of the screen. "I already scheduled your first class. You don't need to bother with studying. I'm sure you know enough about the COVID19 pandemic as it is."

I almost laughed derisively at the implication that I'd been planning to study for this. Did he think I'd applied for this job? I certainly wasn't going to be doing any overtime. I considered the rest of what he'd said, about Covid 19. That was going to be my special topic from the past. I smiled humorlessly. Someone was going to listen to a class about me sleeping until 10 everyday and not leaving the house? It was hardly the most riveting historical time. Well, good. If my presentation was short and boring, I'd have more time to get to the real purpose of my visiting the people of the future-grabbing a time machine and getting the hell out of here.

Davidson walked out the door without turning back.

Chapter 28

When I woke up the next morning, there was a moment of bliss as I thought of the face of the man I loved. Reality set in a moment later, before I'd finished fully picturing his face. I was in a completely different year, completely unsure of what was going to happen today, and completely alone. I wasn't completely despairing, though. Today was my first chance to take control of the plan, and stop letting the plan happen to me. After the general unease of yesterday, I was more than ready to get myself back on track.

I rolled over in bed, kicking the heavy cotton comforter off of my feet. My full intention was to jump out of bed and start the day, but the bed was so warm, and so soft, and it begged me to stay. Somehow, beds had managed to get even softer in the future. This was like memory foam on steroids. For a moment I closed my eyes, wondering how bad it would be if I just lived the rest of my life in it. I wouldn't have to go out and meet a stranger today, or even put on clothes. I could just let this cloud caress my skin for another day and try again tomorrow.

Despite the absolute genius of that plan, I sighed and forced myself up anyway.

There was a tan wooden wardrobe across from the bed that I hadn't investigated the night before. I opened it to see a row of multi-colored, long-sleeved, floor length dresses. Next to those were long-sleeved shirts and plain slacks. I was beginning to understand why Vlad had stuck with the clothes he knew. It was strange choosing an outfit from a fashion you didn't understand. As someone likely more interested in fashion than Vlad, though, I was sort of excited to try on the clothes. It was like putting on a costume for a play.

I chose a pink dress with big cherries and apples on it. Though a look in the mirror clued me into the fact that it was a ridiculous dress, it was fun. I was in no position to turn down fun. Besides, it clearly wasn't ridiculous for this time or it wouldn't be in my closet. For a second it crossed my mind that Davidson had planted it there to humiliate me, but I dismissed the idea as ridiculous right away. There were way better ways to torture me than picking out an outfit that would make me look stupid. I almost laughed at the absurdity. Besides, I thought I could kind of pull it off. There was no makeup in my room, so all I could do was splash water on my face and wipe away the bits of mascara that had run down my face yesterday. It wasn't my best look, but I had to believe it was acceptable.

Smiling in the mirror, I practiced being likable. If I were going to recruit whoever had requested this lesson to help me, they'd have to think I was someone worth helping.

A knock on the door interrupted my preparations. Was it Davidson? I sighed. I really didn't want to see him today. For one thing, I didn't want him to see my outfit and think I looked dumb. Just because I'd decided he didn't put the dress there to mess with me didn't mean he wouldn't have an opinion on it. The idea of him standing there feeling superior about the fact that he knew the fashion of this time and I didn't made my blood boil. Maybe I would just change into my real clothes from yesterday. No, I was going to keep wearing what I was wearing. What did Davidson know about anything?

When I opened the door, though, I came face to face with a young woman who looked somewhat familiar. I definitely didn't know her, but I'd seen her in passing. I tried to block out her current outfit of a bright yellow floor-length dress with big, puffy sleeves and focus on her face. This new century was a disaster of fashion. Then again, people wore scarves as belts when I was a kid. Oh, I recognized her now. She'd been in the office yesterday, talking to a hologram on the phone.

"Hello, I'm Ariah," she said, smiling sincerely. She had porcelain skin and black hair down her back, reaching her waist. Her face had a friendly quality. I instantly saw her as a friend. I decided not to berate her for participating in my slavery. Just because she worked for the app didn't mean she knew what was going on behind the scenes, right? Maybe she thought I'd signed up for this.

"Hi, I'm Lane," I said instead, gesturing out the door for her to lead the way. I dug through the endless thoughts in my head like I was looking for the M&M's in a bag of trail mix, but I didn't come up with any questions to ask her that might help me. Instead, I just followed as she walked.

She led me past all the gray buildings until we came to a parking lot. Instead of gravel, though, the floor of the parking lot was made out of smooth, white stone. I tapped it with my shoe before I stepped onto it.

"The cars go faster without friction," Ariah explained. That sounded to me like they might have a hard time slowing down, but there was a reason I wasn't an inventor in my own time. Physics had never been my strong suit. Maybe they'd moved beyond the necessity of friction.

I followed her into a black car. It was longer and slimmer than the SUV's they drove in my time, but the interior was fairly similar. There were labeled temperature controls next to my seat. I turned the temperature all the way down, only to gasp when my leather seat became so cold it hurt to sit on. *Now this is the future,* I thought as I adjusted it to a comfortable setting.

By the time I'd adjusted my seat, we were there. The house had to have been right next door for us to get here as quickly as we had, or the cars here were much faster. I supposed the latter wouldn't be too shocking considering everything else I'd seen here.

"Ok, go ahead up. Davidson has arranged everything this time," Ariah said, turning from the front seat to look at me kindly. "If you need help you can come back and get me, but it's super easy. Just touch anywhere on the door and look into the screen and they'll come let you in."

The screen? I gulped and climbed out of the car. I dreaded this meeting as I walked up the simple stone driveway, which looked just the same as any stone driveway I'd seen before. Forget the fact that I didn't know what the hell that stuff Ariah had said about the screen meant, it was bad enough that I was walking up alone to a stranger's door, unsure of what I was really even supposed to be doing here. Shouldn't I have been given some materials to go over in case this person had questions that my personal experiences couldn't answer? I stopped myself. Did I care what this person did or didn't learn about the year 2020? It wasn't like I was really their professor. I only needed to be concerned about the quality of my class insofar as it would affect the person's willingness to help me get back to my own time. Unfortunately, I didn't really know if that would be relevant to them or not. Surely they would be willing to help me as soon as I told them that I was imprisoned here, regardless of the quality of my performance. Unless they already knew the circumstances, and they were perfectly fine with it. No, I couldn't believe that. I'd downloaded the app myself, and I knew I hadn't known the whole story. I had to give this person the benefit of the doubt.

The house looked surprisingly normal as I made it up to the door. The Tucson tradition of keeping a lawn of rocks instead of grass was maintained, even in this time. I wondered how much it was still the same age old problem of keeping grass alive in such harsh temperatures and little rain, and how much it was just an appreciation of aesthetic tradition. It wasn't until I got to the door that it got weird. In the middle of the normal door was some kind of tablet screen, about one square foot. It had a picture of a grinning monkey with the word "Welcome!" I'd never seen a tablet stuck to a door before, but I did have some familiarity with touch screens, so I tapped on it.

The monkey and its message disappeared, showing my face instead. I stared at it awkwardly, resisting the temptation to move until I found the perfect camera angle. The door opened.

"You must be Lane Reid," a young man said. He was lean but toned, with thick black hair and deep brown eyes. If my friends had seen him, they would've demanded I set him up with them. Considering he lived in a different century, though, I thought the age difference might be too inappropriate.

"That's me," I said, shrugging. Maybe this was the time to demonstrate a glowing personality, but I felt uncharacteristically shy, and like my limbs were made of wood. He didn't hold out his hand to shake mine, fortunately, so I kept my arms by my sides. I wasn't sure they were capable of doing anything else at the moment. He invited me in, so I entered the house. There was a TV wall; the entire wall to my left was made of TV screen. I supposed that invention had been inevitable. Still, I had to admit it was kind of cool to see. On a table next to it, I recognized a Virtual Reality headset. I bet it worked better now than the one I'd tried.

"Do you want to sit down?" he asked, sitting on the couch and motioning for me to sit next to him. It was indigo leather, with a panel of metal buttons on the side of its arm. I wondered what they did, but I wasn't here for that. I sat down and put my hands in my lap instead.

Where was I supposed to start with this? I remembered that Gannicus had run through a spiel about choosing IEducator, but I opted out of that one. My goal was to destroy this app, so I thought I could skip advertising for it. It was weird that Davidson hadn't given me any guidance on this, but maybe he'd suspected that I wouldn't go along with his orders anyway. If so, he was probably right.

"Thank you for having me," I said warmly, looking up at the stranger on the couch through my eyelashes. I wasn't quite shooting for seduction, but I did think it would help if he thought I was cute.

I thought that was probably the best I could do. I'd never been great at flirting with strangers. "What's your name?"

"Titan," he replied, the couch squeaking slightly as he leaned in closer. Alright good, maybe I was sensing a little interest there. This just might work. "Maybe you can tell me what it was like for you to live through a global pandemic." He randomly adjusted the long silver chain he was wearing around his neck, pulling it in different directions. I wondered if he even noticed he was doing it, or if it was just a habit.

"Well, it actually wasn't so bad for me personally. I was scared at first, but there comes a time when you really can't live in fear anymore. You kind of have to move on with your normal life. Maybe that's bad, but eventually regular life took back over."

He was listening intently, so I continued. "There was a long time when I couldn't be around my twin sister, that was really hard."

Thinking of Tamryn opened a hole in my heart, and I had to pause before I could speak again. It had been really hard to go that time without being able to see her, but at least I'd been able to talk to her on the phone. Even if I desperately needed to, I couldn't talk to her now. I wondered what she was doing now. I hoped I could get back to see her soon. It didn't feel right for us to be apart for long; decades apart was more distance that I'd ever imagined sitting between us. Before I could stop myself, I considered what would happen if I failed and couldn't get back. When would she stop waiting for me to come back? She couldn't wait long, because she'd know that if I ever got access to a time machine I'd go back to the week that I left. Would she be able to accept that I was gone?

"I could only talk to her on video chat," I continued, swallowing a lump in my throat and trying to focus on the conversation. "That was better than *nothing*, though." Like now. Now we had no connection. Levi must have had to remind her that this was all part of the plan a hundred times. I swiped at my eyes. Here I was again, losing track of my mission here. My first instinct was to shut it down and refocus, but then I saw Titan's face.

He was staring at me intently, his eyebrows furrowed in concern. His hand reached out towards me for a moment, but he hesitated and pulled it back. Adrenaline shot through me. I actually hadn't been trying to make him feel sorry for me as much as I'd simply been feeling sorry for myself. The fear of not getting back to my own time was real. His reaction, though, was more encouraging than sympathy usually could be. If he already felt concerned for me, he might be willing to help me. Hope sparked in me, but I tried to push it away and dwell on my sorrow. The worst thing I could do was move forward too fast and blow it.

"Are you ok?" he asked, his hand twitching as if he might offer it to me. On it, I saw a plain gold ring. A wedding band. Ah, that I could use.

"Have you ever been in love?" I asked instead of answering. My hunch was supported by the dreamy grin that spread across his face.

"Oh, yes," he replied immediately. "My wife is my heart. I would die if I had to go a day without her."

What if you had to go a lifetime without her? If this man or someone else from this time didn't help me, that could be Gannicus's fate. I wanted to pull Gannicus from inside my head and put him right in front of me, just for a little bit, so I could hold him.

"I love someone too," I said quietly. "But he's back at home, in my own time."

Titan looked stricken, then an expression of confusion crossed his handsome features.

"Why did you choose to leave him?" he asked.

This was it. This was the big moment. If I told him I was here against my will, he'd have to help me go free. I hadn't even asked if he had access to a time machine yet, but surely we could straighten everything out as soon as he agreed to help.

"I didn't choose," I said slowly, watching him closely. "I was kidnapped and taken to your time against my will. I'm being enslaved."

Well maybe that was putting it all out there a little too soon, but I couldn't take it back now. I waited. There was a short pause in which Titan started to open his mouth and then closed it again. Was he going to say anything? My stomach turned. Should I say something else? Did he understand? I thought back to when I'd first met Gannicus, and I'd thought he was just an actor. Did Titan think this was all part of the show? No, he looked stricken. He knew I was telling him a horrible truth. My chest tightened and I felt the need to take a deep breath, but he opened his mouth and I didn't want to discourage him from saying whatever he was about to say.

"I'm sorry to hear that," he finally replied, looking down at his hands. "I hope you see him again someday."

I nodded, wiping my eyes and waiting for him to tell me that he was willing to do what it took to reunite two lovers that were torn apart by such cruelty. I didn't need him to have a clever plan, either. Coming up with plans was apparently part of my new job description since I'd gotten involved with the app, so I could certainly manage to figure something out once I knew what resources he had to help me. I just needed him to express his outrage about the situation and commit to doing his part in changing it.

He didn't. Instead, he offered me a bottle of water.

I immediately deflated. What was water going to do to help me? Could I get on a tiny boat and sail across the 16 ounces to my own time? I didn't think so. There wasn't much else I could do besides accept the water, though. I nodded and watched him walk out of the room, closing my eyes against the sudden sting of disappointment. Well, what was I supposed to do now? I considered asking him point blank for help, but that wasn't without risk. What if he tried to report this conversation to the app? Something tightened in my chest. What if he did? I hadn't even thought of that. He hadn't seemed like the type so far, but I thought I'd better leave it alone in case he did decide to rat me out. It was too late to undo what I'd said so far, but I could avoid bringing it up again.

Instead, I thanked him for the water when he got back, and asked a few questions about the strange material it came in. It was some kind of metallic rubbery substance. I resisted the urge to squeeze the bottle and play with it more than I drank from it. We spent the rest of the hour discussing quarantine efforts and the delights of wearing face masks to the grocery store, until my captors came back to pick me up.

Like it had gone with Gannicus, the pickup went smoothly. Titan saw the SUV appear outside the front window, and pointed it out to me. I handed him my nearly empty bottle and headed out the door, expressing something like thanks for his time, I was really enchanted to get to relive a time in my own life as some kind of academic curiosity after getting my hopes up that you were a decent enough person to not throw me back into slavery. Except it was probably more like "Thanks, have a good day!"

Ariah was the one who picked me up, so I smiled at her when I slid into my seat. Maybe I'd convince her to help me, since Titan had been completely useless.

My return to my room was a unique experience in a complete trip through hell. I hadn't consciously realized it, but I had been completely sure that this was going to work the first time. Sure, I hadn't known if I'd make my pitch the first time I met with someone. Once I actually told someone the truth about the app, though, I was sure they would immediately be outraged and join the fight against it. The feeling causing so much pressure behind my eyes right now was something like disappointment, but it was so enmeshed with a complete loss for what to do next that I didn't have a word to accurately describe it. Despair, maybe?

As I looked at the plain white walls and white sheets of my prison, I considered the possibility that I could spend the rest of my life here, at least until I died of some future disease for which I didn't have an immunity. Ok, I didn't like that thought one bit. I hadn't even considered that I could catch a disease from being here. I had certainly considered that I might be stuck here. In fact, I'd played that one out in my head a few thousand times. It wasn't getting any easier to adjust to the idea, though. And I shouldn't start getting used to the idea.

Chapter 29

This was just one "no." It didn't mean that I wouldn't have any more chances to escape. What really got to me, though, when I thought about it, was that Titan had seemed like the perfect mark. He'd really gotten what I was telling him, and had obvious sympathy. He even connected with me on the experience of being in love! What was so crushing about this loss wasn't that I'd tried my plan out on the first person I met and they'd happened to shoot me down. No, that I thought I could definitely handle. It was the fact that I didn't see how I was going to meet another person who connected so well with me and my story in order to try again.

I collapsed on the bed, succumbing to the numbness of the all-white interior of the bedroom. The bed was so inviting, welcoming me home after a difficult day, that tears burned in my eyes. I yanked the ridiculous pink dress over my head, but got stuck pulling it off. This small irritation could have been enough to make me lose it, so I took a slow breath through my nose and tried again, this time starting with the zipper. Once I was free, I pulled the covers over my head and closed my eyes. I wasn't going to give up, but I was going to give myself a few minutes to wallow in self pity before I forced myself to move forward. As long as I was letting myself pout, maybe I could just close my eyes for a second too.

When I opened them again, it felt much later. My room had no windows, so there was no way to tell for sure. Maybe I should just call it a night and go to bed for real. I wasn't tired anymore, though, and I wanted to get started moving on with my plan right away. So instead of laying back down, I slid off the edge of the bed and made my way to a little brown table a few feet away, where I picked up the tablet Davidson had left for me. The time read 14:00. So 2 o'clock. The first thing I was going to do was figure out how to change the time setting on this thing. I wasn't trying to do math every time I wanted to know what time it was.

What was I supposed to do with myself? I had endless time and nothing to do with it. Unsure of what else to do, I went for a walk around the base. I skipped the elevator, taking the stairs instead. I was afraid the elevator was harder to operate than it looked and I'd get stuck.

I didn't run into anyone on the walk, though part of me wished I would. It was better than being lonely. On my way back to my room, I found myself approaching door 33. What if Gannicus was in there, somehow? What if he'd gotten captured trying to save me?

Before I could talk myself out of it, I knocked hard on the door. I waited, my heart in my throat. No one came to answer it.

I was smiling when I turned and walked back to my room. Knowing he hadn't been imprisoned all over again was a consolation I sorely needed. So even though I thought of it, I didn't let myself dwell on the idea that he could've been dead instead.

I didn't know what to do with myself when I got back to my room, so I picked up the tablet and decided to become familiar with it. I settled into a plastic chair next to a small plastic desk in the "classroom" section of my room, flinching slightly at the unexpected cold of the surface. There were only two apps on the tablet: one for internet, and the other for IEducator. Access to the internet could give me a lot of information about this time, even if I just looked at the news. I barely registered that as an option, though. Taking a deep breath to prepare myself, I opened IEducator and pulled up the list of available classes. Who had Davidson taken to this time?

No, I didn't think I wanted to know. What difference did it make, really? I had a plan and I was going to stick with it, regardless of who was here right now. There was no reason to look through it and upset myself. But. Maybe I'd come across a name I recognized and we could start talking about next steps when I got back.

The first class was "Keeping the Doctor Away One Apple at a Time: Johnny Appleseed." Ok, I did recognize that name but only because I'd learned about him 50 times in elementary school. I'd never actually met him. I scrolled down one more.

"Ten Days in a Mad House: Investigative Journalism with Nellie Bly."

That sounded interesting. I thought I remembered learning something about this woman in college, when I'd taken journalism courses. All I remembered was that she wrote an article or something about an insane asylum, which was pretty much already covered by the title of her class. Well, that was that. Time to see if I could figure what kind of streaming services they had in the future.

I scrolled across the screen of the tablet, but I couldn't get the other instructors off my mind. We were all here in this strange, terrible situation together. It couldn't hurt to actually get to know them.

Opening a webpage, I searched for Nellie Bly. Instead of a series of Google results, a video popped up as soon as I typed her name into the search. As the video started, it expanded beyond the screen and out of the tablet, projecting a holographic screen about the size of a computer in front of me. I resisted the urge to jump back, instead focusing on the images in front of me and the sound that was obviously coming from the tablet but sounded more like it was coming from all around me.

"Nellie Bly was a pioneer for female journalists..." a voiceover started, in a soft yet masculine British accent. The video explained how Nellie Bly, or Elizabeth Cochran, her actual name, pursued a career in journalism despite a lack of interest from men in the field, until she met Joseph Pulitzer, who gave her a writing assignment that would have reasonably terrified any number of journalists: she was told to go undercover as a patient to an insane asylum on Blackwell's Island. In the asylum, she discovered that patients suffered a range of horrors, from ice cold baths and spoiled food to beatings. Some of the patients, she found, were only committed because they spoke another language or because they were poor. The video stopped, at this point, to show what looked like a generic warning stating that the footage shown was not taken by a time traveler, but was instead a reenactment, to avoid "altering the pattern of time." It went on to tell how Nellie was released from the asylum by her editor after 10 days. Her story led to an influx of money to the asylums, and a lot of positive changes in the way that the patients were treated from then on. The video was only a few minutes long, and it left me wanting to know what she was like. After all, she'd only been 23 when she went into the asylum. That was barely older than me.

It occurred to me that if I wanted to know more about her, I could do that. As if my fingers had a mind of their own, I found myself opening up the app and seeing the list of classes again. Nellie Bly's class was numbered with "20." Immediately, I wondered if that 20 might indicate a room number.

Well, there was only one way to find out.

My courage faded when I made it to the door marked "20." Like all the others, it was a heavy door with a white painted surface only interrupted by a small peephole in the center. It was more reminiscent of my time than the current year we found ourselves in, considering there was no screen and no pictures of smiling monkeys.

When it came time to finally knock on the door, I hesitated. What if it wasn't her? What if it was someone like Vlad, or Charles Manson or something? Was Charles Manson still alive in my time? I wasn't sure. What if it *was* her? She probably spent so much of her time talking to people who wanted to hear her story, would she welcome a visitor asking her questions? Was "I was just in the neighborhood killing some time and I thought you might like to chat" an acceptable reason to just knock on someone's door? I sighed. I didn't know what to say because I didn't even know why I was here. After spending my whole life as a twin, and even after my twin moved, still living with my parents, I wasn't used to being alone. As much as I was trying to think of a good excuse to go knocking on doors, the truth was that I was lonely. Besides, I liked to think that I saw some of myself in her. In a way, I was undercover right now, going behind enemy lines to try to learn more about the mistreatment of innocent people. Maybe she'd see some camaraderie in that.

I tapped on the door. I didn't want to knock loudly, in case I drew undue attention to myself from the other rooms. I wasn't sure who was behind this door, but I didn't have a *clue* who was behind the others. I wasn't sure I was ready to find out.

There was no answer. Well, that was anticlimactic. I sighed, and I didn't quite know whether it was from disappointment or relief. It was probably a bit of both. I turned to walk back up to my room, but froze when I heard the rush of air that indicated a door opening.

"Hello," said a kind but confident voice. I looked back to see a middle aged woman with graying hair tied back into an intricate bun, a braid wrapped around the top. She looked ordinary in her appearance, but she had a confidence that made her seem somehow more elegant.

"Hi," I said, stumbling slightly as I turned to move back towards the door. "My name is Lane. I just, um." I sucked in a breath as I tried to think of an explanation for why I was here. "I just moved in."

She smiled wryly, understanding despite my deadpan delivery that the ridiculousness of the situation wasn't lost on me. This wasn't your average apartment complex.

"When are you from?" she asked. I didn't think I'd ever get used to the bizarre switch from wondering *when* someone was from instead of *where*.

"2020," I said.

She raised her eyebrows but didn't say anything. Ok, so it was on me to fill the silence. After all, I was the one who'd shown up at her door. She'd probably expect me to have a reason.

"I literally just got here," I continued, raising my voice against a strange shyness that was making me want to retreat into myself. "Like, yesterday."

To my surprise, her eyebrows furrowed in slight confusion before she smiled politely at me.

"I just arrived this morning myself," she said. "I have been trying to figure out what the purpose is of this place and my being here."

I shifted my weight from one foot to the other, almost forgetting there was someone in front of me as I worked out the implications of what she'd just said. She'd just gotten here? Why? Had Davidson brought in multiple new people to his operation here to go with my arrival? I supposed introducing new "talent" was a good way to keep users on the app.

"Dear," Nellie Bly said carefully, watching me warily. "Are you ill?"

I shook my head. My head was starting to hurt a bit, but it wasn't something I needed to complain about.

"Would you like to come inside?" she asked, opening the simple white door wider to reveal the inside of her apartment. It was just like mine, except in place of the dry erase board there was a simple empty chalkboard.

"Sure, thank you," I said, walking just past her into the apartment, where I turned and waited for her direction. She gestured to a small wooden table and its chairs about halfway between the bedroom section and the classroom section of the apartment, and we both sat down.

"It is concerning," she said, putting her hands together primly in front of her on the table. "As soon as I was told the date, I asked if I might be sent home again. The skinny man with the curly hair told me that I would be sent back soon, and I have not heard from him or anyone else since. I wonder whether he cannot send me back right now, or whether he will not."

I grimaced slightly, rearranging my hands on my lap. It was, obviously, the latter. Would it even help her to know that, though? Maybe it would be better if she didn't know what was going on for as long as possible.

She smiled at me encouragingly, and I immediately felt bad for considering keeping the truth from her. She was clearly smart enough to understand, and brave enough to handle it. What more right did I have to know the truth than she did? Anyway, her whole job had been finding out the truth, so she was going to learn it anyway.

"Actually, I do know something about that," I said, making the decision to just push ahead and get her on the same page as me.

I told her the whole story, from how I'd discovered the app in my own time to how it looked like Davidson was just opening up a new location in 2106 to go with his business in 2020. I tried to sound competent as I explained that I'd been selected as a representative for the prisoners of 2020 to find out the location of the time machine so they'd have somewhere to go once they liberated themselves.

"I had a very similar experience when I was about your age," she said.

Her words flowed easily as she briefly told me her story about the asylum. I could tell this was a story she was used to telling, but the pleasant faraway look in her eye suggested that she didn't mind telling it. Though I had to agree with her many readers over the years that it was a great story, a small detail held my attention. Her editor told her he would liberate her from the asylum after 10 days, and he did. That was, unfortunately, where our stories were different. I had no one coming to bail me out of this nightmare. If I couldn't convince a stranger to rescue me, I was probably stuck in this asylum for good. Titan popped into my head and I remembered how close

I'd gotten, and how he'd completely shattered my hopes. I sort of hoped his fiancee would break up with him.

"I will be alert for any intelligence that might help you," she said. "If I meet any of the others," she gestured around the room in reference to the other inhabitants of these dorm buildings, "I will tell them your story and see how we can help with the escape."

Oh shit. The others in this time. Of course those of us in 2020 would come and save them. Someone could just hop in the time machine and bring it to this year, and send them all back to their own times the same way we planned to do in 2020. That wasn't the problem. Adding another pit stop in the timeline wasn't a dealbreaker. No, I was just now realizing that if Davidson could start his business in 2106 and 2020, what would stop him from starting it in 2032 or 1999 or any other year that he took his time machine? Sure, if we waited until he was in 2020 and destroyed his time machine, he'd be stuck in 2020. Until he made a new time machine and started this whole thing over. Shit.

Was there a way to stop someone from doing something for the rest of their life? Besides sending them to jail, which we'd already ruled out because that would draw law enforcement attention we didn't want. Maybe we could report him to the authorities after everyone got sent home. Except that meant that there'd be no witnesses to testify, and more importantly, that would draw legal attention to Gannicus and Levi, which was out of the question. What if we captured him and kept him somewhere so that he couldn't invent anything anymore? I grimaced. That seemed a lot like what he'd done to us, which was just straight up kidnapping. It didn't make me feel better that the only other idea that popped into my head was murder. Was getting rid of Davidson for good the only way to solve this problem? It wouldn't be the first time someone in history had been willing to kill for their freedom. Gannicus hadn't exactly used diplomacy to escape slavery. Goosebumps emerged from my skin at the thought. I wasn't willing to take Davidson out myself, I knew that much. But was I willing to stand by and let someone, maybe even Gannicus, do it? No. I refused to think about this. I was not in charge of this decision. I had to do what I came here to do, and I'd tell the others my concerns when I got home. If I got home.

Right now I was getting tired of the direction of my thoughts. I turned my attention back to Nellie Bly.

"Well, you know all about going behind enemy lines undercover," I said. "Any advice?"

"Look for the good-hearted people. There are always some."

I thanked Nellie for her advice and stood up, sensing an end to the conversation. I made my way back to my door, stopping for a moment when I heard music coming from inside. Instinctually I froze, my stomach dropping. Who was in there? I supposed anyone could've gotten in there, since I didn't have a key and hadn't locked it on my way out. I put my head closer to the door.

I didn't hear anyone moving around in there. I twisted the knob and threw open the door in one panicked motion anyway, since I really didn't know anything for sure. My heart rate started to decrease as I took in the empty room and saw that I'd been right. The music was coming from my tablet, which was lit up in the middle of my thick white comforter.

Without the walls in the way, I could hear now that it was playing a strange type of music, with a drum-like beat that sounded too digital to be made by a real drum. The singer bellowed in a deep baritone about someone breathing lightning. That was the first time I'd heard the slang of the future, and I spent a moment contemplating what it meant. It was too hard to make out all the lyrics to try to piece together the meaning behind the song. I tried to give it a chance, but I decided I hated the music of the future. My kids would definitely not think I was cool when I had them.

I didn't know much about the future, but I didn't think tablets would be created to play music to empty rooms. As soon as I put this together, I shot forward and snatched it up, expecting to see an incoming call from Davidson, since he was the only person who would conceivably have this number. Instead, the screen was lit up with the iEducator icon. Before the song could end, I tried to answer the call. I tried tapping on it and swiping across it, but nothing was working. Finally some combination of swiping worked, and a holographic image of a man appeared above it.

"Hello," he said as soon as I saw him. He was probably in his late thirties, with curly bleach blonde hair. I wondered if I was a hologram for him too. I couldn't help it; I had to swipe my hand across the image of the man in front of me, watching the image break up and reassemble when I pulled my hand back. The future was weird.

"Hi," I said awkwardly, wondering how you were supposed to talk to a stranger in the future who called you randomly and was now a hologram in your room. Could he see the whole room? Could the little holograph version of him spin around in a circle and look at everything?

"I wanted to take your class on the pandemic of 2020, if you're available." He spoke politely and with some hesitation, like this was the first time he'd arranged to take a class. I supposed it had to be, since Davidson had just brought me and the others here. I wondered how much time he spent advertising for the app before he brought in the instructors.

So. My class on the pandemic of 2020. I hesitated. My experience with Titan had left a bad taste in my mouth, and part of me wanted to avoid another interaction with these "customers." After all, if I hadn't convinced Titan, what chance did I have of convincing this guy? How would I know when it was appropriate to tell him about my situation? I'd clearly read things wrong with Titan, and I was lucky that things hadn't gone a lot worse than they did. This new person might report me to Davidson immediately. What would happen then? If Davidson knew that keeping me here alive was a risk, maybe he'd just toss me in the incinerator and be done with it. My hands started to shake at the thought. I couldn't have that. I was very tempted to let the negative thoughts consume me and grant me the opportunity to lay in bed for a week, pretending I was sick with the flu instead of trapped in the future. If I did that, though, I'd be staying trapped in the future. The longer it took me to find someone sympathetic to my situation, the more time I'd waste languishing away here instead of seeing my boyfriend and my family.

I didn't want to be here. I wanted to go home.

"Yes," I said, with as much casual friendliness as I could muster. "I'm available at 9 am tomorrow."

Chapter 30

Ariah was there the next morning, knocking lightly on my door. Despite my hesitation about accepting the class, I was ready, dressed in a long purple dress with lace at the sleeves. Somehow Victorian Chic was the fashion of the early 2100's. Seeing fashion from another time was kind of exciting, I had to admit. It was one of the few parts of my situation that brought me any joy. That and the fact that I knew I was here for a reason, even if I was in the hard part right now. Who knew? Maybe the guy I met today would be the one to hear my story and commit to helping me get back.

I tried not to think about what I'd do when I got back, now that the situation had gotten more complicated. Well, it had always been this complicated, I just hadn't thought of it until now. The fact that Davidson could just move to a new time and start this whole thing over again didn't leave my mind all night, as hard as I tried to remind myself that I needed to focus on one day at a time, and that tomorrow would worry about itself. Was I willing to be a part of it if we needed to... take him off the map? Take care of him? Whatever euphemistic phrase people used to make killing someone seem not as horrifying? I was leaning towards no. How could I live with myself? On the other hand, what was the point of all of this if Davidson could just continue on with his evil plans?

"Good morning," Ariah said when I opened the door, obviously oblivious to the conflict in my mind that threatened her boss's very life. She was wearing blue golf shorts and a white shirt, a simple outfit that made the day's situation seem a little bit more normal. I wondered if that was the appropriate business attire of the day.

Though I had escape on my mind, Ariah and I got to know each other better as we headed to the car. I found myself asking a lot of questions on our relatively short walk, eager to take my mind off of more stressful matters. After very little prying on my part, she shared that she was an only child who'd felt a burden to make something special of herself. I related to part of that story. College had fallen out of fashion by this time, so she finished school at 18 and started working for Davidson's tech company soon after that. Not for the first time, I wondered if she could be an ally. Just because she worked here didn't mean she knew that we were here against our will, right? It was entirely possible that the others she'd transported had been too afraid of retaliation to tell her the truth.

Almost as soon as we sat in the car, Ariah was pulling up to a house. It was unnerving, this instant travel. I didn't even have time to look for a seatbelt. Now that I was here, I gazed out the window at our surroundings. This neighborhood looked more like San Francisco than Tucson, with a street full of brightly colored row houses. Ariah parked on the street and directed me with a pointed finger to an orange one. She shared that orange was her favorite color, and I might have considered whether to tell her that orange was my least favorite color, if there hadn't been too much on my mind. Instead, I was considering whether this whole thing wouldn't be easier if I just skipped meeting this guy who owned the orange house, and tried my luck by telling Ariah the whole story and begging for her to drive me to Davidson's time machine and let me go home.

"Make sure you stay there until I come to get you," she said, as if reading my mind. "Davidson doesn't like it when people get lost." Her tone was friendly, but her smile didn't reach her eyes. Maybe it was my imagination, conjuring a hidden threat where there was only friendly advice. There was something so creepy about saying that Davidson didn't like it, though, that it was hard to convince myself that the chill I felt could be attributed to my own paranoia. There *had* been something there, in her eyes. A deeper meaning to inane words. Startled, I only nodded and slid out of the car.

Alright, so maybe Ariah wasn't the one to talk to about this. That didn't mean I didn't have any hope. I was here to meet someone new, someone who could just as easily be the savior I was looking for. This time when I got to the door with the screen, I knew what to do. This one had a picture of a beach ball. I tapped on it and waited until the man from the hologram call quickly came to let me inside.

The interior of his house was distinctly, strikingly 1970's themed. I was surprised people in this time even remembered the '70's, much less designed their homes based on the decade. The carpet was dark brown, with a large orange rug in the middle. In the middle of the living room was a lowered conversation pit, with tan couches adorned with bright yellow pillows. In my time, it would've been weird to see a room like this. I didn't know if it was better or worse that this room was found in the future. Was this considered antique?

"My name is Warrior," the man said, inviting me to sit on one of the couches.

"I'm Lane," I said, unsure whether he already knew that or not. No one had told me how to act in these meetings, so all I could do was say what felt natural and hope I didn't ruin my plan before I'd even really started. "Your house is nice."

"Does it remind you of home?" he asked, his eyes lighting up. What? Who was I, Marcia Brady?

"No," I replied plainly, though I felt a bit sorry when he glanced at his hands in his lap, disappointed. He wasn't even *close* to my time, and I wasn't going to lie to him. I didn't really know why I couldn't just lie to him, but it felt wrong somehow. I was here to tell him about my time, and it seemed ridiculous to start that off by making things up. To assuage his feelings, or maybe just to ignore them, I decided to change the subject. "Let's talk about the virus."

I told him about the quarantine, about the months that people were expected to stay in their homes unless they worked for a business that was deemed essential. My heart lifted when he asked if people ever went out in those days. I sensed an opportunity to discuss my favorite topic, my love.

"Yes. Actually, I met my boyfriend on an app and we met in person..." I faded out, seeing Gannicus in my imagination. Damn, I missed him.

"He's dead now, huh? If you're from 2020?" Warrior asked academically, as if it was the most natural question in the world. My stomach dropped. I wanted to snap that his stupid '70's interior design was dead. Who would say something like that? I took a deep breath and tried to remind myself that this was 80 years in the future, so he might think there was some emotional distance there. I'd just come from my time a few days ago, but he didn't necessarily know that. There was no reason to lash out at him.

"No," I said instead, even though it didn't even make sense. How did I know if Gannicus was alive in this time? What did that even mean, with his life of time travel? I said it for myself, though, barely aware that someone was listening. "He's alive and he's happy and he's free." Gannicus might not exist in this time, but he was alive and well in mine. That was real right now, in a way.

"That's good," Warrior said, widening his beady eyes to no one in particular like he thought I was crazy and raising his eyebrows to his slightly thinning hair. It was off putting, being the only audience to his facial mockery of me. I was beginning to get tired of entertaining this guy. He made it a lot worse by sliding closer to me on the couch. "It's ok if you feel lonely, though. I could help with that." He placed a hand on my thigh.

My heart immediately rose into my throat. I hadn't prepared for a situation like this. My eyes darted around the room, looking for evidence that someone else lived in this house too, someone who might be called to help if things took a turn for the worse. There was one pair of men's shoes by the entrance to the hallway, which I imagined belonged to him. There were two pictures on the shelf, but they were both of Warrior by himself in various vacation spots. I breathed out slowly through my nose. The tastelessness of his timing made me nervous, like maybe he didn't really care if I was interested or not. No, I was catastrophizing. All I had to do was let him down easy, give him a way out. If I could politely turn him down, maybe we could move on and let this all fall behind us.

I scooted away, sliding across the couch until I was stopped by the arm.

"Oh, that's ok," I said, a friendly smile hiding my tension. "I'm working on myself right now."

I waited for his reaction. To my immense relief, he stayed where he was, shrugging off the rejection. He muttered some form of agreement and shifted the conversation away. I tried to keep from visibly sagging with relief. Warrior might have been a little odd, but apparently he wasn't dangerous.

As we got to talking, he told me he was fascinated by the past. He loved to watch movies from my century, especially once they started Virtual Reality movies. I wasn't quite sure what Virtual Reality movies were, but I thought I could figure it out from the name. Besides, I was here to tell him about my time, and to eventually convince him to help me get back to it. I didn't need to ask him questions about the movies of his time, beyond what questions were required for polite conversation. His favorite movie was *Sandstorm*. I nodded politely, even though I'd never heard of that movie because it hadn't been invented yet. When he told me I was lucky to have lived in my time and then get to experience this one, I didn't argue.

It reminded me of when I'd once told Gannicus it seemed fun to be a teacher, and the expression on his face had betrayed that he disagreed. Little had I known that he wasn't teaching as part of a job, but because he was biding his time until he could set a plan in motion to break free. With all of his thoughtless comments, Warrior was no more ignorant than I was. I hoped I still looked cooler to Gannicus than this guy looked to me, though.

As off-putting as it was to be thrust into a completely new time, it gave me a deeper understanding of Gannicus than I'd had before. Though we'd had countless conversations about our feelings and experiences, this was different. Now I'd actually felt what he'd felt. It was both better and worse, knowing the truth from this side. It was painful to look straight on at the fact that Gannicus had seen me as clueless, participating unknowingly in his suffering for so long. It twisted in my gut. On the other hand, though, I saw how he could have managed to forgive me. It wasn't my fault that I hadn't known. No one, including him, had told me. Just as I had the power to tell Warrior my situation right now, Gannicus had had the opportunity to tell me. For his own reasons, he'd chosen not to. Maybe it was time to stop blaming myself for that.

I suddenly refocused on Warrior when a key phrase in his ramblings grabbed my attention.

"I'm sorry," I interrupted. "Did you just say you have a time machine?" He blinked at me for a moment, as if displeased that this was the reason I'd stopped him from telling whatever boring story he'd been telling.

"Yes," he said sharply. "I have a time machine. Everyone here has a time machine."

Everyone here has a time machine. The beginnings of a plan started to form as hope blossomed in my chest. I didn't think I'd ask Warrior if I could use his time machine. I didn't have any indication so far that I could trust him, and I doubted I was going to get any going forward. Maybe in the near future, though, I could find a way to escape from someone's house and find their time machine.

"Can you show me how it works?"

With some reluctance, Warrior stood up and led me down a hallway to a small room that looked like it might have originally been a large closet. Inside was a machine, designed just like the one I'd taken with Davidson to get to this time. My breath quickened. Here it was. I needed one of these so bad, and there was one right in front of me. I tried not to give away too many of my thoughts. Oblivious, Warrior continued by showing me how to use the dial to set the time and explained how to start it if there was no one on the outside to push the button, though he warned that it was always best to have a buddy when traveling through time.

"Wow," I said, reaching a slow, tentative hand towards the large glass cylinder in front of us. "It would be pretty cool to see how this one works."

"Eh, it's pretty much like all the others," Warrior said, turning and leaving the small room. He stopped just outside the door, tapping his feet on the thick carpet as he waited for me to follow him. I tried not to look too disappointed. I tried not to *feel* too disappointed. After all, this was a positive. Everyone in the future had time machines! I could talk to anyone I met from here on out and if they were inclined to help me, they could. And they would, right? Right? I pushed the doubts aside for the moment.

I followed Warrior back into the living room, listening as politely and attentively as I could while he rambled on about the most boring aspects of his life. Ariah came soon after, to my relief.

Now that I knew these people had time machines, it was only a matter of time before I convinced one of them to let me use it to set myself free. I'd only need it to get home, and then I'd find a way to get it back to them. Surely they'd be ok with that kind of arrangement. Of course, that would be like allowing a stranger to borrow your car. I thought about my own car, and what I would do if someone came to me in desperate need, begging to borrow it. I tried to imagine myself hearing their story, weighing the risks in my head. I cringed. Now that I knew what a desperate situation really was, I liked to think that I'd be willing to help someone who came along and needed me. When I held that up against the image of handing a stranger my keys, though, it fell flat. I needed my car. I had to go places. Uh oh. I wasn't too much less generous than the average person, I hoped, and yet, I wouldn't be able to do it. The chances of someone giving me their machine were looking smaller. Miniscule, in fact. The chances were the size of ant shoes.

When I made it to my room, I stumbled to a chair by my little table and fell down into it. It was time to get realistic. How was I going to get out of here? I considered my family back home, and my stomach clenched. My parents didn't even know where I was. Would Tamryn cover for me? How? If she said that I was staying with her and Levi, they'd still expect me to answer my phone at some point. She'd have to tell them that I broke it. At that point, my parents would want to talk to me about getting a new phone, because I didn't really have new phone money. Would she cave? Admit to them that their daughter had been kidnapped and thrown somewhere into the depths of time, with no obvious way of getting back?

It was too hot in here. I paced the room, looking for a thermostat along the white walls and not finding one. I was starting to wish I'd listened to Gannicus. This had been a stupid plan. I couldn't remember now why I'd thought it had been a good one. I took a deep breath. Well, I tried to. It got stuck in my chest, not going deep enough into my lungs. I leaned forward, putting my hands on my thighs as I tried to catch a full breath. The more I thought about it, though, the worse it got. I closed my eyes and tried to relax. So what, the plan sucked. I'd get a new one.

I wouldn't ask if I could use someone's time machine. Yes! I could take it. Could I take it? Just ask to use the bathroom and throw myself inside, press a few buttons and find my way back? That was stealing, but wasn't it ok in a situation like this? I sighed, massaging the bridge of my nose where I was starting to get a headache. No, it wasn't ok, and I didn't have it in me to steal.

I jumped when the phone rang, blasting that same moaning song from before. Sooner or later I was going to have to change that awful ringtone. I slid it open to be greeted again by Titan.

Not this guy again. The last thing I needed was to be reminded just how much harder this whole plan was to execute than I'd imagined.

"I need to see you again," he said, with startling urgency.

He needed to see me again. Why? I wasn't anyone to him. I was just some girl whose dreams he crushed like 24 hours ago. He must have been really desperate. Was he in some kind of trouble? Was it related to the app? It had to be, or else I imagined he'd ask anyone else for help rather than some stranger from the past. Were there issues with his app account? Another instructor? How on earth was I supposed to help with that? I thought about the time Vlad escaped. I hoped this wasn't going to be like that. And if he needed help getting the app to work, he was definitely calling the wrong person. Not only did I not know very much about their modern technology, but me helping him work on this app would be like a cow helping someone open a butcher shop.

I tried to ask him for details, but he just shook his head. It was a bit of a pet peeve of mine, when people asked me for a favor without telling me what the favor was. It was like they were trying to manipulate me into saying yes, to take away my chance to make a good decision. It was usually because the favor sucked. Nonetheless, I agreed to see him the next day, if only to satisfy my curiosity.

Instead of Ariah, a man I'd never seen before came to pick me up for my meeting the next day. He was certainly old enough to be retired, maybe ten years older than my parents. I wondered if the life expectancy was longer in the future, leading people to work for more of their lives. I hoped that was the case, instead of him just having to work longer than average to continue supporting himself. He said his name was Joffrey. What little hair he had left on his head was white, and he wore thick glasses. I didn't know anything about him, but his smile was genuine. I didn't know if he knew the details of my situation, and I didn't want to know. I was happy enough to see a friendly face, so I followed him out the door and towards the parking lot feeling slightly encouraged.

We made it to the car eventually, slowed by his glacial pace. It didn't bother me; I was in no hurry to see Titan. I'd checked him off the list of people who could help me by now, so why should I want to help him? I didn't want to be mean or bitter when he told me what he needed me for, but I couldn't see myself being particularly thrilled about lending a hand. He'd been nice enough, though. I was going to hear him out at least.

When we made it up to the familiar house, I decided I should be prepared for a longer meeting. Titan hadn't given me details, but he'd seemed serious. And actually, the fact that he hadn't given me any details gave some information too. If it were just a small favor or he wanted to know more about 2020, he'd have just told me. Whatever this was, it was going to take time. I told Joffrey that I might take a little longer than an hour if that was ok. I didn't know if he had the authority to say yes or no, but I asked as if he did.

"You take your time, honey," he said, turning back to the steering wheel as he waited for me to exit the car. Well, that part had been easy, at least. I waved to him when I got up to the house, and he pulled away.

Chapter 31

Titan opened the door before I'd even touched it, apparently eager to see me. He moved his arm out towards me as if to pull me inside, but stopped himself at the last minute. I was glad about that. I wasn't particularly fond of men I barely knew physically pulling me into their houses and shutting the door behind us. Still, I wondered what had happened to make him look so frantic. He handed me a water bottle, practically punching me in the hand with it, and motioned for me to sit on the couch. I tried not to show any hesitation as I complied, watching him sit across from me. He sat and fidgeted for a moment, pulling on the bottom of his blue and white checkered shirt.

"I missed it," he said as soon as he considered us ready. "Lane, I'm so sorry I frogged it."

He what? That had to be some form of new slang. I got that he was saying he messed up somehow. Frankly, though, I was a little annoyed by how cryptic he was being. How did he expect me to help if I didn't have a clue what he was talking about? I raised my eyebrows expectantly, prompting him to continue.

"You said you were a slave. You needed me to set you free. I didn't know what I was supposed to do, so I just let the moment pass. But when I lay in bed next to my wife last night, I thought about you." He stopped. "No, I mean, I thought about your problem. You should be with your love."

Oh. Oh.

This was it. I felt the emotions before my brain really registered what he was saying. My heart swelled with friendly love for this man, who finally cared about me in a world of people who didn't. He was going to help me. This was it. I was going to see Gannicus. My brain started its chant: *Gannicus, Gannicus, Gannicus.* I didn't know what to say, and I was terrified to say the wrong thing. If I scared him away now, then I was well and truly lost. No, I had to hope that wouldn't happen. He meant it. He cared. Relief choked me, and I cleared my throat.

"Thank you," I whispered, grasping Titan's hands for a brief moment before freeing them. "Thank you so much."

I did it. I got someone to agree to help me. I knew where Davidson kept his time machine, so I knew how to send them all back. The plan wasn't so stupid after all. Ha! I'd *told* Gannicus that it would work. I smiled. Gannicus.

Emotion was attempting to paralyze me, but I struggled through it. It was time to get down to business. Anyway, this was the part where I had to make a request that might not be taken well. Sure, he was willing to help. But how much was he willing to do?

"I need your time machine."

Titan stood up quickly and I followed, both of us walking through the house. We passed more wall-size TV's, and an array of strange gadgets in the kitchen. Though I was somewhat curious, I was too excited to ask any questions as we went through. Maybe someday I'd come back here and ask all the questions I had. Eh, I doubted it. Titan didn't stop until we made it to a back room full of metal objects. Judging from the brushes and sponges attached, I gathered they were for cleaning. The glass cylinder in the corner, however, was not.

"This is it," Titan said, leading me to the time machine. It had the same tube-shaped light bulbs and dials as the other two I'd seen. Apparently variety in time machines was unnecessary. "I have to go with you, though. Otherwise I won't ever get the time machine back." He laughed awkwardly, but I sighed in relief. I'd been dreading bringing up the issue of how to get the machine back to him, and this was such a simple solution. I couldn't believe how this was all turning out. Just last night I'd been hopeless.

"Please make sure Joffrey doesn't get in trouble when you get back," I said as we climbed into the machine. Titan's skin was warm against me, but I tried not to be uncomfortable. I had a million thoughts running through my head, but I was glad that I'd remembered the people I was leaving behind, even the ones who belonged in this century. Davidson was the type of person to use people and never consider how it affected them; I wouldn't be. "Joffrey is the man who dropped me off. And make sure you tell them when you get back that I attacked you and ran off."

Titan nodded, the slight shaking motion causing him to shift more against me. It was claustrophobic in this little glass tube, but I reminded myself that it was my ride to Gannicus. With that in mind I'd have climbed into a salt shaker if necessary. Titan asked if I wanted the machine set to a different location, explaining it could travel across distance as well. My plan took me back to Tucson, though, so I told him our location was just fine. Any traveling I had in Tucson could be done the old-fashioned way. The less variables I put into this equation, the better. Instead, I raised my hand in a motion for him to send us off. This time, the weightless feeling of traveling didn't scare me as much. I was just happy to be going home.

Actually, three months before home. I hoped that was the right estimate. I needed a time far enough back that Davidson wouldn't know who I was, but not so far back that he hadn't finished his new prototype yet. I needed to get rid of every time machine that existed in the past.

There was something scary about going back further than the day I'd been taken. I'd seen enough movies with time travel to know that there were at least theoretical risks, like altering the path of time or some nonsense. I didn't really know; I usually slept through science fiction movies. Now I was kind of wishing I hadn't. When we'd both climbed out of the machine, Titan showed me how to operate a time machine myself. He moved to set up the machine for his departure, but I stopped him. For the next minute at least, I had someone with me who ought to know a little more about time traveling than I did. It would be a good idea to ask him what I could.

Like, what if I went back to my own time and Gannicus didn't know me or didn't love me? What if I stepped on a butterfly and then went back to my real time 3 months in the future and suddenly chickens were carnivorous?

"What if I change the future by going back? Like, more than I intend to?" I asked Titan, hoping he'd understand what I meant. I didn't want to give the chicken example, but I would if I had to. His forehead wrinkled.

"But this is your own time, is it not?" he asked.

"Well, no. It's actually three months before. But I have to catch someone off guard. Will I change the parts of the future that are really important to me if I do that, though?" My eyes stared into his, pleading with him to understand. Something clicked as recognition set on his face, and he nodded.

"You won't lose your love," he smiled knowingly. "Just don't interact with your past self. And don't tell people in the past about the future - that could change their actions. Make as little impact as you can in the past, and return to your own time. Good luck." He turned to go back to the time machine, but he stopped. "Actually, this is only for emergencies, but there is one way to make sure you don't change people's future actions."

He stuck his head back into the time machine and waited for me to do the same. He pushed down on a metal box in the machine, and the top of it opened. Inside a little plastic case was a small electronic device shaped like a cotton swab.

"Put this in the ear of someone if you want to erase their memories. Tap it for each day you want to erase. It can be dangerous if it's overused, so be careful." He placed the metal cotton swab back into its container and handed it to me.

"Thank you, Titan," I said. That was the only thing I knew to say, but I wanted to say more. Without him I might have been trapped in the future for the rest of my life. That was a heavy favor that he'd done for me, and I didn't know how to thank him for it at all. I just wanted him to have the happiness that he deserved. "I hope things work out for you."

"You too, Lane," he said simply, climbing into the machine after setting the dials. I waved, even though the glass of the door wasn't very clear and I didn't know if he could see me. Suddenly, the machine was gone. If I wanted to make it back to my own time, I'd have to find another one. Luckily, that was all part of the plan.

By the time I made it to the IEducator base, I was coated in a thin layer of sweat. I was lucky that we'd popped up in a part of Tucson that I recognized, because I didn't have my phone to look up directions. I wasn't sure if the base was searchable on my phone's maps anyway. Wearing this weird future dress had been an enormous mistake, though. It felt like a thousand degrees, and the big pattern of cracked eggs all over the skirt was drawing unwanted attention, even earning me a few honks on my walk. I might have asked Titan to drop me off at the base, but I was hesitant to tell him the whole plan. Besides, it wasn't like I knew the coordinates. So I'd had no choice but to walk the whole way, which turned out to be about three miles.

When I made it to the base, I wasn't concerned about getting in. This was before they'd met me, so I was protected by anonymity. I hadn't even downloaded the app yet. Taking a deep breath and putting my shoulders back, I approached the guard shack with confidence. I'd had a three mile walk to consider what I'd say, and I was feeling confident.

"What's all this?" I asked the guard, just to gauge his level of intensity. I wanted to know if he'd answer simple questions, or get straight to telling me to leave. My guess was that he wouldn't be too aggressive. He couldn't have been more than seventeen, with an unfortunate amount of acne and brown hair to his shoulders.

"This is a dormitory for," he started quietly, but I cut him off. I had already determined he wasn't a threat. Unfortunately for him.

"I've heard of this! Thanks for your help," I said, walking past the tower and onto the base. My heart rose in my throat as I wondered if maybe I'd been too bold, assuming he wouldn't come after me. I relaxed pretty quickly though, when he just raised his voice slightly, not bothering to leave the guard shack. He stuttered an admonition, begging me to come back because he wasn't supposed to allow people in, but I pretended not to hear him. I'd be back before he could wonder why I was there. I was taking a chance that he'd be too afraid of getting in trouble to report my entrance to more competent security. It was a risk I had to take.

As soon as the sight of the back of his head assured me he was no longer watching, I took off running across the parking lot. I supposed I had unlimited time, but the nervous pain in my stomach demanded that I get to the building I was seeking *right now*.

I flew past identical buildings, counting them as I went past, listening to my feet hitting the concrete. I kept an ear out for the sound of pounding steps behind me, but in my terror it was hard to tell the echoes of my own footsteps from anything more threatening. I was lucky enough not to see or hear anyone, despite my best efforts to stay aware of my situation. When I got to the right building, I slowed down to take a necessary breath before I tore up the stairs. It was good to take a breather and take stock of the situation. It was also necessary, because it felt like someone was squeezing my calf muscles very tightly. By the time I got to the third floor, I had switched from running to creeping, each step becoming more terrifying than the last.

Before I could talk myself out of it, I knocked on door 33.

Chapter 32

My heart pounded when I felt more than saw the doorknob turning. Apprehension hit me in the chest, hard. Was this a mistake? Would I risk having him in the future if I saw him now in the past? I told myself that the reason I was here was not just to visit, and seeing him was an element of my plan. I even thought it might be true. Right or wrong, it was sending my heartbeat into overdrive. Part of me wanted to turn and run. Part of me wanted to tear the door off its hinges because it was taking so long to open, and I wanted to see him *now*.

There he was. I took a step back, lightheaded, as I took in his tall, muscular body and the kind face I knew so well by now. I wondered if he'd be willing to go along with me, even though he didn't even know me.

"Tamryn?" he said when we made eye contact. "What are you doing here?"

Of course! He thought I was Tamryn. I'd been through this exchange before. This time, I thought it better not to correct him. I was sort of disappointed that he wouldn't know I was his future love, but that wasn't actually important right now. I knew how to erase his memories from the day, but it was an unnecessary correction. There was no reason to sit here and explain the whole story when he'd forget it all by the time I saw him again. He'd have his whole life to know me; he didn't need to meet me right now.

"Yeah, I know, it's weird that I'm here," I said, inwardly cringing at how little I sounded like Tamryn. Why was it so difficult to imitate someone I'd spent my whole life with? "But I need your help."

He studied me for a moment, and I tried not to shrink back from his attention. Even if he spent all day staring at me, he wasn't going to guess that Tamryn had a twin sister. That would be an absurd assumption to make, even if it happened to be true. I was anxious all the same, resisting the urge to bounce on my toes.

"What event brings you here?" he asked, just barely squinting his eyes. He was so beautiful. My stomach flipped in response, rejoicing at the chance to see the man I loved. I'd really thought I never would again. It was strange, watching him interact with me this way. He thought he knew me, but he had no idea. He had no idea that one day he'd know the shape of my lips like he knew his own face in the mirror, or that I'd know the place on his stomach where he was ticklish and the way his voice sounded when he quietly sang along to "Thunder Rolls" by Garth Brooks. It almost seemed like he should know me, instinctually. Like the string that connected us should pull him into me right now. I smiled kindly at him, as if I felt nothing but friendship for this angel in front of me. It was the acting performance of a lifetime just to resist kissing him.

"It's better if you don't ask questions," I said in response. "We have to pick up one more person before we go."

Without another word, Gannicus closed the door behind him and followed me, down the stairs and to the next building. I didn't know where our next ally was, but he did. That was why he got to come on this little trip. Well, that and the fact that I couldn't stop myself from visiting him, even though he didn't know me yet. If I had to choose a tour guide in this place, he was the obvious choice.

"Where's Dr. Chien-Shiung Wu?" I asked quietly, watching carefully for any unexpected visitors. I'd had to ask a little louder than the whisper I would have preferred, since he was way ahead of me, walking ahead and turning around the stucco corners of the building. Before I could repeat my question, he waved me forward and led the way to room 12.

"Allow me to introduce our purpose. She knows me," he said when we got to the door. "What do you need from her?"

There was no way to give him the whole explanation quickly enough right now. I didn't know everything about Dr. Wu or her work on the Manhattan Project; maybe I'd get a chance to ask her. I did know, from a passing story Gannicus had told me, that he'd heard Davidson had asked her help in developing a time machine prototype. We didn't even know if she'd said yes. More than that, I didn't know now if she'd say yes to helping us.

"I just need her to come with us."

I ducked out of sight under the staircase while Gannicus discussed the situation with the physicist. Without knowing the story, she might not be willing to come along. My heart beat a quicker rhythm as I waited impatiently to see whether or not Gannicus would return alone. If she wouldn't go with us, I'd have to come up with some way to convince her. Before I could entirely lose my patience, Gannicus appeared in front of the stairs, an elderly Chinese woman in a white jacket standing behind him.

"Thank you for your help," I said, shaking her hand. It was a bit presumptuous, but I had to imagine that if she'd come this far she was open to hearing my plan. For a moment I was self-conscious about my outfit, but this woman had lived through the 90's. She was aware of bad fashion. "I need your help destroying a time machine. I wouldn't know enough about the technology to do it right, and I'm hoping you do. We don't want it to be a problem that's easily fixed." She smiled meaningfully.

"I believe I can help with that," she said, stepping back to let me lead the way. I suddenly relaxed, rolling back my tense shoulders. This was working.

It might have been nice to have a larger team assembled, but I was afraid to take too long briefing a whole crew. Besides, I couldn't take the chance that someone here would be hostile to the plan and report us. I was anonymous to Davidson in this time, and I wanted to stay that way.

When we made it to the parking lot, I was suddenly struck by the realization that I didn't have a car with me. I'd walked here. In my egg dress. Now I'd have to walk back in my egg dress, but it got worse than that. I'd have to tell my two new guests that *they* had to walk three miles, in the Tucson heat. And one of them was in her 80's. There was nothing for it. I couldn't exactly call an Uber. The sight of the gate guard across the parking lot made my heart sink further. How was I going to get two people out of here without him reporting us? We would just have to wait until he left.

I explained the issue with the guard apologetically, but Gannicus and Dr. Wu didn't seem phased. I reminded myself that at this point they were probably already working on their own escape plan, which might have involved bloodshed. After my role in the plan was done, it still might. I didn't actually get to hear too much about their plan at the meeting before everyone had suggested that I be used as bait. The three of us sat on the side of the first building, where we'd be unlikely to be seen by the people who lived on the base. While we waited, I briefed my team on the plan. We'd find both of Davidson's time machines, send everyone home, and destroy them. Davidson wouldn't be able to start the app in a new time without them. Unless he reinvented it. That was what I'd realized with Nellie Bly.

"Shit," I whispered, earning two confused looks. Yikes, I hadn't meant to say that out loud. I shook off the embarrassment and went straight to explaining the problem. "I'm planning to destroy Davidson's time machine, but that's only a temporary solution. What's to stop him from making another one?"

Dr. Wu smiled. I hadn't been expecting that response.

"As long as Davidson is in this century when you destroy his machines, he won't be creating anything. He didn't invent anything."

What?

My face must have betrayed my confusion, because she continued.

"Davidson isn't from this time. He wasn't the one who actually invented the time machine. When he brought me from my own time, expecting from my reputation as the First Lady of Physics that I'd be able to help him create a new time machine prototype, he told me. I suspect he was boasting about his ingenuity. He told me that he'd grown up in a world where time machines existed, but they were heavily regulated due to their ability to drastically alter the future. Unfortunately for us, his father was high up in the agency that maintained the machines, and Davidson managed to use his father's access to get his hands on one. He brought the machine to your lifetime and introduced himself as its creator. From there he could change anything he wanted. Despite his lack of ability to invent something of his own, he is very intelligent, and his plan has been successful this far. Clearly."

A small light of encouragement burned in my chest. Davidson couldn't just create a new time machine if we destroyed his. He didn't know how. I didn't have to find a way to lock him up or kill him (not that I'd really been too committed to that idea anyway). All I had to do was make sure he was in 2020 when our revolt happened.

Chapter 33

It was at least an hour before the guard left, crossing the parking lot and disappearing through a door in one of the first buildings. I felt myself finally relax the tension I'd been holding since we started waiting. I'd started to get nervous that they would give up on the plan if the guard took too long to leave, and I wouldn't have been able to blame them. It had been a bit of an undeveloped idea. But it worked. As soon as he closed the door, we left our hiding spot and started moving. Considering one of my teammates was at least 80, speed wasn't on our side. I imagined a rope holding me to the base as I tried to resist the urge to sprint across the parking lot, sticking with my new team instead. With every step I felt like the target on our backs grew. I would have taken Gannicus under the fence like we'd snuck on base before (or after, I supposed. I had traveled back in time), but I was afraid that Dr. Wu's age would make that method too difficult. No, we were lucky we'd gotten an opportunity to slip out of the front gate, or we might not have gotten out at all.

Making it to the main road was cause for celebration in itself, but it didn't solve half of our problems. It was hotter than hell, the park was a few miles away, and I didn't know how far our group would make it.

I got an idea that I did not like. I stuck my thumb up like I'd only seen in movies, inviting strangers in passing cars to take pity on us and let us into their cars. Did anyone hitchhike anymore? Or was that just a way to end up in chunks in the back of some psycho's freezer? If it were just me, I would never have considered it. I thought Gannicus might have a pretty good chance in a fight, though, if it really came down to it. All things considered, hitchhiking was the best option, if someone would take us. And for some reason, someone did.

My stomach rolled in apprehension when a rickety brown truck pulled over beside us. My instincts screamed for me to run, but this wasn't the time to worry about strangers.

"Need a ride?" a middle-aged woman asked as she rolled down her window. She was wearing a plaid shirt and had a messy blonde ponytail. Her eyes narrowed slightly at my dress, but the expression was quickly replaced with one of welcoming. Her wary look at Gannicus stayed much longer, though. I could understand her hesitation, given how I was just thinking that Gannicus could beat up whoever it was that decided to stop for us. But it wasn't like he was going to!

Despite her hesitations, the driver didn't say anything about him. She just jerked her head towards the back seat of the truck, indicating that we should get in. Gannicus and I climbed into the back, with Dr. Wu sitting in the front. We were quiet as she started driving, and I stared at the light shining through the window on the blonde in Gannicus's hair. Just being near him made my heart swell with disbelieving joy. As much as I wanted to kiss him or even hold his hand, I couldn't believe how lucky I was just to be sitting next to him again. I didn't care that he didn't know me yet. I knew him. That was enough for now. Besides, we had work to do.

Rather than tell our driver where we were going, I gave her turn-by-turn directions. Her eyes glanced back at me in the rearview mirror with increasing frequency as we got deeper downtown and the surroundings got less friendly. I understood her concern, but I didn't have an explanation to give her. If I made something up and she saw through it, she'd kick us out of the car for sure. Unless she asked, I wasn't risking it.

As we got closer to the park, my foot tapped anxiously on the plastic floor cover. How long would she go before she gave up and said she had to drop us off? She'd already gone out of her own way, that much was obvious. At some point in the hitchhiking interaction, didn't the driver pull up to the side of the road and tell the passengers it was time to get out?

"This'll do," I finally said when I couldn't take it anymore. We were just coming up to the neighborhood that held the park, and I decided that was close enough. I pointed to one of the run-down houses. There seemed to be something extra creepy about hitchhiking to a sketchy park, and this way she would hopefully believe we'd just needed a ride home. With nothing but a dubious look, she pulled the truck over where I'd indicated.

We thanked her for her help, standing on the sidewalk until she drove away. The truck rumbled down the street, its tires on the road the only sound breaking the silence of a still spring day. It was only when she was gone that Dr. Wu turned towards me with raised eyebrows.

"This is where they hide the time machines. I also wish this wasn't the place they chose," I said quickly in explanation, walking in the direction of the park.

By the time we got to the concrete building, I was starting to become terrified that the time machine wouldn't be there. I knew Davidson had one of them, because I'd left him in the future. There had been two when I'd been taken, though, so there should be one left here. Trying to understand the movement of the machines through time was starting to scramble my brain, but I thought it made sense. There were two time machines. Davidson and I took one to the future. I took a completely different time machine back home, and Davidson was still with his time machine in the future. So, there should have been one time machine left here. That was right. I was tempted to babble about these details to my team, but it was important that they thought I knew what I was doing. So instead, I approached the door with all the confidence I could muster.

Unfortunately, it was locked. The lock required a four digit code to open, which was great, because it meant that I had a one in 10,000 chance of guessing the code right. I sighed. I should have thought of something like this before, but I was so distracted by the excitement of even getting this far that I hadn't thought it through well enough. I glanced at Gannicus and Dr. Wu, hoping they hadn't noticed our issue. They had eyes and brains, though, so they immediately saw the problem.

"One in 10,000 odds," I said to the silence.

"I doubt that," Dr. Wu said, as Gannicus stepped closer, putting a hand on the concrete wall to lean in and inspect the lock. He moved aside to let her investigate, apparently encouraged by her comment. I was, too. "Odds are he picked a code that means something to him."

That was good! We could use that. But she continued.

"Something that he would know and other people wouldn't."

Oh, damn. Maybe we couldn't use that.

I tried to think like Davidson. If it were three digits I'd say the code was 666, because he was evil. I considered trying 6666 anyway just on the miniscule chance that it was right, but then I'd have to explain what I was doing and why, and that would have been too embarrassing. Instead, I ran my fingers over the rubbery buttons uselessly, somehow hoping that if I just kept staring, the answer would jump out at me. It couldn't, though. I didn't know anything about Davidson. I didn't know his first pet's name or the street he grew up on or his birthday, not that any of those would do us any good. I said as much to my group, but Gannicus locked his eyes on me with an intensity that seemed promising.

"His day of birth contains too many numbers. However, his *year* of birth is a different matter."

I wanted to kiss him. Well actually I'd already been wanting to kiss him, because he was so cute and I loved him so much. Right now was even better, though, because I got to see that he was not only cute and my beloved, but also absolutely brilliant.

"Yes!" I said too loud. I glanced around the park, but as far as I could see there was no one here to listen. "Do you know the year he was born?"

Gannicus and I looked at each other, our enthusiasm fading slightly. We couldn't even estimate based on the age he looked like, because he was born in a completely different century than this one. I was starting to get tired of all these hurdles appearing in our plan. Why couldn't overthrowing an evil inventor/human trafficker be easier?

"I believe I do," Dr. Wu said. "Well, he told me once." She paused to remember. "It was in the 2190's."

That was good enough for me. I tapped in the numbers, going through each year.

2190. No. 2191. No. 2192. No. 2193. No. 2194. No. 2195.

A little red light at the top of the number panel flashed green, and the padlock holding the door eased open. 2195. Huh. Another cursed year for humanity to add to history's collection. With some fear of what I'd find inside, I pushed open the door.

There was nothing in the room, except for one time machine. I turned towards Gannicus with a smile that had too much familiarity. The love that was flashing out of my eyes was so bright it could have blinded him. A slight furrow in his brow was the only response I got, but it told me to tone it down. He didn't know why I was looking at him with that kind of adoration, but it looked like he could tell that I was. I switched back into celebration mode. We'd gotten inside, and the machine was here.

Dr. Wu inspected the machine, instructing me to shatter the bulbs first, and then showing me how to dismantle the wires on the underside of the machine. I watched her explanation carefully, knowing that when the time came, I'd have to do it myself. I didn't ask her about her part in developing it, but I could see her familiarity with it. I didn't have quite the same familiarity. It was a lot easier to break something than it was to create it, though, so I was comfortable. She explained the mechanics of the machine, and how she understood time travel was theoretically possible, but I honestly didn't get it. Rather than ask, though, I just used the word "cool" a lot and nodded. I knew how to destroy it, and that was enough.

"Let me know when you're done with me, Tamryn, so I can take off," Gannicus said, peeking out one of the high windows. It dawned on me that he was planning his escape. Panic shot through me.

How could I keep him here for three more months, when I could let him go free right now? He could start working on the others' counterattack, gathering weapons for them. Or I could send him back to his own time right now, and save him from the potential dangers of this turning into a physical fight for freedom? Wasn't it immoral to store him for my future use like some kind of farm animal? When I looked at him, standing there trying to envision a life in this time, I realized I knew exactly what he would want. He would want me to send him back to the base for a few months, because that was necessary to win him a life with me, his love. If I just waited a few months, he could be at the base preparing the others for their escape plan, none of them having any idea that I would show up. In just a few months their plan could take off, with a little help from me. And Gannicus would get to know me. Yes I wanted that out of selfishness, but that wasn't the only reason. He wanted me too. I had to make this decision for him, and this was the one he would want.

"Can I talk to you for a minute?" I whispered to Dr. Wu. She glanced at Gannicus and nodded, leading me out of the building. Only once we'd gone a few paces away did I start. "Can you make sure he gets back to the base? I have to wipe his memory." She raised her eyebrows. "I love him. He doesn't know me yet but he will. He can't remember any of today or it could ruin everything." I didn't know how it might ruin everything, just that I couldn't take that chance. If he remembered this when he met me, how would that change our relationship? How would he be different? It was too delicate.

Dr. Wu held my hands in hers, looking into my eyes carefully.

"I'll take care of him for you," she said. I smiled and thanked her.

Gannicus was just coming out of the building when I finished. I smiled easily at him, though it hurt to keep a secret from him even for this short amount of time.

"Come on," I said, going back into the building. He and Dr. Wu followed. Just like Titan had shown me, I found the memory device. I set the dials for my time, so I could rush into the machine as soon as I was done. I walked over to Gannicus and gave myself a moment to stare at him, wallowing in the strange sense that I knew so much of his future that he didn't know yet.

"I have to put this in your ear," I said carefully, holding up the device. He hesitated, but finally grinned and leaned forward.

"Go ahead," he laughed.

"I love you, I love you, I love you," I whispered, sticking the device just inside his ear. He started to turn in confusion, but I tapped the end of the device, feeling a button press down. His eyes went blank, sending a shudder through me.

I didn't have time to consider it. I turned and bolted for the machine, closing the door and hoping the prototype worked. I remembered Davidson had said it might not, but I didn't have another way to get back to my own time. Dr. Wu had said that Davidson asked her for help on it. She hadn't said whether she'd agreed or not. I pressed the button, sending myself through time.

Chapter 34

I stepped out of the time machine, wondering if it had worked. When I didn't see Gannicus or Dr. Wu, I had to believe it did. I sighed in relief when I saw the second machine next to mine. This meant Davidson was back from the future, and both time machines were in 2020 now. He could try to start the app again, but he'd have to rebuild a time machine from scratch. I imagined that would be no easy feat.

I approached the other machine, watching it warily as if someone was going to come out the doors any moment. Considering I could see inside the glass, though, that was nothing more than an irrational hesitation. There was nowhere to go but forward, so I pushed Davidson's older machine on the ground as hard as I could, rewarded only by the sound of a small crack. Ok, so shattering the front glass was futile. Instead, I walked out of the concrete room, scanning the patches of grass and dirt until I found a large rock. With any large rock, there was some chance of finding a scorpion underneath. My skin crawled. As far as I'd come, though, being held back by what might be hiding under a rock was laughable. Fine dirt coated my hands as I lifted the rock and carried it to the time machine.

Just like Dr. Wu had instructed, I smashed the light tubes with the rock until they were all shattered. Then I battered the thin metal on the bottom of the machine that protected the wires, peeling it away when it was weakened. I tore through the wires until I was satisfied that no one would be using this machine to travel. Digging my toes against the ground for leverage, I pushed the machine against the ground and out the door into the grass. It was lighter than I'd feared, considering I'd been a little afraid I wouldn't be able to move it at all. Still, my arms strained against its weight.

The dirt didn't help the machine move forward, and my breaths were turning more into gasps the further I pushed it. I wasn't sure enough that I'd destroyed the machine beyond repair enough to leave it behind, though. Instead, I towed the machine across the park and left it in the middle of the street. Someone would have to move it unless they wanted to destroy their car by crashing into it. It wouldn't have to sit in the gutter long before people started taking scrap metal from it. Some time after that, if I was lucky, the city would cart it away. I felt a little bad about littering, but Davidson was a kidnapper and a murderer. If I compared myself to him, I was still doing pretty good.

I gave the machine a last kick before I left it there, the Tucson sun glaring off the glass and putting spots in my vision. A rush of energy hit me and I felt the strange urge to kick it again, to stomp on it, to take out on it all the fear and pain and frustration that I'd felt in the last few months. It wasn't all bad, though. If it weren't for this time machine, stolen from the future and brought into my world, I never would have met Gannicus. I would take all of those emotions over and over again as many times as I had to if it meant meeting him. So I left that machine behind, and headed for the little gray building that housed my other machine. This one I couldn't just break. I had to take it with me. That was a little more difficult. I didn't know what else to do, so I grabbed the top edges of the cylinder and dragged, wincing as the metal bottom edge scraped the ground. I made my way out of the room, muscles already straining against the awkward angle I was using to pull the thing.

Now what was I supposed to do with it? I couldn't drag it all the way to the base where the others were. Was that even the right place to take it? The others had their own escape plan, and I didn't know how my part mixed with that yet. That was irrelevant, though, because I didn't have a way to transport this thing anywhere anyway. I paced around the grass, staring at the graffitied building across the street as I wondered whether I could get away with hitchhiking again. No, it only got riskier the more I did it. Besides, how would I explain the time machine?

I was beginning to think there was no other option when my foot landed on a strip of glass. My body recognized it before my brain did and my heart skipped at my fortune. My cell phone. Amanda and her crony must have tossed it here after David took me. With my heart in my throat, I called Tamryn.

"H-hello?" she said anxiously. I answered with a "hello" that failed to address the significance of what we'd experienced. Her next question was breathy with relief. I wondered what she'd thought when she'd picked up the phone. "Where are you?"

"I'm in a park in downtown Tucson."

I'd been resting against the time machine for some time when I finally saw Tamryn's car pull up at the other end of the park. They were here. To them it might have been a few hours that I'd been gone, but to me it had been days. And it felt a lot longer. Tamryn got out of the car first, followed by Levi and Gannicus. Tamryn started walking quickly towards me, but she was soon passed by a giant man hurtling past her, heading towards me at a dead sprint.

Tears of joy warmed my eyes as Gannicus got closer. I broke into a run to meet him. We both laughed with relief and elation when he lifted me off my feet and kissed me. I threw my arms around his neck and laid my head on his shoulder after, telling him over and over again how happy I was to see him.

"I thought you were gone," he said as he set me down, peppering my skin with small kisses. "I knew it was the most foolish plan I had ever agreed to as soon as you were out of my sight. When I went in to bring you back, though, you had already gone."

He went in after me? I squeezed him tighter, shaking from the excitement of the meeting and the thought of what could've happened to him if he'd been caught.

"You could've died," I whispered, running my fingers over the handsome stubble that was growing on his chin.

"I died as soon as I realized you were gone." I closed my eyes and rested my head on his chest. For a moment, there was nothing but the two of us. I'd just seen him an hour ago, when he didn't know who I was, but this was different. This was us.

Gannicus's reaction made my heart ache. I'd had my moments when I'd begun to doubt the success of our plan, but at least I'd known that I was alive. If I had been in his position, I would've spent the last hours in agony, worrying that he'd never find a way to make it back. I was reminded again how many ways it could have gone differently.

I looked up when I heard Tamryn's feet crunching in the dirt as she approached. Gannicus released me from his embrace to let me hug Tamryn and Levi too. I told them what had happened since I'd been gone.

"You met me before?" Gannicus grinned when I got to that part of the story. By now we'd made it to the broken-down playground equipment at the park, and we were sitting at the base of a hot yellow slide. "I knew you looked familiar." I playfully shoved him in the chest.

"That's because you thought I was Tamryn," I replied. "Both times!" Tamryn and Levi laughed, standing in the wood chips across from us.

Even as we tried to get back to business, to discuss our next steps, Gannicus and I couldn't stop staring at each other. It was as if we thought we'd lose each other again unless we watched carefully. If I glanced away from him to see Tamryn or Levi, I leaned against him protectively. I never wanted to leave him again. Whatever we did next, we'd have to do it together.

We allowed ourselves time to catch up before we tried to load the time machine into the car. It was too big, so Gannicus and I waited in the park while Tamryn and Levi went to get my dad's pickup truck for it.

Chapter 35

As much as they'd missed me, the others hadn't been sitting around waiting while I'd been in the future. When Levi and Tamryn came back with the truck, there was more inside of it than the usual empty water bottles and CD cases. There were weapons. From a wood stock M14 rifle to a long, sleek katana, Levi and Gannicus had been working on a collection of weapons that would give pause to any guards at the dorm who might try to stop us. There was hardly enough room in the backseat of the truck's small cab for Gannicus on a normal day, and now it was ridiculous. We looked over at each other and smiled as we piled weapons on our laps. There was nowhere else to put them.

I hoped we wouldn't need a single one of them.

Now that I was back, the plan was moving along with no time for rest. There was a meeting tonight at the base, with all of those who were tired of being held captive by Davidson. They'd been training for a potential battle for years, and tonight was their chance. I thought it was likely that if I hadn't made it back, tonight would still happen. They'd been preparing to fight, and my bringing the time machine was just one element of that. Still, I was glad I'd had a part to play, and that if—when—they succeeded in winning their freedom, they'd be able to really go home.

We killed the last hour or so of daylight by trying to eat something. I wasn't sure if I'd managed even half a bite of my Eegee's hot dog before I pushed it aside. I couldn't eat. My stomach was already burning through itself, digesting the horrible ways that tonight could go wrong. Fortunately Gannicus was suffering from no such sickness. He finished it for me. When it was finally time to go to the base, I was glad. We knew what we were doing, and it was time to just do it.

As soon as the base was on the horizon I could see that we weren't the only ones who had been preparing for something. It seemed that after my little break in, the IEducator crew had decided to increase security. Instead of one person manning the guard shack, there were three armed guards waiting at the front gate. Oh no. If they'd secured the front more carefully, had they secured the rest of the perimeter?

I resisted the urge to ask Levi to drive faster. He was going at a reasonable pace, and we didn't want to draw attention to ourselves. The truck crept away from the front entrance, through the anonymous desert miles. I strained my eyes for signs of more guards, but there were none. There was nothing out here but the same fence I'd snuck under. Huh. So Davidson had no idea how I'd gotten onto the base. That was a bit of good luck.

The sound of the truck doors opening felt like they'd break the sound barrier. My eyes flashed around us, but there was no indication that anything had changed. It was all in my head. I pushed the door closed so slowly and carefully that it didn't close all the way, but instead stuck out at the edge. That was good enough. I wasn't willing to make any more noise than I absolutely had to. The others were moving gently too, as if we were all standing on a frozen lake in early spring and didn't know how long it would hold. At least, I imagined that was what it would be like to stand on a frozen lake. I was from Arizona.

For now, we left the time machine hidden in the sage bushes under and around the truck. It was risky, but dragging it in with us was riskier still. Once the confrontation was winding up, Tamryn would bring in the time machine. I wasn't sure how I felt about that part of the plan. Sure, it was better than her actually holding a weapon and having one pointed at her. But did she have to be here at all? I wished she were in her little apartment, where none of this could hurt her. I'd suggested she just wait outside with the machine, but she'd asked how she was supposed to know when to come in, and I hadn't had an answer to that. I'd thought of bringing everyone out to her, but I wasn't sure I could get everyone out with any kind of efficiency. So this was what I got instead.

Levi snuck under the fence first. I squeezed my arm in my fingers, digging my fingernails in against my anxiety while I stood just by the fence and watched. *Electric fence. Electric fence.* It was a random thought, and a morbid one. It wasn't true. He made it to the other side of the fence just fine.

I went next. Gannicus stood behind me, watching the base through the chain link as if there was any information he could pick up through the darkness. I noticed the new moon as I picked myself up off the ground and swiped the dirt off of my jeans. I was glad to see it. We needed all the protection from being seen that we could get.

Levi and I lifted the bottom of the fence up for Gannicus as he shuffled under, army crawling on his stomach under the metal. His long hair brushed the dirt. My eyes soaked up the battle ready excitement in his, but I couldn't get myself to feel his enthusiasm. It was nice that he was ready, but I was scared out of my gosh damn mind.

Gannicus knew the areas that the guards and other non-historical employees were rarely found. Scouting out these areas was one of the parts of the ongoing escape plan, and many of our allies had played their part in developing the mental map we now followed. We were unlikely to be seen if we kept to the back side of the base and the edges of the outermost buildings, where the fence was outlined in desert. I'd snuck onto the base before, and doing it again was no big deal. So why had my heart taken up permanent residence in my throat? With every step I waited for a gunshot to ring out in the air, or the sharp sting of a tranquilizer dart to steal my consciousness. With every step I strained my ears for a cry for help from Tamryn, or a painful grunt from a wounded Gannicus. With every step we got closer to the meeting room, and not a single bad thing happened.

We filed into the recreation room and shut the door behind us. The room was already filled with people.

"Diplomatic leaders to the right," the man across the room from us, at the front of the crowd, said in a historic British accent. His powdered wig waved on his shoulder as he gestured lazily, and a few people began making their way in that direction. I jumped when I recognized a man whose curly beard and sideburns I'd only seen before in a picture of a bust. Something told me I knew it was him, though. Homer. After writing the epic battle of *The Iliad*, maybe he was about to live one of his own. I was hoping diplomacy would take the day this time. Homer had been known for centuries at being so good with words, after all. And he wasn't the only one heading to the front line diplomacy team. There were about 5 of them now. Gannicus looked at me as their small group formed.

"That'll be you," Levi said, putting his hand on Gannicus's arm in a supportive gesture. I froze. Splitting up wasn't part of the plan. What *was* the plan? I tried to focus on breathing in through my nose and out through my mouth. My head snapped towards Levi, my eyes brimming with questions.

"This is what we want," Levi said, giving a small nod in reassurance. "We're hoping if we just talk to the security guards they'll let us go."

Let them go. They'd been training the less experienced members of their team for a year, memorizing guard rotations, stockpiling weapons, and recently having late night meetings when there was a chance the guards would just agree?

When I suggested there might be an issue with that logic, Levi shook his head and smiled grimly.

"Something about bringing an army behind us makes it so we're not exactly asking nicely. Besides, as much as we hope for Plan A, we have to be prepared for Plan B. If they knew we'd all come together against them, we'd never have another chance. It's now or never."

I nodded that that made sense, even as I put that whole line of thinking behind me and moved on to other matters. As a group of medics was organizing in another little corner of the room, a man with a curled gray ponytail and lush white coat pushed himself towards the front of the crowd.

"Attention!" he yelled, earning surprised looks from most of the people in the room who immediately turned their heads to grant his request. A few people were too busy fervently discussing their battle plans, but most of us were listening. That seemed to be enough for him.

"Revolutionaries," he said. No one seemed phased by being labeled this way, probably because it was somewhat accurate. I wondered if anyone else noticed the slight cringe on his mouth when he said it, as if he was afraid of what the word meant as it came out of his mouth. "Let us rethink this movement."

I willed the murmur that erupted to die down. I felt sorry for this man who was already wiping the sweat off of his forehead. Just because his idea was bad didn't mean he was. Maybe he was just afraid we'd fail. Instead of dying down, the noise escalated, like I knew it would. A few people shouted, demanding to know what he thought he was suggesting.

"Perhaps we do not know who the true enemy is! Perhaps Davidson is a decent enough ruler, who would be willing to make changes if he only had the opportunity. Not all kings deserve the guillotine! Anyway, friends, some of us were rulers ourselves. Who will be next?" he stammered his words defensively, as if it were him we were approaching with weapons. Before I could ask, Levi leaned in to give a hushed explanation.

"Louis XVI. He said he was in favor of the reforms of the French Revolution, but he didn't follow through. The people got tired of waiting for him to sign over their rights, so they took him and his wife Marie Antionette to Paris where they could keep a better watch on them. Then he tried to run but he got caught so they killed him."

I raised my eyebrows slightly at this abridged history lesson. Louis XVI was still being shouted down, and it wasn't long before he lowered his face and slipped away from the front of the room, towards the back and closer to where Levi and I were standing. My heart hurt. Sure, he was ridiculous if he was trying to defend Davidson to all of these people who deserved Davidson's head in a gift bag. But it sounded like he was scared of ending up next on the death list, given the trauma of his past. If we won, after all, he'd be sent back to his own time to face the execution that he'd been pulled from. I wanted to look over at him and give him some small smile of encouragement, but I couldn't bring myself to do it. It was like I was made of stone. I just kept my face away, moving to join the medic team. I could feel the right side of my face burning, as if his presence just outside of my peripheral vision was red hot. I tried not to think about it.

Instead, I focused on the team I'd joined. The alternative had been to join the fighting force, since the diplomacy team was necessarily small. I didn't do well with medicine, but I thought I'd do even worse with killing people. I accepted a first aid kit, following along in my head as a kind older woman with her brown hair tied back showed me how to wrap a wound. She introduced herself as Florence Nightingale, which I supposed I could have guessed. The medical team had first aid kits, and the fighting force was weighed down with way more weapons than we'd brought with us tonight. There were only two people I knew of who had managed to escape the base. In those weeks where Gannicus and I had been apart, it was clear he'd done more than pine for me. He'd been assembling supplies for his army.

I looked over to see him talking with his small group, and my heart somehow swelled and deflated at the same time. This was it. He'd been training and preparing for this, and he was ready. His confidence radiated off of him in the relaxed set of his shoulders. I only peeled my eyes off of him when I heard a door to my right open, but when I turned to look it was closed. I must have imagined it.

"It's time," Levi said, holding a sleek black AR-15. He gave a low whistle and waved his arm to the crowd of people in the middle of the room, who hadn't joined a more specialized team. They were the infantry, I supposed. And my sister's husband, who she hadn't even wanted to be involved in this situation, was their leader. I felt a pang of regret at having gotten any of us involved. Then I felt a pang of guilt for starting to regret doing the right thing. This wasn't an extracurricular activity. Levi wasn't involved in this because I was bored one day and wanted to occupy my time. This was more than that. He was here for the same reason I was, for the same reason any of these people were holding a weapon or a first aid kit. Everyone here deserved freedom, and they deserved justice. We all had a part to play in getting there.

The diplomats filed out of the room first. The room was so crowded that the small movements of each person following suit felt like a tsunami rushing forward. Levi was practically walking backwards out the door he was turning around so often, checking on his team with a grim look on his face. I looked around me, at the people who were waiting their turn to exit out the door. Some had stoic expressions, like they were determined to push on and nothing was going to cause them to hesitate from that course. A few faces, though, betrayed apprehension or even fear. A hand wiping away sweat here, a chest rapidly rising and falling there. These were the small signs that despite everyone's determination, this wasn't going to be easy. And even if we tried not to be, we were scared.

The medical group left last, so I held my place as the room cleared. When the last weapon bearer went through the door, his sword clipping the door frame, we took our cue to follow. I tightened my grip on the black fabric handle of my little first aid kit, hoping I wouldn't have need for gauze or antiseptic or stitches. I shuddered at the thought. As far as I was concerned, the best I was prepared for was giving out a bandaid. Maybe it wouldn't even come to that. I tried to tell myself that there was no way the guards would have any problem with letting us go, and the more that I thought it, the more I believed it. We marched across the quiet sidewalk in the dark, passing a few quiet buildings.

The feet of the last of the infantry crunched on the beds of rocks as they hurried towards a clearing in the buildings. It was nothing more than a small picnic area surrounded by dorm buildings, with a few concrete tables and attached benches. There was a nondescript metal trash can off to each side, one with a piece of graying gum attached to the rim. The night air had a hint of summer heat, but a feeble breeze blew small strands of hair around my face. I could see Gannicus and the few other diplomats facing a guard, who was frantically speaking into his walkie-talkie. This was not the beaches of the *Iliad*, but it was the battle ground we got.

I knew my place was with the medical team, but Gannicus was up there. I had to know what was going on. I pushed through the crowd, muttering apologies when I ran into people. A few others from the back or middle of the pack were also creeping forward, straining to hear what was going on. I didn't go all the way up to Gannicus, because I didn't want to get in the way. He was doing a job that might come down to life or death, either for him or the others gathered here. There was no way I'd do anything to distract him if I could avoid it at all. So I stopped when I was close enough to hear, though I was still more towards the middle of our little crowd.

"We do not wish to be here," Gannicus was saying. His tone was tired, and he was emphasizing the words like this wasn't the first time he'd said them.

"Y-y-you guys have it good here," the guard replied, his eyes wide. He was repeatedly pushing a button on the side of his walkie-talkie. I assumed it was to summon backup, but they were already here. Six more guards were approaching us, three from the left and three from the right. They were coming up from behind the first guard, so he didn't see them right away.

I did. I saw them, with their guns raised towards us. Those weren't tranquilizer guns. My stomach rolled. I wanted to scream for Gannicus to back away, to turn and run.

"Fellow men," a man from the diplomat group said. He was dressed in a black t-shirt and black pants, but the bow in his braided ponytail suggested he was influenced more by the fashions of the 1770's than the 2020's. "We have no reason to harm you, nor you us. We just want to go home. There are far more of us than there are of you. Is this job worth your life?"

The guards just stared, and a few of them adjusted their grips on their guns. Sighing, Harriet Tubman addressed them next. She looked pointedly at the first guard, the one who had summoned the others. He was standing in the middle with his hand on the gun in his holster.

"You," she said. She stepped towards him, but when she saw his fingers wrap around the gun at his side, she stepped back again. He relaxed slightly. He looked to be about 30, and his wide-eyed, inexperienced expression and extra weight around his midsection suggested that he was not the rugged Texas Ranger he wanted to be. "Do you have a family?"

"No. We're not here to talk about that," he said shakily, lowering the tenor of his voice as if to sound more authoritative. It came off more as confused than anything else.

"Alright," she said calmly. She kept looking right at him, like the others weren't even there. "Well, I do. I have a family, and they love me and I love them. And I, and the rest of us here, will do what we have to do to get back to them. We would rather it not come to anyone getting hurt. Your bosses won't hold it against you that you let us go, not when you were so outnumbered. This is one of those rare moments where doing the right thing and the easy thing are the same thing."

There was a pause. The guards looked at each other, questions in their eyes. Then, the first guard shrugged. He let his hand fall from its place on his holster. One by one, the others lowered their weapons.

"Get out of here," one on the right said begrudgingly, even sheepishly. He averted his eyes from us as he jerked his head in an indication that we should leave.

I deflated in relief. A rushed breath of air escaped multiple people around me at the same time as they lowered their weapons. Gannicus turned and found me with his eyes, and we gave each other small smiles of disbelief. That was it. After all of the horror and planning, Plan A had actually worked. Looked like I didn't need those bandaids after all.

More guards were approaching our crowd, but that was to be expected. It was their job to investigate disturbances, after all. I tried not to let myself get worried. They met with the guards who had agreed to let us go, and were calmly discussing the situation. It didn't look like anyone planned to overrule the decision.

A crackling sound sent a chill up my spine. Before I could even identify the source, the sound was followed by a piercing siren. I slapped my hands over my ears against it, and I wasn't the only one. The sound shot through me, straight into my bones. It faded quickly, though, and was replaced by a voice. It was coming from a dusty speaker at the top of a wall to my right.

"Attention guards. I have been informed that there has been an insurrection. This cannot be tolerated. We have a business to run."

I recognized that voice. I hated that voice. Amanda.

"Mr. Davidson will be on location soon, as will I. In the meantime, hear this. Any of you who we have so graciously brought from your own times to live with us here, you still have a chance to show your gratitude. Put down your weapons and go back to your dorms. I will give you five minutes. No questions asked, no grudges held. After that five minutes, there's a new offer. This one is to our guards. $200,000 a head for every person you stop permanently. Five minutes starts now."

Chapter 36

Everyone froze. After a second, the guards turned their heads slightly, looking at each other. More were filing in from other parts of the grounds, and I was shocked to see how many people were hired to keep watch these days. The new guys didn't say anything either, just waited for someone else to break the silence.

$200,000 to kill a person? That was a lot of money. Life changing money, even. But enough to kill someone? No way. Surely they must have been thinking that, telling each other just by their facial expressions that this was absurd, that they should quit. This was their cue to realize that they'd been working a morally bankrupt job thus far, but that didn't mean it was too late to change. There was absolutely no way that they would be willing to kill innocent people for some money.

And yet. They'd been working this job this far. Did I really think all those guards were hired in case a random member of the public stepped onto the base? Davidson had hired more guards than the president. They knew. They knew now and they'd known then, that this was not your average security job.

I knew. I knew before their hands started reaching for their guns that they were going to take the money.

It didn't make it any easier when the guns came up and pointed at us again. Gannicus was right in the front. If they started firing, it wasn't hard to guess where they'd start. My heart started pounding in my ears. What could I do? I was afraid any sudden movement would startle them, and we still had our five minutes. Maybe if I crept up to him slowly, without drawing any unnecessary attention, I could convince him to walk away with me. No one else in the crowd was moving, though, so I had no choice but to stand still. If someone moved, it might indicate that we weren't a united front, that some people were leaving. It might give people in the crowd the push they needed to give up and go back to their dorms. I didn't know if I could blame them if they did, but I didn't want to be the reason they did.

The first person to break the silence wasn't part of either group. A door opened behind us to the left, apartment 100. A man with shoulder-length hair despite his receding hairline came out, shaking his head in disgust at the scene before him.

"What is the purpose of this?" he asked, his sharply pointed nose wrinkling. "They won the day they brought us here. Enough of this nonsense."

I expected the group to treat him the way they had treated Louis VXI, and some of them did.

"Go back into your hole, Hobbes!" a woman shouted, the tight sternness of her voice matching the immaculate brunette bun on the back of her head. "You're not a part of this."

Hobbes? His statement was starting to make sense. I knew enough to know that Thomas Hobbes based his social contract theory around a belief in absolutist monarchies, and thought a ruler could do basically anything to his people as long as he didn't unjustly kill them. I wondered what he'd think if he knew what happened to Vlad.

It was encouraging to see that some in our crowd were incensed by Hobbes' outburst, and still dedicated to our plan. But that wasn't the only response I saw. Some people were looking back at the dorms hesitantly, or holding their weapons more loosely by their sides as they surveyed the guards. I should have anticipated their hesitation. Sure, there were about 40 or 50 of us, but by now there were something like 20 guards gathered. Even if we did win, we wouldn't win without casualties. If they were one of those casualties, maybe it wouldn't be worth it. Just because Gannicus and Levi were willing to die for their beliefs, in their last lives and in this one, didn't mean everyone was.

As if I'd spoken my arguments aloud, a few people turned and quietly walked away from our group. They didn't look back at us once. They just skittered away in little groups of two or three, one after the other. When the first group started to walk away, a tall man with a lean, muscular build shouted at them, "With your shield or on it!" It didn't change their minds, only made them move away from our group faster. When the running had died down, I would have estimated that we'd lost about 15. It gave me a sour feeling in my stomach. What did they expect? When they were given weapons, did they think that they were just props? Did they think we were here for fun? I shuffled forward and picked up a pistol that someone had left behind, just in case. I was supposed to be on the medical team, but maybe I'd be needed for more than that now.

The part that annoyed me the most was that even though people were abandoning us, we were still going to fight for their freedom too. Gannicus was up there on the front lines, a rifle slung across his back and a blade in a sheath at his side, prepared to go down fighting for people who were too cowardly to stand with him.

It felt like it had been more than five minutes, but I watched a guard anxiously pull out his phone and check the time, only to return it to his pocket.

Was he checking the time remaining in my life? Once I let the thought seep in, it turned into a downpour in my mind. When our "five minutes" were up, they were going to start shooting at this crowd. Levi was in this crowd. Gannicus was in this crowd. *I* was in this crowd. If I had to choose between my loved ones being killed or myself, of course I'd choose to die for them. But that didn't make the idea of my life being torn away by a bullet through my flesh any less terrifying. I'd already been sweating, but now I was starting to feel clammy and nauseous, like I might panic or faint. I took a deep breath and steeled myself. This was the time to be brave. Whatever was meant to be was going to happen. I said a prayer for all of us here.

"Ok, now you have to decide," Levi said loudly. He moved past a few people until there was no one between him and the guards. "Put the guns down and walk away."

"That isn't going to-" a guard began, raising his gun higher and pointing it at Levi.

A shot rang out.

Before I could register what had happened, before I could scream or cry or wonder if my brother in law was gone, I saw the bullet go through the guard's head.

Then I screamed.

The guard collapsed, his gun clattering on the ground.

Two of the guards fired their weapons at the crowd.

At us.

More shots blasted out from our side, and then, or maybe at the same time, from theirs. My ears rang. I froze. Then I snapped my head back and forth, searching. Gannicus was still on his feet. He'd moved back, whipping his head around deliberately in a search for better position.

A warm splatter of water hit my face.

It wasn't water.

Chapter 37

I gagged. I stared. The man next to me screamed, clutching his arm in agony. His hand was filling with blood where it sat on his bicep. I recognized him. Meriwether Lewis!

"Lewis!" I gasped. Shots and groans rang out around me, but I was in a fog.

"Help him!" a woman yelled. I looked at her. She was the woman who'd shown me how to use the first aid kit. Now she wanted me to treat a bullet wound?

I wanted to be good at this. I so desperately wanted to help. But I didn't have a clue what she was asking. What did I know? About anything?

"I don't know what to do!" I screamed, holding my hands out towards Lewis helplessly.

"Bring him!" she shouted, turning and walking back the way we'd come out here, until she got to a bench. A few other members of the medical team were already there, preparing their supplies and making room for the wounded to come trickling in.

I put my hands on Lewis's arm, putting as much pressure on the wound as I could while walking him over. Pressure was important. It stopped people from bleeding out. The blood on my hands was just paint. It was red paint. I took a deep breath through my mouth and told myself that I was just touching red paint, I wasn't touching a gaping, bleeding wound.

"It-" I tried to get words out around the lump in my throat. I didn't want to be here. I didn't want to be here. I was going to die. We were all going to die and there was nothing to do about it and I just wanted to run as fast as I could as far as I could. But I had a job to do, and I was going to damn well try. I choked out words of encouragement. "It's going to be alright."

"I believe you," he said, with something between a wince and a smile. I gave him my own attempt at a smile back.

We sat him down on the bench, and I waited while the woman inspected the wound. Her head snapped up at me when she realized I was still waiting.

"Go get somewhere for us to lay these people down," she said, gesturing with a shake of her chin that we were in desperate need of space.

Ok, I could do that. I remembered seeing yoga mats in the rec room. I wasn't sure how sterile those were, but a bench didn't seem much better. Besides, we weren't wrapping their wounds in the yoga mats, we just needed somewhere so they wouldn't have to stand up.

I started to run back towards the rec room, but I stopped cold when I saw a small group approaching the battle from behind the picnic tables. There was Amanda. And there was Davidson. Behind them was our old friend Louis XVI.

That *rat*! That disgusting vile worthless piece of... I couldn't even think of anything right now so I just envisioned my raw hate towards him to fill in the blank. He'd betrayed us. That was how Amanda had known. That was why she'd offered that deal to the guards. He must have chosen a new side after he'd been shot down by our side. No, that was a poor choice of words. Rejected. Shot down was what he'd be if I found out his ratting on us led to any harm coming to Gannicus.

I surveyed the area until I saw Gannicus. He was carrying a wounded man I didn't recognize back to the medical area. Ok, he was safe. I kept looking. Levi was crouched behind a metal trash can, searching for his next target.

They were fine. I had a job to do now.

It was surreal, running across the sidewalk by myself in the dark. My life had been completely normal, until one day it just wasn't.

Until one day I saw people die. I saw my brother-in-law take the first life of this battle.

I supposed it made sense. Levi was from the American Revolution. America hadn't won by fairly approaching the British army and announcing their intentions. They'd hidden in the woods and fought guerilla warfare. Levi had actually given the guards much more warning than that. They had pointed their guns at him. He did the right thing, and he did it to protect me and the others.

But that didn't change the way it had felt. One minute the guard was there, and we were all on this earth interacting with each other. The next, the life left his eyes and he slumped to the ground. I was still there, Levi was still there, but that guard would never be there again. He was gone, just like that.

I stepped into the rec room and turned to look for the yoga mats before a wave of nausea rolled through me, worse than I'd ever felt. I was expelling vomit all over the graying red carpet before I even registered it.

When it was over, I spit on the ground, wiped my mouth, and went to get the yoga mats. The sour taste was still in my mouth, and the sting of bile in my throat was choking me, but there wasn't time to make a big deal of that.

I grabbed a chunk of the 5 yoga mats, dividing them up between my two hands, and ran out the door.

I squeezed the mats tighter as I approached the picnic area. My fingernails dug into the spongy material as I watched a few groups of people fighting, grappling on the ground or stabbing. Most people had ducked behind poles or trash cans or anything else they could find, and were watching the carnage with their chests heaving. I jumped when a gun went off, but I didn't even know who had fired it. Gannicus was still alive. It looked like I'd caught him in a brief moment between opponents, because he was just running over to tend to Columbus, who was shrieking about the wound in his side.

It was too hard to tell from my vantage point whether it was caused by knife or bullet, but at this point it didn't much matter. Gannicus pressed his hands to it firmly, yelling out for someone on the medical team.

Levi was still alive too, crouching behind the corner of a building just outside of the action, whispering to a woman crouched beside him and pointing at the scene as if they were planning their next move.

Ok. So everyone I really loved was ok for now. I allowed myself the slightest relief, the tiniest decrease in tension. Until I heard a sound like glass dragging on the ground and turned to see Tamryn coming up the path to my left.

She was too early! She was supposed to wait until the fighting was over. But how could she have known when the fighting was over? I gritted my teeth. She wouldn't have been able to wait for our call, not with the two people she loved most in the world risking our lives out here. It was a gift to me that she'd waited at all, instead of barreling in right behind me. Now she was here though, and I needed to get her the hell away. Great, we had the time machine. That was what we needed to get everyone home after all this. She'd done her part and now she could leave.

I made my way towards her, wondering if I could convince her. I sucked in a breath that wasn't deep enough, straining against my lungs for more air. That was just the anxiety. I willed myself to breathe slower. If I asked Tamryn to leave, would she? Maybe she would if I agreed to leave too. I would. I looked at her face and knew instantly that I'd leave if it put her out of danger. I'd already done a lot to help. It was enough.

We made eye contact, and I shook my head immediately. *Get out of here*, I meant to say. She probably knew what I meant, but she didn't acknowledge it. Instead, her eyes, wide with worry, were surveying the picnic area as she got a little closer and it came into her view. We didn't need twin telepathy for me to see the way her eyes darted desperately, begging for a glimpse of him. There he was, Levi, darting forward and shooting one of the guards in the neck. Tamryn and I both looked away when the bullet made contact and the blood started to flow. Her face was red and her eyes were watery when I looked back at her. Yeah, she was right. This was the most horrible thing either of us had ever experienced, by a lot. I wondered if I was in shock, or else maybe I'd be full-on panicking right now. It was a bit disturbing that if I was honest, I had to realize that I was proud of myself for handling it all, for facing down horror I'd literally never even dreamt of before and finding a way to be alright.

But then I turned my head and had a real reason to panic.

Davidson, who had just been standing by a table blocked from the fighting by two guards, saw Tamryn and her time machine. As if he didn't even have to think about it, like this was a game he'd played before and he knew this was the time he was going to beat this level, he lifted the gun at his side and pointed it at my twin sister.

I didn't know it before, but I had never really known dread before that moment.

Sure, I knew now what it was like to walk into battle, or to face Vlad and think he'd be the last thing I'd ever see. Those weren't moments I'd ever want to relive. But at least in those moments, I was whole. My body was held to the earth by gravity. This wasn't like that.

This was like when you fall off your bike, right before you hit the ground and you have just a second to think "Oh shit, this is gonna hurt." It was like that, if the bike was right on the edge of the Empire State Building and you knew you'd crack each one of your bones and feel each break individually at the bottom. Or if you suddenly sunk to the bottom of the ocean, and your lungs were screaming for air, but there was none to be found.

She was going to die. My best friend, my sister, was going to get shot by an enemy I'd exposed her to and die in my arms. My body turned to ice.

Human beings were resilient. I knew that. I knew that people often underestimated their ability to survive emotional trauma, that they found a way to live through the worst moments of their lives and somehow come to the other side of it. I also knew that I was not one of those people. This was not one of those things that I would ever get over. Yes, maybe I would physically survive. I'd find myself waking up everyday and face the horror of remembering that I'd lost her, and eventually somehow even find a way to stumble out of bed. I'd learn to exist. But I knew for a fact that I would never genuinely smile again. There was no reason to smile if the world didn't have Tamryn in it. There was no reason for anything. There was no me without her. I could not do this. I could not do anything.

The moment stretched on. It didn't really, though. Somehow my despair was condensed into a few neat seconds. I didn't realize that despite the chill in my blood, and the pounding in my head, I hadn't really believed he was going to pull the trigger.

Because when he did pull the trigger, I collapsed in shock.

I didn't faint. I wanted to. Instead I dropped to the ground, distantly feeling the blunt force of my knees crashing into the concrete below me.

God, please, not this. Not her.

Chapter 38

Somewhere between Davidson holding up the gun and pulling the trigger, I'd started screaming. I hadn't stopped. I stopped now. The bullet had left the gun, and by all understandings of time and physics should have reached Tamryn by now. It didn't.

She was standing there, alive. I didn't know what to do with all the emotion that coursed through me, the heat behind my eyes and the swelling in my chest. *Thank God.* She was ok. I was ok. I put my face in my hands, and my hands smelled like sweat and felt like sweat. That wasn't important. My eyes snapped up to see again that she was alive, as if I could've tricked myself and hallucinated her back to life. She was still there, but her facial expression was wrong. Her face was twisted in an expression I couldn't find the brain power to interpret. Instead I turned around and saw why the bullet hadn't hit her.

It had hit him. He was there on the concrete now, his blonde hair strewn across the hard ground. Gannicus. When he'd heard me scream, he must have immediately come to the rescue, jumping in front of Davidson before he could kill Tamryn.

No. No! No! That wasn't fair! That wasn't—that wasn't—it wasn't. It just couldn't be happening. I'd already made it through hell. I'd come back to earth. As if it was happening, though, I stumbled off of my knees and clambered over to him, tripping once or twice on the way. Once it was actually a person I tripped over, and I didn't turn to see who it was. A rush of irritation pulsed through me, and I wanted to scream at that person for lying on the ground in my way. Didn't they know he was hurt? No, probably not. They were probably dead.

Bile rushed into my throat, but I swallowed it back immediately. My love was here. He was on the ground. He was on the ground bleeding because of me, because I'd screamed and he'd heard and run to save my sister. I wished I could take the bullet for him. I didn't want it to be her in Davidson's line of fire, and I didn't want it to be him. Why couldn't it have been me? If he didn't survive this I didn't know how I would either. I loved him. I *loved* him. I loved him. I kept thinking it over and over, even mumbling it, like an incantation that would save his life. Some things were too bad to be true. This was one of them. I squeezed my eyes shut and opened them again. Please let this just be a dream. My limbs seemed only distantly connected to my body, but somehow they made it over to Gannicus anyway. They must have propelled themselves.

Where was the wound? Levi was leaning over Gannicus. I could just see that he had Gannicus's shirt ripped open. He was in my way. I pulled on his shoulder, trying desperately to see past him, to see if Gannicus was ok.

"I need to see him!" I said, and my voice sounded so shrill and foreign to me. Levi turned towards me with a serious, almost blank expression. It was concerned, yet competent. I wished I could siphon a bit of his peace for myself, just to slow my panicked breaths.

"Get me one of the medical bags," he said.

What? I needed to see Gannicus right now. I didn't have time to get him a bag. He blinked quickly, assessing my lack of response.

"Now!" he yelled.

It was the yelling that turned my brain back on. Levi didn't ever yell at me. This was the most important thing he would ever do for me. He was a paramedic, and this was what he did for a living in his new life. Right now he needed a medical bag, if he was going to save the love of my life. I could give him that. I could do that. I ran for the medical area, even though my knees ached and I was half-blind with a blur of tears in my eyes.

There was a man lying on a bench, and even though I recognized him, he was so changed by his wounds that he was hard to recognize. His face wasn't even white, it was gray. It was hard to tell if he was breathing. I didn't even know his name. His stomach was soaked in blood, but there was no one tending to him. Maybe he wasn't breathing after all. I had a moment to register that he was dead, and I recognized him, and I'd never really know him. There was time to say a quick prayer for him as I grabbed the first aid bag lying on the ground next to him, but that was it. Then I sprinted back to Levi and Gannicus. Tamryn was there now, standing behind Levi with her hand on his shoulder.

Levi turned and deftly pulled the bag away from me, unzipping it and pulling out a plastic wrapper. He tore it open and removed what looked like an oval of Saran wrap. I gasped when I stopped following his movements and turned to Gannicus, who had a big, terrifying wound in his chest. No. He had to be ok. I needed him. We'd waited two millennia to find each other. A few months couldn't be all that we got.

"Will he live?" I asked, gripping Levi's shoulder too hard. Levi didn't flinch, but applied the plastic substance to Gannicus's chest, sealing the wound.

"Hope so," Levi muttered, his attention on his task.

There wasn't a particular noise that drew my attention away from Levi and Gannicus. It might have been a grunt of pain off to the side, or the clatter of a weapon landing on the ground. Something in the low din of misery around us brought me back to the present, and I remembered that there was a reason I'd almost watched my twin sister die, and why now I was left praying that the man I loved would survive.

Davidson.

I had to stop him. Either he considered shooting Gannicus enough action for one day or realized it wasn't safe to draw so much attention to himself, or some evil reason I couldn't even imagine, but he was standing by his two guards again. I thought he was watching us all, but I avoided his eyes. If we made eye contact then I'd definitely be back on his radar, and that wasn't what I needed. What I needed was to kill him before he thought to kill me first.

No one else had shot him yet, probably because with the two guards standing right next to him, whoever tried to kill him would be the next to hit the ground bloody after him. That was their issue. I had to finish this. A part of me was holding back, asking myself if I was really capable of killing someone right now, but I told it to shut up. Davidson had threatened Tamryn's life and almost taken Gannicus's. It was time for him to die. If that was too much for me, then I'd have to deal with those emotions afterwards.

I saw a weapon or two abandoned on the ground, but they were too close to Davidson. If he saw me lean down and pick one up, he or the guards would probably make sure I didn't even get to stand up all the way before they shot me. No, I needed to be smart about this. He needed to think that I was doing something else, that killing him didn't register in my mind. What would I be doing if I weren't doing this? Looking after Gannicus. That wouldn't work, though, because that didn't get me any closer to a weapon. What else? Getting medical supplies. That was far enough away that maybe he wouldn't be watching me the whole time, and I'd have time to collect a weapon on the way.

I ran the short distance, my body tense in wait for the feeling of a bullet to rip into me. The longer I was out here, the higher my chances of getting killed by Davidson or anyone else. It was like I could feel the possibility simmering over my skin, causing an anxiety that was more physical than mental. There was nothing to do about that but keep moving. I made it to the medical area pretty quickly, and found Florence Nightingale sewing a wound on the arm of a man I didn't recognize. He had his hair in a long blondish braid, which was sitting over his right shoulder while she attended to the left.

"There," she suddenly said, motioning with her eyes towards the ground by our feet. "Benjamin took it from one of the guards." Benjamin must have been the man she was treating, because he nodded knowingly.

On the ground was a long green and black rifle. The barrel sort of looked like it was made out of PC pipe. I wasn't sure what it was, but it wasn't a regular gun. I lifted my eyes towards her in confusion, and she glanced at Davidson before looking back at me and smiling grimly.

"It's a tranquilizer gun. Just like they used on us. Shooting him with it would be poetic justice, if you ask me. If you try to shoot him with a real gun, the guards might shoot back. If you spare his life, though, we might be able to end this thing with a little less bloodshed."

A strange emotion darted through me, something like relief or hope. That was when I realized that despite my most ardent intentions, I was never really going to be able to kill Davidson. I could do it in direct self defense, but in this situation, with him just standing there now, I knew I'd spend the rest of my life wondering if there had been another way. I didn't know how I felt about this revelation about myself. Sure, I supposed it was a positive that the idea of taking a life wasn't something I could decide lightly. On the other hand, Davidson had threatened the lives of the people I loved the most. How could I even hypothetically let him get away with that? There was no reason for these considerations. It hadn't happened that I'd been faced with the chance to shoot Davidson with a real gun in reasonable conditions, so I had no idea what I'd do. Trying to imagine it was only withering my confidence, in a time when I needed that more than anything.

I picked up the gun, and finally looked at Davidson. He wasn't looking at me. He had glanced at Amanda, and actually laughed at something she said. That little moment gave me time to get the gun and move to a wide pole near the edge of the picnic area, where I could see Davidson if I poked my head out. He was back to surveying the area, and I didn't know if he could see me. I was off to the side enough that hopefully the others would keep him distracted.

If Florence was right, then I would fire this gun, Davidson would go down, and then we'd just have to take down a few more guards and send everyone home.

If she was wrong, then I would fire this gun, Davidson would go down, and one of the guards would immediately shoot and kill me.

Chapter 39

As I felt the smooth plastic of the gun, I considered that I could completely miss. I didn't even know what would happen in that scenario. Unfortunately, that was a very possible scenario, since I didn't have much experience with these things. With dart guns or regular guns, actually. This gun had a sight on it, though, and I'd always been pretty decent at carnival games or arcade games that required shooting. It was just aiming. Lining up the sight with my target.

So that's what I did. I lifted the gun up to my eye, praying desperately that Davidson wouldn't turn and see me hiding here and kill me on the spot. I lined it up so I was looking at his heart, because I'd heard on TV once that you should aim for the chest because it was the biggest target and you were most likely to hit it. I closed one eye like people do on movies, then opened both because that felt weird. That was worse, so I closed the left eye again.

Well, here I went. I was either signing my death warrant or taking out the biggest threat we had. Or some other third option, which I couldn't imagine but could be better or worse than either scenario. The truth was, I had no idea what was going to happen. But I thought of Gannicus, and the crushing disbelief I felt when he was shot, followed by an unbearable pain. We'd had enough of that. We'd had enough pain. It was time for us to go out and have dinner together, to date for real. To worry about enjoying each other, and not about whether Davidson would ever find him. We deserved a life together, and we'd fought so hard to find it. Then I thought of the others, who had been torn away from their loved ones and never even gotten a chance to say goodbye. They'd been forced into a new world, and taken advantage of every moment that they'd been here. As soon as they'd gotten their bearings, they'd come together to plan a battle for their freedom. I lowered the gun.

I didn't know how to shoot a gun. I wanted revenge on Davidson, to be the one to take him out of the fight. That wasn't my glory to have, though. Not because Davidson hadn't hurt me too, because he had. He'd scarred me in ways that I didn't know if I'd ever really get over. But this was our one shot to catch him off guard, and if I missed, we might be done for. It would be like a benchwarmer taking a shot at the buzzer of a tied game when her star teammates were open. The others had been preparing for this battle, and they were ready to take Davidson down. I just had to let them.

So, instead of pulling the trigger and hoping for a miracle, I surveyed the area until I saw Sergeant Ralph Brown, who had been a soldier in WWI. He was one of the few people I'd met when we were all setting up to enter this battle. Right now he was crouched behind a picnic table, reloading his rifle. His gelled black hair brushed the top of the table as he worked. Him. He knew how to shoot. I didn't know him well, but the people I did know well were busy healing wounds. There was a confidence in the set of dark brows that confirmed somewhere inside me that he could do this.

Before I could think of the risks and ask myself if I might get hit by any stray bullets, I darted out from behind the pole. I clutched the tranquilizer gun like it was a shield, crouching low until I made it to the picnic table. Ralph nodded at me solemnly, and went right back to his weapon.

"Excuse me," I said quietly, even though it was too loud around us with groans of pain, gunshots, and grunts of effort, for Davidson to hear me from this distance. "This is a tranquilizer gun. Do you want to shoot Davidson? Florence Nightingale and I were thinking that if we used this instead of a real gun, the guards might be less likely to—"

I stopped, because he took the gun out of my hands before I finished. He propped it up on the picnic table, aiming it for Davidson.

"You got it," he muttered, as if he couldn't pay full attention to his words when he was focusing on his shot.

What if we were wrong? What if the guards fired immediately and I'd just passed the death onto this man that I barely knew? Maybe I should have just shot Davidson myself. That way the consequences would have been on me, no matter what they were. I held my breath when Ralph Brown pulled the trigger.

I kept holding my breath when the dart pierced into Davidson's neck.

I held my breath when Davidson stumbled, and started to collapse. I watched the guards so hard it made my eyes dry, waiting for them to reach for their guns. The air rushed out of my lungs when they did lift their guns, and pointed them at Ralph Brown. And at me.

For one small moment, I let myself close my eyes. If death was coming, there was no reason I needed to see it, right? It would be just like going to sleep. Death by gunshot was quick. Before I could even feel the pain, I'd be dead. I told myself there was nothing to be afraid of, so why was I so scared I couldn't feel my legs? *I love you, Tamryn. I thought. I couldn't say it to her but I could think it. *I love you, Levi. I love you, Gannicus. I love you, Mom and Dad and*—

It was weird that I was still alive. Bullets were pretty fast. I opened my eyes when I realized I hadn't heard the guards fire a weapon.

Just as I opened my eyes, someone did. It wasn't a guard, though, and it wasn't at me. In fact, it was right *next* to me. Ralph Brown shot the guard on the right with the tranquilizer gun, firing almost as soon as the guards had lifted their guns. I wished I could take the dart back, make him undo it. There were *two* guards standing there. Yes, one of them crumpled to the ground next to Davidson. The other one didn't, though. He was perfectly conscious and capable of shooting back. Finally getting ahold of myself, I ducked behind the concrete bench. I didn't know if it would protect me because it didn't cover my whole body, but maybe I'd get lucky and they'd aim for the part of me that was blocked by the bench. Then I waited. Hadn't I just experienced this? Wasn't one almost shooting enough? I felt like the stuffed clowns at the arcade, the ones you throw balls at and try to knock down. They just kept coming back up and it started all over again. But I hadn't been hit yet. Maybe that would continue.

I looked at the guard through the gap between the bench and the table. He wasn't aiming anymore. I stood up all the way, ignoring the existence of other guards and threats in my disbelief. He had his hands up in surrender. No one moved.

One guard in the middle of our battlefield was the first to retreat. He was facing a short-haired brunette woman who I immediately recognized from Saint's Day at Sunday school as Joan of Arc, until he suddenly took a step back and lowered his weapon. She watched him warily while he continued to step back until he reached the buildings on the right side of us, and then he took off into a run.

The others followed suit. Either they realized that it wasn't worth the risk to their lives, or they thought they weren't likely to get paid now that Davidson was down, but suddenly they weren't looking to collect on the reward for our heads anymore. Some of them ran, but most of them just walked, watching us carefully. They didn't know for sure that we would let them leave after they'd tried to take our lives. *I* didn't even know for sure if we would. Somehow, though, they managed to leave, and we were left with just us.

Just us and the time machine that Tamryn had brought. We'd actually done it. We'd won.

Chapter 40

As soon as I wasn't waiting for a bullet to tear through at any moment, I ran for Gannicus. He was still lying on the concrete, and Levi was crouched by his side, monitoring him for any changes. Levi looked up when heard me approach.

"We need to get him and the others to the hospital now," he said, gesturing his head slightly towards the medical area, where two ambulances were waiting. I started. Who'd called them? What if the police were coming too? I looked around, at all these people who were so close to getting home. The time machine was right there. We'd gone through all of this carnage to send them all home. What if we got arrested for it? It was illegal to shoot people, I knew that much. It was self-defense, but we'd gone in with weapons ourselves. It would be hard to sell that we were nothing but innocents, even though I felt strongly that it was true.

"It's ok," Levi said, watching the horror flash across my face. "I just called in a favor. The guys won't report anything."

The guys in question, a handful of paramedics and EMT's, were already ushering the most badly wounded onto gurneys. One of them, a tall man with thinning brown hair, came straight to us, giving a small grim smile as a greeting to Levi. The expression was gone as soon as it came, replaced by a serious intensity in his face that both calmed and terrified me. He was here to take Gannicus.

"I'll go with him," I said immediately, holding my hands out uselessly as Levi and the EMT started working on getting Gannicus onto a gurney. I was so desperate to help, but I didn't have a clue what to do. But they were trying to load my baby into an ambulance, to try to save his life, and I was sick to my stomach and in my heart and in my eyes and in my brain. At least I could sit in the ambulance with him. That would have to help.

"You can't," Levi said haltingly, as if the words were reluctant to leave his mouth. I deflated, and then I swelled with frustration. My chest hurt, and I spilled words as if I could alleviate the pressure.

"Is that against the rules? Who cares? We can do it just this once. You're not reporting this whole thing to the police, you're breaking the rules already. Just let me be with him. It'll help him. He's probably s—" I tried to say that he was probably scared, but the words stuck in my throat painfully.

The EMT was watching my display with a professional sympathy, but I thought I saw a hint of confusion when he glanced at Levi, as if he didn't know why Levi was being so cruel. Or maybe I just imagined that was what he was thinking.

"It's not that," Levi said, elevating the gurney from the ground so they could wheel my love away from me. "You're the only one who knows how to run the time machine. Someone has to stay and get everyone home."

Damn. I didn't have much to say to that. There were plenty of smart people capable of getting everyone organized and ready to be sent home, and I could see now that they'd already started. Joan of Arc had started knocking on doors with efficient intensity, urging anyone who'd been hiding to come out and get in line. Benjamin, who was now wearing a shoulder sling and seemed to be relatively recovered after Florence's medical attention, was ushering newcomers to a table. At the table, a few women I didn't recognize were writing down notes from each person that approached them, and then handing the finished notes back to the person, who was then urged to join the line. The line was leading towards the time machine, which was in the hallway just next to the picnic area, where Tamryn had left it. She'd come back to it, and was waiting for me to start sending people home.

I sighed. Everyone else had immediately started doing their part, and now it was time for me to do mine. I pressed a light kiss to

Gannicus's forehead, imagining that I could put all the power of my love into that kiss, and use it to heal him. If I had had time, I would have wanted to tell him that I could spend the next two thousand years thanking him for saving my sister, and it would barely be a start to the gratitude that he deserved. I would have told him that he was so brave, and that because of that bravery, from the very beginning of this nightmare for him and the others, they'd managed to rescue themselves. I would have told him that he was my world, and I was so ready to start living in it. Once we made it through this, we'd get to the good stuff. Friday night dates at the fair, sharing wedding cake on our first anniversary, welcoming babies. The worst was over, and the best was yet to come. But I'd have time to say all of that. For now I said a prayer for him instead, and stood back from the gurney. He was going to be okay. There was something about Levi's equanimity as he carted Gannicus away that told me that.

I watched them load him into the ambulance, motioning for Tamryn to come over.

"We have to do something about Davidson," I said.

This was one of the harder issues to solve. There was always the option of calling the police, but it would be hard to prove his crime after we sent most of the witnesses away. We'd be tied up with the trial for years, and everyone who did witness his actions would be prevented from moving on with our lives. Besides, what if the jury didn't believe us? This wasn't your everyday crime. No, I wasn't taking that chance. I was about to express my complete lack of ideas when Gannicus groaned slightly. He waved his hand for my attention.

My heart skipped, and I climbed into the back of the ambulance. I had to lean over his face to hear the words he was trying to whisper.

"My time," he breathed.

His time for what? To die? My blood ran cold.

"No, you can't leave me. Don't talk like that," I said, putting my hand to his clammy cheek.

"No," he said, just as quietly. "Take him... to my time."

Oh. Of course. I wished I'd understood him the first time, so that he didn't have to exert himself to say it twice. I looked back at Levi, but Levi didn't seem terribly concerned. Gannicus was already hooked up to an IV and I didn't know what else back there, so maybe it was ok that he'd been talking. So instead of panicking about Gannicus, I climbed down onto the ground and thought about his idea. Now that Gannicus would be staying with me, there was an opening in the gladiator ranks. Davidson had shown himself today to be comfortable with a weapon, and he did have a history of time traveling. It was perfect. It was justice, just exactly as he deserved. I wondered for a moment if it was too much, sending him to such a perilous century. As I surveyed the area around us, though, at the wounded being loaded into the ambulances, and the others working so hard to find their way home, I decided I was ok with Davidson taking on that particular challenge. If he'd thought being forced to survive in another century was good enough for these people, I thought it was good enough for him.

To no one's surprise, Levi immediately agreed. I let him argue the merits of the plan to Tamryn, who seemed to have an even harder time accepting it than I had, judging from their expressions, and made my way to the front of the line that had gathered by the time machine. Each person had a slip of paper with the day and location they were going back to, and all I had to do was work through the line, plugging the dates into the controls of the time machine and letting them exit when we got to their destination. The line continued: Mikhail Bulgakov of the Soviet Union, Ernest Hemingway, and Elvis. I just about peed my pants on that last one, but I tried to play it cool. I thought that I mostly succeeded. I was just moving on to the next person, a short older man with thick white hair, when Joan of Arc asked if she could talk to me off to the side. I agreed, and let the man know that I would be back in a minute.

"Some of them do not want to return," she said quietly.

"What do you mean?" I asked stupidly, just because what she'd said hadn't registered with me yet. "They want to stay here?"

She just nodded. What was I supposed to do about that? We had some bigger guys here who could drag people into the time machine, but I didn't see much reason to do that. Would it be such a bad thing if they just stayed here? They'd have to start new lives, but I thought my new job might have resources for people who were trying to get back on their feet after being the victims of human trafficking. Maybe we could get them settled in a new life in 2020, if that was what they chose.

"Might they stay? I have no way to aid them, for I am determined to return. However, if those of you from this time were willing to guide them—" Joan said after a moment, proposing the solution I'd just been working around to myself.

"Yes," I said quickly. "We'll find a way to help them."

Almost as soon as the words had left my mouth, Joan took off, rounding people up into one section by a picnic table. Those must have been the people who wanted to stay. The process ran smoothly after that, as everyone worked together to keep the lines organized and moving. I smiled when I encountered my old friend Dr. Wu, who was next in line to go home.

"Thanks for taking care of him for me," I said, referencing a memory that was both months ago and just yesterday, and not knowing whether it felt like either one. This had been just about the longest day of my life, and it wasn't going to end any time soon. Still, I was glad to see a familiar face.

"We all did our part," she replied, handing me the slip of paper with the time she wanted to return to, even though I was sure she knew how to work the machine herself. She could hardly go back and send the machine here with no one in it, and that was where I came in. I didn't know what to say, so I half-turned towards the machine behind me in a hint that we could get inside and go whenever she was ready. She soon filled the silence though. "Maybe one day you'll be in history books too."

I laughed, considering. Making history required taking chances and having strong beliefs that you were willing to fight for. I liked to think that I'd demonstrated some of those traits in the last few months. Right now, though, I was tired. Mentally, I felt like falling asleep and crying at the same time. Physically, my legs ached and I would have killed for a foot massage. As thrilled as I was to have been a part of the team, I needed a break before I had another adventure. Besides, I'd seen what kind of trouble people could get into from being remembered by history.

"I think I hope not," I finally said, as we climbed into the machine.

Returning Dr. Wu was uneventful, but my attention was grabbed immediately on my return. As soon as my ears started picking up sounds from my own time again, I was startled by a confused-sounding groan to the left. I turned my head to see the two men who had been guarding Davidson, holding him up by the arms. He was starting to come to, the effects of the tranquilizer wearing off.

"You'd better be getting on before he regains his strength," one of them said.

Chapter 41

"We got everything taken care of. I left Davidson in a heap in the time of the slave revolts, just like we planned. I went back to 2106 and sent them all back too, like we did with everyone here. Well, except the people that didn't want to go back. Tamryn volunteered to work out the logistics of getting them started on new lives here. I think we really—wait, no, shh. Don't do that."

Gannicus had started to try to sit up to take a better look at my face, and I thought it would be best to discourage that. He'd just woken up after surgery to find himself in a brightly colored hospital room, lit up with fluorescent lights and permeated with the smell of disinfectant. He didn't look so good. His face was colorless, and his hair was slightly wet with sweat where it stuck to the side of his face. The hospital gown he wore covered his wounds, but I knew they were there. The wires coming out of his body reminded me of the trauma he'd suffered, as if it was something I would ever forget.

"H-here," I thought he whispered, but it was hard to tell. His voice was so hoarse that whatever he said would have sounded more like the growl of a wounded tiger than the words of a man. Still, the way he started to lift his hand towards me was enough invitation that I didn't need the words. Was it ok if I laid down with him? For a moment, I had a hideous image of laying down on top of the IV and ripping it out of his arm. Would blood spurt everywhere? I didn't know. I avoided medical TV shows because they scared me. I focused on his eyes instead. They were a little cloudier than usual, his focus eased away by the drugs they'd given him to ease his pain. The cloudiness didn't bother me, as long as it meant that he wasn't hurting. I could still read the love in his eyes, and I knew he wanted me close to him as much as I wanted to be close to him. So I slipped into the side of the bed, nearly hanging off the sharp edge as I struggled to find a comfortable position around the wires. Somehow I managed it.

I couldn't lay my head on his chest, for obvious reasons. Instead, I barely rested my head on the edge of his shoulder, holding most of the weight of my head with my own neck. It was going to hurt in a few minutes; I could already tell. That was ok. This was the beginning of the good times.

From the beginning of our relationship, we'd been fighting against his situation. Even before I knew about it, it strained our connection. Once I found out, I couldn't help but doubt his feelings for me. Even now I thought that had been the right decision, to let him decide for himself, with real freedom to make the choice. Still, it hadn't been easy going through my days with the ache in my chest that meant he was gone. Since then I'd flown on a plane for the first time in my life, faced down a CEO who was willing to kill for his own success, survived a trip to the future, and fought in a war. Never in my life had I fought for something as hard as I'd fought for him, and for us. The hard times in my past had been nothing but inconveniences, and I was lucky for that. No part of me wished that I could go back to those days, though. Life was only easy back then because I'd had no idea what I'd been missing. I didn't know who I was capable of being, or who I would one day love.

Now it was different. This wasn't easy. Gannicus was still majorly injured, despite the fact that his prognosis was good. When I smelled the shoulder that my head rested against, I didn't just smell the slight vanilla scent that I loved so much from him. Instead, I smelled disinfectant and the plastic-like cloth of the hospital gown, and the sanitized malaise that always filled hospitals. Where I would normally listen to nothing but the quiet thump of his heart and the sound of our peaceful breaths, now I heard the sharp rhythm of the heart monitor. Instead of thinking wistfully about how many kids we might have, I was thinking about how if he hadn't jumped in front of the bullet that put him here, I might be burying my twin sister. No, this moment wasn't easy. It was more than that. It was worth it.

"I love you," I whispered, and let the slow beep of the monitors send me to sleep.

Chapter 42

"That's everything," Levi said as he closed my car trunk six months later. He, Tamryn, and my parents would be following Gannicus and me in a caravan to my new apartment. Gannicus had found one in the same complex, but wouldn't be able to move in for another week. My new boss had been kind enough to let me defer my start date until Gannicus had had time to heal. It had been a slow, long process, and I'd found something to love in every minute of it. Nursing him back to health had given me an excuse to spend all my time with him, and I didn't mind that one bit. His landlord had put his rent on hold for the first month or so while he lived with my parents and me. Watching them all get to know each other had been a little nerve-wracking at first, but seeing the way they formed inside jokes and eagerly shared stories of history, I started to feel bad that I hadn't introduced them sooner.

In the past couple of months, the story of IEducator had been constant news. At least one employee had reported the events to the cops, and we'd all sat through countless interviews rehashing our role in Davidson's disappearance. The prosecutor decided it wasn't worth pursuing a case against us given the witnesses in our favor, and we'd eventually been let off the hook. The news cycle covering the app's involvement in human trafficking had been an enormous asset for us; we had been declared innocent in the eyes of the public, and that was hard to undo.

The story died down as quickly as it had risen, which was fine by me. The questions about what happened to Davidson started to wear on me right away, and it took a few months before I stopped having dreams about what might have happened to all of us had he not lost the fight. The less I had to spend my days talking about it all, the better.

Besides, I didn't need to be hailed as a hero. All I wanted was to do the right thing and make my life mean something, and I had. Now that Gannicus and I were moving to Phoenix, I was going to start a career that would let me continue that mission. I'd seen and even experienced the degradation and injustice of human trafficking, and I couldn't think of a better use of my skills than to work to combat it.

"You ready?" I asked Gannicus, jingling my keys in my hand.

He nodded enthusiastically and waved to my family as he climbed into the car. I was more than happy to put off the goodbyes until they left us in Phoenix. He reached for my hand after I started the car, intertwining his fingers with mine.

Though neither of us wanted to discuss it at the moment, it was fortunate that my new employer had locations all over the globe. In the somewhat near future, Gannicus and I would be apart while he pursued his own career: he was going into the Army, to try to become a member of the Special Forces Green Berets. We'd move together wherever he was sent, but I couldn't very well go to bootcamp with him. We were both excited about his choice, but we weren't ready to face the idea of separation. Still, it was a long way off. He couldn't go to bootcamp until he fully regained his strength, but we didn't know how long that would be. With how hard he'd been working at his rehabilitation, the doctors liked to say that he'd be stronger than before he'd even gotten shot. That didn't surprise me at all.

The Saguaro cacti waved to me as we flew across the desert, making our way to our new home. I reflected on the time I'd spent after graduation, wondering if I'd ever leave home and build a future for myself that made me proud. All those months I'd spent, agonizing about whether I'd ever find a career, or if I'd be able to start a family of my own. Only now did I realize it wasn't just the future that I hadn't had enough faith in, it was myself.

It didn't matter. The days of uncertainty were gone. I might not know what would happen next, but I knew that whatever came, I could handle it. I'd watched and waited for my opportunity to start my life. Here I was now, pursuing my dreams with the man I loved most in the world.

All it had taken was time. And everything I was made of.